RAVE REVIEWS FOR
NEW YORK TIMES BESTSELLING
AUTHOR CHRISTINE FEEHAN!

THE SCARLETTI CURSE
"The characters and twists in this book held me on the edge of my seat the whole time I read it. If you've enjoyed Ms. Feehan's previous novels, you will surely be captivated by this step into the world of Gothic romance. . . . Once again, Ms. Feehan does not disappoint!"

—*Under the Covers Book Reviews*

DARK GUARDIAN
"This book has it all and then some. A true keeper!"

—*Romantic Times*

DARK LEGEND
"Vampire romance at its best!"

—*Romantic Times*

DARK FIRE
"If you are looking for something that is fun and different, then I recommend you pick up a copy of this book."

—*All About Romance*

DARK CHALLENGE
"The exciting and multifaceted world that impressive author Christine Feehan has created continues to improve with age. By introducing this new band of Carpathians, she is setting the stage for more exhilarating adventures to come."

—*Romantic Times*

CHRISTINE FEEHAN

LAIR OF THE LION

LEISURE BOOKS NEW YORK CITY

A LEISURE BOOK®

September 2002

Published by

Dorchester Publishing Co., Inc.
276 Fifth Avenue
New York, NY 10001

Cover art by John Ennis.
www.ennisart.com

ISBN 0-8439-5048-X

Printed in the United States of America.

Visit us on the web at www.dorchesterpub.com.

"COME HERE TO ME."

A shiver went down Isabella's spine despite the heat of the pool in which she was submerged. She wrapped her arms around her breasts. "I have no clothes on, *signore*."

His gaze burned over her. Hot. Possessive. The merciless eyes of a predator. "It was not a request. I want to see every inch of you. Come here to me now," *Don* DeMarco growled.

Isabella was weary of being afraid. "And if I do not obey?" she asked softly, uncaring what he might think, uncaring that he was the most powerful *don* in the land, uncaring that he was soon to be her husband.

"Isabella." He breathed her name. That was all. Just her name. It came out an ache. Hungry. Edgy with need.

Her heart contracted, and everything feminine in her reached for him. "Don't do this," she whispered, a plea for sanity, for mercy. "I just want to go home."

But she had no home. She had no lands. Her life as she had known it was gone. She had nothing left but her deadly bargain with this powerful, dangerous lion of a man who would soon wed her . . . and eventually destroy her.

The hard line of his mouth softened, and he murmured, "You *are* home, *belleza*. Are you afraid?"

Other books by Christine Feehan:

DARK GUARDIAN

DARK LEGEND

AFTER TWILIGHT

DARK FIRE

THE SCARLETTI CURSE

DARK CHALLENGE

DARK MAGIC

DARK GOLD

DARK DESIRE

DARK PRINCE

*With much love for my sister Denise,
who has always shared my love of books.
You've always brought me great joy.*

LAIR OF THE LION

Chapter One

The wind was shrieking through the narrow pass, bitter and cold, piercing right through her well-worn cape. Isabella Vernaducci pulled the long fur-lined cape closer around her shivering body and glanced anxiously at the high cliffs rising sharply overhead on either side. It was no wonder the *don's* army had never been defeated in battle. It was impossible to scale those terrible cliffs that rose straight up into air, like towers reaching to the clouds.

There was a shadow lurking within Isabella, an impression of danger. It had been growing steadily stronger in the last few hours as she traveled. She ducked her head into the horse's mane in an attempt to gain some relief from the unrelenting wind. Her guide had deserted her hours earlier, leaving her to find her own way along the narrow, twisting trail. Her horse was nervous, tossing its head and jumping skittishly from side to side, showing every sign it wanted to bolt as well. She had the sensation that something was pacing along beside them, just out of sight. She could hear an

1

occasional grunt, almost like a cough—a strange noise she'd never heard before.

Isabella leaned forward, whispering softly, soothingly into the ears of her mount. Her mare was used to her, trusted her, and, although its great body was trembling, the animal made a valiant effort to continue forward. Icy particles stung both horse and rider, like angry bees piercing flesh. The horse shuddered and danced but moved stoically forward.

She had been warned repeatedly of the danger, of the wild beasts roaming freely in the Alps, but she had no choice. Somewhere up ahead of her was the only man who might save her brother. She had sacrificed all to get here, and she would not turn back now. She had sold everything she had of value to find this man, had given what remained of her money to the guide, and had gone the last two days without food or sleep. Nothing mattered but that she find the *don*. She had nowhere else to go; she *had* to find him and be granted an audience with him, no matter how elusive, no matter how dangerous and powerful he was.

His own people, so loyal they refused to help her, had warned her to stay away. His lands were enormous, his holdings vast. Villages and townships whispered of him, the man they looked to for protection, the one they feared above all others. His reputation was legend. And lethal. It was said he was untouchable. Armies attempting to march into his holdings had been buried by snow or rock slides. His enemies died swift and brutal deaths. Isabella had persisted despite all warnings, all accidents, the weather, every obstacle. She would not turn back no matter how the voices in the wind howled at her, no matter how icy the storm. She *would* see him.

Isabella glared up at the sky. "I will find you. I will see you," she declared firmly, a challenge of her own. "I am a Vernaducci. We do not turn back!" It was silly, but she felt convinced that somehow the owner of the great *palazzo* was commanding the very weather, throwing obstacles into her path.

A noise like grating rock captured her attention, and, frowning, she swung her head around to look up at one steep slope. Pebbles were bouncing down the mountain, picking up speed, dislodging other rocks. Her horse leapt forward, squealing in alarm as a shower of debris pelted them from above. She heard the chink of the horse's hooves as it scrambled for purchase, felt the great muscles bunching under her as the animal fought to stay on its feet amidst the rolling rocks. Isabella's fingers were nearly numb as she gripped the reins. She couldn't lose her seat! She would never survive the bitter cold and the wolf packs that roamed freely through the territory. Her horse crow-hopped, stiff-legged, each movement jarring Isabella until even her teeth ached from the impact.

It was desperation more than expertise that kept her in the saddle. The wind lashed at her face, and tears were torn out of the corners of her eyes. Her tightly braided hair was whipped into a frenzy of long, silken strands, pried loose by the fury of the coming storm. Isabella kicked her mare hard, urging it forward, wanting to be out of the pass. Winter was fast approaching, and with it would come heavier snowfalls. A few more days and she never would have made it through the narrow pass.

Shivering, teeth chattering, she urged the horse along the winding trail. Once she was out of the pass, the rising mountain on her left side dropped away to a ledge that appeared crumbling and unstable. She could see jagged rocks far below, a drop-off she had no hope of surviving should her horse lose its footing. Isabella forced herself to remain calm even as her boot scraped along the mountainside. Small rocks tumbled from above, rolled and bounced on the narrow ledge, and careened off into empty space.

She felt it then, an oddly disorienting sensation, as if the earth shimmered and twisted, as if something better left alone had awakened upon her entrance into the valley. With

3

renewed fury the wind slashed and tore at her, ice crystals burning her face and any part of her skin that was exposed. She continued riding for another hour while the wind came at her from all directions. If blew fiercely, viciously, seemingly directing itself toward her. Overhead, storm clouds gathered rather than move swiftly away with the wind. Her fingers tightened into fists around the reins. There had been a hundred delaying tactics. Small incidents. Accidents. The sound of voices murmuring hideously in the wind. Strange, noxious smells. The howling of wolves. Worst was the terrible far-off roar of an unknown beast.

She wouldn't turn back. She couldn't turn back. She had no choice. She was beginning to believe the evil things said about this man. He was mysterious, elusive, dark and dangerous. A man to avoid. Some said he could command the very heavens, that the beasts below did his bidding. It didn't matter. She had to reach him, had to throw herself on his mercy if that was what it took.

The horse rounded the next bend, and Isabella felt the breath leave her body. She was there. She had made it. The *castello* was real, not a figment of someone's imagination. It rose up out of the mountainside, part rock, part marble, a huge, hulking *palazzo*, impossibly large and sprawling. It looked evil in the gathering dusk, staring with blank eyes, the rows of windows frightening in the lashing wind. The structure was several stories high, with long battlements, high, rounded turrets, and great towers. She could make out large stone lions guarding the towers, stone harpies with razor-sharp beaks perched on the eaves. Empty but all-seeing eyes stared at her from every direction, watching her silently.

Her mare shifted nervously, sidestepping, tossing its head, eyes rolling in fear. Isabella's heart began to pound so loudly it was thunder in her ears. She had made it. She should have been relieved, but she couldn't suppress the terror welling up inside her. She had done what was said to be impossible. She was in sheer wilderness, and whatever manner of man lived here was as untamed as the land he claimed dominion over.

Lifting her chin, Isabella slid from the back of the horse, clinging to the saddle to keep from falling. Her feet were numb, her legs wobbly, refusing to support her. She stood still for several moments, breathing deeply, waiting to recover her strength. She stared up at the *castello*, her teeth worrying her lower lip. Now that she was actually here, now that she had found him, she had no idea what she was going to do. White wisps of fog wound around the *palazzo's* columns, creating an eerie effect. The fog stayed in place, seemingly anchored there despite the ferocious wind ripping at her.

She walked the horse as close to the *castello* as she could manage, tying the reins securely, not wanting to lose the animal, her only means of escaping. She tried patting the mare's heaving sides, but her hands were clumsy and burning with cold. "We made it," she whispered softly. "*Grazie.*" Hunching deeper into her cape, she pulled the hood up around her head and was swallowed by the garment. Stumbling in the vicious wind, she made her way to the steep steps. For some reason she had been certain the *castello* would be in a state of disrepair, but the steps were a solid, shiny marble beneath her feet. Slippery with the tiny ice particles on them.

Huge lion heads were carved on the great double doors, incongruous so far out in the Alpine wilderness. The eyes were staring fiercely, the manes shaggy, and the great muzzles open, revealing fangs. The knocker was inside one mouth, and she was forced to put her hand in past the teeth. Taking a deep breath, she reached in, careful not to cut her flesh on the sharpened spikes. She let the knocker fall, and the sound seemed to vibrate through the *palazzo* while the wind lashed at the windows, furious that she had escaped into the comparative shelter of the rows of columns and buttresses. Shaking with cold, her legs weak, she leaned against the wall and tucked her hands inside her cape. He was within the walls of the *castello*. She knew he was home. She *felt* him. Dark. Dangerous. A monster lying in wait . . . He was watching her. She felt eyes on her, malevolent, malicious, venomous eyes. Something evil lurked in the bowels of the *palazzo*, and with her peculiar sensitivity, she felt it like a fist around her heart.

The compulsion to run back into the fury of the storm was strong. Self-preservation told her to stay in the shelter of the large *castello*, but instead, everything inside her rose up in rebellion. She couldn't make herself knock again. Even her tremendous willpower seemed to desert her, and she actually turned toward the lashing wind, ready to take her chances there. Then Isabella clamped down hard on her wayward imagination. She was not going to panic and run back to her horse. She actually grasped the heavy doorframe, her fingernails digging in hard to hold her in place.

The creak of the door warned her. Soft. Ominous. Forbidding. A portent of danger. The interior beyond was dark. An elderly man dressed in severe black stood looking at her with sad eyes. "The Master will not see anyone."

Isabella froze where she was. Seconds earlier she had wanted nothing more than to run back to her horse and ride away as fast as she possibly could. Now she was annoyed. The storm was growing in a frenzy, sheets of ice slamming to earth, white crystals covering the ground almost instantly. As the door began to swing closed, she thrust one booted foot into the crack. Jamming her ice-cold hands into her pockets, she took a deep breath to calm her trembling body. "Well, he will have to change his mind. I shall see him. He has no choice."

The servant stood impassively, staring at her. He neither moved out of her way nor opened the door wider to allow her entry.

Isabella refused to look away from him, refused to give in to the terrible warnings shrieking at her to run while she still had the chance. The storm was full-fledged now, the howling wind hurtling pieces of ice that felt like spears even into the shelter of the covered entryway. "I must put my horse in your stable. Please direct me immediately." She lifted her chin and stared the servant down.

The manservant hesitated, glanced into the darkened interior, and then slipped out, closing the door behind him. "You must leave this place. Go now." He was whispering, his eyes restless and his gnarled hands shaking. "Go while you still can." There was desperation in his eyes, pleading. His voice was a mere thread of sound, almost unheard in the bitter shrieking of the wind.

Isabella could tell that his warning was genuine, and her heart stuttered with fear. What was so terrible within that this man would send her out into an icy blizzard to take her chances with raw nature rather than have her enter the *palazzo*? Where his eyes had been blank before, they were now filled with trepidation. She studied him for a moment, trying to judge his motives. He had a quiet dignity about him, a fierce pride, but she could smell his fear. It oozed out of his pores like sweat.

The door opened a crack, no more. The servant stiffened. An older woman poked her gray-haired head out. "Betto, the master has said she must come in."

The male servant sagged for a fraction of time only, his hand shooting out to the doorframe to steady himself, but then he was bowing low. "I will see to your horse myself." His voice was flat, revealing no emotion at all at his being caught in a lie.

Isabella looked up at the high walls of the *castello*. It was a fortress, nothing less. The great doors were large and thick and heavy. Her chin rose, and she nodded at the older man. "*Grazie tanto* for going to so much trouble for me." *To warn me.* The unspoken words hung between them.

The man lifted an eyebrow. She was clearly an *aristocratica*. Women such as this one rarely even noticed a servant. He was shocked that she didn't berate him for his lie. That she seemed to understand he was desperately attempting to help her. To save her. He bowed again, hesitated slightly before turning toward the icy storm, then squared his shoulders in resignation.

Isabella stepped across the threshold. Alarm triggered her heart to thud wildly. A thick stench of evil permeated the *castello*. It was a cloud, gray and somber and edged with malice. She took a deep, calming breath and looked around her. The entryway was quite spacious, tapers burning everywhere to light up the great hall and dispel the darkness she had glimpsed. As she stepped inside, a wind whipped down the corridor, and the flames leapt in a macabre dance. A hiss of hatred accompanied the wind. An audible hiss of acknowledgment. Whatever it was recognized her just as surely as she recognized it.

The interior of the *castello* was immaculately clean. Wide-open spaces and high, vaulted ceilings gave the impression of a great cathedral. A series of columns rose to the ceilings, each ornately carved with winged creatures. Isabella could see the apparitions winding their way upward. The *castello* preyed on the senses—the artwork rich, the structure impressive—yet it was a trap for the unwary. Everything about the *palazzo* was beautiful, but something unearthly watched Isabella with terrible eyes, watched her with malignant hatred.

"Follow me. The Master wishes you to be given a room. The storm is expected to last several days." The woman smiled at her, her smile genuine, but her eyes held a hint of worry. "I am Sarina Sincini." She stood there a moment waiting.

Isabella opened her mouth to introduce herself, but no sound emerged. All at once she was aware of the utter silence in the huge *palazzo*. No creaking of timbers, no footsteps, no murmur of servants. It was as if the *castello* were waiting for her to utter her name aloud. She wouldn't give her name to this hideous *palazzo*, a living, breathing entity of evil. Her legs gave way, and she sat down abruptly on the marble tiles, close to tears, swaying with a dark dread that was a stone in her heart.

"Oh, *signorina*, you must be so tired." *Signora* Sincini immediately wrapped an arm around Isabella's waist. "Allow me to help you. I can call a manservant to carry you if need be."

Isabella shook her head quickly. She was shaking with cold and weak from hunger and the terrible journey, but the truth was, it was the unnerving feeling of a malignant presence watching her that filled her with dread, that caused her already shaking legs to collapse beneath her. The feeling was strong. Carefully she looked around, trying to appear composed when all she wanted to do was run.

Without warning, from somewhere close by a roar filled the silence. It was answered by a second, then a third. The horrifying noise erupted from every direction, near and far. For one terrible moment the sounds blended and surrounded them, shaking the very ground beneath their feet. The roars reverberated throughout the *palazzo*, filling the vaulted spaces and every distant corner. A strange series of coughlike grunts followed. Isabella, standing with *Signora* Sincini, felt the older woman stiffen. She could almost hear the servant's heart thudding loudly in tune to her own.

"Come, *signorina*, we must get you to your room." The servant put a trembling hand on Isabella's arm to guide her.

"What was that?" Isabella's dark eyes searched the older woman's face. She saw dread there, a fear betrayed by the woman's slightly trembling mouth.

The woman attempted to shrug casually. "The Master has pets. You must not leave your room at night. I will have to lock you in for your own safety."

Isabella could feel terror welling up inside her, sharp and strong, but she forced herself to breathe through it. She was a Vernaducci. She would not panic. She would not run away. She had come here for a purpose, risked everything to get to this place, to see the elusive *don*. And she had done what all others had failed to do. One by one the men she had sent out had turned back and told her it was impossible to continue. Others had come back to her facedown on the back of a horse, with hideous wounds much like a wild animal might inflict. Still others had never returned at all. Time and time again her inquiries had been met with silent shakes of heads and signs of the cross. She had persevered because she had no other choice. Now she had found the lair, and she had entered it. She could not quit now, could not allow fear to defeat her at the last moment. She had to succeed. She could not fail her brother; his life was at stake.

"I must speak with him tonight. My time is running out. It took me far longer than I expected to reach this place. Really, I must see him, and if I don't leave soon, the pass will be closed, and I won't be able to get out. I have to leave immediately," Isabella explained in her most authoritative voice.

"*Signorina*, you must understand. It is not safe now. Dark has fallen. Nothing is safe outside these walls."

The wealth of compassion in the woman's faded eyes only increased Isabella's terror. The servant knew things she did not and obviously feared for Isabella's safety.

"There is nothing to be done but to make you comfortable. You are shivering with cold. A fire is burning in your room, a warm bath is being prepared, and the cook is sending food for you. The Master wants you to be comfortable." Her voice was very persuasive.

"Will my horse be safe?" Without the animal, Isabella had no hope of covering the many rugged miles between the *palazzo* and civilization. The roars she had heard were not those of wolves, but whatever made the noise sounded dreadful, hungry, and doubtless had very sharp teeth. Isabella's brother had given her the mare on her tenth birthday. The thought of the horse being eaten by savage beasts was horrifying. "I should check."

Sarina shook her head. "No, *signorina*, you must stay in your room. If the Master says you must, you cannot disobey. It is for your own safety." This time there was a distinct warning note in the sweet voice. "Betto will see to your horse."

Isabella lifted her chin defiantly, but she felt that silence would serve her better than angry words. *Master. She* didn't have a master, and she had no intention of ever having one. The thought was nearly as abhorrent as the murky feeling pervading the *palazzo*. Pulling her cloak closer around her, she followed the older woman through a maze of wide halls and up a winding marble staircase, where a multitude of portraits stared at her. She could feel the eerie weight of eyes watching her, following her progress as she made her way through the twists and turns of the *palazzo*. The structure was beautiful, more so than anything she had ever seen, but it was an icy kind of beauty that left her cold. Everywhere she looked she saw carvings of enormous maned cats with razor-sharp teeth and ferocious eyes. Great beasts with shaggy hair around their necks and down their backs. Some had huge webbed wings spread to launch them into the sky. Small icons and large sculptures of the creatures were scattered throughout the halls. In an alcove recessed into one of the walls was a shrine with dozens of burning candles before a fierce-looking lion.

A sudden thought made her shiver. Those roars she'd heard could have been from lions. She had never seen a lion, but she certainly had heard of the legendary beasts that were reputed to have torn countless Christians to pieces for the entertainment of Romans. Did the people in this terrible place worship the beast? The devil? Things were whispered about this man. Surreptitiously she made the sign of the cross to protect her from the evil emanating from the very walls.

Sarina stopped beside a door and pushed it open, stepping back to wave Isabella through. Glancing at the servant almost for reassurance, Isabella stepped across the threshold into a bedchamber. The room was large, the fireplace roaring with the warmth of red and orange flames. She was too tired and drained to do more than offer a murmur of appreciation for the beauty of the long row of stained-glass windows and the carved furniture. Even the huge bed with

11

the thick quilt only penetrated the edge of her awareness. She had poured every ounce of her courage and strength into getting to this place, into seeing the elusive *Don* Nicolai DeMarco.

"Are you certain he will not see me tonight?" Isabella asked. "Please, if you would just let him know the urgency of my visit, I am certain he would change his mind. Would you try?" She stripped off her fur-lined gloves and tossed them onto the ornate dresser.

"Just by your coming to this forbidden place, the Master knows that what you seek is of great importance to you. You must understand, it is not of importance to him. He has his own problems to deal with." Sarina's voice was gentle, even kind. She started to move out of the bedchamber but turned back. She looked around the room, out into the hall, and then back at Isabella. "You are very young. Didn't anyone warn you away from this place? Weren't you told to stay away?" Her voice held a scolding note, a gentle one but a reprimand all the same. "Where are your parents, *piccola*?"

Isabella crossed the room, keeping her face turned away, afraid the sympathetic note in the woman's voice would be her undoing. She wanted to crumble into a pathetic heap and weep for the loss of her family, for the terrible burdens that had fallen onto her slim shoulders. Instead, she clutched at one beautifully carved post of the giant bed until her knuckles turned white. "My parents died a long time ago, *signora*." Her voice was tight, unemotional, but the hand gripping the post tightened even more. "I have to speak to him. Please, if you have any way to get word to him, it is very urgent, and my time is very short."

The servant moved back into the room, firmly closing the door behind her. At once the terrible, oily thickness that permeated the air of the *palazzo* seemed to be gone. Isabella found she could breathe more freely, and the tightness in her chest eased. She noticed a strange scent rising from the surface of the hot water in the tub prepared for her, a clean, fresh, floral fragrance she had never before encountered. She inhaled deeply and was grateful for the cup of tea the serving woman pressed into her trembling hand.

"You must drink this immediately," Sarina encouraged. "You are so cold, it will help to warm you up. Drink every drop—there's a good girl."

The tea did help warm her insides, but Isabella was afraid nothing would ever warm her thoroughly again. She was shaking uncontrollably. She looked up at Sarina. "I really can manage. I do not want you to go to any trouble. The room is lovely, and I have everything I could possibly want. By the way, I am Isabella Vernaducci." The bed looked comfortable, the fire cheerful and warm. Despite the inviting, steaming water in the tub, the moment the serving woman left her alone, Isabella intended to fall onto the bed, completely clothed, and just go to sleep. Her eyelids drooped no matter how hard she tried to stay awake.

"The Master would want me to help you. You are swaying with weariness. If my daughter was far from home, I would want someone to aid her. Please do me the honor of allowing me to assist you." Sarina was already pulling Isabella's cape from her shoulders. "Come, *signorina*, the bath is hot and will warm you much more quickly. You are still shivering."

"I'm so tired." The words slipped out before Isabella could stop them. "I just want to sleep." She sounded young and defenseless even to her own ears.

Sarina helped her undress and urged her into the hot water. As Isabella slid into the steaming tub, Sarina loosened the silken braids and fanned the younger woman's hair out. Very gently she massaged Isabella's scalp with her fingertips, rubbing in the homemade soap that smelled of flowers. Gradually, as the heat of the water seeped into Isabella, her terrible shaking began to lessen.

Isabella was so tired, she knew she was drifting as the servant rinsed her hair and wrapped her in a heavy robe. She stumbled to the bed as if in a dream world, half aware of her surroundings and half asleep. The feel of Sarina working at the knots in her hair, smoothing the long tresses, then replaiting the heavy mass as Isabella lay quietly was comforting, something her mother had done when she was very young. Her long lashes drifted down, and she lay passively on the bed, the robe around her naked body soaking up the excess dampness from her bath.

A knock on the door failed to rouse her interest. Even the aroma of food couldn't capture her attention. She wanted to go to sleep, exhaustion taking over and pushing out all worries and fear. Sarina murmured something she couldn't quite catch. She just wanted to sleep. The food was taken away, and Isabella continued to drift, the beauty of the room, the comforting crackle of the fire, and Sarina's hands in her hair lulling her into a sense of well-being.

From far away, insulated in her dreamlike state, Isabella heard Sarina gasp. She tried to open her eyes and managed to peek out from beneath her lashes. The shadows in the room had lengthened alarmingly. The rows of tapers on the wall had been snuffed out, and the flames in the fireplace had died down, leaving the corners of the bedchamber dark and unfamiliar. In one corner she made out the shadowy figure of man. At least she thought him human.

He was tall, broad-shouldered, with long hair and slashing eyes. Flames from the fire seemed to blaze red-orange in his hot gaze. She could feel the weight of his burning gaze on her exposed skin. His hair was strange, a tawny color that darkened into black as it fell to his shoulders and down his broad back. He was watching her from the shadows, blending in so she couldn't discern him clearly. A shadow figure for her dreams. Isabella blinked to try to bring him into sharper focus, but it was too much trouble to rouse herself from her dreamy state. Her body felt like lead, and she couldn't even find the energy to drag her exposed arm beneath the robe. As she lay, trying to make out the shadowy figure, her vision blurred still more, and his large hands appeared to be claws for a moment, his great hulk moving with a grace not quite human.

She felt exposed, vulnerable, but as hard as she tried, she could not manage to rouse herself. She lay facedown on the bed, staring apprehensively into the darkened corner, her heart slamming painfully hard.

"She is much younger than I had imagined. And much more beautiful." The words were said softly, as if merely mused aloud and not for anyone's hearing. The voice was deep and husky, a blend of seduction, command, and a throaty growl that nearly stopped her heart.

"She has much courage." Sarina's voice came from the other side of her, quite close, as if she might be hovering protectively, but Isabella didn't dare check, afraid to take her gaze off the shadowy figure watching her so intently. Like a predator. A great cat. A lion? Her imagination was running away with her, mixing reality with dreams, and she wasn't sure what was real. If *he* was real.

"She was foolish to come here." The lash in his voice stung.

Isabella tried to force her body to move, but it was impossible. It occurred to her that something had been in the tea, or perhaps in the scented bathwater. She lay in an agony of fear, yet she was hazy and dreamy, removed from the fear, disconnected, as if she were watching all this happening to someone else.

"It took great courage and endurance. She came alone," Sarina pointed out gently. "It may have been foolish, but it was courageous, and nothing short of a miracle that she could accomplish such a feat."

"I know what you are thinking, Sarina." A singular weariness tinged the man's voice. "There are no miracles. I should know. It is better not to believe in such nonsense." He moved closer, looming over Isabella so that his shadow fell upon her, engulfing her completely. She couldn't see his face, but his hands were large and enormously strong when he caught her up in his arms.

15

For a horrified moment she stared at the hands gripping her with such ease. One moment the hands seemed to be great paws with razor-sharp nails, and the next, human hands. She had no idea which was the illusion. Whether this was real or a nightmare. Whether *he* was real or a nightmare. Her head lolled back on her neck, but she couldn't lift her lashes high enough to see his face. She could only lie helplessly in his arms, her heart pounding loudly. He tucked her beneath the quilts, robe and all, his movements sure and efficient.

His palm cupped the side of her face, his thumb stroking a gentle caress over her skin. "So very soft," he murmured to himself. His fingers slid down her chin to push the thick rope of hair from her neck. There was unexpected heat in his fingertips, tiny flames that seemed to ignite her blood, and her entire body felt hot and achy and unfamiliar.

The strange roars began again, and the *castello* seemed to reverberate with the hideous sounds.

"They are restless tonight," Sarina observed. Her hand tightened around Isabella's, and this time there was no doubt she was being protective.

"They feel a disturbance, and it makes them uneasy and therefore dangerous. Be most careful this night, Sarina." The man's warning was plain. "I will see if I can calm them." With a sigh, the shadowy figure turned abruptly and stalked out. Silently. There was no whisper of clothing, no footfalls, absolutely no sound at all.

Isabella felt Sarina touch her hair again, fuss with the quilt, and then she drifted to sleep. She had dreams of a great lion relentlessly stalking her, padding after her on huge, silent paws while she ran down a maze of long, wide corridors. All the while she was watched from above by silent winged harpies with sharp, curved beaks and greedy eyes.

Sounds penetrated her strange dreams. Strange sounds to go with her strange dreams. The rattle of chains. A rising wail. Screams in the night. Restlessly Isabella snuggled more deeply into the quilts. The fire had died down to orange embers glittering brightly. She could just make out the pinpoints of light in the darkened room. She lay staring at the colors as an occasional draft breathed life into tiny flames. It was several minutes before she realized she was not alone.

Isabella turned over, peering through the darkness to the shadowy figure seated on the edge of her bed. As her eyes adjusted, she could make out a young woman rocking herself back and forth, her long hair tumbling around her body. She was dressed simply but elegantly, obviously not one of the servants. In the darkness the gown was an unusual color, a deep blue with a strange star-burst pattern, something Isabella had never seen before. At Isabella's movement, the woman turned and looked at her, smiling serenely.

"Hello. I didn't think you'd wake up. I wanted to see you."

Isabella fought the fog surrounding her. Carefully she looked around the room, searching the shadows for the man. Had he been a dream? She didn't know. She still felt the brush of his fingers against her skin. Her hand crept up to slide over her neck to capture the sensation of his touch.

"I'm Francesca," the young woman said, a hint of haughtiness in her voice. "You mustn't be afraid of me. I know we're going to be great friends."

Isabella made an effort to sit up. Her body didn't want to cooperate. "I think there was something in the tea," she said aloud, testing the idea.

A tinkling laugh escaped the curving mouth. "Well, of course. He cannot very well have you running around the *palazzo* discovering all the long-kept secrets."

Isabella fought the haze, determined to overcome her terrible drowsiness. She pushed herself into a sitting position, clutching the slipping robe, suddenly aware she had no other clothes. For the moment it didn't matter. She was

17

warm and clean and out of the storm. And she had reached her destination. "Are there secrets here?"

As if to answer her, the chains rattled again, the wails rose to a shriek, and from somewhere far away came a rumbling growl. Isabella pulled the covers more closely around her.

The woman laughed merrily. "It is a secret how I was able to get into your room when your door is locked securely. There are many, many secrets here, all so deliciously wicked. Have you come to wed Nicolai?"

Isabella's eyes widened with shock. She pulled the heavy robe even more tightly around her. "No, of course not! Where did you get such an idea?"

Francesca gave another tinkling laugh. "Everyone is talking about it, whispering in the halls, in their rooms. The entire *palazzo* is speculating. It was such fun when we heard you were on your way. Of course, the others wagered you would never live through such a journey or that you would turn back. I hoped you would make it!"

Isabella's mouth trembled, and she bit down carefully on her lower lip. "The *don* of the *palazzo* was aware I was coming, and he sent no escort to meet me?" In truth she could have been killed. "How is it you even knew?"

The woman shrugged carelessly. "He has spies everywhere. He knew long ago that you wished an audience with him. He never sees anyone he doesn't wish to see."

Isabella studied the young woman. She was approximately Isabella's age yet seemed quite childlike and mischievous. In spite of the circumstances, Isabella found herself smiling. There was something contagious in Francesca's saucy grin. "What are those terrible noises?" The sounds didn't appear to bother Francesca in the least, and Isabella found herself relaxing a bit.

The woman laughed again. "You will get used to it." She rolled her eyes. "Silly, really. Sometimes it goes on for hours." Francesca leaned forward. "How did you get here? No one can come here without an invitation and an escort.

Everyone is dying to know how you did it." She lowered her voice. "Did you use a spell? I know several spells but none strong enough to protect anyone from the perils of this valley. Was it difficult to get through the pass? Everyone says you did it on your own. Is that true?" Francesca fired the questions at her in rapid succession.

Isabella chose her words carefully. She knew nothing of these people, didn't know if they followed the dictates of the Holy Church or were devil-worshipers. It didn't sound good that Francesca dabbled in spells, and worse that she would admit it aloud. Isabella half expected a bolt of lightning to crash down from the heavens.

"I did come through the pass," she admitted. Her mouth was dry. Beside the bed was an ornate pitcher filled with water, along with a delicate fluted glass. Isabella stared at the water, afraid that if she drank it, it might contain something to send her back to sleep. Her fingers twisted in the covers. She thought carefully about her trip, how difficult it had been, how she had felt as she overcame each obstacle. "It was exhilarating and at the same time frightening," she answered truthfully. Now that she knew the *don* had been aware of her plight all along, she was even more pleased that she had done what so many others had failed to do.

Francesca bounced on the bed, laughing softly. "Oh, that is too rich. Wait until the others hear what you said. 'Exhilarating'! That is too perfect!"

In spite of the strangeness of the conversation, Isabella found herself smiling, because Francesca's laughter was so infectious.

A ferocious roar shook the *palazzo*. A hideous, high-pitched scream of agony mingled with the terrible sound. It echoed throughout the vast *castello*, reaching to the highest vaulted ceiling and the deepest hidden dungeons and caverns the *castello* guarded. Isabella clutched the robe to her, staring in frozen horror at her closed door. The scream was cut off abruptly, but a terrible din followed. From every direction wild animals bellowed, and she covered her ears

19

to block out the sounds. Her heart was pounding so loudly it sounded like thunder, mixing with the chaos. She turned her head toward Francesca.

The woman was gone. The bed was smooth, the quilt without a crease where she had been sitting. Isabella swung her gaze wildly around the room, searching out every corner, trying desperately to pierce the darkness. As abruptly as the terrible noise had started, it stopped, and there was only silence. Isabella sat very still, afraid to move.

Chapter Two

Isabella sat quietly in the bed, the robe wrapped securely around her, staring at the door until dawn streaked rays of light through the long row of stained-glass windows. She watched the sun begin to rise, watched the colors leap to life and bring a certain animation to the images portrayed in the windows.

She stood up and wandered across the room, drawn to the colorful panels. She had been in many of the great *castelli* when she was a child, and all of them were awe-inspiring. But this one was more ornate, more intricate, more everything. In her room alone, a mere guest room, was a small fortune in art and gold. It was no wonder the armies of the Spanish and Austrian kings and those who came before had sought entrance into this valley.

Isabella found the small chamber reserved for morning ablutions and took her time, going over in her mind each argument she would use to persuade *Don* DeMarco to aid her in saving her brother. *Don* DeMarco. His name was whispered by powerful men. It was said he had the ear of the most influential rulers in the world and that those who did not listen or heed him ended up disappearing or dead. Few saw him, but it was rumored that he was half man, half beast and that within his valley strange, demonic apparitions aided him. The gossip included everything from ghosts to an army of wild beasts under his command. Isabella remembered her brother, Lucca, telling her every story and laughing with her over the absurd rumors people were so willing to believe.

She looked around her room carefully. Crosses were hung on either side of her door. She moved closer to examine the door itself. The carvings on it were of angels, beautiful, winged creatures guarding the bedchamber. Isabella smiled. She was being fanciful, but the rumors of demonic creatures and an army of wild animals she had laughed over with her brother seemed far closer to reality now, and she was grateful for the plethora of angels standing guard at her door.

The room itself was large and rife with ornate carvings. Several small etchings of winged lions hung on the walls, but most appeared to be of angels. Two stone lions guarded the great fireplace, but they looked rather kindly, so she patted their heads to make friends with them.

Isabella could not find her clothes anywhere and with a sigh of frustration opened the enormous wardrobe. It was packed with beautiful gowns, gowns that looked as if they were new, made just for her. She pulled one out, her hand trembling as she smoothed the full skirt. The frocks looked as if her favorite dressmaker had sewn them. Each one, everyday wear and fancy ball, was her size and made with lace and soft, flowing material. She had never had such fine dresses, not even when her father was alive. Her fingers caressed the fabric, touching the tiny seams in reverence.

In the bureau she discovered intimate items carefully folded, with flower petals strewn throughout each drawer to keep them freshly scented. Isabella sat on the edge of her bed, holding the garments in her hands. Had they been made for her? How could such a thing be? Perhaps she had been given another young woman's room. She looked around the enormous bedchamber once more.

It didn't contain the personal accessories she would expect to find in someone's private chambers. She found herself shivering. All at once the beautiful gowns seemed a bit sinister, as if *Don* DeMarco, knowing she was coming, had devised his own disreputable plans for her. Francesca said the news of her imminent arrival had traveled well ahead of her, yet the elusive *don* had not sent out an escort. None of it made sense to her.

How had Francesca managed to come into her room despite the locked door? Mulling over the puzzle, Isabella dressed slowly in the plainest gown she could find, feeling she had no choice. She couldn't very well go to meet the *don* without a stitch of clothing on. She knew that many *castelli* and the great *palazzi* had secret passageways and hidden rooms. That had to be the answer to Francesca's abrupt arrival and departure. She took a few minutes to examine the marble walls. She could find no evidence of an opening in any of them. She even examined the large hearth, but it seemed solid enough.

Her breath caught in her throat when she heard a key turn in the lock of her door and it was pushed open. Sarina smiled at her. She was carrying a tray. "I thought you would be awake and quite hungry by now, *signorina*. You didn't eat at all last night."

Isabella glared at her. "You put something in the tea." She backed away from the older woman until a wall brought her up short.

"The Master wanted you to sleep through the night. His pets can be frightening if you are not used to their noise. Besides, you were so tired from your journey, I think you would have fallen asleep even without aid. And I explained last night that you could not roam freely throughout the *palazzo*. It's not always safe," Sarina said, repeating her warning of the night before. She didn't seem in the least remorseful.

The food smelled wonderful, and Isabella's empty stomach rumbled, but she stared at the tray suspiciously. "I told you last night that my errand is urgent. I must see the *don* immediately. Has he agreed to an audience?"

"Later today. He is nocturnal and rarely sees anyone in the morning hours unless it is a dire emergency," Sarina answered calmly. She placed the tray on the small table in front of the fire.

"But it is an emergency," Isabella said desperately. *Nocturnal?* She turned the strange concept over and over in her mind, trying to make sense of it.

"It isn't to him," Sarina pointed out. "He will not change his mind, *signorina*, so you may as well eat now while you have the chance. The food is excellent and without any herb to aid you to sleep." When Isabella continued to stare at her, she sighed softly. "Come, *piccola*, you'll need your strength for what lies ahead."

Isabella crossed the room reluctantly to stand beside the chair. "I couldn't find my clothes, so I put on one of the gowns I found in the wardrobe, *signora*. I trust I did not do anything wrong."

"No, the Master provided clothes for you, as he knew yours had been ruined on your journey. Sit, *signorina*, and eat. I'll tend your hair for you. You have such beautiful hair. My daughter would have been about your age. We lost her in an accident." There was a tightness to her voice, and although the older woman was behind the chair where Isabella had seated herself, she knew the housekeeper had made the sign of the cross.

At least they all weren't devil-worshipers in this valley. Isabella sighed with relief. "I'm so sorry for your loss, *signora*. I can only imagine how terrible it would be to lose a child, but *mia madre* died of the fever when I was but six, and *mio padre* was carried home from a hunting accident. I only have *mio fratello* now. And I do not wish to lose him, too."

She didn't add that both she and Lucca believed her father's hunting accident, which subsequently caused his death, had been no accident but a serious bid by their neighbor, *Don* Rivellio, to begin the takeover of their lands.

"You met *mio sposo*, Betto, last night on your arrival. He stabled your horse for you. The animal was very tired. He is a good man, and should you need anything, he will aid you." Sarina lowered her voice, almost as if she thought the walls had ears. As if she were a conspirator.

Isabella wrapped her hands around the hot cup of tea. She inhaled deeply but found no trace of any herb she could identify as medicinal. "He seemed very nice, and he was kind to me." She looked up at Sarina. "Did *Don* DeMarco enter my room last night while I slept?"

Sarina stiffened, her hands stilling as she was placing the dishes closer to Isabella's chair. "Why do you ask such a thing?"

"I had strange dreams, that you were here in my room and he came in."

"Are you certain? What did he look like?" Sarina turned to tidy the bed, keeping her back to the younger woman.

Isabella thought the housekeeper's hands were trembling. She took a cautious sip of tea. It was sweet and hot and tasted perfect. "I couldn't see his face. But he seemed . . . large. Is he a big man?"

Sarina fluffed the quilt, then smoothed it carefully. "He is tall and enormously strong. But he moves . . ." She trailed off.

"In silence," Isabella supplied thoughtfully, almost to herself. "He was here last night, in this room, wasn't he?"

"He wished to make certain you had suffered no injury on your journey." Sarina prompted her to eat, pushing the plate toward her. "Our cook becomes very upset when we don't eat what she provides. Already we sent back your meal last night. She has prepared this especially for you. Please try it."

Isabella hadn't eaten a real meal in so long, she was almost afraid to take a bite. Her stomach protested at first, but then the strange, honeyed cake simply melted in her mouth, and she found she was quite hungry. "It is good," she praised in answer to Sarina's expectant expression. "What was that terrible scream I heard? That was no dream but someone mortally wounded." She was reluctant to tell even Sarina about Francesca's visit, uncertain whether it would make trouble for the young woman. She liked Francesca and needed at least one ally in the *castello*. Sarina was sweet, and very good to her, but her loyalty was definitely to *Don* DeMarco. Everything Isabella said, everything she did, would be dutifully reported. Isabella accepted that as Sarina's duty. Her father had been *don* over his people. She knew what loyalty the title commanded.

"These things happen. Someone was incautious." Sarina shrugged her thin shoulders almost carelessly, but as she turned away, Isabella saw that her face was pale and her lips were trembling. "I must go. I will return for you when it is time." She was already halfway to the door, clearly not wanting to continue the conversation. Before Isabella could protest, the door was firmly closed, and she heard the key turn in the lock.

Isabella spent a good portion of the morning napping. She was still tired and drained from the exhausting journey, and every muscle in her body seemed to ache. She had studied every inch of the room and the stained glass and again searched for hidden passageways, then finally threw herself onto the bed. She was fast asleep when Sarina returned, and they had to hurry, Isabella taking care of her rumpled appearance, Sarina dressing her hair and clucking at her like a hen.

"You must hurry, *signorina*. You do not wish to keep him waiting too long. He has many appointments. You are but one."

"I didn't mean to fall asleep," Isabella apologized. The older woman opened the door for her, but Isabella was suddenly reluctant to step into the corridor, remembering the terrible, overwhelming cloud of evil she had encountered the previous evening.

Isabella was "different." Lucca told her to keep her strange premonitions and oddities to herself, never to allow anyone to know that she was "sensitive" to things beyond what the eye could see. But Lucca and her father had relied on her feelings when they were looking for allies, when they sought others to join their secret societies to protect their lands from continual assaults by outside rulers.

"Signorina," Sarina said softly. "We cannot take a chance on being late for your appointment. He will not grant you another."

Isabella took a deep breath and followed Sarina out the door, patting the angels for good luck as she slipped past. She looked up just as a young serving girl threw water from a golden goblet into her face. The water splashed down her cheeks to drip into the neckline of her dress. Isabella stopped dead in her tracks, staring in numbed shock at the girl standing in front of her.

A sudden silence fell as all work ceased and servants gaped in horrified fascination. The water continued to drip down Isabella's gown, running between her breasts like beads of sweat.

"Alberita!" Sarina chastised the girl, frowning severely, although laughter was evident in her sparkling eyes. "The holy water is sprinkled on one's person, not thrown in one's face! *Scusi, Signorina* Isabella, she is young and impulsive and does not always listen well. The holy water was for your protection, not your bath."

Alberita dropped a slight curtsey in Isabella's direction, gaping up at her in horror, her face ashen, tears in her eyes. *"Scusi, scusi! La prego* do not tell the Master."

"I am most grateful for the protection, Alberita. I shall go to meet my destiny with no trepidation in my heart. Assuredly I have extra protection from any who would seek to harm me." Isabella had to struggle to keep from laughing.

Sarina shook her head and carefully wiped Isabella's face.

"It's good of you to be so understanding. Most others would have demanded she be flogged."

"I have no more status than you, *signora*," Isabella confessed, unashamed. "And I do not believe in flogging. Well," she muttered under her breath, "perhaps *Don* Rivellio could use a good flogging."

Sarina's mouth twitched, but she didn't smile. "Come, we mustn't be late. *Don* DeMarco has a busy schedule. Be certain you are properly respectful."

Isabella glanced at her, certain the older woman was laughing at her, but Sarina was leading the way through the wide corridors and archways. They hurried past several servants working. She noticed that they all looked at her with solemn faces, some of them with tight smiles. All of them made the sign of the cross toward her as if blessing her.

Holy water and blessings from the servants. Isabella cleared her throat. "*Signora*, is *Don* DeMarco a member of the Holy Church?" Her voice wavered a little, but Isabella was proud of the fact that she had managed to get the words out without stuttering. She had a sinking feeling that maybe all the rumors about the *don* were true after all. She sent up a quick, silent prayer that *Don* DeMarco and God were on good terms.

Sarina Sincini did not answer but walked quickly ahead of her, leading the way into a large open court with winding staircases rising off it in several directions. In the center of the court was a fountain that soared nearly to the second story. It provided Isabella with a measure of relief to see that each cutaway section of the fountain was topped with a cross. At the base of each circular column, however, was the inevitable lion, broad and muscular, with a tawny mane tipped in black. Still, the sound of water splashing was soothing, and the intricate carvings of kindly figures around the top of the fountain provided more assurance.

Isabella wanted to linger and examine the large sculpture, but Sarina was halfway up one of the winding staircases. As Isabella hurried up the seemingly endless stairs, she gazed at the array of portraits on the wall. One, the face of a man, was so beautiful it made her ache inside. His eyes held pain, deep sorrow. She was mesmerized by his eyes, wanting to hold him close and comfort him. The feeling was strong in her that she knew him, that she recognized those eyes. Isabella looked past the portrait to the next one. She recognized that face immediately. Francesca's laughing eyes gazed back at her, mischievous and happy. The painting must have been done fairly recently, as Francesca seemed nearly the same age as she was now. Who, exactly, was she, Isabella wondered. A young cousin of the *don*? The artist had captured the essence of her, her warmth and sunny disposition. Isabella took courage just looking at the sweet face. She squared her shoulders and hurried after Sarina.

They took many twists and turns through numerous hallways and darkened alcoves, passing more stained-glass windows and intricately carved arches. Isabella wanted to explore everything. The *castello* in the daylight seemed more open and airy and far less of a threat than it had the night before. She no longer sensed the thick, oily impression of evil.

Finally they reached the far end of the *palazzo*, a distance from the main rooms. She caught glimpses of rooms filled with books and sculptures and all sorts of intriguing things she would have liked to examine, but Sarina continued to hurry through the maze of corridors. Isabella was truly lost as they made their way up a third flight of wide, curving steps to a balcony and a double door straight ahead. Isabella stopped abruptly in front of it, not needing Sarina to tell her she was in *Don* DeMarco's private lair.

"This entire wing of the house is the Master's. No one is allowed entrance unless he has issued an invitation."

"What of the servants?" Isabella asked, curious. She was staring at the huge, intricately carved double door graced with a lion's head complete with shaggy mane and piercing eyes. The muzzle seemed to come right out of the carving, open mouth displaying sharpened teeth. But there was something different about this lion, something very different from the others. This lion looked intelligent, cunning, menacing. It was almost as if the portrait of a man had been made into the carving of a lion. She could almost see the human beneath the frightful mask.

"You must go in," Sarina prompted.

Isabella continued to stare at the carving, scarcely hearing the older woman. She reached out and touched the ferocious muzzle with a gentle fingertip, almost caressing it, something inside her responding to the look in those eyes.

"*Signorina*, take hold of the handle and go inside," Sarina urged her in a soft hiss.

Isabella's heart began to pound as she gazed in horror at the doorknob—another snarling lion's head. She was afraid, now that she was actually here, that the *don* would turn her down and she would have nowhere else to go. "Come in with me," she whispered softly to the housekeeper, a plea that cost her a great deal in pride.

"You must go in alone, *piccola*." Sarina patted her shoulder encouragingly. "He is expecting you. Have courage." She began to walk away.

Isabella reached out to her before she could stop herself, clutching desperately at the woman's dress. "Is he as they whisper of him?"

"He is both terrible and kind," Sarina answered. "We are accustomed to his ways, to his appearance. Others are not. Be one he can be kind to. He has not much patience, so go in quickly. You look beautiful, and you have shown much courage." She reached past Isabella, grasped the ornate doorknob, and twisted it.

Isabella had no choice. She entered the room slowly. Her heart was beating so loudly, she feared he might hear it. She tried not to look intimidated or stiff with anger. She needed to be humble. She repeated that to herself several times. She *had* to be humble, not speak her mind or allow her wayward tongue to run away with her. She couldn't afford to be the wild girl-child breaking every rule in her father's

house, running free in the mountains when no one was looking, playing tricks on her beloved brother at every turn,
continually earning her father's disapproving frown as he
turned away from her in disappointment.

She held tightly to her memories of her brother, Lucca.
He had often aided her in her rebellious ways, her best
friend and confidant despite their father's pleading that she
act the part of a lady. She knew she would have been wed
long before now if her father had had his way, sold to some
older *don* to aid the war chest. Lucca wouldn't hear of it.
Several times she had dressed as a boy and accompanied
him on hunting expeditions. He had taught her to wield a
sword and a stiletto, to ride as well as a man, even to swim
in the cold waters of the rivers and lakes. Long after their
father died, her brother had protected her, loved her, and
watched over her. Even when they were desperate for
money, he had never once thought of selling her to one of
the many suitors. And she would never, ever abandon Lucca
in his hour of need.

Isabella lifted her chin. Lucca had taught her courage,
and she wouldn't fail him now in her last, desperate attempt
to save him. She moved into the darkened interior of the
room. A fire blazed on the hearth, but it couldn't compete
with the heavy draperies blocking out every vestige of light
from the windows. She saw two high-backed chairs in front
of the fire, but the room was huge, with high, vaulted ceilings and so many alcoves and archways an army could have
been hiding. Even the blaze in the large fireplace had no
hope of shedding light into the shadowy recesses.

For a moment she thought herself alone as the heavy door
swung closed, locking her in the room. Then she felt him.
She knew it was he. The *don*. Mysterious. Aloof. She sensed
him there in the darkness, the weight of his stare. Intense.
Calculating. Burning. Afraid to cross the wide expanse of
marble floor to one of the high-backed chairs, Isabella shivered in spite of her determination not to show her fear.

Then she froze, standing perfectly still, her gaze riveted

to the deepest shadows, a darkened alcove where she made out the shape of a man. He stood tall, and on his forearm perched a falcon, a raptor with a wicked beak and talons that could pierce, rend, and shred delicate skin. Its round, beady eyes were fixed on her intently. The bird stirred as if it might fly at her face, but the man spoke softly to it, his voice so low she couldn't make out the words. He stroked the falcon's neck and back, and it settled down, though it never took its gaze from Isabella.

No matter how hard she tried to pierce the darkness to see the man clearly, she could not. When he turned slightly to touch the bird, he appeared to have long hair, swept back from his face and secured at the nape of his neck with a leather tie, yet it was still wild and shaggy, looking like a mane in disarray. But the cloak of darkness shielded most of him from her so that she couldn't tell what he truly looked like. His face was completely hidden, so she had no idea of his age or features. But as she continued to stare, the flames from the fireplace seemed to leap into his eyes, and for a moment she could see the reflection shimmering through the darkness.

His eyes glowed a fiery red, and they were not human. Cold gripped her, and Isabella wanted to turn and run from the room.

"You are Isabella Vernaducci," he said from the dark alcove. "Please be seated. Sarina has brought tea to steady your nerves."

His voice was pleasant enough, but his words immediately pricked her pride.

She swept across the room regally, a woman of stature, of importance, her head held high. "I do not recall having unsteady nerves, *Signor* DeMarco. However, if *you* feel nervous, I shall be happy to pour a cup for you. I trust the tea is free of any herbs that might cause you to become . . . *drowsy.*" Isabella sat in a high-backed chair, taking time to arrange the long skirt primly over her legs and ankles. She cursed herself silently. Her pride might lose her her hard-won audience with the *don*. What was wrong with her that she bristled in his company? What did it matter what he said, what he thought of her? Let him think her nervous and weak if that was what he wanted. As long as she got her way.

Don DeMarco allowed the silence between them to lengthen. She could feel the weight of his disapproval, the weight of his stare from the shadows.

Trying to salvage the situation, Isabella looked down at her hands. "Thank you for the garments. I had very little in the way of proper clothing with me. The room you offered me is beautiful and the bed comfortable. I could not have asked for better care. *Signora* Sincini took excellent care of me."

"I am happy to see that the gowns fit you. Are you rested from your journey?"

"Yes, *grazie*," she said demurely.

"It was foolish of you to venture into danger, and if your *padre* was alive, I'm certain he would see to it that you were punished for such folly. I am inclined to take on the responsibility myself." His voice was velvet soft, playing along her nerve endings like the brush of fingertips, warming her skin, and she was thankful for the heat of the fire to explain the blush stealing into her face. He was chastising her, yet his voice was nearly a physical caress, and for some reason, Isabella found herself extremely susceptible to it.

"You were warned repeatedly not to come to this place. What kind of woman are you that you would risk your reputation, your life, making such a journey?"

Her fingers curled into two tight fists, and her fingernails dug deeply into her palms. She had the feeling he was watching her closely from the shadows, that his eyes caught that tiny telltale rebellion. Surreptitiously she pushed her hands out of sight beneath the skirts of her dress.

"I am a desperate woman," she admitted, trying unsuccessfully to peer into the darkness. He looked a large, powerful being, not quite human. The bird of prey perched on his arm, staring at her with round, beady eyes, added to her nervousness. "I had to see you. To plead for *mio fratello's* life. I sent messengers, but they were unable to reach you. I know you can help him."

She swallowed the unexpected sob threatening to choke her. "He is in the dungeons of *Don* Rivellio. He has been sentenced to death. *Mio fratello*, Lucca Vernaducci, has been imprisoned for nearly two years, and the conditions are appalling. I have heard that he is ill, and I came here to plead with you to save his life. I know you have the power to have him pardoned. One word from you, and *Don* Rivellio would release him. If you do not wish to openly ask for such a favor, *è possibile* you could arrange for his escape."

She blurted the words out desperately, unable to hold them back a moment longer, and she leaned forward toward the dark corner. "Please do this, *Don* DeMarco. *Mio fratello* is a good man. Do not allow him to die."

There was a long silence. Nothing moved in the room, not even the falcon. *Don* DeMarco sighed softly. "What is he charged with?"

She hesitated, her stomach a tight knot. She should have known he would ask. How could he not? "Treason. It is said he conspired against the king." It was only fair to answer him truthfully.

"Is he guilty? Did he conspire against the king?" he asked, the softest of growls emerging from his throat.

Her heart jumped wildly. Her teeth tugged at her lower lip. "Yes." Her voice was low. "Lucca believed we should overthrow all the other countries seeking to rule us, that no foreign government would care about our people. But what harm can he do now? He is ill. Our lands, our properties—everything we have—has been confiscated and given to *Don* Rivellio. The *don* wishes Lucca dead so that there be no question that he retain our properties. In truth *Don* Rivellio had Lucca arrested for reasons of his own, and he has profited greatly. It is to his advantage to dishonor our name and dispose of *mio fratello*."

"At least you have it in you to tell the truth of your brother's crime."

She lifted her chin haughtily. "Our name is an honored one."

"It was until *tuo fratello* became too loud in his professions of a secret society. Such a thing is not to be talked of to everyone in a tavern."

Isabella hung her head, twisting her fingers together. Her father and brother had been adamant that the society was gaining ground, small pockets of men amassing the power to defeat outsiders. They refused to bow down to any government, distrusting the motives of foreigners pledging alliances. They swore *omertà*—an oath to the death.

"There was no proof!" she said. "*Don* Rivellio *paid* those men to say what they did. Lucca never talked. *Don* Rivellio wanted others to believe he had so that those in the secret circle might well assassinate him. He was charged with treason and sentenced to death." Her gaze was hot with suppressed fury against the *don*. "Lucca was tortured, but he gave no names, incriminated no others. He *never* talked."

"Has it occurred to you that by coming here you might have placed yourself in the same untenable position as *tuo fratello*? I might be allied with *Don* Rivellio. What is there to prevent me from turning you over to him and repeating your treasonous words? It certainly would be far easier than what you propose, and it would gain me not only the *don's* gratitude, but he would also owe me a favor. The world of power operates on intrigue and favors." His voice had dropped another octave, and she shivered despite the warmth of the fire. Surely no one had ever conveyed such menace in such a soft voice.

She lifted her chin defiantly. "I am well aware of the risk I'm taking."

"Are you?" The two words were low, almost a whisper of sound. Ominous. Threatening. "In truth I do not think you have any idea." The silence stretched between them until Isabella wanted to scream. The falcon on the *don's* arm stared at her with merciless eyes. "What kind of man would send his sister to plead for his life? He must have known you were risking your own by coming here."

Her teeth tugged at her lower lip. "In truth he would be angry with me if he knew. But I felt I had no choice."

"Did you plead so eloquently with *Don* Rivellio?" This time his voice conveyed something else, something nameless, but it stirred a terrible dread in her heart. She saw his white teeth flash, as if he snapped them at the mere thought of such a thing.

She wanted to give him whatever answer he needed to hear to encourage him to help her, but she had no idea what he would prefer, so she settled on the truth. "No, I could not force myself to do such a thing. Are you going to help me?" She couldn't stem the impatience in her voice.

"What are your intentions if I do not?"

At least he hadn't dismissed her immediately. "I shall attempt a rescue myself."

He did stir then, white teeth gleaming at her from the darkness. Mocking amusement. "I see. And if I do agree to aid you in this plan to free your guilty *fratello*, what is in it for me? You have no land to give me. You have no money. Your loyalty toward *tuo fratello* is commendable, but I doubt I would elicit the same from you. How did you plan to repay me? Or did you expect me to risk my life and the lives of my soldiers for nothing?"

"Of course not." She was shocked that he would think such a thing of her. "I'm a Vernaducci. We pay our debts. I have *mia madre's* jewelry. It is worth a small fortune. And my mount. She is well bred. And I myself am a hard worker. You may not believe I'll give you the same loyalty, but in exchange for *mio fratello's* life, I'll work hard for you. I ran our home, so I'll have no trouble becoming a *domestica*, as I know what is expected." She stared steadily into the shadows of the alcove, digging her nails even deeper into her palms while her heart beat out a wild rhythm.

"I do not wear jewelry, and I have many horses. I also have many *domestici*, all quite loyal and very capable of doing their jobs."

Her shoulders sagged. She hunched in the chair, struggling desperately not to cry. But she continued to stare into the darkened alcove, not wanting to break contact with her only hope.

"What else are you willing to do in exchange for the life of *tuo fratello*?" The words were soft. "Will you trade your life for his?"

At once her mouth went dry, and her heart nearly stopped. She thought of the unearthly scream of agony she had heard in the middle of the night. The terrible roar of the beasts. Did he sacrifice women to the lions for some pagan god? Did he watch humans being torn to pieces simply for his own perverted pleasure? She knew there were many in power who committed terrible atrocities. "I think you know I would do anything to save him," she answered, suddenly very afraid.

"Once you give me your agreement, there will be no going back on your word," he cautioned.

"You will have him pardoned?" She tilted her chin, putting on a show of bravery.

"You will trade your life for that of *tuo fratello*? I have your word of honor?"

She stood up quickly; she could not stay still. "Gladly," she said defiantly, proudly, every inch a Vernaducci. Even her father would have been proud of her in that moment.

"And I can trust the word of a woman?" His voice was soft, almost caressing, even as he insulted her with his question.

Her eyes flashed at him in a small flare of temper. "My word is not given lightly, *signore*. I assure you, it is every bit as good as yours."

"Then it is done. You will remain here, in my *palazzo*, and the moment we are wed, I shall secure your brother's

37

release." There was a grim finality to his words.

She gasped aloud, a soft protest. It was the last thing she had expected. Her eyes widened as she tried to peer into the darkened alcove. To see him, to see his face. She *had* to see him. "I don't think it is necessary to wed. I'm quite happy to remain a *domestica* in your *palazzo*." She curtsied deliberately. "I assure you, *signore*, I am very hardworking."

"I have no need of another *domestica*. I have need of a wife. You *will* wed me. You have given me your word, and I will not release you." That strange, low growl rumbled from deep within his throat, and the bird on his arm shook its wings restlessly, as if suddenly nervous or about to attack. Its beady eyes stared at Isabella as relentlessly as did the eyes in the shadows.

Isabella's heart stuttered, and she gripped the back of the chair to steady herself, but she gazed intently into the alcove, refusing to be intimidated. "I did not ask to be released, *Don* DeMarco. I merely attempted to point out I was not expecting you to marry me. I have no dowry, no land, nothing to bring to the match." She should have been sagging with relief that he wasn't feeding her to his lions, but instead she was more frightened than ever. "*Mio fratello* is ill. He will need care. He must be brought here immediately so that I can nurse him back to health."

"I will not tolerate interference from your brother. He would not want you to trade your life for his. He must believe our match is one of mutual affection."

After all she had been through, her relief was so tremendous that Isabella feared she might collapse. She could feel tears clogging her throat and swimming in her eyes, and she turned away from the *don* to stare into the fireplace, hoping he wouldn't notice her weakness. She waited until she was certain she could control her voice.

"If you save *mio fratello*, I will not have to feign affection for you, *Don* DeMarco. It will be so. I have given you my word. Please make the arrangements. Every moment counts, as Lucca's health is failing, and *Don* Rivellio has ordered his death at the end of this moon's cycle." She sank back into the chair to keep from collapsing into a pitiful heap on the floor.

"I would not make promises you cannot keep, *Signorina* Vernaducci. You have not yet seen your bridegroom." There was a grimness to his voice, a hard, implacable warning.

He moved forward then—she *felt* him moving rather than heard him—but she didn't turn her gaze away from the fire. Suddenly she didn't want to see him. She wanted to be alone to give herself time to regain her strength and courage. But her legs were far too shaky to carry her from his quarters. He strode into the edge of her vision, tall and muscular, a powerful, fit male, reaching upward to allow the falcon to settle onto a perch built into an alcove far from the fire. And then he was walking toward her. As he approached she became aware of how silently, how quickly, how fluidly, he moved.

He reached for the small teapot on the table between the two chairs. For one horrible moment Isabella saw a lion's huge paw with dangerous claws. She blinked, and the paw, only an illusion of her terrified imagination, became his hand. She watched as he poured the liquid into two cups and handed her one.

"Drink this. You will feel better." His voice was gruff, almost as if he regretted the small kindness.

Gratefully closing her hands around the hot cup, she accidentally brushed his skin with her fingertips. At the slight contact a whip of lightning leapt into her bloodstream, arcing and crackling, sizzling hot. Shocked, she nearly jumped away from him, her startled gaze flying upward to lock with his.

Chapter Three

Isabella found herself staring into strange, liquid amber eyes. They were mesmerizing. A cat's eyes. Wild. Mysterious. Hypnotizing. Blazing with some emotion she couldn't fathom. His pupils were intensely pale and unusually elliptical in shape. Still, she felt she had seen those eyes somewhere before. They weren't altogether unfamiliar to her, and she relaxed, a small smile curving her mouth.

His hand suddenly cupped her chin, forcing her to continue to meet his fierce gaze. "See me, bride. See your bridegroom. Take a good look at the bargain you have made." His voice had a deep, rumbling note to it, that undertone of growling she had noticed before.

Isabella did as he said. She began to inspect him. His hair was thick and oddly colored. Tawny, almost golden, it framed his face and fell below his shoulders, where it darkened to appear as black and shiny as a raven's wing. The need to touch the thick luxurious mass was so strong, she actually lifted her hand and did so in the lightest of caresses.

He caught her wrist in a hard, unbreakable grip. She could feel his great body trembling. His eyes became turbulent and dangerous, watching her with the unblinking, unnerving stare of a predator locked onto its prey. She saw his features then, the long, obscene scars etched into the left side of the face of an angel. Wicked and frightful, they ran from his scalp to his shadowed jaw, four of them, as if some wild animal had raked his cheek, tearing the flesh right down to the bone. And he did have the face of an angel, absurdly handsome, a face any artist would want to capture on canvas for all time.

His grip tightened until she thought he might crush her bones, his eyes becoming wilder, narrowing dangerously, fixing on her face as if he were about to leap upon her and devour her for some terrible misdeed. He bent toward her, his perfectly sculpted mouth snarling, a warning growl rumbling in his throat.

As she continued to gaze at him, his features changed, blurring oddly so that for a moment she thought she was staring into the face of a great beast, its muzzle open to show sharp white teeth. The eyes, however, remained somehow familiar to her. She stared directly into those eyes and smiled. "Are you going to have tea with me?"

His body was very muscular, far more so than that of any man she had ever encountered, his sinews defined and rippling with strength beneath his elegant shirt. His thighs were twin columns of power, like oak tree trunks. He was tall but well proportioned, frightening in his size and the power he exuded.

Those amber eyes stared at her for several heartbeats. He slowly released her wrist, the warmth of his palm lingering on her skin. Isabella twisted her fingers into the folds of her skirt to prevent herself from rubbing at the marks on her wrist. Her pulse throbbed in a rhythm of fear and excitement. It was silly the way her wild imagination persisted in seeing him as the strange, leonine carvings in his home. And it was equally silly that the outside world thought him a demonic beast because of a few scars.

Isabella was no frightened child to faint away because he bore evidence of surviving a vicious attack. Deliberately she took a sip of tea. "You do not disappoint me, *signore*, or frighten me, if that is your intention. Do you think me so weak or young? I am no child to have fear of a man." Although he was much more intimidating than she wanted to admit. And he clearly had enormous strength. He could crush her easily should he make the effort. It was impossible to judge his age. He was no boy but a full-grown man, bearing the weight of his title and the burden of ensuring his people's welfare on his broad shoulders. And now that of her brother. She had brought him yet another encumbrance, and the thought made her feel guilty. "Please do have some tea. I would hope to become better acquainted with you."

"Tell me what you see when you look at me." His voice was quiet, a mere thread of sound, a whisper of velvet and heat. Yet it was a command from a powerful being.

To steady her nerves, Isabella took another sip of the hot, sweet tea. It was laced with honey and fortified her. "I see a man with many burdens to bear. And I have brought him another. I'm sorry for that, but I cannot allow *mio fratello* to die. You were my only hope. I didn't wish to complicate your life further." Her words were sincere.

Don DeMarco hesitated as if uncertain what to do. He finally seated himself in the chair opposite her. Isabella smiled warily at him, offering a tentative olive branch. "I fear you have made a poor bargain, *signore*. *Mio padre* spent a good portion of his life frowning and shaking his head in disapproval of my behavior."

"I can well imagine the truth of that." Irony laced his voice, and she could feel the weight of his relentless stare.

Isabella felt the brush of butterfly wings in her stomach, and heat curled slowly through her bloodstream. She knew little of the relations between a man and woman. She didn't even know if he would want her in that way. But she couldn't seem to look at him without her entire body clenching with a heat and fire she'd never felt before. It was uncomfortable and frightening. And she didn't want anyone dictating to her, curtailing her activities. She was accustomed to doing as she pleased with few restrictions.

She tilted her chin. "I do not obey the dictates of others very well."

His low, amused, caressing laughter startled her. It slipped inside her and wrapped around her heart. "Is that a warning or a confession?" he asked.

Her gaze touched his, then slid away shyly. She had the feeling he rarely laughed. "I think it was more of a warning. I've never been able to understand the meaning of the word *obey*." She took another sip of tea and regarded him over the rim of the cup *"Mio padre* said I should have been born a boy." The hand hidden in the folds of her skirts twisted the material tightly. She was terribly nervous, far more so than she had even been. *Don* DeMarco was not at all what she had expected. She could have dealt with a stuffy old man, even one with greedy, lust-filled eyes. *Don* DeMarco was incredibly handsome, more than handsome, and she had no idea how to deal with him.

"It has been long since I sat and talked with another like this," he admitted softly, some of the tension easing out of him. "My meetings are not social, and I never take dinner with members of the household." He sat back in his chair, stretching his long legs toward the fire. He should have looked relaxed, but he still looked a wild animal, restless in its cage.

"Why not? Dinner was always my favorite time of the day. *Mio fratello* would tell me such wonderful stories. It was difficult for me when *mio padre* decided I needed to learn certain feminine accomplishments and locked me indoors. Lucca would tell me as many wild tales over dinner as he could think of to make me laugh."

"Were you often locked in?" His voice was mild enough, but something in his tone made her shiver. Clearly he didn't like the idea of her father locking her in, but it was perfectly fine that he had done so.

"Often enough. I liked to roam the hills. *Padre* was afraid I would run into wolves." Truly, her father had been afraid he would never find his wild child a wealthy husband. Isabella pushed the thought away swiftly, lest the *don* see the fleeting sadness in her eyes. His intent stare seemed capable of reading every nuance of her posture and expression.

Don DeMarco leaned toward her and gently brushed some tendrils of her hair away from her face. The unexpected gesture made her pull away from him, and something sharp scratched her from her temple to the corner of her eye. The edge of his ring must have scraped her skin. She gasped with the sudden pain, reaching up to cover the damage with her palm.

He stood up so fast, his teacup went crashing to the floor, shattering and spilling its contents. The puddle took on the ominous shape of a lion.

At once Isabella's heart pounded fearfully, and she tilted her head to look up at the *don*. His eyes blazed dangerously, his mouth looked cruel, edged with a snarl, and that curious growl rumbled in his throat. The scars along his cheek became red and vivid. Once again the strange look of the lion blurred with his face so that for a moment she was staring at a beast and not a man.

"What do you see now, *Signorina* Vernaducci?" he demanded, a kind of fury running through his body, filling the room with danger. Even the falcon on its perch flapped its wings in alarm. *Don* DeMarco's fingers tangled in the hair at the nape of her neck, holding her still, holding her prisoner.

She blinked up at him, bringing him back into focus, unsure what she had done to warrant such a reaction. "I'm sorry, *signore*, if I have offended you in some way. I meant no insult." In truth she couldn't even remember what she had said that could have set him off. His fingers were a tight fist in her hair, yet there was no pressure, just the sharpness

44

of his ring digging into her skin. She stayed very still.

"You have not answered my question." His voice was pure menace.

"I see you, *signore*." She stared steadily into his catlike eyes.

Don DeMarco remained still, his gaze locked with hers. She could hear her own breathing, feel her heart pounding. He let out his breath slowly. "You have not offended me." His fingers left her hair reluctantly.

"Why, then, are you so upset?" she asked, puzzled by his strange behavior. Her skin throbbed where his ring had pricked her.

His fingers settled around her slender wrist, prying her hand from her temple. A thin trail of blood trickled down her face. "Look at what I have done to you through my clumsiness. I injured you, perhaps scarred you."

Relief flooded her as she understood that he was angry with himself, not with her, and she laughed softly. "It's a small scratch, *Don* DeMarco. I cannot believe you would be upset over such a trivial thing. I've skinned my knees numerous times. I do not scar easily," she added, aware he was probably sensitive because of his own terrible scars.

She tugged at her hand to remind him to release her. "Allow me to clean up the tea and pour you a fresh cup."

His thumb was stroking her sensitive inner wrist as he towered over her. The sensation was shocking, little tongues of fire licking up her arm, spreading over her skin until she was burning with some unnamed need she had never experienced. His eyes were staring at her with far too much hunger.

Don DeMarco's fingers tightened possessively around her wrist. "You are no *domestica* in my home, Isabella. There is no need for you to clean up the mess." He bent toward her, a slow, unhurried assault on her senses.

Isabella's body clenched in reaction to his nearness. He came even closer, until his wide shoulders blotted out the entire room around her. When she inhaled, he was there in the air, filling her lungs. He smelled wild. Untamed. Masculine. His eyes seemed to devour her face. She couldn't look away from him, nearly hypnotized by his gaze. When he lowered his head to hers, his strangely colored hair brushed her skin with the sensation of silk. She felt his tongue at her temple, a moist caress as he removed the trace of her blood. The touch should have repulsed her, but it was the most sensual thing imaginable.

An abrupt knock at the door spun him around, and he leapt away from her with a catlike movement that took him halfway across the room, landing so lightly she didn't hear his feet on the tiles. There was something menacing in the set of his shoulders. His hair was a wild mane flowing down his back, shaggy and untamed despite the cord securing it. Muscles rippled beneath his shirt. He stalked to the door and wrenched it open.

At once Isabella felt the dark stench of evil pouring into the room, shadow streaming in like filthy water, fouling the air. She carefully placed her empty teacup on the table, rising as she did so. She saw only Sarina's anxious face as the servant hurried into the room. The older woman was looking past *Don* DeMarco to the puddle of tea and broken crockery on the floor.

"*Mi scusi per il disturbo, signore*, but those wishing an audience with you are waiting. I thought perhaps you had forgotten them." Sarina curtseyed slightly, not looking at the *don*. Instead she was examining Isabella's face, her expression distressed.

Self-consciously Isabella covered the scratch on her temple with her palm. Even as she did so, she turned in a slow circle, trying to pinpoint the exact location from which the cold, ugly sensation of evil was originating. It was so real, so strong, her body began to shiver in reaction, her mouth went dry, and she could feel the frenzied pounding of her heart. Something was in the room with them, something Sarina didn't appear to notice. Isabella saw the *don* lift his head warily, as if he was scenting the air. Unexpectedly the falcon began to flap its wings. Isabella swung around to look at the bird.

Sarina was already at the table, bending to pick up the broken teacup. Isabella felt a sudden surge of hatred in the room, black and fierce. She threw herself forward just as the raptor let out a scream and launched itself straight at Sarina's exposed face. Isabella landed on the older woman, driving her to the floor, covering her with her own body, hands over her own face as the falcon struck at the servant with outstretched talons.

A roar shook the room, a terrible, inhuman, beastly sound. The falcon uttered a high-pitched squawk as it slashed Isabella's back, shredding the fine fabric of the gown and digging long furrows in her skin. Isabella couldn't prevent a cry of pain from escaping. She could feel the bird's wings beating above her, fanning her. Sarina was sobbing, praying loudly, wretchedly, not even trying to escape the weight of Isabella's body.

Isabella turned her head to look for the *don*. He wasn't in her line of vision, but, to her horror, an enormous creature had crept into the room through the open door. It stood only a few feet from her, its head down, its eyes staring at her intently. It was a lion, nearly eleven feet in length, at least six hundred pounds of roped muscle and sinew, with a huge golden ruff tapering to a thick mane of black running halfway down its tawny body. The luxurious crest added to the beast's impression of power. The animal stood completely still. Its paws were huge, its gaze fixed on the two women. The lion was the biggest, most frightening thing Isabella had ever seen. She couldn't have imagined the animal in her worst nightmare. Sarina and she were in mortal danger.

And the falcon had ripped open her skin, the smell of blood an invitation to the beast. The thought came unbidden to her that something evil had orchestrated the event.

Isabella knew that neither she nor Sarina could escape. The animal would strike with lightning speed. She forced breath into her body. She would have to rely on the *don*. Trust him to tame the beast. Or slay it. As she stared into the wild, feral eyes, she vowed to be unafraid. The *don* would not allow the beast to harm them.

The lion took a slow step forward, then froze again in a classic prelude to an attack. She couldn't look away from the eyes so focused on her. She *would* believe in the *don*. He would come to their aid. Tears blurred her vision, and she blinked rapidly, desperate to keep her wits about her.

Hands caught at her, gentle hands that lifted her into strong arms. Then she was cradled against the *don's* chest. She buried her face in his shirt, terror rendering her incapable of speech. For the first time in her life she was close to fainting—a silly, feminine reaction she abhorred. She wanted to see if the lion was gone, but she couldn't find the courage to lift her head and look.

Don DeMarco reached to help Sarina to her feet. "Are you injured?" he asked the older woman in a gentle voice.

"No, just shaken. *Signorina* Vernaducci saved me from harm. What did I do to upset your bird? He has never flown at me before." Sarina's voice quavered, but she brushed off her skirts in a determined, businesslike manner, not once looking directly at the *don*.

"He is unused to so many strangers in his territory," *Don* DeMarco answered gruffly. "Leave that mess, Sarina. *Signorina* Vernaducci is injured. We must see to her wounds." He was already moving swiftly through the room and out into the corridor, Sarina traveling in his wake.

Shaking uncontrollably like a ninny, Isabella was mortified at her own behavior. It was beyond bearing. She was a Vernaducci, and Vernaduccis did not carry on when embattled. "I'm sorry," she whispered, appalled at her lack of control. She was crying in front of a servant, in front of *Don* DeMarco.

"There, there, *bambina*, we will take the sting from those wounds," Sarina crooned to her as if she were a mere babe. "You were so brave, you saved me from terrible injury."

They were rushing down the stairs, the *don's* body fluid and powerful, not jarring her in the least. The lacerations were painful, but Isabella was crying from relief, not pain. First the falcon and then the lion had been terrifying. She hoped the four-footed beasts didn't have freedom of the castle. Surely the one she saw had escaped from a cage somewhere on the grounds. She took a deep breath and forced herself to calm down.

"I am sorry for my foolish weeping," she apologized again. "Really, I'm all right now. I'm quite capable of walking."

"Do not apologize to me again," *Don* DeMarco said grimly. His golden eyes moved over her face in a dark, brooding perusal. There was an underlying harshness to his voice, a nameless emotion Isabella had no hope of identifying.

She gazed up at him, and her heart stilled. His face was a mask of bitterness, his expression without hope. He looked as if his entire world had crumbled, every dream he had ever had smashed beyond repair. Isabella felt a curious wrenching in the region of her heart. She lifted a hand and touched his shadowed jaw with gentle fingertips. "*Don* DeMarco, you persist in thinking me a glass bauble that will shatter when dropped. I'm made of sterner stuff. In truth, I wasn't weeping from pain. The bird merely scratched me." She could feel the burning and throbbing now that her terror had receded, but reassuring the *don* seemed of paramount importance.

The golden eyes blazed down at her, possessively, settling on her mouth as if he wished to crush her lips beneath his. He stole her breath with that look. Isabella stared up at him, mesmerized, unable to glance away.

With exquisite gentleness he finally placed her on her bed, rolling her over so that she was lying on her stomach, the long lacerations exposed to his probing gaze. She felt his hands on her, pushing aside the material of her gown, ripping it down to her waist. It was shocking and more than unseemly to have *Don* DeMarco see her like this, and in her own bedchamber. Isabella squirmed with embarrassment, reaching instinctively for the coverlet. She could feel the cool air on her bare skin, and her back was painful, but she was humiliated that she had wept and nearly fainted and now her gown was down around her waist.

The *don* caught her hand to prevent her from wrapping herself in the quilt, and he whispered something ugly under his breath. "These are no small scratches, Isabella." His voice was harsh, yet the way her name rolled off his tongue was a velvet caress.

"I will take care of her." Sarina's tone bordered on shocked outrage as she bent over the younger woman to examine the wounds.

"She is to be my bride, Sarina." There was a bite to the *don's* voice, a self-mocking note that brought a fresh flood of tears to Isabella's eyes. "You will see that she comes to no further harm."

There seemed a hidden meaning in his words, and Isabella sensed an understanding passing between the two, but she couldn't catch the drift. Her back was throbbing and burning, and she just wanted them both to leave her alone.

"Of course, *Don* DeMarco," Sarina said softly, compassion in her voice. "I will watch over her. You must meet with those waiting. I will see to *Signorina* Vernaducci personally."

Don DeMarco bent so that his mouth was next to Isabella's ear, so that the warmth of his breath stirred tendrils of her hair and whispered over her skin. "I will set in motion the plans to fulfill our bargain at once. Do not worry, *cara mia*. It will be done."

Isabella closed her eyes, her fingers curling into two tight fists as Sarina began to work on the ragged wounds on her back. The pain was excruciating, and she didn't want *Don* DeMarco to feel it with her. He was already in enough pain. She sensed the torment buried deep within his soul, and she hated that she was adding to his burdens, burdens she had no hope of understanding but knew instinctively were on his broad shoulders.

Whatever Sarina was doing drove the breath from Isabella's body, so she couldn't form an answer to the *don*. Small beads of sweat broke out on her brow. She thought she felt his lips brush her skin, right over the scratch on her temple.

A sound of distress rumbled in his throat. "I did this," he stated somberly.

Isabella felt that the small scratch was the least of her worries, yet it seemed enormously upsetting to the *don*. "You saved us from a lion, *Don* DeMarco. I'm scarcely worried about such a trivial mark."

A small silence followed, and she felt the sudden tension in the room.

"You saw a lion?" Sarina asked softly, her hands still on Isabella's shoulder.

"*Don* DeMarco, I was not mistaken, was I?" Isabella asked. "Although I admit I have never seen such a creature before. Do you truly keep them as pets? Aren't you afraid of accidents?"

The silence stretched out endlessly until Isabella stirred, determined to look at the *don*. With an oath, *Don* DeMarco spun on his heel and in his usual silent way stalked from the room.

"I did see such a beast in the room with us, *Signora* Sincini. I am telling the truth. Didn't you see it?" Isabella asked.

"I did not see anything. I was looking at the floor, terrified the bird would rip out my eyes. Falcons are trained to attack the eyes, you know."

Isabella felt tears welling up again. "I made the *don* angry, and I don't even know why." She couldn't bear to think about the implications of a bird deliberately being trained to attack humans. Or about lions wandering inside the *palazzo*. Or about the *don* stalking away, disgusted with her behavior. She squeezed her eyes shut tight, her tears leaking

51

onto the quilt, her head turned away from the housekeeper.

"*Don* DeMarco has much on his mind. He was not angry with you. He was worried, *piccola*, truly. I have known him many years, since he was a babe."

The lump in her throat prevented Isabella from answering. She had traded herself to the man in return for her brother's life. She had no idea what was expected of her, no idea how to act or how he would treat her. She knew nothing of him but dreadful rumors, yet she had tied her life to his.

"I'm so sorry this happened, *signorina*." Sarina's voice held a wealth of compassion. "I feel it's my fault that you were injured."

"Call me Isabella," she whispered. She kept her eyes closed, wanting to sleep, wishing Sarina would offer her the tea with herbs in it. She thought about suggesting it, but her back was on fire, and she couldn't seem to find enough air to breathe and talk at the same time. "Of course it was not your fault. It was an accident, nothing more. The bird became upset. I saw it flying at you, and I leapt upon you. In truth, I was afraid I might have injured you when I drove you to the floor." She didn't mention the terrible sensation of evil entering the room, that black, choking entity that had been all too real to ignore.

Sarina touched the angry scratch on Isabella's temple. "How did this happen?"

Isabella fought to keep her voice steady. Her back throbbed and burned. "The *don* was being very sweet, but his ring caught my skin. It was an accident, certainly not important." She clenched her teeth to keep from blurting out how badly her back hurt.

Sarina turned to answer a knock at the door, then closed it quickly against prying eyes. She mixed the herbs she had sent for and carefully applied the poultice to the long lacerations. Isabella nearly screamed, sweat breaking out on her body, but then the cuts went blissfully numb, and she could breathe again. But she was still trembling in shock and reaction. There was another knock on the door, and this time a servant handed Sarina a cup of the blessed tea.

Isabella had to be helped into a sitting position, surprisingly weak from the experience. She smiled wanly at Sarina. "Next time, let's ask Alberita to pour a *bucket* of holy water over my head before I leave my room." She cupped her hands around the warmth of the teacup, trying to absorb the heat.

Sarina laughed shakily in relief. "You are a good girl, *signorina*. Your *madre* is no doubt smiling down upon you from heaven. I thank you for what you are giving the *don*. He is good and deserving."

Isabella took a sip of the tea gratefully. It immediately eased her terrible tremors. "I hope you still say that when he finds me running wild in the hills and scowls fiercely because I do not arrive to dinner on time."

"You will make him a good wife." Sarina patted her leg gently. "As soon as you drink the tea, I will help you undress. You will sleep peacefully, *bambina*."

Isabella hoped it was the truth. She wanted desperately to close her eyes and escape into the enfolding darkness. The relief she felt that *Don* DeMarco had agreed to rescue her brother was tremendous. She would put aside her concerns about his strange pets and hope that she could persuade him to rid the *castello* of the creatures at a later date.

Isabella drank the sweet, medicinal tea and did her best to help Sarina remove the tattered gown. Then she lay on her stomach on the soft mattress and allowed her eyelashes to drift down. Sarina bustled around the room, removing all evidence of the terrible incident and lighting several aromatic candles to dispel the gathering shadows and provide a soothing fragrance. She stroked Isabella's hair until the *don's* betrothed was drowsy, and then she left, locking the door carefully.

Isabella awoke to soft whispers. A gentle feminine voice was calling to her. The room was dark, and the flickering candles were nearly burned down completely, the wax in oily pools and the flames sputtering and smoking.

She turned her head and saw Francesca sitting on her bed, anxiously wringing her hands and peering at her. Isabella smiled sleepily. "What's wrong, Francesca?" she asked, her voice as reassuring as she could make it under the circumstances.

"He hurt you. I never thought he would hurt you. I would have told you to run away, Isabella, really. I like you. I would have warned you away if I thought for even a moment that—" There was childlike quality to Francesca's voice, as if she spoke the simple, guileless truth.

The medicine from the tea was still in Isabella's body, making her feel dreamy and weightless. "Who do you think hurt me, Francesca? No one hurt me. It was an accident. Not important at all."

There was a small silence. "But everyone is saying he struck you, slashed terrible gashes in your body, and would have devoured you if Sarina had not stopped him by entering the room." Tears welled up in Francesca's eyes, and she folded her arms across her chest and rocked back and forth as if to comfort herself.

"Surely you do not mean *Don* DeMarco," Isabella said drowsily.

Francesca nodded. "I have heard many such stories of his cruelty."

"Who would say such terrible things? I can assure you, Francesca, *Don* DeMarco was a perfect gentleman, and he saved my life. Sarina's life, too. Surely his people do not hate him enough to tell such tales. That's cruelty itself. They should live under the rule of a man such as *Don* Rivellio if they wish to learn the difference." Isabella sought to reassure the young woman, but the conversation disturbed her. She had heard all the whispered warnings; even the *don's* own servants had attempted to bless her as she sought an audience with him. Perhaps there were things she didn't know. "Have *you* ever found him to be unjust or cruel? A man who would slash a woman to ribbons and devour her?"

"Oh, no!" Francesca hastily shook her head. "Never! But I pulled down the quilt while you were sleeping, and I saw your back. Surely it will scar. How could this have happened?"

"The falcon became frightened and attempted to attack Sarina. I was in the way. It looks much worse than it really is." Isabella was beginning to wake up despite the medicine. She felt stiff and uncomfortable and needed to visit the alcove. It was a struggle to sit up. Francesca, watching her with great interest, moved aside to give her more room to maneuver.

Isabella raised an eyebrow at her and glanced down at the quilt wrapped around her bare skin. Francesca grinned impishly at the show of modesty and looked up at the ornate ceiling. That quickly her mood changed, and she was beaming.

Isabella moved slowly, catching up the robe Sarina had thoughtfully laid out for her. Like all the other garments provided for her, it was made of a soft fabric that clung to her curves. Thankfully, her back was still numb enough that the material didn't aggravate her wounds.

She became aware of the same moaning and wailing she had heard the previous night, coming from the hallways of the *castello*. She also heard that strange, grunting cough. "What kind of animal makes that sound?" she asked Francesca, already fairly certain of the answer.

Francesca hopped to her feet restlessly and shrugged. "A lion, of course. They are everywhere in the valley, in the *palazzo*. They are the guardians of our *famiglia*. Our guardians and our keepers." She sighed, obviously bored with the subject. "Tell me of life outside this valley. Down the great mountains. What is it like? I have never been anywhere other than this place."

More and more Isabella believed that Francesca was younger than she appeared. Whose truant child was she that she wouldn't reveal her full identity? Recalling her own wayward childhood, Isabella decided not to press the point and frighten off her new friend. "I have never been in mountains such as these," Isabella told her. "The *palazzi* in other places I have been are much like this one but not as ornate."

"Have you ever been to a ball?" Francesca asked wistfully.

Isabella returned from the alcove to stand by the chair in front of the hearth. The fire had burned down, leaving smoldering embers. The faint light cast an eerie glow on the wall behind her. She turned her head to look at her own shadow, her thick braid falling past the curve of her bottom in the flowing robe. She did a slow pirouette, watching her shadow on the wall, wincing as her back protested. "Yes, more than one. I do love to dance."

Francesca tried a spin, holding her arms out as if she were dancing with a partner. Isabella laughed, turning to look at Francesca's shadow, but the glowing embers weren't strong enough to cast the young woman's silhouette on the wall alongside Isabella's.

"It will be fun having you here," Francesca said. "You can teach me all the proper steps. I've had to make up my own."

"It will have to be another night, when my back doesn't hurt, but I'd love to teach you to dance. Does *Don* DeMarco dance, Francesca?"

Francesca swayed this way and that, turning one way and the other as she danced around the room. "There has been no music in the *palazzo* for a long time. I love music and plays and dance and all the young men in their finery. I have never seen such things, mind you, but I have heard tales. We do not entertain here."

"Why is that?" Isabella asked, trying not to smile at Francesca's exuberance.

"The lions, of course. They would not tolerate such activities. They rule here, and we obey. They would not accept so many visitors, although they are quiet tonight. They must be accepting you, or they would be roaring in protest as they did last night. When you stuck your hand into the lion's mouth, he judged you, friend or foe. Those seeking Nicolai's favor must first stick their fingers inside the lion's mouth. If he bites, Nicolai knows they are the enemy, and they cannot enter."

Isabella stared into the embers of the smoldering fire, frowning as she did so. Francesca must be mistaken. She was a young woman, unbridled in her thoughts and actions. She must be making up stories or repeating gossip as she had earlier, when she believed the *don* had slashed Isabella. "Ruled by lions? How can humans be ruled by a lion? The beasts are wild and dangerous, and they were used by barbarians to kill people of faith. But, those in power commanded the lions, not the opposite." She shivered when Francesca did not reply. "How many lions are in this valley?" she asked.

There was no answer. Isabella turned her head, and Francesca was once more gone from the bedchamber. Isabella sighed. She would be certain to ask the girl the next time she saw her just where the secret passageway was. It would most likely to be a useful piece of information to have.

Chapter Four

"Isabella." Sarina shook her shoulder gently but insistently. "Come, *bambina*, you must wake now. Hurry, Isabella, wake now."

Isabella lifted her lashes and stared up into Sarina's kind face. "What is it? It's not yet light." She moved carefully, the lacerations on her back more painful now that the medicine had worn off. She tried to keep from wincing. "Is something wrong, Sarina?"

"You have been ordered to leave this place. The supplies are packed, and your escort is waiting with your horse." Sarina refused to meet Isabella's eyes. "He will not relent, *signorina*. Hurry now. He has said you must leave immediately. I must tend to your back."

Isabella tilted her chin defiantly. "We have a bargain. The *don* is a man of his word, and I insist that he keep it. I will not leave this place. And he will rescue *mio fratello*, Lucca."

"The messengers have been sent to secure your brother's

freedom," Sarina assured her. She was pulling clothes out of the wardrobe.

"There is the matter of our marriage. I believe he offered for me. He ordered our marriage. He cannot go back on his word."

"It was not announced." Sarina still wouldn't meet her gaze. "I must put salve on your wounds. Then you must dress quickly, Isabella, and do as *Don* DeMarco has ordered."

"I don't understand. I must see him. Why is he sending me away? What have I done to displease him?" Isabella had a sudden inspiration. "The lions were quiet last night. Doesn't that mean they are coming to accept my presence?"

"He will not see you, and he will not change his mind."

Sarina tried to hide her distress, making Isabella wonder what consequences of the *don's* decision she feared. She had no doubt that Sarina was well versed in all the legends about the *don* and his *palazzo*.

Isabella took a deep, calming breath. Well, if *Don* DeMarco didn't want her as his bride, then perhaps both of them had made a lucky escape. She had no intention of ever conforming to a husband's wishes. Not now. Not ever. "My back is fine this morning, *grazie*. I do not need medicine."

She rose stiffly and deliberately took her time washing, hoping the *don* was pacing in his rooms, anxious for her departure. Let him be anxious and have to wait on her pleasure. Ignoring the clothes Sarina had laid out for her, she dressed in her old, worn clothing. She needed nothing from *Don* DeMarco other than that he keep his word and rescue her brother.

"Please understand, he wishes you to have the clothes. He is providing a full escort to the pass, supplies, and several men to take you on to your home." Sarina tried hard to be encouraging.

Isabella's eyes flashed fire. She had no home. Don Rivel-

Christine Feehan

lio had confiscated her lands and all things of value, other than her mother's jewels. But she dared not use her last treasures except as a final resort to try to bribe the guards holding Lucca. Still, she was far too proud to point out the obvious to Sarina. Isabella had come to *Don* DeMarco expecting to become a servant in his *castello*. If he wished to throw her out, she certainly wasn't going to beg him to take her as his bride, or even for sanctuary. She had been born the daughter of a *don*. She may have run wild at times, but the blood of her parents ran deep in her veins. She had plenty of pride and dignity, and she wrapped both around her like a cloak.

"I have no need of anything the *don* has offered. I made my way to the *palazzo* alone, and I can certainly find my way back. As for the clothes, please see to it that those in need receive them." She met Sarina's eyes steadily, every bit as proud as the *don*. "I am ready."

"*Signorina....*" Sarina's heart clearly ached for the young woman.

Isabella's chin rose higher. "There is nothing to say, *signora*. I thank you for your kindness to me, but I must obey the orders of your *don* and leave immediately." She had to leave quickly or she might humiliate herself by bursting into tears. She had elicited a promise from *Don* DeMarco to save her brother, and that, after all, was the only reason she had come. She would think of nothing else.

Not his broad shoulders. Not the intensity of his amber gaze. Not the sound of his voice. She would not think of him as a man. Isabella glanced at the door, her features set and determined.

Sarina opened the door, and Isabella swept through it. At once the cold hit her, piercing and deep and unnatural. It was there again—that sense of something malignant watching her, this time in gloating triumph. Her heart began to pound. The hatred was so strong, so thick in the air, it took her breath away. She felt the weight of its ugly presence.

60

But Isabella could not worry any longer about those living with something evil in the *castello*. If the *don* and his people didn't know or care what was dwelling within their walls, it was none of her business. Looking neither right nor left, not waiting to see if the housekeeper followed, Isabella hurried through the maze of halls, relying on her memory to find her way out. She was terrified of leaving yet equally terrified of staying.

The unnatural cold air followed her as she made her way through the wide halls. It stabbed at her as if to run her through with an ice-cold sword. It clawed at the wounds on her back, seeking entrance to her soul. She couldn't prevent a shudder of fear, and she imagined she heard the echo of taunting laughter. As she walked down the long, twisting stairs, a ripple of movement followed her, and she could have sworn the portraits on the walls stared at her. The burning tapers in the halls flared from strange wind gusts and splattered waxy, macabre apparitions onto the floor, as if her adversary were maliciously celebrating her departure with gleeful delight.

She felt a wrenching sensation in the region of her heart as she walked out of the *castello* into the biting wind of the Alps. She took a breath of the clean, fresh air. At least the horrifying feeling of something evil watching her was gone once she was outdoors. Men and horses were waiting for her to join them. Without warning, the lions began to roar, from every direction—the mountains, the valley, the courtyard, and the bowels of the *palazzo*—creating a frightful din. The sound was hideous and terrifying, filling the air and reverberating through the very ground. It was nearly worse than the black feeling inside the *castello*.

The horses panicked, fighting the riders, bucking and snorting, heads tossing warily, eyes rolling with fear. The men murmured to the animals in an attempt to calm them. Snow fell in steady sheets, turning everyone into ghostlike mummies.

"You have plenty of food," Sarina assured her, quickly

hiding her shaking hands behind her back. "And I put salve in the pack."

"Thank you again for your kindness," Isabella said without looking at her. She would not cry. There was no reason to cry. She cared nothing for the *don*. Still, it was humiliating to be sent away as though she mattered not at all. Which was true, Isabella supposed. She no longer had lands or a title. She had less than did the servants in the *castello*. And she had nowhere to take her sick brother.

Isabella ignored Betto's helping hand and swung into the saddle by herself. Her back protested alarmingly, but the pain around her heart was more intense. She kept her face averted from the others, even grateful for the snow that would hide the tears glittering in her eyes. Her throat burned with regret and anger. With sorrow.

Determinedly she dug her heels into her horse and set the pace, wanting to put the *palazzo* and the *don* far behind her. She didn't look at the escorts, pretending they weren't present. The lions continued roaring a protest, but the snow, falling faster, helped to muffle the sound. She was aware that the men and horses were extremely nervous. Lions hunted in packs, didn't they? The breath left Isabella's lungs in a sudden rush.

Unless that was the terrible secret the valley guarded so well. So many of those men loyal to the Vernaducci name had been sent out to find this valley within the Alps, yet they had never returned. It was whispered *Don* DeMarco had an army of beasts to guard his lair. Were they hunting her now? The horses gave every indication that predators were near. Isabella's heart began to pound.

Don DeMarco had acted strangely, but surely he wouldn't be so upset with her that he would want her dead. What had she done that warranted her removal from the *castello*? She hadn't asked the *don* to marry *her*; he had been the one to insist on it. She had been willing to work for him, had offered her loyalty to him. If he had simply changed his mind about taking a wife, would he want her dead?

Isabella glanced over to the captain of the guard, attempting to gauge his level of anxiety. His features were hard, stony, yet he urged the riders to greater speed, and it was apparent that all the men were heavily armed. Isabella had seen men like the captain before. Lucca was one such man. His eyes moved restlessly over their surroundings, and he rode easily in the saddle. But he rode like a man expecting trouble.

"Are we hunted?" Isabella asked, her horse falling into step with the captain's mount. She was feigning calm, but she would never completely forget the sight of that lion, its hungry stare fixed on her.

"You are safe, *Signorina* Vernaducci. *Don* DeMarco has insisted upon your safety above all else. It is our lives should we fail him."

And then the lions fell silent. The quiet was eerie and frightening, worse than the terrible roars. Isabella's heart pounded, and she tasted terror in her mouth. The snow swept down, turning the world a startling white and muffling the chink of the horses' hooves on the rocks. In truth, Isabella had never seen snow until she came into these mountains. It was icy cold and wet against her face, hanging on her eyelashes and turning men and mounts into strange, pale creatures.

"What is your name?" Isabella needed to hear a voice. The silence was eating away at her courage. Something paced silently alongside them with every step the horses took. She thought she caught glimpses every now and then of movement, but she couldn't make out what it might be. The men had closed ranks, riding in tight formation.

"I am Rolando Bartolmei." He waved at the second man riding close by. "That is Sergio Drannacia. We've been with *Don* DeMarco all our lives. We were boys together, childhood friends. He is a good man, *signorina*." He glanced at her as if trying to make a point.

Isabella sighed. "I am sure he is, *signore.*"

"Must you leave so quickly? The storm will pass soon enough. I can assure you, our valley is quite beautiful if you would but give it a chance." Captain Bartolmei glanced again to the rider on his left. Sergio Drannacia was taking in every word. Clearly, neither understood why she was leaving so abruptly, and they were trying to persuade her to stay.

"*Don* DeMarco ordered me from the valley, *Signor* Bartolmei. It is not by choice that I am leaving in such a storm." Her chin was up, her face proud.

The captain exchanged a long look with Sergio, almost in disbelief. "You were allowed into the valley, *signorina*—a true miracle. I would have hoped you would be able to see more of this great land. Our people are prosperous and happy."

That the people could be happy under the circumstances was difficult to believe. Isabella took a deep breath. "The night I arrived, I heard a terrible scream, and the lions roared. Someone was killed that night. What happened?" She wanted to appear calm, as if she knew more of the mystery than she actually did.

The captain exchanged another quick look with Drannacia, who shrugged his broad shoulders. "It was an accident," the captain said. "One of the men became careless. We must remember that lions are not tame. They are wild animals and must be respected as such."

Isabella listened to the tone of his voice. It was tight and clipped. She had learned much from her father and brother by thus listening for the small nuances in a voice. The captain did not fully believe his own explanation. He was uneasy with the beasts pacing silently, unseen, beside them, and talking of accidents did nothing to ease the tension. It stretched out endlessly until nerves were screaming.

They rode for perhaps an hour, the storm slowing them down. Visibility was poor, and the wind began to howl and moan, filling the ghostly silence left by the ceasing of the lion's roars. Isabella pulled her cape tightly around her in an attempt to ward off the relentless cold. It seemed to invade her body and turn her blood to ice, and she shivered continually. Wet and miserable, her hands numb with cold despite her gloves, she was nearly thrown when her mount stopped without warning, rearing halfheartedly. Trying to calm her horse, she peered through the heavy veil of snow.

Isabella's heart nearly stopped. She caught a glimpse of something large, covered in snow, but still showing patches of golden tan and black. Eyes glowed through the white, icy crystals, eyes full of wicked intelligence. Her breath caught in her throat, and she froze, her hands falling to her sides as the horse sidestepped and began backing up nervously.

The captain leaned over, caught the reins of her mount, and swung both horses around. "The animals are guarding the pass!" he shouted. "They're not going to allow you to leave."

There was something very sinister about the way the large beast stood on the narrow ledge at the entrance to the pass, its eyes fixed on her. Its gaze was intent, targeting her, recognizing her. It was mesmerizing and terrifying at the same time.

"It isn't the single beast you can see that you must worry about. Lions are pack hunters. Where there is one, there are many. We must take you back." The captain was still leading her mount. His voice jolted Isabella out from under the spell of the predator, and she reached forward hastily to retake control of her horse. The captain needed his hands free; his own horse was plunging and snorting nervously.

It was nerve-wracking to ride nearly blind through the heavily falling snow, with her mount trembling and sweating in fear and the other animals bucking and snorting, blowing out great clouds of vapor in their terror. That peculiar, coughlike grunt would sound to their left, then a few minutes later to their right, then behind and ahead of them. Her escort was unnaturally quiet, eyes straining through the snow to catch glimpses of the elusive hunters.

Isabella was just starting to breathe again when she felt the disturbance in the air. She looked up at the sky, expecting to see something predatory overhead, but only the white flakes floated down. All the same, she and the men were not alone. Something other than a pride of lions had followed them from the *palazzo*, and it was angry that they had turned back, heading away from the pass. She could feel intense hatred and rage directed at her, a black wall of evil bent on her destruction. Isabella couldn't identify what it was, but she felt it all the way to her bones.

She began to shake, her body reacting to the intensity of that animosity. It was personal—she felt it. And something terrible was going to happen. She was helpless to prevent it, but she knew it was coming.

Almost at once the lions began to roar again. The beasts were very close, and the sound was deafening. The horses panicked, bucking and plunging, rearing and spinning, and chaos reigned. The slope was icy, and the animals slid and crashed into one another, trumpeting in fear. Men fell into the snow and covered their heads to protect themselves from the slashing hooves. Isabella's mount whirled around and slipped on the steep grade, sliding dangerously and ultimately toppling over. She tried to kick herself free, but it was impossible with the folds of her skirts, and she hit the ground hard, the thrashing, fallen horse pinning her leg beneath it.

The pain in her back was excruciating, driving the breath from her body and overriding any harm that may have been done to her leg. For a moment she couldn't think or breathe; she could only lie helplessly while her horse thrashed desperately, trying to regain its footing.

The captain leapt from the back of his plunging mount and caught Isabella's horse's reins, yanking the animal up. The horse stood trembling, head down. The captain jerked Isabella up out of the snow, ignoring her inadvertent cry of pain, shoving her behind him, his sword drawn out of his scabbard. Pandemonium surrounded them, but the captain issued orders, and his men caught the horses that had not run free into the storm, and they stood, shoulder to shoulder, a solid wall of protection around Isabella.

"What is it, Rolando?" Sergio asked, his eyes straining to see through the blinding snow. "Why are they attacking us? I don't understand. Why would he send her away, his only chance at salvation? If she wasn't the one, they never would have allowed her alive through the pass."

"I don't know, Sergio," the captain said. "They allowed her through, then prevented her from leaving. We are doing as they wish, taking her back to the *castello*, yet they are hunting us."

Isabella shook her head. "*They* are not hunting you. *It* is hunting me, and it is using the animals to do its bidding." *Just as it had directed the falcon to target Sarina.* Isabella knew she was right. Something wanted her out of the valley. Whether it was the *don* or something else, the hatred was directed at her.

The captain swung his head around to stare at her, his features very still, his eyes alive with curiosity. He was silent for so long, Isabella was afraid he thought her crazy. She pressed a hand to her rolling stomach but stepped to his side, her chin high.

"What are you talking about?" he demanded, a man in command, a man determined to do his duty and needing all information available to him. "What is hunting you? I don't understand."

She had no way of explaining what it was, because she didn't know. She only knew that it was real and malignant. "I felt it earlier when the *don's* falcon attacked Sarina. Something is driving these attacks. That's why I asked about the death that night. I thought it was possible that something similar had happened."

"I know of no such thing," the captain denied, but he was looking around him warily. His fingers abruptly bit into Isabella's arm, thrusting her farther away from him, her only warning. He stepped squarely in front of her so she was forced to peek around his solid bulk. Her breath left her lungs in one continuous rush.

She saw the huge lion through the snow. All stealth and power, head lowered, shoulder blades protruding, its blazing eyes focused directly on her. The lion seemed to flow over the ground, stalking her in slow motion. Although men and horses surrounded her, it looked only at her, staring with deadly intent.

The horses were rearing and plunging, dragging their riders with them in all directions as they tried to escape. The men were forced to abandon their mounts in order to protect themselves and Isabella. The odor of fear was pungent. Sweat broke out on their bodies, but to a man they stood frozen in place while the storm raged around them.

The lion suddenly exploded into a dead run, its speed unbelievable, smashing into the circle of men, swiping with razor-tipped claws, so that they ran for their lives, leaving a clear path to Captain Bartolmei, Sergio Drannacia, who stood shoulder to shoulder with him, and Isabella. The beast leapt, hundreds of pounds of solid muscle, going straight for Isabella. Sheer terror found a home in her heart, in her soul. She stood frozen, watching death come to her.

A second lion emerged from the storm, a great shaggy beast with a thick golden and black mane. Larger and even more heavily muscled, it roared a challenge as it intercepted the first lion, distracting it from reaching its prey. The two lions slammed into each other in midair, crashing together so hard that the ground shook. At once the fight became a frenzied battle of teeth and claws. Ferocious and mesmerizing, the roars reverberated through the air, drawing other lions. Blazing eyes burned brightly through the snowflakes.

Isabella watched the second lion closely. It was well muscled, in its prime, and obviously intelligent. She could see it driving in again and again for the weakened areas where blood already marked the other male. The sound of bones crunching chilled her, horrified her. In the end, the large predator held the smaller lion helpless in its grip, teeth buried in the throat until the fallen animal strangled.

Captain Bartolmei signaled to Sergio. "Now!" They both leapt toward the victorious lion, swords ready.

"No!" Isabella shouted, brushing past the two men to place her body between them and the lion. "Get away from him."

The men stopped abruptly. Silence fell, leaving the world white and dazzling, and nature held its breath. The lion swung its great head around, its muzzle still bloody. The eyes fixed on her, blazed at her, a peculiar amber that seemed to glow with knowledge and intelligence. With sorrow. "No," she said again very softly, her gaze trapped in the lion's. "He saved us."

As she stared at the great cat, the wind gusted and blew snow all around them, momentarily blinding her. She blinked rapidly, trying to clear her vision. The wind blew the snow aside, and she found herself staring into wild amber eyes. But the victorious lion was gone. The amber eyes belonged to a human predator. She was no longer seeing a lion standing over the fallen beast, but *Don* Nicolai De-Marco. He stood tall and straight, his long hair blowing in the wind, snow falling on his broad shoulders and elegant clothes.

Isabella's stomach somersaulted, and her heart melted. She blinked to remove the snowflakes from her lashes. The *don's* tall frame blurred and wavered so that his long hair seemed a golden, flowing mane around his head and shoulders, deepening in color from tawny to black as it cascaded down his back. His hands moved, drawing her attention, and the illusion had her looking at two huge paws. Then the *don* moved, and the strange, wavering mirage disappeared, and she was once more looking at a man.

He glanced down at the body of the defeated lion, and she saw the shadows in his eyes. He hunkered down beside the great cat and buried one gloved hand in the thick fur, his head bowed for a moment in regret. Behind him was a small army of men on horseback. *Don* DeMarco rose to his feet and signaled the riders to hunt for the runaway horses.

He walked right up to Isabella and took her hand in his. "Are you injured, my lady?" he asked softly, gently, his amber eyes capturing hers, holding her prisoner, setting butterfly wings fluttering deep inside her.

Mutely Isabella shook her head as she looked down at her hand in the palm of his, almost afraid she would see a great paw. His fingers closed around hers, and he pulled her close to the warmth of his body. Her body was trembling in reaction, and as hard as she tried, she couldn't stop herself. *Don* DeMarco removed his cape and swirled it around her shoulders, enfolding her with his body warmth. He reached back toward the line of men, and his horse responded to the silent signal, trotting to him instantly.

His hands spanned her waist and lifted her easily onto the saddle. "What happened here, Rolando?" he asked, and that strange growl rumbled, a distinct threat, deep in his throat.

Isabella shivered and snuggled deeper into the heavy cloak. It was no wonder the *don* occasionally looked like a lion, with his long hair and shaggy cloak. It was made of the pelt of a lion. The *don's* mount smelled the beasts surrounding them, but it was steady, not in the least nervous. Isabella wondered if it was used to the wild scent because of the cloak.

"The pass was guarded, *Don* DeMarco," the captain explained. He stared past the *don*, not quite meeting his eyes. "We turned back, and this one attacked us. A rogue, no doubt." He indicated the lifeless lion in the blood-soaked snow. "In the blinding snow, we could have made a terrible mistake, Nicolai."

Isabella had no idea what he meant, but the captain's voice shook with emotion.

Nicolai DeMarco easily swung onto the back of the horse, settling Isabella close to his chest, his arms sliding around her while he grasped the reins. "Would it have been so terrible, my friend?" He turned the animal back toward the *castello*, obviously not wanting an answer. Isabella stirred in his arms, a restless movement that brought her body right into his.

She tilted her head and looked into his eyes. "You're going the wrong way." Her tone was every bit Vernaducci, as haughty as the expression on her face. "My sense of direction is quite good, and the pass is in the opposite direction."

He stared down into her face for so long she didn't think he would answer. She became aware of the movement of the horse as it rocked their bodies together. There was strength in his arms, and his hair brushed her face like silk. She wanted to tangle her fingers in the mass, but, instead, she curled her hands into two fists to prevent such folly. His mouth, beautifully sculpted and sinfully inviting, drew her gaze. She decided it was a mistake to look at him, but she was already caught in the heat of his stare and couldn't look away.

Nicolai touched her face gently, but Isabella felt the stroke through her entire body. "I'm sorry, Isabella. I found I'm not nearly as noble as I would like to think. I cannot give you up."

"Well, I just want you to know that I've completely changed my opinion of you." She ducked beneath the thick cloak to get out of the biting wind. "And it isn't for the good."

His laughter was soft, almost too low for her to catch. "I will have to do my best to change it back."

When she looked up at him, there was no sign of humor in his face. He looked sad and weighted down. Lines were etched into the angles and planes, and he appeared older than she had first thought. Isabella couldn't prevent her hand from creeping upward to touch his face, to brush gently at the harsh lines. "I'm sorry about the lion. I know you have some connection to them, and you felt the loss greatly."

"It is my duty to control them," he answered without inflection.

Her eyebrows shot up. "How can you possibly be responsible for controlling wild animals?"

"Suffice to say, I can and I do," he said tersely, dismissing the subject.

Isabella's teeth came together in protest. Was she going to have to get used to being summarily ignored? In her home she had done much as she pleased, taken part in heated discussions, even political ones. Now her life had changed not once, but twice, on the whim of the same man. It would have been far easier if he hadn't been so attractive to her. Beneath her long lashes, her eyes flashed at him, a flare of temper she struggled to control. "You aren't getting off to a very good start, *Signor* DeMarco, if changing my opinion of you is your intent."

He looked startled for a moment, as if no one had ever voiced displeasure with him before. Captain Bartolmei, riding close to his *don*, turned his head away, but not before Nicolai caught the sudden grin. Sergio, on the other side, went into a spasm of coughing. The *don* swung his head in the soldier's direction, and the chortling sound immediately ceased. Nicolai tightened his arms around Isabella.

Isabella was drifting, safe and secure in the warmth of the *don's* arms. But she became aware of tension among the three men. Truly, it was more than the three men. It extended to the columns of men, as if they were all waiting for something to happen. Isabella closed her eyes and allowed her head to find a niche on *Don* DeMarco's chest. She didn't want to see or hear anything more. She pulled the cloak over her head.

The feeling of dread persisted anyway. It grew with each step the horses took. It wasn't a feeling of evil, but more of anticipation, of expectation. It seemed that each of the riders knew something she did not. With a sigh of resignation she threw off the hood and glared up at the *don*.

"What is it? What is wrong?" He looked more distant

than ever. Isabella pushed down the temper that always got her into trouble. *Don* DeMarco was the one making all the decisions. If he was already regretting his little whim of returning her to the *palazzo*, that was his problem, and he could look as grim as he wanted, but she wasn't going to feel guilty.

Nicolai did not answer her. Isabella studied his face and realized he was concentrating completely on something else. She noticed the captain and Sergio riding closer to their *don*, protectively. She turned her attention to his hands, so steady on the reins as he guided the horse through the snow. Isabella sat up straighter. *Don* DeMarco was *not* guiding the horse. Sergio and the captain were doing so with their own mounts. The *don's* total attention was centered deep within himself, and he didn't seem to be fully aware of anything around him. Not even Isabella.

His expression caught her interest. He was struggling internally—she sensed it—yet his face was a mask of indifference. Isabella knew things. She had always known them, and right now she was very aware that Nicolai DeMarco was fighting a terrible battle.

She knew the lions were still pacing alongside the two columns of riders, much farther away than before but still there. Was the *don* controlling their behavior in some way? Did he truly have such an ability? The idea was terrifying. No one in the outside world would ever accept such a feat. He would be condemned and sentenced to death. Rumors were one thing—people loved gossip, loved to be deliciously frightened—but it would be an altogether different proposition if *Don* DeMarco could actually control an army of beasts.

Isabella became aware of the horse beneath them. Where the animal had been steady before, it was becoming increasingly nervous, dancing, tossing its head. The cloak enfolding her in its warmth seemed almost to have come alive, so that she smelled the wild lion, felt the brush of its mane against her cheek.

73

Don DeMarco reined in his mount, halting the columns of riders. She could feel the change in his breathing, the air moving through his lungs in a rush, his breath warm on her neck. Then the captain signaled the two columns of riders to continue to move forward toward the *palazzo*. The storm effectively muffled the sounds of the horses and riders as they disappeared into the white, swirling world.

Nicolai touched Isabella's hair, his hand heavy and large as it ran down her head and back. The stroke was incredibly sensual, and Isabella shivered. He leaned into her so that his mouth was close to her ear. "I regret I cannot escort you all the way back to the *palazzo*, but Rolando will see to it that you arrive safely. I have other pressing duties." That peculiar growling note rumbled deep within his throat, sensual and frightening at the same time. Easily, fluidly, he swung down from the horse, one hand lingering on her ankle.

Isabella's breath caught in her throat. She was wearing boots, but she felt that intimate touch right through her body. "There are lions, *Signor* DeMarco. I feel them around us. You can't be out here on foot," she pointed out anxiously. "Nothing can be so important."

"Captain Bartolmei will see you back to the *castello*. Sarina is waiting for you, and she'll be sure you are well cared for in my absence. I'll return as soon as possible." The wind was blowing hard. The *don's* hair flared around his face, thick and shaggy, gold at his crown, darkening to almost black as it cascaded down his back. "Isabella, stay close to the captain until you are safe within the walls of my home. And listen to Sarina. She wants only to protect you."

"*Don* DeMarco," Captain Bartolmei interrupted. "You must hurry."

All the horses were snorting and dancing nervously. Isabella's mount was rolling its eyes in fear, tossing its head up and trying to back away.

Isabella reached out and caught Nicolai's shoulder. "You

have no cloak, and it's freezing out here. Please come with us. Or at least take back your cloak."

Don DeMarco looked at the small gloved hand on his shoulder. "Look at me, my lady. Look at my face."

She heard the swift intake of breath, of fear, by the two men guarding them. She didn't spare them a glance, looking only at Nicolai. For some reason she couldn't fathom, he was breaking her heart. He looked so aloof, so utterly alone. She boldly framed his scarred face with her palms. "I am looking at you, *mio don*. Tell me what I am to look for." Her gaze drifted over his face, taking in the handsome, sculpted lines, the deep scars, the blazing intensity of his amber eyes.

"Tell me what you see," he commanded for the second time, his expression wary.

"I see you, *Don* Nicolai DeMarco. A very mysterious man, but one some would call handsome." Her thumb stroked a lingering caress over his shadowed jaw. Isabella found she couldn't look away from his hot gaze.

"Would you be one of those calling *Don* Nicolai DeMarco handsome?" he asked, his voice even lower than before, so that the wind whipped it away almost before she caught the words. His hand moved up to his jaw, covering the exact spot where her thumb had caressed him, holding her touch in the warmth of his palm.

A slow smile curved Isabella's mouth, but before she could answer him, her mount reared back, forcing her to grab at the reins.

Don DeMarco stepped hastily away from the animal, slipping quickly into the shadow of the trees. "Go now, Rolando. Get her home safely." It was an order.

"Your cloak," Isabella called to him desperately as the captain caught at the reins of her horse. Already the horse was in motion, Sergio and the captain urging the animal toward the *palazzo*. She struggled to remove the heavy lion pelt, quickly tossing it back toward where she had last seen the *don*. "Take your cloak, *Don* DeMarco," she pleaded, afraid for him, a lonely figure impossible to see in the whirling storm of white.

Isabella nearly turned completely around on the back of her mount. She actually considered leaping off the horse. There was a desperation in her, a fear that if she took her eyes off the *don*, she would lose him. But as hard as she tried, she could not make out his figure in the snow. She had merely the impression of something large and powerful flowing with fluid grace across the snow. He stooped to pick up the cloak and slowly straightened to watch her go. His frame wavered, became indistinct, as he slipped on the heavy cloak, suddenly taking on the appearance of an untamed beast. She found herself staring into glowing eyes, eyes blazing with fire, with intelligence. Wild eyes.

Her heart stopped, then began to pound in alarm.

Chapter Five

Sarina gathered Isabella into her arms, then led her quickly through the halls and up the stairs to her room. "You have had such trouble, *bambina*. I am sorry. It was good that Captain Bartolmei and *Signor* Drannacia were with you."

"The one they call Sergio?" Isabella asked, struggling to get everyone's name straight. The men had been very nice to her, but neither would yield to her pleas to turn back and aid the *don*. "They left him there alone, in the storm, with no mount and no help should the lions attack him. He was completely alone, Sarina. How could they do such a thing to their *don*?"

She was shivering uncontrollably, cold and wet from the storm, shaken from the approach of the rogue lion, but most of all, fearful for Nicolai DeMarco's safety. "They should have stayed and protected him. It was their duty to protect him first, above all others. I don't understand what is going on in this place. What good are these men if they are disloyal? I wanted to go back to him, but they wouldn't let me." She was furious, *furious,* that the men had prevented her from staying with *Don* DeMarco.

"They *were* protecting their *don,*" Sarina answered softly, and she made the sign of the cross twice as they hurried through the spacious *palazzo.*

"You don't understand. He was alone, surrounded by those huge beasts." Isabella was shivering so hard her teeth were chattering. "They left him there. *I* left him there." That was worse, to think that she had been so frightened by the size and ferocity of the lion that she had chosen the coward's way out. She had scarcely even resisted the soldiers.

"You are not thinking clearly, *signorina,*" Sarina said gently, soothingly. "You would never have been allowed to stay behind. The captains had their orders to see you safely home, and they would have forced your obedience. You are in shock, cold, and hungry. You'll feel much better when you are warm."

As they moved swiftly through the halls of the *castello,* several servants smiled and nodded at them, open relief on their faces. Isabella tried to acknowledge them graciously, not understanding their reaction to her return. Nothing in this place made sense—not the people, not the animals. "Lions don't live up in the mountains. How did they come to be here? Shouldn't someone go out and look for the *don*?"

Sarina remained silent except for her little, soothing, clucking noises. Isabella's room was ready, with a fire burning and a tea tray. The housekeeper helped remove Isabella's cape, gasping as she spotted blood on it. "Are you injured? Where are you injured?"

Isabella stared in dismay at the red smears. She took the cape from Sarina, crushing the material in her hands. *Don* DeMarco had wrapped her in his own cloak. It had lain over hers, smearing her cape with blood. It was the *don* who had been injured. She had shook her head, denying the possibility. He must have gotten blood on his cloak when he knelt beside the fallen lion.

"I am unhurt, *signora,*" Isabella murmured. "Well, my

back is painful. I think I will swallow my pride and ask you to apply the numbing salve." She attempted a weak smile as she allowed Sarina to open her gown and expose the wounds on her back.

Isabella lay on the bed on her stomach, her fingers curling around the coverlet as Sarina carefully prepared the mixture of herbs. "Tell me about the lions, *signora*, and why the *don's* men would leave him alone in a snowstorm with wild beasts surrounding him. There is no alarm in the *palazzo*. I sense unease but not fear. Why is that?"

"Hush, *bambina*. Lie still while I apply this to your poor back. And you must call me Sarina. You will be mistress here now."

"I have not agreed to such a thing. He threw me out once and may very well do so again. I'm not ready to forgive him." Through half-open eyes, Isabella caught Sarina's quick, appreciative smile, but she had no idea what to make of it.

"I think you're just what *Don* DeMarco needs." Very gently Sarina began to apply the numbing potion to Isabella's ravaged back. "You would like to hear the story of the lions, would you? It is an interesting one to tell around the fire at night to frighten the children. It must have a few grains of truth in it, as lions should not be in these mountains. Yet they are here." She sighed. "They are a curse and blessing to our people."

Isabella opened her eyes to look fully at Sarina. "That is a strange thing to say. I saw the *don's* face when he knelt beside the rogue lion and touched it so . . ." She searched for the right description. "Reverently, sadly. He was sad that it was dead. My heart ached for him." Suddenly aware she had revealed too much of her confused feelings for the *don*, Isabella frowned. "Just for that moment, until I remembered how he had ordered me to leave without so much as a reason. He is fickle and prone to changing his mind, obviously not someone to count on." She managed to sound disdainful even while lying on her stomach with her gown pulled down to her waist. A true Vernaducci could manage under the worst circumstances, and Isabella was proud of herself. The world didn't have to know she melted every time the *don* looked her way. "Tell me the story, Sarina. I find it a most interesting topic." And it would keep her from running out into the storm in an attempt to hunt for the *don*.

Sarina began to pat the melting snowflakes from Isabella's hair. "Many, many years ago, in the old times, back when magick ruled the world, when gods and goddesses were called upon to aid the people, three houses of power resided here in this mountain valley. The houses were DeMarco, Bartolmei, and Drannacia. They were of ancient and sacred lineage, well favored and much loved by the gods. At that time, the houses practiced the old ways, worshiping Mother Earth. It is said it was a time of great power. There was powerful magick in the houses. Priests and priestesses, wizards and sorcerers. Some even say witches."

Isabella sat up, intrigued. Carefully she held the front of her gown over her generous breasts. "Magick, Sarina?"

Sarina looked pleased that her tale was chasing the shadows from Isabella's eyes. "Magick." She nodded firmly. "There was peace in the valley, and prosperity. The crops grew, and the houses were happy places. *Le famiglie* were allied, and they often intermarried to maintain the balance of power and defend against all outsiders."

"Sounds sensible," Isabella approved. She could breathe again without the pain in her back. The room was warm and finally thawing out the ice in her blood. She reached for the tea and had to make a hasty grab for her gown.

Sarina smiled at her. "You may as well take that off and wear one of the garments *Don* DeMarco had made for you."

Isabella would have argued, but she wanted to hear the story. "Where do the lions come in?" Obediently she peeled off the dress and stepped out of it. As she opened the wardrobe door and dragged out another gown, she glanced over her shoulder at the housekeeper. "They can't have been here in the mountains all along."

"You are so impatient." Sarina took the dress and carefully eased it over Isabella. "No, there were no lions back then. Let me tell the story the way it is said to have happened. For hundreds of years—maybe even more—the valley was safe from invaders, and although the world changed around them, the people managed to live peaceful and happy lives, practicing their faith wisely."

Sitting on the bed, Isabella drew her legs up beneath her long skirt and hugged herself. "That must have been an interesting time. There's much sense in the workings of nature."

Sarina glared at her, made the sign of the cross, and tapped Isabella's head. "Are you going to listen to me or risk angering the holy Madonna with your nonsense?"

"Does she get angry? I can't imagine her angry." Isabella saw Sarina's expression and quickly hid her smile. "I'm sorry. Tell the story."

"You do not deserve it, but I will," Sarina complied, clearly gratified that her young charge was growing rosy and warm and relaxed after her frightening ordeal. "There came a time when the people became more adept and more daring in their magick. Where once the people were as one, small divisions began to form. Oh, not all at once. It happened over the years."

Isabella took a sip of tea, savoring the taste and heat. She poured a second cup and handed it carefully to Sarina.

Surprised and pleased, Sarina beamed at her, cradling the warm cup in her hands. "No one knows in which house it started, but someone began dabbling in things best left alone. The beauty of the people's beliefs was corrupted, twisted, and something was let loose in the valley. Something that seemed to creep and spread until it reached every house. The magick became tainted, and once evil entered, it began to take shape and grow. It is said the howling of ghosts was often heard, as the dead could no longer find rest. Things began to happen. Accidents affecting each of the houses. The houses began to grow distant from one another. As the accidents increased and people were injured, they began to blame one another, and a great rift formed between the families. Since the houses were intermarried, it was a terrible thing. Brother against sister and cousin against cousin."

Isabella wrapped her hands around the warmth of her own teacup. She was shivering again. She had felt the presence of something evil in the *castello*, yet this was merely a frightening story for children. "That doesn't sound so much different than times are now. Our lands were stolen right out from under us. No one can be trusted, Sarina, not when power is involved."

Sarina nodded in agreement. "There is no changing what is true—not a hundred years ago, and not now. There was the whisper of conspiracy, of evil. The magick was used for things other than good. Crops failed regularly, and one house would have food while another didn't. Where they had shared before, now each tried to keep their treasures in their own holdings."

Sarina took a sip of her tea. The wind was howling outside the walls of the *palazzo*, rattling the windows so the images in the stained-glass windows seemed to move under the onslaught. Outside, despite the early hour, shadows lengthened and grew. A low moan arose, and tree branches waved wildly and scraped against the thick marble walls in protest.

Sarina looked out the colored glass and sighed. "This place does not like talk of the old days. I think remnants of that ancient magick still remain." She laughed nervously. "I'm grateful it is not yet night. Things happen in this place at night, *Signorina* Isabella. We laugh at the old ways and say they are tales made to frighten children and entertain us, but, in truth, strange things happen in this place, and, at times, the walls seem to have ears."

Isabella immediately placed her hand over the housekeeper's in a gesture meant to comfort. "You cannot truly be afraid, Sarina. This room is protected by angels." She laughed softly, reassuringly. "And my guards." She pointed to the stone lions sitting on the hearth. "They are very friendly. They would never allow anything in this room that shouldn't be here."

Sarina forced an answering laugh. "You must think me old and foolish."

Isabella took time to study the housekeeper's face. It was lined but gave the appearance of age rather than worry. But deep in Sarina's eyes was that hint of desperation Isabella had perceived in Betto and in a few other servants in the *palazzo*.

Fear clawed at Isabella, swirling deep in her stomach, a subtle warning. It wasn't all her wild imagination and the aftermath of facing wild beasts. There was something more in the *castello*, an underlying fear the people all seemed to share. But maybe it was just that the story Sarina was telling her went with the wind lashing at the windows and the snow falling relentlessly, trapping them indoors.

"Not old and foolish, Sarina," Isabella corrected softly, "but kind to a stranger. I couldn't ask for more courtesy than you have shown me. It is greatly appreciated, and if telling me this story is upsetting to you, it isn't necessary. I thought it interesting and harmless, a way to pass the time and take my mind off the worry of *Don* DeMarco's being left alone in the storm. But truly, if this is uncomfortable for you, we can speak of other things."

Sarina was silent a moment. Then she shook her head. "No, it's just that I've never liked storms. They seem so ferocious when they move through the mountains. Even as a young girl they made me fanciful. There's no need to worry about *Don* DeMarco. He is well able to take care of himself. But it is good you are concerned for him." Before Isabella could protest, Sarina hastily took up the story. "Where were we?"

Isabella grinned at her. "We hadn't gotten to the lions yet." She attempted to look innocent but failed miserably.

"You are obsessed with the lions," Sarina chastised. "The

magick had become twisted into something dark and ugly. Husbands suspected wives of infidelities. The penalty for such a sin was beheading. Jealousies became dangerous. The valley became a place of darkness. Storms ravaged the mountains. Beasts carried off young children. Some began to sacrifice animals and worship things best left alone. The years continued to go by, and the sacrifices worsened. Children were stolen from houses and sacrificed to demons. No one knew who was responsible, and each house looked upon the other with terrible suspicion."

Wind rushed down the fireplace with a wail of derision. Orange flames blazed and leapt high, taking the shape of shaggy-maned beasts with open mouths and glowing eyes. Sarina jumped, turning to look at the flash of fiery shapes, cringing visibly.

Isabella stared into the fireplace for a long moment, watching the wild flames die back down. Quite calmly she persisted, "How barbaric. Is it true? I know people did do such things in some places."

"According to the old tales, it was so. Who is to say what is the truth and what is legend?" Sarina's gaze strayed to the fire often, but the flames were small, and it burned cheerfully, filling the room with much-needed warmth. "The story has been handed down for hundreds of years. Many things have been added. No one knows if there is any truth to them. It is said that the very weather could be controlled, that such powers were commonplace. Who is to know?"

Isabella was watching the housekeeper closely. Sarina certainly believed the tale of twisted magick, of a religion, a way of life, corrupted into something dark and malignant.

"There came a time when the Christian beliefs began to spread. At that time, the *don* of the DeMarco house was named Alexander. He was married to a beautiful woman, one very powerful in the ways of magick. She was considered a true sorceress. There was much jealousy of her powers by the other houses, and much jealousy of her beauty.

Still, she met someone who spoke to her of this new belief, and she listened. And *Don* DeMarco's wife became a Christian."

Sarina seemed to breathe the word into the room, and, outside the windows, the howling wind stilled, leaving a hush of expectancy. "She became popular with the people, as she continually cared for the sick and worked tirelessly to feed those in need—not just those in her own holding but also the people in the other two holdings. But the more the people loved and followed her, the more jealous the other wives became.

"The wives of the other *dons*, Drannacia and Bartolmei, conspired to get rid of her. Sophia DeMarco was her name. They began to gossip about her and complain to their husbands that they had seen her with other men, that she was flitting about the countryside with the soldiers, fornicating and holding secret rituals of sacrifice. No one really knew much about Christianity, so it wasn't that difficult to frighten the people. They were willing to believe the worst, and the whispers and accusations were finally carried to her husband. It was *Don* Bartolmei and *Don* Drannacia who formally accused Sophia of infidelity and human sacrifices."

Isabella gasped. "How awful! Why would they do that?"

"Their wives had convinced them, whispering continually that they were doing a service to *Don* DeMarco, that it would go a long way to healing the rift between the houses if they had the courage to tell the powerful man just what his unfaithful wife was doing. They said she was making him look foolish and went so far as to accuse her of plotting the death of *Don* DeMarco. The two jealous women paid several soldiers to confess to bedding her. The *dons* believed her guilty and went to Alexander."

"Surely he didn't believe them?"

Sarina sighed softly. "Unfortunately, the evidence seemed overwhelming. It became a witch hunt, with more and more people coming forward, telling tales of devil worship and betrayal. They demanded her death. Sophia pleaded with

Alexander, begged him to believe in her innocence. She swore to him that she had never betrayed their love. But Alexander's heart had turned to stone. He was angry and jealous and bitter, thinking she had made a fool of him. It is said he went berserk and ranted and raved and publicly condemned her." She glanced around the room as if afraid of being overheard. "It happened here in the *palazzo*, in the small courtyard in the center of the three towers."

Isabella shook her head. "What a terrible thing, to have your own husband turn on you." A chill went down her spine at the thought of truly incurring *Don* DeMarco's displeasure.

"She threw herself on his mercy, wrapped her arms around his knees, and begged him to believe her, swearing again and again to him that she loved him and had been faithful. She was sobbing, begging him to soften his heart and see her through the eyes of their love, but he would not listen." Sarina paused. "Once he uttered the words to condemn her, all was lost to the DeMarco *famiglia*. The sky darkened, and lightning flashed across the sky. Sophia stopped crying and grew silent, her head bowed as she realized there was no hope; Alexander had sentenced her to death. She rose to her feet and looked at him with great contempt. She seemed to grow in stature, and she raised her arms to the sky. Lightning flashed from her fingers. She began to speak, saying words the *don* could not understand at first. Then she looked him directly in the eye.

"No one spoke, no one moved. Then Sophia uttered these words. 'You do not look upon your own wife with the eyes of compassion and love. You are incapable of mercy, no better than the beasts in the deserts and mountains. I curse you, Alexander DeMarco. I curse you and all your descendants to walk the earth with the beasts, to be seen as the beast, to be one with the beast, to rip the heart from the ones you love, as you have done to me.' Her face looked cold and was set as stone. She looked at the other two *dons*, and she cursed them, also, that their children would repeat

86

the betrayal of their fathers. As she knelt in front of the executioner, she seemed to soften. 'I will give you this much, Alexander,' she said, 'for my love for you, which has always remained steadfast, and to show you what mercy and compassion are. If one should come along who will see DeMarco as a man and not a beast, one who will tame what is untamable, who will love the unlovable, she will be able to break the curse and save your children's children and all who remain loyal to your house.' "

Isabella twisted her fingers into the heavy coverlet on her bed in protest of what was coming. She almost stopped Sarina, but it was too late. The housekeeper continued.

"Before Sophia could utter another word, she was beheaded. *Don* DeMarco could never take back his angry words. His wife was dead. Nothing would bring her back. Her blood seeped into the ground, and to this day, nothing grows in that courtyard. He buried her, and she remains deep beneath the *palazzo*. But burying her did not free him from his dark deed. He could not sleep or eat. The conditions in the valley worsened. *Don* Alexander grew thin and weary. What he had done to his wife preyed on him. He quietly began to investigate the charges against his wife, as he should have before he condemned her. He became convinced that Sophia was truly innocent, and he had committed a terrible sin, a terrible crime. He had not only allowed his enemies to murder his wife, but he had aided them to do so. He went to the other *dons* and laid before them the horrendous deed they had participated in. And they, too, realized their wives had betrayed them through jealousies."

Isabella jumped up and paced restlessly across the room. "Now you have me feeling bad for all of them, while they all deserved to be unhappy. Alexander most of all."

"He suffered greatly, Isabella. Terrible things happened, and he was helpless to do anything but witness the dissolution of the three houses. He decided to go to Rome. He wanted to find someone to talk to him about the Christian beliefs. He was looking for redemption, for some way to right the wrong he had committed. In the end, he did not undertake the journey alone. The heads of the other two houses accompanied him. They went into the city to find that the Christians had been rounded up and torn apart by lions for the amusement of the crowds. It was an ugly and terrifying scene, watching the animals tear men, women, and children to pieces.

"Alexander went a little crazy and vowed to destroy the lions. He found his way below ground, where they kept the lions. They were in cages, chained, without food, taunted and teased. It was said each lion was confined in a space so small the animal could not even turn around. The guards tormented the beasts, slicing their skin to make them hate all that was human. Alexander went up to a cage with his sword, wanting to sink it into the creature, but instead, he took pity on it. The pity he had not had for his own beloved wife. He could not force himself to kill when he was so guilty. The others tried to convince him, but he would not listen. He insisted the other *dons* get to safety, and he freed the lions from the cages, fully expecting to be torn apart."

Sarina sighed and placed her teacup on the tray. "It is said that when the three *dons* returned to the valley, DeMarco wore scars on his face, and the lions paced beside him. Still, it was not redemption. He could find no happiness, and neither would his children or their children. When they returned, they found the other two houses in ruins. DeMarco pulled the houses together under one holding and sealed the valley from intruders. The three *famiglie* have remained together since, their lives interwoven in prosperity and in hardship. From that time until this time, DeMarco has held dominion over the lions and kept the valley safe from invaders. Some say a great veil, a shroud of mist and magick, covers the valley and hides it from all who would seek to conquer. But from that time to this, no DeMarco has loved without pain, betrayal, and death." Sarina shrugged. "Who knows what is truth and what is story?"

"Well, that's the saddest thing I've ever heard, but it can't possibly be true. Surely there have been happy marriages in the DeMarco house," Isabella said, struggling to remember what she had heard of the DeMarco name. Lucca had often told her tales of the mountain holdings. The stories to scare the children of a lion man who fought entire armies and led a legion of beasts into battle. Stories of betrayal and savage deaths.

"Happy marriages do not always last," Sarina replied sadly. "Come, let us speak of other things. I'll show you around the *palazzo*."

Isabella tried a few times to pry more information out of the housekeeper, but the woman refused to say another word on the subject of lions and myths. Throughout the day Isabella thought often of *Don* DeMarco, alone, out in the snow. No one spoke of him or alluded to him. The *castello* was bustling, the servants working to keep the great halls and multitude of enormous rooms cleaned and polished. She had never seen such magnificence, such richness in a holding, and she wondered anew at the *don's* ability to retain his lands when so many invaders had, time and again, managed to take other holdings.

She ate a quiet dinner with Sarina and Betto, although Sarina was clearly uncomfortable with her insistence that she dine with them. Betto said little, but he was courteous and charming when he spoke. Isabella retired to her room in the evening, drank the required cup of tea, and allowed Sarina to once again apply the numbing salve to her back. The housekeeper spent a great deal of time combing out and rebraiding Isabella's hair, most likely waiting for her to become sleepy. Isabella deliberately yawned several times and made no protest when the door to her bedchamber was locked from the outside. She lay in bed waiting for Francesca, hoping the girl would visit her once the household settled down.

The wailing started an hour or so later, along with low moans and the rattling of chains. The noises seemed to be in the hall outside her room, and Isabella was frowning at the door when Francesca flounced happily onto the end of her bed. Startled, Isabella began laughing. "You must tell me where the secret entrance is," she greeted. "It would come in quite handy, I'm sure."

"There is more than one," Francesca said. "Why did you go away like that? I was afraid you would leave and I would never see you again." For the first time the young woman looked vexed and sulky.

"It certainly was not my choice to go off in a snowstorm," Isabella defended. "I'd never even seen snow until I came here."

"Really?" Francesca turned her head, her dark eyes leaping with interest. "Do you like it?"

"It's cold," Isabella said decidedly. "Very, very cold. I was shaking so much my teeth were chattering."

Francesca laughed. "My teeth always chatter, too. But sometimes, when I was little, I used to slide down the hills on a skin. It was fun. You should try it."

"I'm not so little, Francesca, and I'm not certain of the fun. When my horse threw me off, and I landed in the snow, it was not soft, as I thought it would be. When the snow falls, it seems fluffy, but on the ground it is much like the water of a pond becoming ice."

"I tied skins to my shoes once and tried to slide, but I fell very hard." Francesca laughed at the memory. "I didn't tell anyone, but my legs were black and blue for a week."

"Who makes all that noise?" Isabella asked, curious. The wailing and moaning seemed to be louder than usual. "Doesn't it bother anybody?"

"I think everyone ignores them out of politeness. I tell them to stop, that no one is impressed with such nonsense, but they won't listen to me." She looked indignant. "They think I'm a child. But, in truth, I think it makes them feel important." She looked at Isabella, her dark eyes guileless. "Have you ever taken a lover? I've never had a lover, and I've always wanted one. I think I'm pretty, don't you?"

Isabella sat up, careful of her back, drawing the coverlet

over her knees. Francesca was such a mixture of woman and child. "You're beautiful, Francesca," she assured her, feeling older and maternal. "You have no need to worry. A handsome man will come along and insist on marrying you. How could any man resist you?"

At once the shadows cleared from Francesca's face, and she beamed at Isabella. "Will Nicolai be your lover?"

Isabella took a sudden interest in plucking at the stitching on the quilt. "I know nothing of lovers, never having had one. I do have a *fratello*, a very handsome one *Don* De-Marco said he would come here. His name is Lucca."

"I have always liked that name," Francesca conceded. "Is he very handsome?"

"Oh, yes. And when he rides on a horse, he is dashing. All the women say so. I can't wait for you to meet him." Isabella smiled at the thought. Francesca might be just the person to get Lucca through the coming months. She was beautiful and funny and sweet. "He is ill, and he has been imprisoned in the dungeons of *Don* Rivellio. Have you ever met the *don*?"

Francesca shook her head solemnly. "No, and I don't think I would want to. Is Nicolai going to rescue your brother?"

Isabella nodded, but deep within, her heart twisted. She had left Nicolai DeMarco standing alone in the storm. The wind had howled and blown sheets of white flakes over him, and all she had done was fling his cloak to him. She never should have left him.

"You look so sad, Isabella," Francesca said. "There is no need to worry. If *Don* DeMarco has said he will have Lucca brought here to you, he will do so. He is a man of his word. Truly. He lives by his word. I have never known him to break it."

"Do you know him well?" Isabella asked, curiously, suddenly realizing she knew nothing of the DeMarco family. Francesca gave every appearance of being an *aristicratica*, and she certainly knew all the intrigues of the *castello*. Isabella had presumed she was family, most likely a cousin.

Francesca shrugged. "Who can know the *don*? He rules, and he provides protection, but one does not eat with him or speak with him."

"Well, of course they do." Isabella was horrified at the total lack of concern in Francesca's voice. "*Mio padre* was the *don*, and he certainly ate with us and conversed with us. No one wants to be alone, not even the *don*."

Francesca was silent for a time. "But it has always been so. He's in his rooms until night, and then all within the *palazzo* are confined so he is free to go anywhere, inside or out. He sees no one. His visitors are taken to his rooms to speak with him, but he is never seen. And he certainly does not take food in the presence of others." The young woman sounded shocked.

"Why? He had tea with me."

Francesca leapt to her feet. "That cannot be so. He doesn't eat with others. It isn't done."

Francesca seemed so upset, Isabella chose her words more carefully. "Is it a law of the holding that the *don* cannot eat with others? I don't understand. What of his *madre*? Surely the *famiglia* eats together."

"No, no, never." Francesca was adamant. "It isn't done." She began to pace the length of the room, clearly agitated.

The ghostly wails grew louder, and the moans seemed to rise and fall with the outside wind. "I didn't mean to upset you, Francesca," Isabella apologized gently. "The rules are different where I'm from. I'll learn yours."

"It isn't done," the younger woman repeated. "It is *never* done."

"I'm sorry." Isabella stirred, meaning to slide off the bed. The coverlet slipped precariously, and she looked around hastily for her dressing gown. Francesca was upset, and, although Isabella didn't know why, she wanted to comfort her. She located the garment in the darkness and turned back to the young woman. Her heart sank, and she dropped the robe back onto the chair where she had found it.

That quickly, Francesca had taken the opportunity to escape. Isabella called softly to her, but there was no reply, only the irritating sound of the ghostly wails. She thought about trying to find the secret passageway, but it seemed too much of an effort when she was worried about other matters. She slipped back into bed and lay quietly thinking of the *don*. It made no sense that he was not allowed to dine with another, but then, nothing in the valley made much sense to her.

Isabella lay staring at the wall, unable to sleep despite the darkness. She tried not to worry about Nicolai DeMarco. No one else seemed to feel he was in danger from the terrible storm or from the wild beasts roaming the valley. Isabella sighed and turned over to stare up at the ceiling. After a time she became aware of a sound, a deep sound, almost cavernous. Air rushing through lungs. She had heard that sound before, and it chilled her. Beneath the coverlet, her fingers curled into fists, and her breath nearly stopped.

Slowly, inch by inch, she turned her head toward the door. It had been locked; now it was open. *Something was in the room with her.* She strained to see into the darkest recesses of the room. At first she saw nothing, but as she stared, she finally made out a huge bulk crouched a few scant feet from her. The head was enormous, the eyes glowing at her. Watching her.

Isabella watched the beast right back. Now her heart was pounding so loudly, she was certain it could hear. She looked only at the eyes. They stared at one another for endless moments, and then the eleven-foot lion simply padded silently out of her room. She watched the door close. Isabella sat up gingerly and stared at the closed door. It hadn't been her imagination; the lion had been in the room with her. Perhaps someone had deliberately opened the door to allow it in, hoping it would kill her as its ancestors had killed the Christians.

The wailing was driving her crazy; the sound of chains rattling seemed to fill the hall outside her room. The noise went on and on until Isabella jumped out of bed in exasperation and dragged on her dressing gown. She was annoyed enough at her wayward imagination without the continuous howling of ghosts and ghouls or whatever was making such a fuss. Even the thought of lions prowling the halls of the *palazzo* was not enough to keep her a prisoner in her room. If the beast had wanted to devour her, it had already had a perfect opportunity. She stalked across the room and jerked at the door. To her shock, it was locked again.

Isabella stood there for a long moment, puzzled. A lion could not have locked the door, and surely Sarina hadn't crept back to lock it a second time. She had no idea how late it was, but she set about picking the lock, suddenly furious at having been locked in her room like a naughty child . . . or a prisoner.

Once she had the door unlocked, she flung it open defiantly and stepped out into the hall. She knew the way to the library, and, carefully lighting a taper, she began to retrace the route. The din in the hall was awful. Wailing and moaning and rattling of chains. Totally exasperated, Isabella paused at the entrance to the great study. "Enough! All of you will stop that silly noise this instant! I want no more of it tonight."

At once there was total silence. Isabella waited a moment. "Good!" She flounced into the library, allowing the door to swing closed behind her. Searching the shelves and cubicles, she thought of *Don* DeMarco alone in the snow. Inspecting a painting, she thought of him hunkered down beside the dead lion, sorrow in his eyes. Seating herself in a high-backed chair at the long marble table, she thought of him taking her hand in his. Staring at the ornate script of the thick tome she had chosen, she could think of no one, of nothing, else. He filled her mind and her heart until her very soul seemed bursting with fear for him.

Chapter Six

Isabella turned her head, and he was there. Her heart gave a single leap of joy, then began to pound with alarm. *Don* DeMarco was watching her intently. His amber eyes blazed at her with a smoldering mixture of desire and possessiveness. He was in the shadows, so he seemed indistinct, yet his stare was vivid and brilliant, almost glowing at her.

Very slowly she closed the book she was reading and set it on the table. "I am very happy to see you arrived safely, *Signor* DeMarco," she greeted him.

"How is it I find you lurking about the *palazzo* when you have been instructed to stay in your room at night?" he countered. His tone was a low blend of sensuous and rough. His voice seemed to seep into her pores and light a fire in her blood.

"I do not think I would use the word *instructed*," Isabella countered daringly. "It was most certainly an order."

"Which you completely ignored." His blazing eyes didn't so much as blink. "You chose to skulk instead."

" 'Lurking,' *signore?* 'Skulking'? I fear your imagination is out of control. I am merely reading a book, *Don* De-Marco, not stealing your treasures."

His mouth twitched, drawing her attention to his perfectly sculpted lips. "Sarina had orders. It is necessary to know that the servants obey without question."

Isabella lifted her chin and stared straight back at him, arching one eyebrow as if daring him to chastise her. "Have no fears, *signore.* Your housekeeper did her duty to you and carried out her orders, securely locking me in."

For the first time he stirred there in the shadows, and the movement drew attention to his earlier stillness. Muscles rippled, fluid and sinewy, reminding her of the predatory beasts he held dominion over. He had been motionless; now he exuded tremendous power, tremendous danger. "You are locked in your room for your safety, *signorina,* as you well know." His voice was quite low, a lash of temper held in check.

"I am locked in my room for your convenience," Isabella countered calmly. She folded her hands neatly in her lap to keep him from seeing her fingers twisting together in agitation. If they were to spar, she was not going to run simply because he was the most compelling and intriguing—the most *frightening*—man she had ever met. "Surely you would not have me believe you are so careless as to allow huge beasts to run free in your home. You are an intelligent man. That would be disastrous for several reasons. I suspect locking me in my room is more to keep me out of mischief than for my personal protection against marauding lions."

"And you saw no lions this night?" he asked softly, his voice a caress.

Isabella blushed, her lashes sweeping down to veil her expression. She had the feeling he knew she *had* seen a lion. "None from which I needed protection, *signore.*"

His stare didn't waver, rather became even more focused. The color of his eyes deepened, seeming to burst into flames. "Perhaps you need protection from me." His voice was velvet, purring menace.

Silence seemed to fill the library. She could hear the wind tugging at the windows as if trying to get in. She forced herself to meet that steady gaze defiantly. That she might need protection from the *don* was both shocking and strangely exhilarating.

"How did you manage to escape from your room, Isabella?"

The way he said her name, wrapping it up in a soft caress, sent liquid fire crawling through her body. He was lethal. Wickedly, sinfully lethal. His voice suggested he knew many things she had only heard about. Intimate things his hot gaze demanded she share with him. She could barely manage to breathe when she looked into those eyes, when she saw his tormented face. When she saw the intensity of his desire.

Isabella moistened her lips with the tip of her tongue, the only gesture betraying her nerves. "I certainly am not about to confess anything to you. Suffice it to say, I learned the fine arts one needs for moving about freely when my father used to confine me in my quarters. He often forbade me to go riding."

He smiled, a flash of white teeth, fine laugh lines crinkling the corners of his eyes. "I imagine he often forbade you to do many things."

"Yes, he did," Isabella admitted, trying not to melt right on the spot at his mere smile. There was something about him that tugged at her heart. If she wasn't careful, he could steal her soul and leave her a hollow shell. She leaned forward deliberately, defiantly, locking her gaze with his. "He forbade me all sorts of things, he locked me up continually, and it never did him a bit of good. I went where I wanted to go and did as I pleased. I have never, at any time, been a good or dutiful girl."

The table separated them, polished marble that gleamed a beautiful rose color under the flickering light of the tapers.

Nicolai glided closer, a tall, powerful figure looming over her so that the massive table seemed suddenly inconsequential. Deliberately he placed both palms flat on the surface and leaned his heavily muscled frame toward her so that their faces were mere inches apart.

"Is that a warning, *Signorina* Vernaducci?" His voice was nearly liquid, it was so soft, purring menace and blatant temptation.

Isabella refused to back down. Her pulse was racing, her heart pounding. He was the most handsome and imposing man she had ever seen. Up close he was mesmerizing, and just looking at him robbed her of air. She could see the terrible scars that had ravaged his left cheek, yet she could also see the absolute perfection of his masculine body, of his handsome face. Isabella struggled to drag air into her lungs, struggled not to lift her hand and cradle his scars in her palm. "Yes, *Don* DeMarco. I feel it is only fair to tell you the truth about me."

"Your intention, then, is to defy me?"

Sparring with him would have been much easier if he hadn't been staring at her mouth with such evident fascination. "I offered a lifetime of loyal servitude in return for the rescue of *mio fratello*. I even agreed to become your wife, and your answer was to ruthlessly order me to leave the valley in the middle of a snowstorm," she accused. "I don't think I owe you fidelity."

"You haven't forgiven me yet," he observed thoughtfully. "I thought we had dispensed with your unfavorable opinion of me."

He was so close, she wanted to touch his tempting mouth. His hair was an altogether different enticement, but she was determined to match him stare for stare. She managed her haughtiest tone. "I see nothing in my behavior that would lead you to believe that. I was merely polite, as good breeding commands."

"Really?" His voice was low, one eyebrow shooting up. He grinned at her then. A self-assured, know-it-all, wicked smile. It changed his face completely, chasing away the shadows and the deep lines. He looked young and handsome and sensually appealing. Her breath caught in her lungs, and her heart stopped beating. She could only stare helplessly at him.

Nicolai simply reached out, almost in slow motion, his palm curling slowly around the nape of her neck. His hand was large and hot against her skin, wrapping around the slender column so that his fingers lay against her vulnerable throat.

Fire raced through her body at the touch of his lips on hers. Every muscle clenched tightly. Heat blossomed low and sinfully in her stomach and spread to meet the flames racing through her bloodstream. His lips moved against hers, a slow teasing of senses, awakening her to a world of sensuality. His teeth tugged at her lower lip, an enticement she couldn't resist. She opened her mouth to him. Opened her heart to him. He swept in, masculine, possessive, a fire and a whirlwind consuming her. Her knees actually weakened, and her fingers grasped the marble table for anchor while the storm raged through her. Liquid heat spread, an aching need, curling and throbbing within her.

Isabella dragged herself away from him, horrified at her own behavior, shocked that she wanted to fling herself into his arms. She was very aware they were alone in a room, far from anyone else. The door was closed, and the tapers gave off meager light. She was wearing only a thin gown and dressing robe. Her hair was hanging down her back in a wild and wanton fashion. She wanted him with a desperation she had never known before.

Struggling to control her breathing, Isabella lowered her lashes to veil the expression in her eyes. She looked away from him, unable to meet the intensity of the stark desire burning in his amber gaze. She glanced down at the huge tome with its elaborate scripts, then down at the polished marble—anywhere to avoid his piercing eyes. Her gaze fell on the back of his hand, where he was leaning his palm on the table. Only it was a huge paw. The biggest paw she had ever seen. Intrigued, Isabella bent closer to inspect the five retractable, hooklike claws. The fur was dark and soft. Without conscious thought she stroked a caress over the fur; burying her fingers in the richness. The texture seemed real and more beautiful than she had imagined. Amazed, she looked up to meet Nicolai's strangely colored eyes. At once she realized she was pinning his hand to the table, still immersed in her strange illusion, her fingers caressing his skin.

Color crept up her neck and flooded her face. She snatched her hand away and cradled it against her, holding the warmth of his skin to her heart. "I'm sorry, *Signor* DeMarco, I don't know what got into me." First she had allowed him to be familiar with her, and then she had touched him intimately. What must he think of her?

"If you were again to agree to become my bride, Isabella," Nicolai said softly, his voice whispering along her skin like a purr, "then there would be no need to be embarrassed over the showing of affection."

She lifted her chin, arching a dark eyebrow at him. "Show of affection? I beg to differ with you, *signore*. It was merely curiosity; it overcomes me at the most inopportune times. A small failing I do my utmost to master."

A smile tugged at the hard edges of his mouth. "Curiosity, was it? I hope that I satisfied you, but I would be most willing to continue the experiment should you agree to become my wife."

"I appreciate your sacrifice," Isabella said, her eyes sparkling with laughter. "As for agreeing to be your wife, I have done so once and was treated abominably." She made an attempt at looking pathetic. "As I am a female, weak and rather nervous . . ."

"Ah, the fainting type?" Nicolai supplied helpfully.

"Yes," she lied. "I'm not certain my poor nerves could withstand the strain of such a husband."

He rubbed his shadowed jaw thoughtfully. "I must confess I didn't consider your . . . nerves. Still, I think we may get around the problem if we're careful."

He looked so young and handsome, so completely tantalizing, Isabella felt a curious melting sensation in the region of her heart. He tempted her in so many ways. She felt rather like a moth drawn to the flames. "Is there a specific number of times you intend to drive me from the *palazzo*? I think I'll need the answer to that question before I give consideration to your marriage proposal."

Nicolai shoved a hand carelessly through his hair. Unexpectedly, he winced and quickly dropped his arm to his side. "I believe the one time was enough, Isabella. I am certain it will not happen again."

"You're hurt." She hurried around the table and caught his arm. "Let me see."

Nicolai went completely still at the touch of her fingers. "This is what you want, Isabella? It is possible you will learn things about me you might not wish to know."

"I already know things about you I don't wish to know." Her eyes smiled at him, soft and generous if a little shy.

Nicolai reached out, framed her face gently, his thumbs sliding over her skin with exquisite tenderness. "You have not begun to know me, Isabella. I do not deserve to have you look upon me with such an expression in your beautiful eyes. I am dragging you into a world of danger where you will never know friend from enemy. I despise myself for being so selfish and cowardly that I cannot give you up."

"Well, of course you don't deserve me, *Signor* DeMarco, as I am such a fine catch with my wealth of lands and treasures, my sick brother, and the reputation of my name to bring to our marriage. Now stop stalling, and let me see your wounds. You are being a *bambino*—most unseemly when you are trying to impress me."

"Is it working?" His voice whispered over her skin. He leaned closer so that she smelled a wild, masculine scent, and the warmth of his body enveloped her. She found herself falling into the depths of his strange eyes, mesmerized and dizzy with such an unexpected longing that she froze, pressing a hand to her somersaulting stomach.

He bent to her, his gaze holding her captive, slowly moving closer. At the first touch of his lips, she closed her eyes, savoring the touch of him, the taste of him. His mouth took possession of hers, and the world seemed to rock, shift, and move until it fell away and she was burning inside and out.

His arms circled her waist and drew her to him, into the shelter of his body, gently, carefully, but tightly, so that she was pressed against him. She could feel his every muscle imprinted on her body. She went boneless, pliant, and melted into him, a part of him, catching fire so that she hungered for him.

Isabella felt his breath hitch as she burrowed closer. Immediately she pulled away, glaring up at him. "Let me see." Abruptly she was all business, a Vernaducci, well used to giving orders and having them obeyed. "I know you're injured, and I'm not taking no for an answer. I'm very stubborn."

"It is not difficult to believe that, Isabella," he said wryly. "But it is nothing, a mere scratch. I was careless when I should have been attentive."

Isabella slowly pulled his tunic away from his side to expose his bare skin. She gasped aloud. "You've been attacked by the lions." She touched his skin with trembling fingertips. "I don't know why I believed you would be safe from them. Everyone in the *palazzo* acts as if you are perfectly safe from the beasts."

"I am safe from the lions." His voice was gruff as he turned away, dragging his tunic back over the lacerations.

"Let me tend the wounds. It doesn't look as if you are safe. I thought of you as I wandered through the halls, believing that if you were really safe from the lions, then I would be safe, too. I just had to have faith. Sarina left me a potion that numbs, already made up." She took his hand, entwining her fingers with his. "Come with me."

"It is not at all proper," he warned, a hint of his boyish

grin touching his mouth. "My reputation would be destroyed completely."

Her eyebrows shot up. "I didn't realize you worried about such things. But you are correct, of course. The world might think ill of you. We can't have them whispering rumors and gossiping. Still, I must tend the lacerations, so I guess I have no choice but to agree to marry you, so your reputation remains safe."

"I thank you for the sacrifice," Nicolai said solemnly, but his eyes laughed at her teasing.

"Tremendous sacrifice," she corrected. "And it doesn't mean I have in any way forgiven your absurd and very rude conduct."

Despite the lightness of her tone, Nicolai heard the underlying note of hurt. He tightened his fingers around hers, holding her still beside him. "I had thought to protect you, Isabella, not reject you. *La mia famiglia* has a history of turning on their loved ones. I had no wish to take a chance with your life, *cara*, so I sent you away from me. I am dangerous, far more dangerous than you could possibly know." He brought her hand to the warmth of his lips, his touch soft on her skin. "You should be upset with me for allowing the lions to hold you here."

"The lions?" she echoed. "You believe they were deliberately forcing me to stay within your valley?" The warmth of his breath against her skin made her shiver with helpless need.

Nicolai kept her hand pressed against his lips, as if he couldn't bear to lose contact. "I know that they were. I changed my mind almost immediately once you were out of my sight. They knew. They always know. I'm not noble and courageous. If I were, you would be safe and far away from this place." There was a trace of bitterness in his voice. He rubbed her hand along his shadowed jaw, a small caress, closing his eyes for a moment and savoring the feel and scent of her.

Isabella was silent for a moment, turning his words over

in her mind. Nicolai was serious. He feared for her life. Feared that in some way he might be responsible for harming her. "What history of turning on loved ones, *Don* DeMarco?" Her heart was pounding in her chest, and she tasted fear in her mouth.

The words fell into a vacuum of silence. She stood very close to him, feeling the heat of his body. His thumb stroked a caress over the pulse beating so frantically in her wrist. He moved, his posture protective, towering over her, sheltering her against the echo of danger vibrating in the air. The night seemed to wrap them up, enveloping them in a shroud of darkness.

"Hasn't anyone yet regaled you with tales of how I received the scars on my face? I thought they would all leap at the chance to tell you." A strange rumble was emanating from his throat, somewhere between a purr and a growl.

Isabella tilted her head to look up at him. In the flickering light from the burning tapers, she could see shadows across the left side of his face, hiding the jagged lines etched deeply into his skin. She reached up and gently laid her hand over the scars, her palm comforting. "I don't think you realize how loyal your people are to you. No one has repeated gossip, *signore*, nor do I think they would do so. If you wish to tell me how this happened, please do, but don't feel it's necessary."

His hand covered hers, pressing her palm more tightly to him. His long lashes, the only feminine thing about him, veiled the sorrow in his burning eyes. "Why do you have to be so beautiful? So good?" There was a wealth of despair in his voice.

She felt the pain in his heart as if it were her own, and she ached to hold him, to ease the heavy burdens she had no hope of understanding. Without conscious thought, she leaned her body into his, her soft, full breasts pressing against his chest.

He groaned—she heard it quite clearly—his body tightening.

Nicolai experienced a heavy, aching need that crawled through his bloodstream and invaded every cell, every muscle. His arms slipped around Isabella and hauled her closer still, until there was only the thin barrier of their clothing separating them. Still, it wasn't close enough. His fingers tangled in her long hair, dragging her head back so he could take possession of her lush, inviting mouth. Enormously strong, he crushed her to him, trying to crawl inside the haven of her indomitable spirit. Wanting to lose himself in the perfection of her soft body.

Fire raced through him to her and back again, burning so hot, so fast, the flames were out of control. His mouth was hot with hunger, with need, with a raging desire almost beyond his comprehension. It took him so fast, so ferociously, he was unprepared for the primal lust blossoming deep within him, bursting into a conflagration as the taste and scent of her swamped his senses.

Isabella recognized the wildness rising in him, the terrible hunger and need, as his kiss deepened in masculine domination, taking rather than coaxing her untutored mouth to respond. He swept her away with him into a world of pure sensuality. She went with him willingly, wanting to feel his body hard and hot against hers. Wanting the enormous strength of his arms wrapped tightly around her. She merged with him, heat to heat, her mouth moving against his. She could feel the heavy thickness of him pressed against her, and it excited rather than alarmed her. She reveled as his fist tightened in her hair.

Unexpectedly, his ring scratched her neck, a sharp sting that drew her out of the silken web of erotic passion. Isabella gave a soft cry and lifted her head, staring up into his blazing eyes. She touched her neck, and her fingers came away smeared with a thin ribbon of red.

Nicolai snarled and leapt away from her, a single bound that took him deep within the shadows. His gaze was wild, turbulent, his eyes gleaming eerily like those of a beast. With his wild hair flowing around him, and his impressive size, he gave the appearance of the lions that roamed his lands.

"This is perilous, Isabella." His voice was gruff. A growl rumbled deep within his throat, making him sound untamed, dangerous. "You should not be here."

"There is no need to worry, *signore*." Isabella sounded amused at his trepidation. "I was not the most ladylike in my youth, and *mio fratello*, Lucca, taught me to render a man incapable of harming me. While it is true I would not want you writhing on the ground in pain, I would certainly defend my honor earnestly."

There was a silence while her heart beat out a rapid rhythm. Then a soft, muffled sound began to build in volume. Laughter. Warm, contagious, real. Nicolai shook his head, rather startled at the sound of his own laughter. He couldn't remember a time, even in his youth, when he had laughed. She didn't understand. Thank the Madonna she didn't understand. She stood there in front of him, her young, beautiful face innocent and without guile. Her eyes were wide and staring at him with trust, with the beginnings of affection, with everything he could ever want. She was offering him the world and the joys of paradise. He was offering her death and the fires of hell.

His laughter died away, and he blinked back something wet that was obscuring his vision. "Your brother taught you a manner of rendering a man harmless?" He rubbed his jaw thoughtfully, unobtrusively swiping his eyes to clear them of moisture. "I have not heard of this, a small creature such as yourself able to manage such a great feat. I would like this procedure explained to me in great detail."

Isabella was mesmerized by him, totally charmed. His laughter found its way deep into her heart, lodged there, and made a home. Faint color stole up her neck and tinged her face. "I am certain you know what I mean, *signore*."

"I think it is time you call me Nicolai. If you are considering reducing me to a writhing, painful heap on the floor, it's best that we're friends. I was merely hoping for a demonstration of this procedure. I wish you to teach my entire holding such a useful thing, so that all young women travel with protection and alleviate the worries of their fathers."

Her lashes fluttered, and Isabella twisted her fingers together. "You are jesting with me, *Don* DeMarco."

"Certainly not, *cara*. I am quite excited about this new form of protection that will allow a small woman such as yourself to cause a man of my size and strength to fall helplessly to the floor. Your brother, Lucca, taught you such a useful and invaluable trick? Tell me, Isabella, did he learn such a thing from a master swordsman?"

"You are impossible. I implore you to behave before I'm forced to call Sarina and have her deliver you a good clout on the ear." She tried to sound stern, but her eyes were dancing, and her lips curved enticingly.

He folded his arms across his chest, his gaze fixed on the temptation of her soft mouth. "Sarina believes you safely locked in your room, a well-bred young lady betrothed to her *don*."

Isabella managed a haughty glare when she really wanted to laugh. "You can just fix those horrible gashes in your side all by yourself. I'm going to my bedchamber and will do my utmost to forget this discourse."

"I have been accused of being a gentleman, Isabella, and I must insist on escorting you back to your bedchamber." He leaned close so that his breath was warm against her ear. "I cannot have you skulking about looking for hidden treasures."

Isabella thought herself a safe distance from him, yet in no time he had managed to glide quite close. He was so silent it was frightening at times. Without looking at him, she carefully replaced the tome on the shelf where she had found it. "If you're too frightened to wander the halls alone, I will consent to accompany you." She was proud of that haughty note. She felt it justifiable under the circumstances. His teasing was too appealing. She couldn't look at him without melting. She was in danger of fast becoming one of the very women she despised, clinging to a man and gazing at him in abject adoration. It was too humiliating to be borne.

Nicolai placed one hand on the small of her back as they walked together, side by side, out of the room. She was acutely aware of the heat of his hand so close to her skin. The rippling of his muscles beneath his shirt. The silence of his footfall. His height and the width of his shoulders. Mostly she was aware of his palm burning its way through her dressing robe, branding her.

She could feel the weight of his stare, and she kept her head bent, a small mutiny when he seemed to be taking over her life so quickly.

"I sent word that your brother must be released into my care," he said suddenly.

Isabella's head went up, and her gaze met his immediately. "You did? Thank the good Madonna. I have been so afraid for him. *Don* Rivellio would like nothing more than to see him dead. *Grazie, Signor* DeMarco, *grazie.*"

"Nicolai," he corrected softly. "Say my name, Isabella."

She certainly owed him that much. Her eyes were shining at him; she couldn't help it. She wanted to throw her arms around him and kiss him again. "Nicolai, *grazie.* For *mio fratello's* life."

"You do not owe me anything, *cara,*" he replied gruffly, but he couldn't drag his gaze from the fascination of her perfect mouth. "Rivellio is a powerful enemy and always greedy for more property. I'm surprised he didn't try to secure your lands by offering marriage to you."

Isabella looked straight ahead at the vaulted archways faintly lit by one or two tapers in sconces on the wall. "He did offer," she admitted, and once more she began walking in the direction of her room. "More than once. I refused him immediately. He was very angry. He didn't show it, but I could see it."

"Isabella." He said her name into the night. Whispered it. His voice was gentle, even tender. "You are not respon-

sible for what happened to your brother. Lucca chose to
join a secret rebellion, and he was foolish enough to get
caught. Rivellio used every means possible to attain the
lands he wanted. He wouldn't have been satisfied with your
dowry; he would have had Lucca murdered for the entire
holding."

Isabella let her breath out slowly. "I didn't think of that.
Of course he would have. He probably would have had me
murdered, too, so he could wed another who would bring
him more wealth."

"I suspect you are correct. He would allow a decent
length of time to go by first, of course. Either that or he
would have locked you up for his convenience and told the
world you had died. It isn't unheard of."

The idea chilled her. The casual, matter-of-fact way he
said it chilled her. Isabella had always had the protection of
her status, her birthright, name, and property. Her family
watched over her protectively. She had heard of the bru-
tality a woman could suffer at the hands of an unprincipled
man, but she had never thought overmuch about it.

When they arrived at her bedchamber, the room was
warm with the glowing embers of the fire. Isabella was all
business as she located the salve, but her stomach was
churning at Nicolai's words. She knew nothing of the *don*.
He was younger than she had thought and much more handsome than she ever could have imagined. He possessed a
charisma and charm she found enthralling. His voice and
eyes mesmerized her. His sexual magnetism was almost
more than she could resist.

"I frightened you, *cara*, with my thoughtless words. I can
assure you, I do not intend to lock you in a dungeon while
I marry other unsuspecting women for their fortunes. One
wife is enough for me. Especially when she is unpredictable
and skulks around my *palazzo*, hunting for my treasures."

"It is said you meet with many men, yet they do not see
you."

He caught her arm, pulling her close to him. "Who told

you such a thing?" Golden eyes blazed at her, tiny flames burning brightly in warning.

Isabella rolled her eyes expressively, not in the least intimidated. "It is common knowledge. Many gossip absurdly both in and outside this valley. But when I had an audience with you, you stayed mostly in the shadows." She laughed softly. "Skulking. I believe you were skulking in the shadows."

His harsh expression softened, and his eyes laughed at her teasing. Their voices were soft in the night. As if by mutual agreement neither wanted to awaken something from slumber that was better left alone. As it was, they were in their own world, locked together by the darkness and something intangible they shared. "I may have been skulking, for want of a better word. I love the night. Even as a child I felt I owned it." His eyes burned over her, amber flames gleaming brightly. "The night belongs to me, *cara*. I see what others do not. It holds a beauty and a fascination and, most importantly, a freedom I cannot have in daylight hours. I am most comfortable at night."

He was telling her something important, yet she was unable to grasp the meaning behind his words. Fleetingly remembering Sarina's calling him nocturnal, Isabella looked up at the perfection of his masculine features. "You are unnaturally handsome," she observed critically, without guile, "yet you seem not to know it. Why do you keep so much to yourself? Is it merely the way of your *castello*?" She enjoyed his company immensely and hoped he would continue to be a companion to her.

Nicolai hesitated, his first moment of indecision. He raked a hand through his hair, his body jerking as he lifted his arm. "You must meet the other women and begin to learn what is necessary to run the *palazzo*. I do not want a wife in name only. I expect you to take an active interest in your home and its people."

"I helped run *mio padre's* holdings, so I certainly will have no problem learning about this one." It was ten times larger than anything she had ever seen, but Sarina had already befriended her, and Isabella was certain the woman would help. It seemed a daunting task, but Isabella liked challenges, and she had confidence in her own abilities. She lifted her chin as she touched the edge of his tunic. "I was hoping we could share some meals together." Very gently she lifted his shirt to reveal the claw marks where the lion had raked his skin. "Hold this." She caught his wrist and pressed his palm against his shirt to keep it in place and away from the lacerations.

Nicolai watched her intently, the pupils of his eyes so pale they were luminous in the darkness. Her fingers brushed his skin gently, soothingly, lingering just a bit too long. His entire body clenched and tightened and ached with need. His breath caught in his throat, and his blood heated to a molten pool. He tore his gaze from her face, from her tender expression. The way she looked at him was almost too much to bear. His teeth snapped together in frustration, and a low growl escaped. "I should have insisted on sending you away."

Her gaze jumped to his face. "Why?" The question was stark. Innocent. Far too trusting.

It drove him mad. "Because I want to lay you down on the bed, the floor, anywhere at all, and make you my own." The words escaped before he could stop them, before he could take them back. He didn't know if he wanted to shock her or frighten her or warn her.

"Oh." The single word slipped out softly.

She didn't sound shocked or frightened. She sounded pleased. He saw the smile Isabella tried to hide.

She kept her gaze glued to the lacerations on his ribs, which matched those on the left side of his face. "How did you get these marks?"

Nicolai hesitated again, then sighed softly as he relaxed. "I was tussling with one of the lions, and I was a little slow." She was turning him inside out, and he wasn't prepared for the intensity of his emotions. Where before he had wanted her to know everything, now he merely wanted her to want him more than life.

He was lying. Isabella knew it. She glanced up at his set face. It was the first time he had told her an outright lie. His lashes were long and dark and feathery, completely at odds with his gleaming eyes, burning with such fierce intensity. She was gentle as she smeared the salve along the lacerations. "*Signor* DeMarco, I do not mind silence, but I object to untruths. I would ask that you would consider my request that if we're to be wed—"

"We are to be wed, Isabella." It was a command, uttered with complete authority.

"If that is so, *signore*, then I would ask that you refrain from speaking if you are inclined to tell me a falsehood. I want you to promise me that you will at least give consideration to my request."

"I will tell you this much truth, Isabella," he said softly. The air around them stilled, gathering powerful charge. Danger vibrated between them. "The one you should fear the most is standing before you. That is truth, the absolute truth. Heed my warning, *cara*. Never trust me, not for a single moment, if you value your life."

Isabella was afraid to move. Afraid to speak. He believed every word he had uttered to her. There was menace in his voice. And sorrow. And regret. But more than those things, there was the ring of truth.

Chapter Seven

They were all watching her. Isabella tried not to pay attention at first, but as Sarina showed her around the *palazzo*, she became more aware of the covert looks, the whispers following her from room to room. The atmosphere in the DeMarco holding was different from that of any she had been in, and she decided it was the people who made the difference. They were servants for the most part, polishing each room until it gleamed, but they did so as if they owned the *palazzo*.

Their loyalty to the *don* ran deep and seemed ingrained in every man, woman, and child she saw. They watched her intently. Eagerly. Each of them made it a point to say something encouraging to her, something complimentary about the *don*. They made it clear they were eager that she remain in the valley and marry their *don*. Isabella noticed that they smiled at one another, and all seemed close. The *castello* should have been a happy place, but, with her extreme sensitivity, she felt an undercurrent of unease.

A shadow hovered over the entire holding. An anxiety lurked just beneath the surface of apparent happiness. Eyes slid away from her, held secrets and traces of fear. As she moved through the great halls, suspicion began to seep into her pores and soak into her heart and soul. It was insidious, a tiny alarm at first, but it grew and spread like a monster of distrust until even Sarina seemed not an ally, but an enemy.

Isabella took a deep breath and halted, tugging at Sarina. "Stop for a moment. I'm feeling ill. I need to sit." Her mind was churning and spinning, making it impossible to think clearly. She seemed strangely out of sorts, wanting to snap in agitation at anyone near her. They were near a sweeping staircase, and Isabella sank gratefully onto the bottom step, pressing her hands to her throbbing temples, trying to stop the creeping sickness of mistrust and suspicion.

At once the housekeeper halted and leaned over her solicitously. "Is it your back? Do you need to rest? *Scusi, piccola*, I rushed taking you through the *palazzo*. It's so large, and I wanted you to know where everything is so you'd feel more comfortable. I should have been more careful, but it's so easy to get lost here." She brushed back Isabella's hair with a gentle hand. "I must let *Don* DeMarco know at once. He's arranged for the wives of Rolando Bartolmei and Sergio Drannacia to meet with you today. He wishes you to have friends and feel comfortable here. This is your new home, and we all want you to feel welcome."

"No, I'm fine. I'm looking forward to meeting them." Focusing on Sarina's face, Isabella realized how childish and silly she was being. Living in a large, unfamiliar *palazzo* far from home, without anyone she knew, must be affecting her nerves. She might very well turn into the fainting type if she wasn't careful. She forced a smile. "Really, Sarina, don't look so anxious. I promise, I'll be fine."

"*Signorina* Vernaducci." Alberita curtseyed in front of her, quite a feat when she was briskly swiping at walls with a broomstick. "It's good to see you again." She was beaming at Isabella even as she leapt enthusiastically at the cobwebs.

Watching the young servant jump up and down, not even getting close to the vaulted ceilings, Isabella began to relax again. The normal rhythm of a *palazzo* was there, despite the enormous size, despite the undercurrents. Little Alberita, with all her antics, was a part of something Isabella recognized. At a very early age she had helped to run her father's *palazzo*. More than once she had dealt with servants whose enthusiasm cheered the household far more than their work contributed. Isabella's strange mood dissipated as happiness bubbled up inside her.

Sarina sighed aloud. "She will never learn, that one." Although she tried to sound severe, her tone was brimming with mirth. She and Isabella looked at one another in total understanding. Laughter spilled between them, and their merriment put smiles on the faces of the servants within hearing.

A loud crack was the only warning. Then Alberita's broken broom handle flew through the air, right at Isabella's head. Alberita shrieked. Sarina shoved Isabella. Isabella found herself sprawled on the floor, and the broom handle smashed against the wall just above her and dropped, rolling until it hit her body.

Alberita flailed her hands wildly, shrieking so loudly that servants came running from all directions. Betto caught the remainder of the broom before it could harm anyone and set it carefully aside. Sarina hissed a sharp order, and Alberita clapped a hand over her mouth to stifle her screams. Still, she burst into hysterical weeping.

Captain Bartolmei rushed in, one hand on his sword hilt. He pushed the servants aside and caught at Isabella, dragging her up from the floor and pushing her behind him, shielding her with his body. "What happened?" His voice was harsh.

"An accident, no more," Sarina hastily explained.

Some of the servants began to murmur as if distressed or frightened. "The broom flew at her!" one woman yelled.

"That is silly, Brigita, and an utter falsehood," Sarina reprimanded sharply.

"Alberita attacked her!" another accused.

When Alberita howled a denial and cried all the harder, Captain Bartolmei crowded protectively closer to Isabella. "We must report this immediately to the *don*."

Isabella took a deep breath, desperate to regain her composure. She feared she might laugh at the complete absurdity of the situation. She dared not, for it would humiliate the weeping girl even more. "I think young Alberita should be taken to the kitchen and served a calming cup of tea. Is there anyone able to escort her to the kitchen, Sarina?" Isabella smiled serenely, moving confidently out from behind the captain. "*Grazie*, Captain, for your quick action, but, of course, we can't disturb *Don* DeMarco with something so small as this accident. It was merely a broken broom. Alberita is very enthusiastic in her work."

Determinedly she went to the young girl, ignoring the captain's restraining hand. "Your hard work is much appreciated. Go with Brigita, now, Alberita, and get a nice cup of tea to steady you."

"You must be more careful, girl," Captain Bartolmei snapped. "If anything should happen to *Signorina* Vernaducci, we are all lost."

Isabella laughed softly. "Come now, Captain, you'll have the people believing I was terrified by a broom."

Rolando Bartolmei found himself unable to resist her mischievous grin. "It wouldn't do to have that happen," he agreed.

"Rolando?" The voice was young, trying to be imperious but wavering alarmingly. "What is going on?"

The servants, Isabella, and Captain Bartolmei turned to face the newcomers. Two women, obviously *aristocratiche*, stood beside Sergio Drannacia, waiting for an explanation. But it was the tall, handsome man behind them who caught Isabella's attention and stole the breath from her lungs.

Don DeMarco was utterly motionless. His long hair

flowed around him, shaggy and thick. His eyes blazed with fire, the eyes of a predator, focused, intent on prey. For a moment his image shimmered, so that a lion seemed to stare relentlessly, mercilessly at the man standing so close to Isabella.

The very air in the room stilled, as if any movement, any sound, could trigger an attack. The servants hastily stared at the floor. Captain Bartolmei bowed slightly, averting his eyes.

The two women turned to look behind them. At the sight of the *don* one of them screamed, her face completely white. She would have slumped to the floor if Sergio Drannacia hadn't caught her and steadied her.

It was Isabella who moved first, breaking the tension. "Is the woman ill?" She hurried through the small group of servants, around the women and Drannacia, and made straight for *Don* DeMarco. She looked up at him. "Shouldn't we offer her a bedchamber?"

Captain Bartolmei took the woman from Sergio, giving her a small shake. He bent his head and whispered fiercely to her, his face stiff with embarrassment.

Betto clapped his hands and gestured to the servants, scattering them quickly, sending them back to their duties. "Tea is served in the drawing room," he announced to his *don,* and he melted away as only a well-practiced manservant could.

"There is no need of a bedchamber," Captain Bartolmei answered grimly. "My wife is perfectly fine. I apologize for her conduct."

The young woman turned her head away, but not before Isabella saw tears glittering in her eyes at the harsh reprimand she had received from her spouse. Captain Bartolmei's wife kept her head down as they walked through the halls to the drawing room.

In truth, Isabella felt sorry for the girl. More than once her father had publicly censured her. She knew the utter humiliation of such a deed. She knew what it cost in strength and pride to have to face those who had witnessed the reprimand.

The *don* matched his longer strides to Isabella's, his hand resting lightly on her arm, his body quite close to hers. "Would you care to explain why the captain was holding your hand?" His voice was low but purred with a menace that sent a shiver down her spine. His palm slid along her arm to take possession of her hand, his fingers threading tightly through hers.

Her startled gaze jumped to his face. "Is that what it looked like? How awful. He was worried for my safety and kept pushing me behind him." Isabella shook her head. "No wonder his wife became hysterical. What must the poor woman think?"

Something dangerous flickered in the depths of his eyes. "Why would you care what she thought? Isn't what *I* think of paramount importance to you both?"

She tightened her fingers around his and leaned closer. "You, I know, have a brain in your head. I'm certain it would occur to you that the last thing your friend the captain would do is hold my hand in front of the servants." She rolled her eyes toward the ceiling, a trace of humor in her voice.

"If you came upon your husband holding the hand of another woman, what would you do?" Nicolai asked, curious, suddenly amused by her reaction. She hadn't even considered that he would be jealous or angry or in any way upset by seeing another man so close to her. She had faith in his ability to reason, never once considering that a jealous man was by definition unreasonable.

She tugged on his hand, forcing him to stop. She went up on her toes and whispered in his ear. "If he truly were holding her hand, I would crack a broomstick over his thick skull very, very hard." Her voice was so sweet, so low and sensual, for a moment the words nearly didn't register.

Then Nicolai shocked himself and his guests by laughing aloud. Real, heartfelt laughter. It rumbled in his throat and spilled into the room, making every servant within hearing distance smile. It had been long since they'd heard their *don* laugh. The sound instantly dispelled the tension running high in the *palazzo*. Sergio and Rolando exchanged a quick, amused smile.

"*Signorina* Vernaducci, may I present my wife, Violante?" Sergio Drannacia said quietly, his arm wrapped around a woman who looked to be several years older than Isabella. "Violante, this is Isabella Vernaducci, betrothed to *Don* DeMarco."

Violante curtseyed, a smile curving her mouth, but her eyes were wary, speculative, as they ran over Isabella's figure. "So pleased to meet you, *signorina*."

Isabella nodded an acceptance of the introduction. "I hope we become great friends. Please call me Isabella."

"And may I present my wife, Theresa Bartolmei," Rolando Bartolmei added.

The young woman dropped a slight curtsey, lowering her lashes. "It is an honor to meet you, *Signorina* Vernaducci," she murmured softly, her voice wavering slightly.

Theresa Bartolmei was about the same age as Isabella. She carried herself as an *aristicratica* yet seemed very uneasy in the *don's* presence. She was so jittery, she made Isabella nervous. The woman didn't look at *Don* DeMarco, keeping her gaze steadfastly on her feet other than the brief glance she had directed toward Isabella.

Isabella forced a smile, moving closer to Nicolai. It irritated her that so many people treated him so strangely. "*Grazie, Signora* Bartolmei. It is wonderful to meet you. Your husband was very kind to me when we were traveling on the roads to the pass. And today, with the accident, he did his duty by protecting me. I appreciated it very much."

Isabella was an innocent, yet she wrapped Nicolai up in an intimacy he had never shared with any other in his life. His body stilled, hardened. He held her in front of him, not daring to move when he would have preferred to retreat and leave his childhood friends to make conversation with

the women. He was afraid he might shatter if he moved.
There was a roaring in his head, a painful ache in his body.
Fire raced through his bloodstream. Worse than his physical
reaction to her was the way she was wrapping herself
around his heart, until just looking at her hurt.

His hands tightened possessively on her arms. It was all
that kept him anchored. Sane. It was all that prevented him
from sweeping her into his embrace and carrying her off to
his lair, where he could indulge his every fantasy with her.
The others were talking; he heard their voices but as if from
a great distance. For Nicolai, there was only Isabella and
the temptation of her mouth, of her soft body with its lush
curves. Her laughter and her quick mind. No one else ex-
isted or mattered. He was becoming obsessed. He was fast
losing control, and that was inherently dangerous. For a
DeMarco, control was everything. Completely, utterly es-
sential.

He bent his head until his mouth brushed against her ear.
"I should have been the one to rescue you, your true hero."
There was an edge to his voice when he had wanted humor.

Isabella dared not look at Nicolai, but she leaned against
his broad chest so that he kept his dark head bent to hers.
"He merely protected me from a runaway broom." She
whispered the words against the corner of his mouth, her
breath teasing his heightened senses.

He had known she would find a way to lighten his heart.
Her eyes danced with shared humor, locking them together.
He found he could breathe again. His fingers curled around
the nape of her neck, then drifted to her shoulder and down
her back, a gesture meant to thank her where he had no
words.

"It is a pleasure seeing you both," he said softly to the
two ladies, "but I must ask to be excused, as I have many
duties to attend."

The wives of his captains stared resolutely at the floor,
once again setting Isabella's teeth on edge. Nicolai's hand

swept down Isabella's hair in a light caress. "Be happy, *cara mia*. I will see you later."

She caught his wrist boldly. "You don't have time for a cup of tea?"

There was a collective gasp of shock. Even the two captains stiffened. Isabella felt the color rise in her neck and face. The simple question was treated as if she had made a terrible breach of etiquette.

Nicolai ignored the others, his vision, his world, narrowing until there were only the two of them. His large hands framed her face, and his gaze drifted hungrily over her. "*Grazie, piccola*. I wish I had the time. For you, anything." His sensual voice was filled with regret. "But I have kept several emissaries waiting far too long as it is." He bent his head and brushed a kiss against her temple, his fingers lingering a moment on her soft skin. Abruptly he turned and in his silent, deadly fashion walked away.

Isabella turned to find the couples watching her. She lifted her chin and determinedly pasted a confident smile on her face. "It looks as if Cook has prepared a feast for us. I hope you're hungry. *Grazie*, Captains, for bringing me company."

"We'll return shortly," Rolando assured his wife. "We, too, have our duties to attend to." He patted his wife's hand in reassurance before walking away.

Theresa watched him go. She was visibly trembling, her eyes darting around the room anxiously as if she expected a ghost to come flying out of the walls.

Violante looked toward her husband, her gaze hopeful. When he merely walked away without glancing back, her shoulders sagged. Almost at once she recovered and seated herself gracefully. "Sergio tells me the wedding is to be within the moon's cycle." Her eyes slid speculatively over Isabella's curvy figure. "You must be . . ." She paused long enough to be bordering on rudeness . . . "nervous."

Theresa pressed a hand to her mouth to stifle her gasp of shock.

Isabella smiled coolly. "On the contrary, *Signora* Drannacia, I'm very excited. Nicolai is most charming and attentive. I cannot wait to be his wife."

Sarina poured the tea, a mixture of herbs and hot water, into the cups. She kept her gaze resolutely on her work, but Isabella noticed the tightening of her lips.

"Aren't you frightened?" Theresa ventured.

"Why ever would I be afraid? Everyone has been wonderful to me," Isabella said, easily portraying a wide-eyed innocent. "They've made me feel very much at home. I know I'll be happy here."

Sarina flashed at her a covert grin as she placed a platter of biscuits on the table. The housekeeper faded discreetly into the background, leaving Isabella to fend for herself.

Despite her youth, Isabella had been in similar situations before. Violante Drannacia was a woman feeling threatened. She was determined to maintain her position, real or imagined, wanting the upper hand with all the other females in the *palazzo*. She was also uncertain of her husband and felt compelled to warn off any competition. Isabella knew the signs well.

Violante patted her hair, looking superior and knowledgeable. It was obvious she easily intimidated Theresa. She leaned closer to Isabella and looked cautiously around the room. "You haven't heard the legend?"

"A fascinating tale. I can't wait to tell my children on a dark and stormy night," Isabella improvised. Which legend? she wondered.

"How can you stand to look at him?" Violante asked, her gaze challenging.

The smile faded from Isabella's dark eyes. She drew herself up, her young face haughty. "Don't make the mistake of forgetting yourself, *Signora* Drannacia. I may not be mistress here yet, but I will be. I won't have Nicolai maligned in any way. I find him handsome and charming. If you can't bear to look at the scars on his face, scars from a horrifying attack, I would ask you not to visit our home."

Violante paled. She pressed a hand to her chest as if her heart had fluttered at the attack. "*Signorina*, you misunderstand me completely. It is impossible to notice scars when we've been taught not to look upon him. You're not from this valley." She took a sip of tea, her eyes bright as they examined Isabella's face. "It is ingrained in us not to stare directly at him, of course."

It took a great deal of effort, but Isabella maintained her composure. The women knew things she didn't, but she would not give the advantage to Violante Drannacia by asking her personal questions regarding the *don* or the *palazzo*. "How fortunate for me." She kept a smile on her face as she turned to Theresa. "May I ask how long you've been married, *Signora* Bartolmei?" She was secretly pleased to see the younger woman look appalled at Violante's behavior.

"Theresa," Captain Bartolmei's wife corrected. "Only a short time. I've always lived in the valley, but not in the holding. My *famiglia* has a large farm. I met Rolando when he was out hunting." A blush stole up her neck at either the memory or the admission.

"The lions didn't bother your farm?" Isabella asked.

Theresa shook her head. "I never saw one until I came here to the *palazzo*." A shadow crossed her face, and she twisted her fingers together nervously. "We heard them, or course, on the farm, but never once in all the years I was growing up did I ever see one."

"Theresa's afraid one might gobble her up," Violante supplied.

Isabella laughed lightly, shifting closer to Theresa. "I think that shows good sense, Theresa. I, too, would prefer to avoid being gobbled up. Have you seen a lion up close, Violante? I had no idea they were so enormous. Their heads are so massive, I think all three of us would fit into one's mouth."

"Well." Violante shivered. "I saw one up close once. Sergio was making a patrol through the valley, and he stopped near our house to take me for a walk. We thought we were alone. We never heard a sound. We just walked right up on it." She cast a sheepish look at Theresa. "I started to scream, but Sergio put his hand over my mouth so I couldn't make a sound. I was terrified it would eat me right up."

The three women looked at one another, then burst out laughing. Theresa relaxed visibly. Violante took a sip of her tea, managing to look regal. "What are you doing about this wedding of yours, Isabella? May I call you Isabella?"

"Please do. The wedding." Isabella sighed. "I haven't any idea. *Don* DeMarco announced it, and that was the last I heard. I don't even know when it takes place. What was your wedding like?"

Violante sighed in happy remembrance. "It was the most beautiful day of my life. Everything was perfect. The weather, the dresses, Sergio so handsome. Everyone of importance was there." She hesitated. "Well, with the exception of the *Don* DeMarco. He met with Sergio beforehand and gave us a magnificent wedding gift. Surely the dressmaker has started on your dress. She must hurry." She patted Isabella's hand. "We would love to help plan it, if *tua madre* isn't available, right, Theresa?"

Theresa nodded eagerly. "It would be fun."

"*Don* DeMarco knows I have no *famiglia* other than *mio fratello*, Lucca. He is quite ill, though, and could hardly plan a wedding. I've lost both of my parents."

"I'll speak to Sarina and see what is being done," Violante said firmly. "We cannot leave the details to *Don* DeMarco, as he is very busy. It gives us an excuse to visit you often."

"You'll never need an excuse," Isabella answered. "Our three houses are connected and always will be, bringing our people and the valley prosperity. I hope the three of us become very close friends. What was your wedding like, Theresa?" The young woman seemed perpetually nervous, and Isabella wanted to put her at ease.

Theresa beamed at her. "It was beautiful, and Rolando was most handsome. We were married in the Holy Church, of course, but afterward we danced all evening under the stars."

"*Scusi, Signorina* Vernaducci," Sarina interrupted with a slight curtsey. "I must take care of a problem in the kitchen."

"We'll manage, Sarina, *grazie*," Isabella assured her and waved her one ally away. She turned back to the other two women, determined to try to make friends. "It sounds wonderful, Theresa. I suppose your parents planned it for you."

"Yes, with *Don* DeMarco," Theresa said, looking uneasy again.

Isabella's stomach did a funny little roll, instantly putting her on guard. While the two women continued to chat, she glanced surreptitiously around the room. They were no longer alone; something had joined them. It was subtle, the outpouring of twisted malice flowing into the room.

Isabella sighed. It was a long afternoon. She kept the conversation going, but it was difficult, as Theresa looked faint if Nicolai was mentioned, and Violante seemed to want to sneer at each new subject with contempt. Isabella was secretly relieved when the captains returned to claim their wives.

Theresa eagerly gathered her things, drew on her gloves, and rose with haste, earning her a frown from her husband.

"Shall I escort you back to your room?" Captain Drannacia offered Isabella solicitously, his hand resting on the back of his wife's chair.

Isabella glanced up in time to see the fear and suspicion on Violante's face. The woman covered her reaction by rising gracefully and smiling at Isabella. "It's been such a pleasure. I hope we can do this again soon."

"I hope so, too," Isabella assured her. "*Grazie*, Captain Drannacia, but I have no need for an escort."

"We'll have to come back soon if we're to help with the wedding," Theresa reminded her. "I've really enjoyed meeting you, Isabella. Please come to my home sometime, too," she added shyly. "For tea."

125

Isabella smiled at her. "I would enjoy that. Thank you both so much for coming to meet me."

"I have duties here in the *castello*, Sergio," Rolando Bartolmei announced regretfully. "Will you see *Signora* Bartolmei safely home for me?"

Theresa looked as though she might protest, but she choked back her objection, staring down at the tips of her shoes instead.

"Perhaps Captain Bartolmei will escort you to your room, *Signorina* Vernaducci," Violante said with unexpected malice, "just to make certain you don't get lost."

Theresa winced visibly and glanced at Violante, clearly shocked.

"I would be happy to escort you," Captain Bartolmei agreed, bowing gallantly, ignoring his wife's pale features.

"That won't be necessary, *signore*, but *grazie*. I know my way around the *palazzo* fairly well now. Sarina has been helping me. I wouldn't want to keep you from your duties." Isabella smiled, but her insides were trembling, a sign something was very wrong. The surge of power had been unexpectedly strong, preying on Theresa's jealousy. Isabella wanted them all to leave, afraid the malevolence was growing. "I appreciate both of you for bringing your wives to meet me."

Captain Bartolmei touched his wife's hand briefly, bowed to the others, and walked out of the room. Sergio Drannacia took Violante's arm and escorted the two women out, first bowing to Isabella.

Isabella sighed softly and shook her head. Holdings were the same everywhere, filled with petty rivalries, suspicions, jealousies, and intrigue. The *palazzo* of *Don* DeMarco, however, was somehow different. Something crouched in wait, watching, listening, preying on human weaknesses. She felt tired and worn out and alarmed. No one else seemed to notice anything was wrong; they didn't feel the presence of evil as she did.

She waited a few minutes longer for Sarina, but when the

housekeeper didn't appear, and shadows began lengthening in the room, Isabella decided to go to her bedchamber. It seemed to be the most restful room in the *palazzo*. She started through the wide hallways, looking up at the artwork, the carvings of lions in various positions, some snarling, some watching intently. Isabella began to feel as if she were actually being watched, a fanciful feeling in the midst of the carvings, etchings, and sculptures.

"Isabella." She heard her name drifting down the hallway. It was spoken so low she barely caught it. For a moment Isabella stood still, straining to listen. Had it been Francesca? It sounded like her voice, a bit disembodied, but it was something Francesca might do. Hide and call to her. At once her heart lifted a bit at the thought of her friend.

Curious, Isabella turned along the corridor and immediately came to a door she knew led to the servants' corridors. It stood slightly ajar, as if Francesca had deliberately left it open to catch her attention. The voice whispered again, but this time so low Isabella couldn't catch the actual words. Francesca seemed on the move, determined to play an impulsive game.

Finding the voice impossible to resist, Isabella slipped through the door and found herself in one of the narrow corridors used by the servants to get quickly from one end of the *palazzo* to the other. Even in her own holding Isabella had never explored the network of servant entrances and stairwells. Intrigued, she began to walk along the hallway, following the twists and turns. There were stairways that led up and across and over and led to more staircases. They were steep and uncomfortable, nothing resembling the ornate stairways that spiraled through the *palazzo*, connecting the various stories and wings together.

There were very few sconces to hold torches, and the shadows lengthened and grew, and a heaviness grew in her heart along with them. She paused for a moment to get her bearings, midway up another steep staircase.

Just as she was going to turn back, Isabella heard the

mysterious whisper again. "Isabella." It was somewhere just ahead. She moved quickly up the narrow, curving staircase, following the soft sound. She had been cautioned to stay away from the wing where *Don* DeMarco kept his residence. Uncertain whether the staircase had twisted back and upward toward his wing, Isabella hesitated, one hand grasping the railing in indecision. She was confused as to precisely where she was heading, which was strange, since she'd always had a remarkable sense of direction. Everything seemed different, and that strange shadow in her heart grew longer and heavier. Surely if she accidentally ended up in the wrong part of the *palazzo*, she would be forgiven. She was a stranger, and the place was enormous.

The soft whisper came again, a woman's voice beckoning her. Isabella again began to climb the endless staircase. It branched off in many directions, led to wide halls and narrow corridors. She had seen none of this with Sarina and was hopelessly lost. She had no idea which floor she was on or even which direction she faced.

A door was partially opened, cool outside air rushing in. It felt good on her skin. Isabella was hot and sticky and out of breath. She stepped out the side door, staring in awe at the sparkling white landscape. She was definitely up high, on the third story, and the balcony was small, just a crescent-shaped overhang with a wide wall for a railing. As she took a step toward the edge, the door swung closed behind her.

Isabella stared at it in shocked surprise. She tried the handle, but the door didn't budge. Exasperated, she pulled on the door, then pounded senselessly until she remembered no one was likely to be near the entrance. She was locked out in the cold wearing only a thin day gown. The balcony was icy, slippery beneath her shoes. The wind tugged at her clothes, pierced her with its icy breath. She suddenly realized she was on the balcony of one of the rounded towers, and below her was the infamous courtyard where a DeMarco had put his wife to death.

"How do you get yourself into these things?" she asked aloud, taking mincing steps toward the balcony railing and gripping the wall surrounding her tiny prison. Clutching the edge, she leaned out, looking down, hoping someone would be in sight and she'd be able to attract attention.

As she rested her weight against the railing, she felt the surge of power, of glee, flowing around her, the air thick with malice. Without warning the tiling crumbled out from under her. She was tumbling through space, her fingers clawing for something solid, a scream ripping from her throat. She caught at the neck of one of the stone lions guarding the sheer side of the *castello*. For a moment she nearly slipped, but she managed to circle the statue's mane with her arms.

Isabella screamed again, loud and long, hoping to attract someone to her plight. She couldn't drag her body up onto the sculpted lion, and her arms ached from hanging. Snow had collected on the marble likeness, making it ice cold and very slippery. Isabella locked her fingers together and prayed for help.

The sun had set, and darkness was settling over the mountains. The wind rose and fiercely attacked her dangling body in icy gusts. She was becoming so chilled, her hands and feet were nearly numb.

"*Signorina* Isabella!" The shocked voice of Rolando Bartolmei came from above her. She looked up to find him leaning out over the balcony, his face pale with concern.

"Be careful." Her warning was a mere croak of sound.

"Can you reach my hand?"

Isabella closed her eyes briefly, afraid that if she looked down she would fall. Looking up was even more frightening. Her heart was pounding, and she tasted terror. Someone, something had arranged her accident. Someone wanted her dead. She had been led right into a trap. Captain Bartolmei was on the balcony. She had to let go of her lion and trust him to pull her up.

"Look at me," he commanded. "Reach up and take my hand right now."

She clutched at the stone lion but managed to look up at her rescuer.

"Are you injured?" Captain Bartolmei's voice bordered on desperation. "Answer me!" This time he used his authority, commanding compliance. His hand was inches from hers as he leaned down to her. "You can do it. Take my hand."

Isabella took a deep breath and let it out. Very slowly she worked at loosening her grip, one finger at a time. Taking a leap of faith, she reached for him. Rolando caught her wrist and dragged her up and over the railing. She collapsed against him, both of them sprawling on the snow-covered balcony.

For a moment he held her tightly, his hands patting her back in a clumsy attempt to comfort her. "Are you injured in any way?" He sat her up with gentle hands.

Isabella was shaking so hard her teeth chattered, but she shook her head firmly. Her skin felt like ice. Rolando removed his jacket and settled it around her shoulders. "Can you walk?"

She nodded. If it got her to her bedchamber, a warm fire, a cup of hot tea, and her bed, she would crawl if need be.

"What happened? How did you come to be in this place?" He helped her to her feet and guided her out of the wind, back into the servants' corridors.

"*Grazie, Signor* Bartolmei. You saved my life. I don't think I could have held on much longer. I thought I heard someone I know calling to me. The door closed behind me, and I was trapped." Subdued, Isabella followed his lead through the network of stairs and hallways until they were once again in the main section of the *palazzo*. "Please send Sarina to me," she said as they stopped in front of her door. Her feet were so numb she couldn't feel them. "I would prefer that you not say anything. I shouldn't have been exploring." Before he could protest, Isabella ducked into her room, murmuring her thanks once again.

She closed the door quickly before she humiliated herself by bursting into tears. Isabella flung herself facedown on the bed. The fire was already roaring in the fireplace, but Isabella didn't think she would ever be warm again. She wrapped her hands in the coverlet and shook helplessly, uncertain if it was from sheer terror or from the bitter, piercing cold.

Sarina found Isabella shaking uncontrollably, her hair wet and tangled, her gown soaked and streaked with dirt. Most alarming was the fact that Captain Bartolmei's jacket covered her.

"My hands and feet are burning now," Isabella said, struggling not to weep.

The housekeeper took charge immediately, drying her young charge, dressing her hair, and tucking her beneath the quilts after a cup of soothing tea. "Captain Bartolmei's coat shouldn't be in your room. Did the servants see you wearing it? Did you run into any of them as you came through the *palazzo?*"

"Don't you want to know what happened?" Isabella turned her face away, sickened that she had been so close to death, yet all the housekeeper seemed worried about was propriety. "I'm certain someone saw us. We weren't trying to hide."

Sarina patted her gently. "It is necessary to be cautious, given your status, Isabella."

Isabella flinched, having heard the words many times from her father. "I'll try to arrange it so that the next time I'm nearly killed, it won't be food for gossip."

Sarina looked horrified. "I didn't mean—"

Nicolai DeMarco stalked in without warning, interrupting whatever the housekeeper had to say. His amber eyes blazed with heat. "Is she injured?"

Sarina kept her gaze fixed on Isabella, who turned her

head toward the sound of the *don's* voice. "No, *signore*, just very cold."

"I wish to speak with her alone." Nicolai made it a decree, circumventing any protest Sarina might make.

He waited until his housekeeper had closed the door before taking the chair she had vacated. His palm cradled the back of Isabella's head. "Captain Bartolmei tells me you nearly fell to your death. What were you doing up there, *piccola?*"

"Certainly not leaping to my death, if that's what you think," Isabella retorted without her usual spirit. "I was lost." Her lashes drifted down. "I followed the voice. The door locked. It was cold." Her words were low, her sentences disjointed, and made no real sense to him. "Aren't you going to ask why Captain Bartolmei's jacket is in my bedchamber? Sarina seemed overly concerned with it." There was distress, hurt in her tone, despite the fact that she tried valiantly to hide it. "I've already had the lecture on being more discreet when I'm falling to my death, so if you don't mind too much, I'll pass on another one."

"Go to sleep, *cara mia*. I have no intention of being angry with you or Rolando. On the contrary, I'm in his debt." He stroked a caress down her hair, bent to brush a kiss against her temple. "Captain Bartolmei is investigating how such a thing could have happened and will report to me. You have nothing to worry about. Sleep, *piccola*. I'll watch over you." Nicolai abandoned the chair to stretch out beside her on the bed, curving his body protectively around hers.

"I think this would earn you another lecture," he teased softly, his breath warming the nape of her neck. "But I don't intend for you to have nightmares, *bellezza*, so I'm going to stay for a while and chase them away for you."

"I'm too tired for conversation," she said without opening her eyes, pleased that he'd called her beautiful. There was comfort in the strength of his arms, the hard frame of his body. But Isabella didn't want to talk or think. She wanted to escape into sleep.

"Then stop talking, Isabella." He nuzzled her hair with his chin. "I have four dignitaries waiting to be received, and I'm here with you. That should tell you how much you mean to me. I *need* to be with you right now. Go to sleep, and let me watch over you."

Where she had been ice cold, inside and out, heat blossomed and spread. She snuggled deeper beneath the coverlets and fell asleep with a smile curving her mouth.

Chapter Eight

In the next few days that went by, no one mentioned the incident with Captain Bartolmei. If anyone had witnessed Isabella's bedraggled appearance and the captain's coat around her shoulders, they were being discreet. She saw little of *Don* DeMarco, as he had many duties and often consulted with his two captains and counselors. People came continually to the *don*, asking for favors, expecting him to solve problems from domestic arguments to affairs of state. Isabella spent her time learning her way around the *palazzo*. She worked at getting to know the servants, learning their names and faces and strengths and weaknesses.

Sarina was often at Isabella's side, explaining how things were done, what was considered unchangeable law, which things were the *don's* personal preferences, and what could be changed should Isabella decide she would prefer it.

They finished conducting an inspection of storage when they heard a commotion in the lower hall. Voices were raised in anger, and a child cried shrilly. Together, Sarina and Isabella rushed down the stairs to see Betto shaking a young boy. Betto's face was twisted with rage, a terrible mask of malignity as he shouted accusations at the child. A crowd of servants surrounded him, but no one dared defy his authority.

Sarina gripped Isabella's arm, her fingers digging into the young woman's skin. "What's wrong with him? He never raises his voice. Betto is always calm and reliable. He would not act in such a way, especially not for the servants to see." The housekeeper was horrified. She stood frozen, her mouth gaping open, her eyes wide with shock. "What's gotten into him? This isn't my Betto. This isn't like him at all."

The words echoed in Isabella's ears. She had seen Betto, a kindly soul, bustling about the *palazzo* in the course of his duties. Dignified. Efficient. The epitome of the discreet manservant. *This isn't Betto.* Sarina had been married to him for most of her life. Knew him intimately. His behavior was so out of character, so bizarre, his own wife didn't recognize him.

Isabella remained very still, studying Betto's stiff, jerky movements. The elderly servant's features were distorted with hatred and rage. He shook a bony fist at the young boy, cuffing the child's ear. A torrent of curses exploded out of his mouth, foul words, vicious and cutting. *This isn't Betto.*

Tears streamed down the child's face, and he struggled wildly to pull away from the old man. His mother, a pretty young woman named Brigita, stood wringing her hands and weeping. "Let him go, Betto. Please let Dantel go. He was only playing. He would never steal from *Don* DeMarco."

"If you had been watching him the way you should have been, you daughter of a whore, the no-good brat wouldn't have been stealing the Master blind."

Sarina gasped and clapped a hand over her mouth. She swayed and went so pale Isabella was afraid she might faint. Isabella circled the housekeeper's waist with one arm to help hold her up. "Betto." Sarina whispered his name softly, tears glittering in her eyes. Her voice was broken, reflecting the state of her heart.

Isabella could feel the hostility in the room. The mother's anxiety and anger were rising rapidly in direct proportion to Betto's bizarre behavior. The loud cries and shouting had brought other servants running. They were all murmuring, some supporting the distressed mother and others supporting Betto. Isabella remained still, reaching for something beyond what she was seeing with her eyes. She blocked out the sounds of fury, the loud, incensed words, until they were a mere buzz of angry bees in the background.

She found it then. Subtle. Insidious. The touch so delicate it was nearly impossible to detect. It wasn't strong as before, as if it had changed tactics, but the taint of evil was there just the same. It flowed through the room, touching everyone in its path. It fed the emotions, lived on the anger and hostility. It was breathing hatred into the *palazzo*, setting friend against friend. She felt its glee, felt the swell of power as it spread its poison throughout the room.

Isabella held up a hand for silence. One by one the servants turned to look at her. She was an *aristicratica*, born to a higher station, and she was betrothed to their *don*. None dared disobey her. As the faces turned toward her, the rage in the room darkened to a black, ugly malevolence, more potent than anything she had every faced. It was tangible, filling the air to the vaulted ceilings. She could see the animosity on the faces staring at her. Her heart began to pound as the anger was twisted and directed straight toward her.

"Sarina, you know Betto as he really is, through the eyes of your love," Isabella directed her statements to her one ally in the room but spoke loudly enough for all to hear. "Something must be terribly wrong. Perhaps he is ill and needs our help. Go to him, and use your love to guide him back. We will all help." She smiled at the servants and slipped away from Sarina to go to the young mother. She took both cold, nervous hands in her own to connect them together. "Think, Brigita. Betto would not normally say such foul things to you. Has he ever treated you or your son so cruelly? Been so harsh?" To keep the maid's attention focused on her rather than on the weeping child, Isabella spoke softly, persuasively, staring directly into the young woman's eyes.

Brigita shook her head. "He has always been kind to Dantel and me. This is so unlike him. When my husband died, he provided food for us and gave me a job here." Her voice wavered, and she burst into fresh tears.

"It is so unlike Betto, isn't it?" Isabella reinforced. "I thought it was something such as that." She patted Brigita's back encouragingly. "Betto is such a good man. Sarina is very much afraid something is wrong with him. Perhaps he is ill. We must all come to his aid now, when he needs us most."

The young woman nodded fearfully, not wholly convinced as she looked at the old man who was trembling with an unnatural rage.

Isabella crossed the room to Betto's side with a great deal more confidence than she felt. Smiling serenely, she gently removed the older man's hand from the boy's arm and pulled the child to her. Without looking at Betto, she knelt to put herself on eye level with the child. "Dantel, your *madre* has told me how good Betto has always been to you. Is that the truth? We all know you were not stealing. Betto knows it, too; he hasn't lost his faith in you. This is a misunderstanding, and things have been said in anger." She gently wiped the tears from the boy's face. "We need your help right now, Dantel. I know you are very brave, like the lions here in the valley, brave like your *don*. Your *madre* believes you are brave, and Sarina says it is so. You must tell me of Betto's kindness to you. Tell everyone."

Dantel sniffed several times, his large dark eyes staring into hers as if he dared not look at Betto or he would burst into tears again. His little body straightened, and he puffed out his chest. "I am very brave," he conceded. "If you need my help, *signorina*, I will do as you wish." His dark gaze flicked to his mother, who was still wringing her hands in indecision.

"We all need your help. Tell us how Betto has been kind to you."

The little boy glanced uneasily at Betto. "He carved me a lion and set it on my bed on my birthday. He didn't know I saw him, but I follow him all the time."

"Why do you follow him?" Isabella asked.

"I like to be with him," the boy admitted. "I saw him carving the lion, so I knew he had given it to me." He smiled at the memory, his gaze shifting hesitantly toward his mother. "And once when we didn't have enough food, and *madre* was crying because she was so hungry and she had given me the last of our food, he brought us all kinds of things to eat." His voice became stronger. "He taught me how to ride a horse."

"He taught my son, too," another servant chimed in.

"And he cared for old Chanianto until he passed on," another said. "Remember how he washed him and kept him clean? He even fed him soup when the old man was too weak to feed himself."

The atmosphere in the room had changed subtly. The servants were smiling at Betto. Sarina went to her husband, put her arms around him, and held him close to her, fiercely protective. Then it was Betto who was weeping. He crushed his wife to him and wept as if his heart were breaking. Dantel's mother made a soft sound of distress. Tears glittered in the eyes of several other servants looking on.

Dantel ran to wrap his arms around the old man's legs. "It's all right, Betto!" the boy exclaimed. "I love you!"

"Forgive me," the old man said, his voice ragged, his throat raw and clogged with tears. "I meant none of those foul things, Dantel. You're a good boy, much loved by all in the *palazzo*. Much loved by me. In truth, I don't know what happened to me, why such filth spewed from my mouth. I'm so ashamed." He sat down abruptly on the gleaming marble tiles, his knees giving out, carrying Sarina to the floor with him.

The old woman clung to him, holding him close, laughing a little at the absurdity of two elderly servants sitting on the floor. Crying over the terrible fright to both of them, Betto put a hand to his head. "Brigita, forgive me. I don't know what happened. I knew your *madre* and your *padre*. They were wed in the Holy Church." He shook his head, holding it in his hands, groaning in abject humiliation.

"I was bad," Dantel burst out. "I was playing with the statue, and I knew it wasn't mine. I dropped it, Betto." He began to weep again. "Don't cry, Betto. It isn't your fault. I did take it."

"Betto is ill," Isabella said, ruffling the boy's hair to comfort him. "You didn't steal, Dantel, and we all know it. Betto just needs to rest, and we'll all look after him. Sarina will need your help to carry things to him and entertain him while he's resting. Run off with your *madre* and comfort her while we get Betto into bed. Later you can help Sarina bring his food to him. It is time we all served Betto and repaid his many kindnesses."

"I will," Dantel said staunchly, looking very important. He reached for his mother's hand. "Call me when you need me, Sarina, and I'll come right away."

Isabella and Brigita both reached for Sarina and Betto at the same time, helping the couple get to their feet. As Betto staggered, still holding his wife tightly, Isabella felt anew the presence of the dark, malevolent entity. She felt a swell of venom, of concentrated hatred directed solely toward her. Pressing a hand to her midsection, Isabella turned her head toward the entrance of the room, looking up toward the ceiling as if she might actually see her enemy.

Brigita and Dantel took three steps toward the wide entryway to the room. Isabella leapt after them, her warning dying on her lips. She was too late. The beast was crouched in the large hall, its eyes fixed on mother and son, a snarl on its face, the tip of its tail twitching as it lay in ambush.

It was a huge lion, with a magnificent mane that surrounded the massive head and draped down the length of its back, wrapping around its belly.

Several of the servants screamed. Some ran back into the large room and attempted to hide behind furniture, while others stood frozen and began praying loudly. Immediately Isabella felt the surge of glee, of power. Two of the men caught at swords hanging on the wall, arming themselves and standing their ground reluctantly. They looked absurd, a pitiful defense against such a mighty enemy.

"Stop!" Isabella hissed. "All of you, be silent! Hold perfectly still." She began to move very slowly, inching her way around Sarina and Betto, ignoring them as they both made a grab at her arm to stop her.

Isabella was trembling violently, but she knew it wouldn't matter where in the room she was if the beast should decide to attack. The lion was capable of mauling or savaging everyone there. Its speed was undisputed. It was huge, invincible. The two swords were ridiculous weapons against the animal with its large teeth and razor-sharp claws. She had no real idea of what her plan was, only that something deep within her heart and soul drove her forward.

Isabella inserted her body between the lion and its prey. The lion's gaze immediately fixed on her. She met the stare with one of her own. The moment their eyes locked, realization hit her like a fist. Two entities stared back at her from the gaze of the lion. One was untamed and confused, the other hostile and enraged. She narrowed her focus, determined to hold the lion motionless and ignore the nameless terror burning in its eyes.

"Sarina, go for *Don* DeMarco." She kept her voice soft and soothing. It wobbled in spite of her determination to keep calm. "If you value the lives of those of us here, move very slowly until you make your way across the room. I'll hold the lion's attention, and you get to the other entrance. Once you are out, hurry."

Sarina's hand reached out as though she could drag Isabella back to safety. Betto took the trembling fingers and squeezed them in reassurance. None of the other servants moved, no one uttered a sound, no one seemed to breathe.

Isabella didn't turn her head to see whether Sarina had done as she asked; she had to believe the housekeeper would find the courage to do as she had bid. She didn't dare break eye contact with the lion. The great beast was shuddering with the need to leap upon her, to rend and tear, to sink its teeth deeply in her flesh and hear the satisfying crunch of bones. It was only Isabella's focused stare that prevented the animal from attacking.

The lion's need to kill was so great, Isabella could feel it deep inside her own heart. The conflict in the animal was so considerable that she felt sorrow for it, an aching pang in contrast to the terror welling up inside her. She refused to blink, refused to turn away, as much for the sake of the beast as for her own life. It was confused and fighting itself as the surge of dark power thrust at its instincts continually, urging it to kill. Kill Isabella. Kill everyone.

The lion shuddered again, a terrible trembling, and crawled forward toward Isabella, belly to the ground, eyes focused on her, fixed and staring. Roped muscles rippled along its massive body. Saliva dripped from the huge fangs as it snarled at her, a warning, almost a pleading, a dark challenge. The beast's breath was hot on her body, but she didn't move a muscle.

Behind her, the servants stirred in panic, close to running, but Betto stopped them with an imperious hand raised and a quick shaking of his head. Any sudden movement or noise might trigger the lion to attack.

Isabella could feel tiny beads of sweat running down the valley between her breasts. Her heart was pounding in her ears. She tasted fear in her mouth. Her knees threatened to buckle, but she stood her ground, staring into the round, gleaming eyes, determined not to run. Her mouth was so dry she wasn't certain she could speak if she had to. The animal was enormous, so close to her she could see the variations in his fur, silver, black, and brown woven so tightly it appeared to be a silky black. She could see eyelashes, whiskers, two scars slashed deep into the giant muzzle.

"I'm with you, Isabella. Have no fear." The voice was soft, almost sensual. Nicolai stepped slowly, carefully to Isabella's side. His hand enveloped hers, tightened around her fingers, connecting them physically. Isabella didn't dare take her gaze from the lion, but even so, she knew Nicolai was watching the beast intently, his amber eyes blazing with fury, concentrating on holding the creature in place. She could almost feel it as he began slowly, forcibly, to impose his will on the animal.

Isabella fought beside him, understanding the battle as no other in the room could. She understood then the immense concentration and focus it took for Nicolai to communicate with and control the untamable. The lions weren't docile or domesticated, they weren't pets, they were wild animals meant to be hunting prey and living far from human society. To keep them from following their natural instincts, Nicolai used a tremendous amount of energy at all times. He was in some way a part of them, bound to them, and the lions considered him the head of their pride.

The lion wanted to obey. The creature seemed to be fighting some inner battle. Isabella continued to stare into its eyes, her compassionate nature reaching out to the huge cat. She felt her own strength pouring into Nicolai. He seemed enormously powerful. She could feel his body close to hers, vibrating with tension, with effort. Isabella began to feel a strange affection for the lion, almost as if she couldn't separate Nicolai from the beast. Her expression softened, and her mouth curved.

She knew the exact moment when the taint of twisted power was defeated and retreated, leaving the unfortunate lion to face Nicolai alone. She felt the withdrawal of the black hatred, felt the darkness shimmering away from her mind, and then the room was empty of malice. Normal. It was still fraught with tension, the smell of fear, but nothing fed the intense emotions with rage and loathing. She began to breathe again, and her body shook with reaction.

The lion hung its head, turned, and padded silently down the corridor toward the stairs leading to the lower regions of the *castello*. Isabella burst into tears. She turned away from the *don*, from the servants, with every intention of rushing to the privacy of her bedchamber, but her legs refused to carry her anywhere.

Nicolai's strong arms crushed her to him, enfolding her close, protectively. He buried his face in her abundance of hair. "What were you thinking? You shouldn't have gone near that lion. Something was wrong with it—couldn't you see that?"

He was virtually holding her up. If he let go, Isabella would have slumped to the floor in a heap. She buried her face in his shirt, trying to hold back the sobs wracking her from head to toe. Now that the immediate danger was past, she was falling apart. No matter how strongly she admonished herself to stop crying and not humiliate herself in front of the servants, Isabella continued to weep and tremble. She clung to him, an anchor of safety in a world of danger.

"What has gone on here?" Nicolai's voice was imperious, commanding.

The sudden hushed silence penetrated Isabella's near hysteria, and she peeked around *Don* DeMarco to observe the others in the room. The servants were silent, uneasy, staring at the floor, the ceiling, out into the hall. Looking anywhere but at their *don*. Sarina was looking at Isabella, studiously averting her gaze from Nicolai.

It was enough to stop the flood of unwanted tears. Isabella wanted to shake the entire lot of them. Nicolai DeMarco had just saved their lives, yet they wouldn't even look at him. She turned to face them, her fingers entwining firmly with his, her posture protective, her glare furious and accusing as she stared at Sarina.

143

Sarina sighed softly and made a visible effort to steel herself before she looked fully at *Don* DeMarco's face. She gasped and crossed herself. "Nicolai!" It was a measure of her shock that she was so familiar as to call him by name.

Betto instantly looked up, crossed himself, and a smile tugged at his mouth. "*Don* DeMarco, it's an extraordinary day. Look at you, my boy." He beamed, his grip on his wife strong. "Look at him, Sarina. A handsome boy grown into a handsome man." He sounded like a proud father.

Isabella was confused. Sarina and Betto were staring at *Don* DeMarco as if they had never seen him before. Tears glittered in Sarina's eyes. "Look at him," she encouraged the other servants. "Look at *Don* DeMarco."

Isabella turned her head to look up at him. He looked the same to her, a sculpted model of masculine beauty even with the four raking scars that seemed only to define his courage. He epitomized strength and power. Had none of his people noticed how truly handsome he was? Could none of them see his integrity? His honor? It was so plain to see, no mystery, a man willing to carry burdens and protect others. Surely they were not all so petty that the scars were impossible to look upon. Isabella thought they gave the *don* a rakish appearance.

The low murmur of astonishment had Isabella whirling back to face the servants. Some crossed themselves. Some wept. All were staring at Nicolai as if he were a stranger, but they were beaming at him, eyes shining, smiles happy. It made no sense, and it made *Don* DeMarco uncomfortable. Sad, even. Isabella caught the shadows in the depths of his eyes.

Perhaps in his childhood they all thought him remarkably handsome, and now, because of his scars, they avoided looking at him. Of course he was saddened and embarrassed to be the center of such attention. Isabella wanted only to comfort him. She circled his neck with her slender arms, brought his head down toward hers, and stood on her toes so that her mouth could reach his ear. "Take me out of here, please, Nicolai."

He lifted her into his arms, picked her up as if her weight were no more than that of a child. For a moment he was motionless, with the stillness of a predator, his face buried in her hair, and then he moved, powerful muscles bunching beneath his clothing, his stride silent and sure as he glided through the long halls to her bedchamber.

Isabella felt his mouth on her neck, his lips velvet soft, a brush of a caress, no more, but edgy need was crawling into her body. She tilted her head up to his in blatant invitation, wanting the rush of fire, wanting to blot out everything but the feel of him, the scent of him.

His mouth found hers instantly, hot and possessive. His fist tangled in her hair, pulling her head back as his booted foot kicked the door closed behind them, sealing them away from the rest of the household. "It was quick thinking to hold the lion from attack, but very dangerous. I don't know how you managed it, but you must never do such a foolish thing again. You terrify me with your courage." He pressed her against a wall, his body hard against hers. Nicolai kissed her again, hard and wild, hunger rising fast and furiously. "You terrify me," he whispered against the corner of her mouth.

She slid her hands boldly beneath his tunic, wanting to feel his skin. Her mouth roamed his face, his throat, hungrily, flames racing through her bloodstream so that she could think only of him. His scent, his taste, his touch.

His mouth captured hers in a series of long kisses, deep and elemental, a wildfire out of control. Nicolai spun her around and tipped her onto the bed, a low growl escaping from deep within his throat. The sound only inflamed her more. Kissing him wasn't enough. It could never be enough.

His teeth tugged at her lip, her chin, the smooth line of her throat. Nicolai followed her down to the bed, his body pinning hers to the coverlet, hard and hot and very masculine. She could feel his every muscle imprinted on her, the thick, hard length of him urgent and demanding. She closed her eyes and gave herself up to the fire of his mouth, to the need of his body and the hunger in his mind. That quickly, they seemed to be raging out of control, unable to think coherently, only to burn for one another, need one another. His tongue swirled in the hollow of her throat, trailing fire down to the swell of her breasts.

Isabella gasped as his teeth scraped gently, teasingly over her sensitive skin. He caught at the string at the neckline of her blouse and pulled until it loosened, giving him access to satin soft skin. He pushed the material off her shoulders, his fingertips lingering on her skin. It wasn't enough. He wanted to see her, needed to see her. Nicolai dragged the blouse farther down her body until her breasts were completely exposed to him, thrusting upward, her nipples hard and beckoning in the coolness of the air. His gaze was hot, appreciative, moving over her with raw possessiveness and stark desire. Her breasts were lush, firm, an invitation into a world of excitement where nothing else could reach them.

"Isabella." He breathed her name softly, gently, in reverent awe. He had such need of her, right at that moment when she brought him such terror and joy. His head pounded with need; his body roared for release. "I can't think of anything other than making you mine." And he couldn't. Not his honor. Or hers. Not the lions, or the curse, or propriety. He needed to taste her, to bury himself deep within her. There was so much passion in her, so much life. So much courage.

A groan escaped his throat, and he bent his head to her lush offering. His hair brushed her skin like a thousand tongues, enclosing her in a world of sensation. His mouth, hot and strong, closed over her breast.

Isabella gasped with sheer pleasure, a soft cry emerging from her throat, her body arcing more fully into his. She wrapped her arms around his neck and cradled his head to her while he suckled, his tongue dancing and teasing and stroking caresses. His mouth pulled strongly until she felt the sensation everywhere, a liquid heat burning low, pooling, aching, coiling tighter and tighter until she wanted to cry from sheer pleasure.

His hands moved over her skin, cupping her breasts, his thumbs teasing one nipple while his teeth gently tugged on the other. He traced her ribs, became impatient with her gown, and simply ripped it from her body, tossing it aside, exposing her more fully to him.

"Nicolai!" Her gaze jumped to his face.

It was a small protest, but his hand had found her thigh, was stroking her skin, moving up to push tightly between her legs. He found her damp invitation and pressed his palm to her. Holding her gaze with his, he deliberately brought his palm to his mouth and tasted her.

Her eyes widened in shock. Her body burned. Liquid heat dampened the tight curls between her legs, and she shifted restlessly. "What are you doing?" Whatever it was, she didn't want him to stop.

"Whatever I want," he answered softly. "Whatever you want." Nicolai bent his head again, this time to the underside of her breast, his tongue tracing her ribs. His hand caressed her leg as he did so, moving upward to stroke her tight curls. Slowly he pushed his finger into her tight entrance, watching her face, his hair on her soft stomach, his tongue swirling in her belly button.

Her body clamped tightly around his finger, muscles clenching hard, and his body shook with the need to mount her. She lifted her hips to meet the finger pushing deeply into her. It was his undoing, that small, uninhibited act. She was so sensuous, so sexy and natural, his need consumed him. Nicolai heard a roaring in his ears. His head was pounding, his body so hard and uncomfortable he could think of nothing else but taking her. "I think of you when I lie in bed, and my body grows hard like this." He took her hand and brought it to the front of his breeches. "I sit at my desk and think of you, and you do this to me. I can't walk or eat or even dream without this aching need. Put me out of my misery, *cara*. Let me have you."

Her hand rubbed the front of his breeches, and he groaned again, his great body shuddering with pleasure. She kissed his chin, the corner of his mouth. "I want you in the same way," she admitted.

He fastened his mouth to hers, hard and hungry and edgy with need. Nicolai tore at his breeches so that he sprang free, the hard, thick length of his erection, his entire body burning and aching with need. He caught her knees and thrust them apart to give him better access. His hands found her small bottom and dragged her to him until he was pressed against her damp, hot entrance. Teeth clenched against the need to thrust hard, he began to push slowly into her. He was careful, when every cell in his body cried out frantically to be frenzied and mindless, to sate his wild hunger. His thick velvet knob disappeared inside her to be surrounded by her hot, tight sheath. He groaned with the effort to take his time, to be gentle with her.

He was much larger and thicker than his finger. Where before there had been sheer pleasure, now Isabella felt her body stretching, a burning, stinging sensation. She gasped and clutched his broad shoulders. "You're hurting me."

For one terrible moment he didn't care. Nothing mattered but burying himself in her, deep and fast and hard. Relieving the terrible, aching, throbbing need. His skin crawled with hunger. His fingers tightened, biting into her hips, and he threw his head back, his long hair wild, his amber eyes blazing at her. She belonged to him. Only to him. No other would have her and live.

Isabella blinked and found herself staring into the muzzle of a lion, felt its hot breath, saw the flames in its hungry eyes. Her face went white, and she stared into those gleaming eyes, her heart pounding, her body frozen in terror.

"No, *Dio*, Isabella, no!" She heard his voice as if from far away. "Look at me. See me. Right now, *cara*, you must see me."

His hands framed her face—hands, not paws. His mouth found hers—his mouth, not a gaping muzzle. Tears were on her face, but she was uncertain if she had shed them or if it had been he. He was holding her tightly to him, kissing her gently, tenderly. "I would not harm you for the world, Isabella." His hand was pressed against her damp curls, as if he were soothing her from the pain he had caused with his invasion.

Her teeth tugged at her lower lip in distress. "I think I'm too small for you, Nicolai. I'm so sorry." There was shame in her eyes.

He cursed softly, then kissed her again. "You are perfect for me. It is my duty to prepare your body to accept mine, Isabella. I wanted you too badly. We will go much slower next time. There are many ways to make you more comfortable." As he spoke he gently pushed his finger inside her, a slow stroke that made her gasp. Withdrawing, he replaced the first with two fingers, stretching her carefully. He pushed deep inside her, watching the shadows leave her eyes. Her body was slick and hot and soft, open to him. Her hips found the rhythm of his fingers, rising to meet him eagerly.

Suddenly his head went up alertly, as if he had heard something she had not. He withdrew his fingers from her body and caught at the coverlet, rolling her into it. "You're about to have company, but we aren't through here, *cara*. Not by any means. You are to wed me soon, Isabella. I want you in my bed." He was fast doing up his breeches and straightening his clothes. "What are we to do with this gown?"

He wasn't nearly as calm as he would have liked her to think. Isabella took great satisfaction in watching him struggle to breathe normally. A small, contented smile flitted across her face. "Perhaps we could say you were wounded and I sacrificed my beautiful gown to provide bandages." She found some solace in knowing that her body wasn't the only one throbbing and burning for release.

He thrust the shredded dress into her wardrobe. The material was frothy, and he was forced to bunch it up. It spilled out several times before he was finally able to close the door to hide it. Isabella pulled the coverlet up to her mouth to muffle her laughter.

"I am saving your reputation," he pointed out, trying not to laugh himself at the absurdity of fearing his housekeeper when he had faced a lion without flinching. "When I was a small boy, Sarina could lecture me as no other in the *castello*. Do not think because she has aged that she is any less fearsome. She has a cold eye and stern voice. You will not escape unscathed should she catch us."

Isabella lifted an eyebrow, then assumed her most innocent and guileless expression—the one she had perfected as a young girl when her father took her to task. Observing her very believable expression, Nicolai groaned. "You wouldn't dare blame me."

"*I* have no knowledge of such things." She even sounded innocent. "You are my betrothed and my *don*. I only do as you bid me." Curious, she looked at him. "How do you know it is Sarina coming?"

He shrugged his powerful shoulders. "I have good hearing and an acute sense of smell." He bent to nibble her neck. "You smell so wonderful I could eat you."

For a moment their eyes locked, and Isabella melted inside. There was a quick knock on the door, and Sarina entered carrying a tea tray. She gasped as she saw the *don* sitting on the edge of Isabella's bed. Hastily she averted her eyes from him, going very pale. "I'm sorry, I had no idea you were in here, *Don* DeMarco." Still she managed to sound disapproving. "I came to help Isabella prepare for bed. It is much too late for her to have visitors." She set the tray on the nightstand beside the bed and busied herself pouring tea, pursing her lips as she did so. "And male visitors shouldn't be in her bedchamber without my presence."

"Male visitors shouldn't be in her bedchamber at all," Nicolai commented dryly.

Isabella would have laughed at Sarina's scolding at any other time, but she couldn't abandon him, not when Sarina wouldn't even look at him. She reached for his hand and held it tightly. "I was nearly hysterical after the confrontation with the lion, Sarina. Nicolai was good enough to soothe me, as we knew you were busy with Betto. How is he?" Without thinking, she brought Nicolai's hand to her mouth, pressing her lips against his knuckles.

Sarina watched her. Instead of evincing disapproval, her eyes widened in surprise, and pure joy spread across her face. She took a deep breath and looked directly at the *don*. At once her expression softened. "It is a wonderful and great gift to look upon you, *Don* DeMarco. I had given up hope."

Nicolai touched his face, then reached out to touch Sarina's. She didn't flinch but beamed at him. "How is this possible?" he asked. His hand slipped from Isabella's as he reached to frame his housekeeper's face.

Fear blossomed in the woman, and she stepped away from him. Immediately he dropped his hands to his sides, his handsome face hardening perceptibly.

"Take her hand," Sarina instructed softly. "*Don* De-Marco, take Isabella's hand."

He did so, and lions roared. The sound erupted throughout the *castello*, reverberating through every floor so that for a brief moment the walls of the *palazzo* shook. Sarina didn't even flinch as the sound died away, leaving a vacuum of silence.

"It is Isabella," the housekeeper said. "It is Isabella."

Isabella had no idea what either of them was talking about, but Nicolai kissed her right in front of Sarina. A slow, lingering kiss that heated her blood and melted every bone in her body. He stared into her eyes for a long, endless moment. She saw the flare of desire, of possessiveness. She saw affection.

Isabella smiled and traced a fingertip over his perfectly sculpted mouth. They were becoming closer. No matter

151

what strange things were taking place in the *castello*, they were becoming friends. If she was to marry him, she wanted more than merely the heat between them.

"Good night, Isabella. I trust you have had adventures enough for one evening," he said tenderly, his eyes alight with mischief. "No roaming the halls, seeking out ghosts."

"She is a good and obedient girl," Sarina said staunchly. Her hand felt for the key in the pocket of her skirt and patted it for reassurance.

"Is she now?" Nicolai rose in his fluid, graceful manner, all power and controlled coordination, gliding across the room silently. He paused at the door. "Obedient to whom, I wonder."

Sarina watched the door close behind him and turned back to stare in disapproval at Isabella's bare shoulders. "What has been going on in here?"

Chapter Nine

Isabella had the grace to blush. "Nicolai is very handsome," she observed casually. It didn't come out casually. She barely recognized her own voice. It was soft and sensual and totally unlike her.

Sarina's eyebrows shot up. "It is good you find the *don* attractive, Isabella, but he is a man. Men want certain things from women. Nicolai is no different. Did your *madre* explain to you what is expected of a woman when she weds?"

Isabella sat up, holding the slipping coverlet with one hand and accepting the cup of tea with the other. Sarina began to brush out Isabella's long hair. The action was soothing. "*Mia madre* died when I was quite young, Sarina. I asked Lucca, but he said it was my husband's duty to teach me those things." Color crept up her neck into her face. She had the feeling the *don* was teaching her already, before he should.

"There are things that go on in the bedchamber between a man and wife, perfectly natural things. Do as he tells you,

Isabella, and you will learn to enjoy what others do not. My Betto has made my life wonderful, and I believe Nicolai will do the same with you. But these things are done *after* you are wed, not before."

Isabella sipped her tea, thankful she didn't have to reply. She wanted Nicolai with every fiber of her being. It didn't matter that things hadn't gone perfectly; her body still burned for his. She didn't dare tell Sarina what had transpired in her bedchamber.

Isabella lay awake for a long while after Sarina left, hoping Francesca would come to visit her. She was restless and wanted company. Sarina's tongue-lashing had been far milder than Nicolai had led her to anticipate, and she was grateful Sarina had treated her as a daughter or a friend. But she couldn't talk to Sarina about Nicolai.

She sighed and rolled over, the quilts tangling around her body. She should have dressed in her bedclothes, but once Sarina left, Isabella lay naked, her body burning, the memory of Nicolai's mouth pulling strongly at her breast and the feel of his silken hair sliding over her skin, uppermost in her mind. She ached, she burned, she was unsettled and edgy. She wanted all the things Sarina had hinted at. She wanted Nicolai's tongue stroking her skin, his fingers buried deep inside her.

It was useless lying there, unable to sleep. She sat up, allowing the coverlet to fall to her waist so that the air cooled her hot skin. She pulled her long, thick braid around and loosened her hair, shaking her head so that it brushed her skin the way his had, cascading past her waist to pool on the bed. Her body clenched as the silky strands caressed her body. She groaned softly in sheer frustration.

If she hadn't been so aroused, she would have asked Sarina why the servants treated their *don* so abominably, but she could only think of him. Nicolai DeMarco. Isabella threw back the covers determinedly and rose from the bed. Padding naked across the room, she stretched her hands out toward the fireplace, the only light left in the room. She had never stood naked in front of a fire and found it sensual.

Had he changed her in some way? She had never felt like this, hot and heavy and so aware of her own body. She had been naturally curious about what went on between a man and a woman, but no man had ever affected her as Nicolai did. She liked touching him, liked how hard and solid his body was. Isabella sighed and patted the guardian on the hearth behind its shaggy mane.

There was no noise, no sound, nothing to warn her, but she turned her head, and Nicolai was standing there, on the far side of the room, part of the wall open. His eyes glittered in the darkness, blazed with the leaping flames from the fireplace. Isabella's heart began to pound. He looked every inch a predator, as frightening as one of his lions. She felt vulnerable without her clothes and rather wanton. She ducked her head to bring her long hair swinging around her body like a cape.

"You shouldn't be here," she managed to say.

His hot gaze drifted possessively over her body. One breast peeked out at him through the fall of silken hair, but she didn't notice. "You're right. I shouldn't." His voice was husky, and his body hardened with a savage ache.

"Sarina said we should not be together until we are wed," she blurted out, the only thing she could think of to say.

"Don't look so afraid, *cara*. I intend to be propriety itself. It would help if I could wrap you in a robe. You're rather tempting standing there with the firelight touching you in intriguing places." He picked up the robe flung over a chair and crossed the room to stand close to her.

Isabella could feel the heat radiating off his skin. Off her skin. Her body clenched and went liquid at the sight of him. He seemed to be the very air she breathed, his scent in her lungs, in her mind. "I didn't mean to tempt you." She didn't know if that was the truth. If she had any sense at all, she would run. At the very least she should cry out for Sarina. Instead, she stood very still, waiting. Hoping. Exhilarated.

He bent his head slowly to her. She watched the long fall

of his strangely colored hair, much like the mane of a lion. She wanted to bury her hands in it and feel it, but she stood, mesmerized, watching his head come closer to her. His tongue flicked the nipple peeking through the veil of her hair. His hand cupped her bare bottom, drew her closer to him, so that he could take her breast into his mouth. Hot and moist, his mouth closed around her, suckled strongly, greedily. His fingers kneaded her buttocks, a slow, sensual massage that left her weak and aching with need. Her hands came up and cradled his head, her fingers delving into the thick mass of his hair.

"What are you doing to me?" she whispered, closing her eyes as his hands skimmed her body possessively and cupped her breasts.

His palm slipped around the nape of her neck. "Something I shouldn't. Put on the robe before I forget all my good intentions." He draped the robe around her, cinching it tightly. "I have a surprise for you. I knew you wouldn't be sleeping." He bunched her hair in his hand, pulled back her head, and fastened his mouth to hers. His kiss rocked her world, sending a firestorm rushing through her body. When he lifted his mouth from hers, they could only stare wordlessly into one another's eyes.

Isabella touched his face, her fingertips caressing the deep scars. "Are we going somewhere?"

He grinned at her, a little-boy, mischievous grin. "You'll need shoes. I knew you wouldn't even ask me questions—you'd just come with me. You love adventures, don't you?"

Isabella laughed softly. "I can't help it. I should have been born a boy."

His eyebrows shot up, and he reached out to slip a hand inside her robe, his palm cupping the weight of one breast, his thumb caressing the nipple. "I'm very glad you were born female." There was a catch in his voice, a small rasp betraying the urgent demands of his body.

Isabella stood very still, trying not to melt at his touch, trying not to fling herself into his arms. "I suppose I'm very glad I was, too," she admitted while her blood heated and pooled into a throbbing ache.

"Didn't Sarina tell you to stop me when I touched you like this?" He bent his head to brush a kiss across her trembling mouth as he reluctantly withdrew his hand from the warmth of her body. "Because if she didn't, she should have."

"I can't remember right now," Isabella admitted, feeling dazed. She looked around for a distraction. "I knew there was a secret passageway. There was one in our *palazzo*. I used to play in it as a child."

"I am not here to seduce you, Isabella, but to take you on a great adventure."

"Good, because I do recall now that Sarina made it very clear that there is to be no seduction before we are wed." She was excited at the prospect of going with him and hastily pulled on her shoes. "Should I put on a gown?"

His amber gaze gleamed at her, moved over her body, left her weak. "No, I like knowing you're wearing nothing beneath the robe. No one will see us." He took her hand. "You'll be safe with me." He carried her fingertips to his lips, his breath warm on her skin. "I don't know how safe I'll be with you."

Her heart was pounding loudly, but she went without hesitation. "I'll look after you, *Signor* DeMarco, have no fear."

"I had good and noble intentions," he told her as they moved into the narrow hidden corridor. "It isn't my fault that I found you without attire." His white teeth flashed at her, that boyish smile that stole her heart. "I thought that only happened in my dreams."

"Do you often dream of women without clothes?" There was the smallest bite to her voice, despite her obvious amusement.

Nicolai glanced down at her, his grin widening. "Only since I've met you. Hold tightly to my hand; otherwise, I won't be responsible for any exploring it might do."

Isabella laughed, and the light, carefree sound traveled through the maze of hidden corridors, awakening things better left alone. "Your hand has no direction unless you give it leave," she pointed out.

He wiggled his fingers so that they brushed enticingly against her hip. "No, they are entirely on their own in this matter. I plead innocence." He brought her hand to the warmth of his lips. "I love your skin." His teeth nibbled gently at her knuckles, his tongue swirling a caress over the pulse in her wrist.

Her eyes were wide and dark as she looked at him, half in love, half afraid.

Don DeMarco smiled at her. "You'll love this, Isabella."

She blinked up at him, shocked at the way her body seemed to belong to him. His every gesture, every movement, tempted and seduced her. "I'm certain I will."

She followed him through the long tunnels of stairs and passageways, her hand tightly in his. She was acutely aware of the power he exuded, the supreme confidence, the width of his shoulders and the strength of his body. She was aware he made no sound when he walked. None. She heard only the soft padding of her own shoes on the floor.

Nicolai pushed at a section of the wall, and it slowly swung outward. He stepped back so Isabella could see. The cold hit her first, an icy blast that pierced her robe and went straight to her skin, but then she was staring in awe at the countryside. It was a pristine, glistening white. Snow hung in the trees and covered the slopes. Icicles spiraled from the eaves of the *palazzo*. The full moon reflected off the snow, turning night into day. The mountains sparkled like jewels, a breathtaking scene she would never forget.

"You're shivering," he said softly. "Let's get you under the furs." He scooped her up close so that his body heat could seep into her.

Isabella relaxed in his arms as if she belonged there. He carried her to where two horses were waiting, harnessed to what looked like a carriage on runners. He placed Isabella on the padded seat, settled next to her, and tucked thick furs around her. "What is this?" She had never seen such a thing before.

"Betto made me one when I was very small. He carved the wooden runners and secured them to an old conveyance my parents didn't use anymore. It was smaller than this one, but it went over the snow fast. I had this one made recently and thought we should try it out."

Isabella snuggled deeper beneath the furs, curling her fingers together in an effort to stay warm. Nicolai tugged a pair of fur gloves from the pocket of his jacket and put them on her hands. They were far too large but very warm, and the simple, thoughtful gesture sent butterfly wings fluttering in her stomach.

"Are you warm enough?" he asked. "I can get another fur if we need it."

Isabella shook her head. "I'm very warm, *grazie*. What exactly are we doing?"

"It feels like flying might feel." He shook the reins, and the horses began a slow walk, dragging the carriage behind them.

As the animals picked up speed, the conveyance began to skim over the snow, gliding smoothly through the white crystals. Isabella clutched at Nicolai's arm and lifted her face to the wind. It was beautiful. Perfect. The two of them were locked in a world of white, skimming over the snow fast enough to make her heart soar.

The countryside was beautiful, the air crisp and fresh. Isabella found herself laughing as they raced along, the moonlight casting a silvery sheen on the branches overhead. Nicolai stopped the carriage atop a slope, his arm pulling her close to him. Below them was a small pond, already frozen so that the ice gleamed.

"It's truly beautiful," Isabella said, looking up at him. "*Grazie*, Nicolai, for sharing this with me."

His hand bunched in her hair. "Whom else would I share it with?" He looked away from her, out over the sparkling ice. His features were still and harsh. "No other would dare to come with me."

"Why?" Isabella pressed one gloved hand to his scars and stroked his skin to warm him. "Why are they all so silly? You are so good to them. Why do they fear you, Nicolai?"

"They have great reason to fear me, just as we all feared *mio padre*." He turned his head to look down at her, his amber eyes brooding. "If you had any sense, you would fear me, too."

She gave him a soft, trusting smile. Her furred fingertips traced his frown. "Do you want me to fear you, Nicolai? If you want such a thing, you must give me a reason."

He stared into the guileless innocence of her dark eyes for a long moment. "Isabella." Her name was a soft whisper in the night. Gentle. Tender. He bent to find her mouth with his, taking possession, his tongue probing, insistent.

Beneath the thick furs Nicolai slipped his hand inside her robe to find her breasts. "I dreamed of taking you out here in the snow, in the moonlight." He kissed the corner of her mouth, her chin. "If I asked you, Isabella, would you give me your body?" His mouth wandered lower, down the line of her throat, nudging her robe aside so that it gaped open for him. His hands fit her rib cage, his thumbs resting on her taut nipples.

"Why, Nicolai?" There was something sad, something desperate, driving him. "What are you afraid of? Tell me."

He rested his head against her bare breasts. "I hurt day and night. I can think of nothing but you. Nothing else, *cara*. But I don't know if relieving the ache in my body is going to do much for saving my soul." He slipped his arms around her and clung tightly, as if she were his safe anchor. "I didn't want to love you, Isabella. There is more danger in that than you can possibly imagine." He closed his eyes. "I want to give you the world, but in truth, I am taking your life."

She held him to her, stroking his hair. "I can't help you, Nicolai, if you don't tell me what's wrong." She kissed the top of his head and held him tighter. "Out here, where we're alone and the world is made of ice and gems, can't you tell me? Don't you know me well enough yet to know I fight for the ones who belong to me? I risked everything to save Lucca. Why would I do less for you?"

"You would run screaming from this place, from me, if you knew the truth." There was bitterness in his voice, in his heart. "The lions wouldn't allow it, and I would have to hold you prisoner. In the end I would destroy you as *mio padre* destroyed *mia madre*." He lifted his head and stared into her eyes. "As he nearly did me."

She saw torment in his amber gaze. Anger. Fear. Determination. Emotions swirled up from his soul to burn in his eyes like a flame.

The chill Isabella felt had nothing to do with the cold. She tugged at his hair. "Tell me, then, Nicolai, and we will see if I am a frightened *bambina* to run screaming from the man to whom I am bound."

His hands caught her slender shoulders, fingers digging into her flesh. He gave her a little shake, as if the intensity of his feelings was more than he could bear. As he did so, she felt the sharp stab of needles puncturing her shoulders. Her breath caught in her throat, but she choked back the soft cry of distress before it could escape. She looked down at her left shoulder, at his hand.

Clearly she saw a huge lion's paw, retractable claws. The claws were curved and thick and sharp, the tips digging into her skin. It was no illusion but a reality she couldn't ignore. A part of her mind was so shocked, so horrified and frightened, all it could do was scream. Silently. Locked in her head, deep in her mind where only Isabella lived, she screamed silently. And she wept. For herself, for Nicolai DeMarco. With pity for them both. Outwardly she was a Vernaducci, and, male or female, a Vernaducci did not give in to hysteria. She struggled for control and sat very still.

Nicolai had not uttered a falsehood. There was danger here, mortal danger. It vibrated in the air around them. The horses began to grow restless, tossing their heads and sidestepping. Isabella could see their eyes rolling wildly as they scented a predator.

She took a deep breath and let it out. "Nicolai." She said his name softly and lifted her gaze to meet his eyes.

They blazed at her. Wild. Turbulent. Deadly. Flaming with passion, with fire. She refused to look away from him, to see him as the others saw him. "What did your *madre* do when your *padre* told her the truth?" The cold had been numbing her pain, but at her question, the paws flexed, and the claws dug deeper. Thin ribbons of blood trickled down her shoulder.

"What do you think she did? She ran from him. She tried to escape. She couldn't even look at me once she knew what I would become." His voice was a raspy growl, as if his throat itself was altered and it was difficult for him to speak.

"I look at you and see a wonderful man, Nicolai. I don't know what is happening here, but you are no beast without thought or conscience. You have tremendous control and the ability to think, to reason. I have no intention of running from you." She felt the claws retract. She felt the wildness in him subside.

The horses felt it, too. They settled down and stood quietly, blowing softly, white vapor streaming from their nostrils.

Nicolai looked down at her soft skin, and a growl escaped him. He swore viciously, brutally, clapping the fur to the wounds. "Isabella. *Dio*. I can't risk you, not for myself, not for the others. I thought if I didn't love you, if I didn't feel anything, you would be safe, but I've never felt so deeply about anything." He looked stricken, pale beneath his dark skin. "What have I done to you?"

"You aren't risking me, Nicolai. Don't you realize that yet?" She pressed close to him, her lips finding his. He was stiff with his fear for her. "It is my risk to take. Mine alone. You can't force another to you. Love has to be freely given." She kissed him again, small kisses along the line of his jaw, the corners of his mouth, teasing, coaxing until he gave in because he couldn't stop himself.

Nicolai gathered her close and welded them together, his mouth dominating hers, kissing her until fire raced between them, burning out of control, a storm every bit as intense as his turbulent emotions. His hands framed her face, and he stared down into her eyes. "I'm so afraid to believe in you, Isabella. If something goes wrong and I can't control it . . ."

"What choice do you have?" Isabella tried to prevent her tiny shiver, but he missed nothing, not the slightest detail about her, and he pulled the furs close, tucking them around her. "You have to control it. Do you know how it happens? Why? Are you aware of it happening?"

He raked a hand through his hair in agitation. "I have always accepted what I was born with. A gift, a curse—I don't know. The people believe the old legends, and they hope for a miracle. They think you're that miracle. I only know I have always been able to talk to the lions. They are part of me. I wasn't afraid of it or ashamed of it. I knew it made me different, and I knew *mia madre* didn't want anything to do with me, but I can't remember when she did, so it wasn't that bad a thing. Sarina and Betto were always there. And I played like any boy with my friends Sergio and Rolando."

She leaned into him, because he seemed to need more comfort than she did. Her shoulders stung, the only reminder of what had happened. He was so charismatic that, without those small wounds, she would never believe it had. Somehow he managed to steal his way into her heart until she ached for him, ached for the pain reflected in his eyes. "Your *padre?*" she prompted.

Nicolai sighed and gathered the reins into his hands. "He withdrew from everyone, became more savage until even I could not see the man *mia madre* planned to flee. He found out before she could leave the *palazzo*. He hunted her through the halls, up and down the stairs. She ran to the great tower, out into the small courtyard. I knew what might happen, so I followed him, to stop him, but he was too far gone. Then he turned on me." He touched the scars on his face with trembling fingers, a man remembering a boy's nightmare. He fell silent, staring out over the sparkling pond.

"The lions saved you, didn't they, Nicolai?" she said softly.

He nodded, his face hardening perceptibly. "Yes, they did. They killed him to save my life."

"When you were a small boy, did the beast in you ever come out?"

Nicolai shook the reins, and the horses began to walk. "No, not ever. But that day, in the *castello*, my life changed for all time. Not even Sarina could see me anymore. When they look at me—my friends, my people—they see something else. All of them." He looked down at his hands on the reins. "I see my own hands, but they do not. It's a lonely existence, *cara*, and I had hoped never to pass such a thing on to my child."

"I see your hands, Nicolai." Isabella rested one gloved hand on his. "I see your face and your smile. I see you as a man." She rubbed her head against his shoulder in a small caress. "You aren't alone anymore. You have me. I'm not running from you. I'm staying with you because I want to stay." And, God help her, she did want to stay. She wanted to hold him in her arms and comfort him with her body. She wanted to chase the shadows from his eyes and banish the nightmare that had ended his childhood.

He put the reins in one palm and enveloped her hand with the other, tucking it beneath the heavy furs to keep her warm. They rode in silence, in the white, cold world, with the moonlight beaming down on them and the snow glistening like a gem field.

Isabella rested her head against his shoulder and stared up at the sky. The wind blew softly, sending little snow flurries flying from the tree branches. She felt the tug of it in her hair, on her face. As the conveyance glided over the snow, cutting through the wind, she felt a sense of freedom she had never had. It did feel as if they were flying, and she laughed softly, clutching the furs to her. "I love this, Nicolai. I truly do." Her laughter floated away on the wind, beckoning. Beckoning.

An owl flew out of nowhere, straight at one of the horses, talons outstretched as if it might rake the vulnerable eyes. The horse reared, screaming, a cry of terror that echoed through the silent world. Both horses went wild, plunging and bucking, streaking through the snow, racing down the slope and through a small stand of trees.

The conveyance tipped over, spilling them out onto the ice-cold ground. Somehow Nicolai managed to wrap his arms around Isabella. She clung to the thick fur rug, and as they rolled, it wound around them both, helping to protect them from the collision. They rolled to the bottom of the hill, a tangle of arms and legs and hair. Snow was everywhere, clinging to the fur, to their clothes, between their shivering bodies, even on their eyelashes. When they came to a stop, the wind knocked out of them, Isabella was lying on top of Nicolai, his arms wrapped around her head to protect her.

"Isabella!" Nicolai's voice shook with concern. "Are you hurt?" His hands moved over her body, searching for injuries.

She could feel laughter bubbling up out of nowhere and wondered if she was the first Vernaducci in history to become hysterical after all. "No, really, Nicolai, I'm just shaken up a bit. What about you?"

He was already looking around for the horses. She felt him stiffen just as the laughter inside her faded, replaced by a creeping fear. Her hands tightened on the fur rug, and she looked cautiously around them. She glimpsed movement in the trees, sleek shadows, glowing eyes.

Nicolai very gently lifted Isabella off him. "I want you to make for the nearest tree. Climb up it and stay there." His voice was calm, low, but held unmistakable authority. The *don* giving an order.

Isabella looked around desperately for a weapon, anything at all, but found nothing. She was shivering violently from the cold. Or fear. She wasn't certain which. The horses stood only a short distance away, shaking, their bodies wet with the sweat of terror. "Nicolai." There were tears in her voice, an aching need to stay with him.

"Do as I say, *piccola*. Get to a tree now." He rose to his feet, dragging her up as he did so, his eyes restlessly probing the thick stands of pine. He lifted his head and scented the wind.

Isabella couldn't smell their enemy, but she caught glimpses of the shaggy, slender bodies as they slunk through the woods. More than that, she felt the taint of something, something malignant, something nameless and far more deadly than a pack of wolves.

"Isabella, move!" There was no mistaking the command or the menace in Nicolai's voice, although he didn't spare her a glance.

She dropped the fur and raced to the nearest tree. It had been years since she climbed, but she caught the lower branches and hauled herself up. Without the protection of the fur, the wind bit at her skin, piercing straight through her thin robe. Despite her gloves, her fingers felt numb as she gripped the branches. She clung there, teeth chattering, and watched with horror the scene unfolding beneath her.

The wolves came out from the trees, their eyes fixed on their prey. Not Nicolai—the pack avoided him but moved toward the tree where Isabella perched. One, far bolder than the others, leapt, growling, its jaws snapping at her leg. A scream escaped as she jerked her leg up, scraping her skin on the tree bark.

A lion's roar shook the valley. Angry. Fierce. A challenge. A good six hundred pounds of solid muscle, the beast leapt into the middle of the wolf pack, swiping at the most aggressive animal with a deadly paw. In desperation, the pack leapt on him, snarling and growling, rending and tearing his back, his legs, his neck, until the snow was dotted with red. The wolves were so numerous, Isabella was certain the lion would fall beneath their weight. The sight was terrifying, the sounds worse.

"Nicolai." She whispered his name into the night, her voice aching and filled with tears. She had no idea how to help him.

The lion shook his massive body, and the wolves went flying in all directions, yelping and crying. The beast leapt after them, swatting at the slower animals so that they screamed in terror and limped off, running away from the larger and more powerful predator.

The lion stood still for a moment, watching them move off; then it shook its shaggy mane and shuddered. Isabella could see that red darkened the fur in many places. The huge mane, thick around its neck, down its back, and under its belly, had protected it from the worst bites, but it was wounded. It turned its head and looked at her. Amber eyes blazed at her, focused and intent.

"Nicolai!" There was joy in her voice. She jumped out of the tree and landed on her backside in the snow.

The massive head went down, and the beast crouched as if to spring. Isabella felt its swelling triumph in the air, dark and venomous, gloating with its power. Her breath stopped, and her heart pounded. She tasted fear. The lion's eyes never left her, the intensity of its concentration terrifying.

Isabella sat in silence, waiting for death. She looked straight into the amber eyes. "I know it isn't you doing this, Nicolai. I know you only wanted to protect me." She said it softly, lovingly, meaning it. "You are not my enemy, and you never will be." Whatever lay in the valley with hatred and cunning, it wasn't Nicolai DeMarco. It used the killing instincts of the beasts, any intense emotions, anger and hate and fear, human or otherwise. It twisted such things to its bidding. Isabella refused to allow it to use her feelings for the *don*. She stared straight into those flaming amber eyes and saw death as it leapt at her. "I love you," she said softly, meaning it. Then, for the first time in her life, she fainted.

A voice called to her, urging her to open her eyes. Isabella lay quietly in a cocoon of warmth. She had the oddest sensation that she was flying. If she was dead, it wasn't all that bad. She snuggled deeper into the warmth.

"*Cara*, open your eyes for me." The voice penetrated her awareness again. Rough with worry, anxious, sensual. Something in the tone melted her insides. "Isabella, look at me."

With a great effort, she managed to lift her lashes. Nicolai was staring down at her face, holding her in his arms while he guided the horses. The conveyance was gliding over the snow at a fast pace, heading straight for the *palazzo*. Nicolai let out his breath in a rush of white vapor. "Don't ever do that to me again."

Isabella found herself smiling, lifting a furred glove to trace the frown on his face. "This was a very exciting adventure, Nicolai. *Grazie*."

"You told me you faint, but I didn't believe you." The accusation was somewhere between teasing and relief. "*Dio*, Isabella, I thought you were lost to me. You were so cold. I was selfish to bring you out here in such clothes. I'm taking you back to the *castello*, and we are packing your things. I'm personally escorting you out of the valley."

To his shock, she burst out laughing. "I don't think so, *Signor* DeMarco." She shifted in his arms to look up at his set face. "You sent me away once and promised you would not do so again. Don't you know what happened? Don't you understand?" She caught his face in her hands. "Together we can defeat it. I know we can."

He used one hand to put her back beneath the furs. "Stay there. You're so cold, I thought you were dead." He guided the horses along a rear wall and signaled to a guard. The conveyance was brought close to the *palazzo*, next to what appeared to be a seamless outer wall.

But the wall swung open at the *don's* touch. Nicolai

thrust her into the passageway and out of sight and waited to give the guard brisk orders to see to the horses immediately. Then he was whisking Isabella through a maze of corridors, holding her close, furs and all.

"The wolves hurt you," she said. "I saw them. I want to help. If not, we must call Sarina. I want a healer to look at you. I have some knowledge of mixing plants, but not enough. I want Sarina or your *castello's* healer to look at you."

The room he entered was hot, almost sultry. Steam rose from a pool of water lapping at the tiles. Isabella stopped talking to stare. She had heard of such things, but the *palazzo* of her *famiglia* had no such wonder.

"You will get in immediately. I'll summon Sarina to attend you," Nicolai said, his voice harsh with emotion as he allowed her feet to touch the tiles.

Isabella circled his neck with her arms, tipping her head back to look into his eyes as she leaned into me. "Nicolai, don't do this. Don't put me away from you. If I have the courage to stay with you and see this through, you must have the courage to believe it can be so."

His hands caught her wrists with every intention of pulling her arms down, but instead he tightened his grip, nearly crushing her bones. His body trembled with the dark intensity of his emotions. "I could easily kill you, Isabella. Do you think *mio padre* did not love *mia madre*? He loved her more than anything. They started out just this way. Everything starts out with love and laughter, but in the end it's twisted into something ugly and wrong. This valley is cursed, and all within it are cursed. Do you think the people stay out of loyalty and love to me? They stay only because if they are away too long from the valley, they die."

She relaxed into him. "Your *padre* did not tell your *madre* what she was facing. He didn't give her the choice. You told me she didn't even know or suspect until well after you were born. You gave me the choice. You told me the risks. I've accepted them. I know nothing of curses, but I do know people. I've been in many holdings, and none of them are like this one. Your people love you. Whatever else you think, believe that. If it is true that they are under a curse and that whatever affects you affects them, then you owe it to them to have the courage to follow this through."

He caught her robe and dragged it from her shoulders. "Look at what I've done to you, Isabella. Look at the evidence of love gone wrong. I did this to you."

Isabella caught at his bloody shirt and held up her smeared hand. "This is what I see, Nicolai. I see evidence of a man risking his life to save mine."

She pulled away from him, dropped her robe to the ground, and walked down the few steps into the heated water until it covered her to her neck. The water was scalding on her cold skin, but she had only so much bravado, and she very much wanted Sarina's comfort. A lecture seemed a small thing to endure in exchange.

Chapter Ten

Nicolai closed his eyes against the tempting sight of Isabella. The steam rising from the hot pool only managed to make her look more alluring, more ethereal. He wanted her with every fiber of his being. Not just her body—he wanted her allegiance, her heart. Her laughter. His fingers slowly curled into two tight fists. She was looking up at him with such trust, her enormous eyes soft and gentle.

His fists knotted harder as his emotions darkened, sweeping through him with an intensity that shook him. He felt the sharp stab of needles in his palms.

Isabella was watching the play of emotion in his eyes. She saw the exact moment the beast won, leaping with red-orange flames into his gaze and burning out of control. She wanted to weep, but she smiled instead. "We will need Sarina, Nicolai, to look at your wounds, as I lack the knowledge."

"I will send her to you," he replied, his voice a mixture of gruffness and sensuality. "I have no need or want of aid."

He forced himself to take two steps back. Away from heaven. Away from peace and comfort. He would not dishonor Isabella or himself when he had only a painful life and a horrifying death to offer her.

When he closed his eyes at night, he saw the terrifying scene over and over again. His mother running for her life, her mouth open wide as she screamed for mercy. Her hair had been loosened from its long braid, and the wind whipped it behind her. He had seen his father, shimmering one moment as a man, the next a massive lion, easily running her down as if she were no more than a deer in the forest or a rabbit shaking before him.

Nicolai always ran toward them in the dream, in a desperate attempt to stop the inevitable, just as he had in real life. A boy with tears streaming down his face—his parents, his life, already lost to him, a small knife gripped in his hand. It had been a pathetic weapon against such an enormous beast. But each time he closed his eyes, it happened again. He always did the same thing, always carried the same knife and always watched the lion leap upon his mother and kill her with one savage bite.

His eyes burned, and his gut clenched in revulsion. Tonight he had stalked Isabella. At the last moment he had come to himself, hearing her call his name. Hearing her voice whisper words of love to him. Of forgiveness. Of understanding. He had allowed the beast in him to rise fully, to consume him as he fought off the wolves. That had never happened before. More and more, as his emotions deepened, intensified, his control slipped, and the beast ate away at the man. As it had consumed his father. A single sound of horror escaped his throat.

"Don't, Nicolai," she pleaded softly. "Don't do this to yourself."

It had taken years for his father to be seen by the people as the beast, but once that happened, it had quickly devoured him. The people had seen Nicolai as the beast since that terrible day in the courtyard when his father killed his mother and attempted to destroy him.

"I nearly killed you." The admission was low, harsh, the truth. "It will happen, Isabella, if I don't send you away. I have no choice. It's for your own protection. You know that."

"I know the lions refused to let me leave through the pass. I know I'm supposed to be with you." Isabella wrapped her arms around herself to keep from shaking. "It is the only thing I know for certain, Nicolai." She looked up at him with her big, innocent eyes. "You're the breath in my body, the warmth and joy in my heart. Wherever you sent me, I would wither and die. If not my body, at least my spirit. Better to have joy burning hot and bright, if only for a short time, than to die a long, endless death."

His expression hardened, his eyes blazing with such intensity it seemed to pierce her heart until she felt actual pain. "The one thing I know with a certainty, Isabella, is that if you stay in this place with me, I will be the one to kill you."

The words hung in the air between them, shimmering with a life of their own. Isabella felt ice-cold terror, even though she was submerged in hot water. She lifted her chin. "So be it." She said it softly, aching for him, wanting to comfort him, wanting the solace of his arms even as the certainty of her inevitable death terrified her.

He turned on his heel and stalked out of the room, leaving her in the water, in the darkness, in an unfamiliar room with nothing to guide her. Isabella put her head down on the pool's tiled edge and wept for both of them.

Sarina immediately appeared and found Isabella with tears trailing down her cheeks. Appalled to hear that the young woman had gone out unescorted with Nicolai, clad only in her robe in the dead of night, Sarina clucked disapprovingly. Even so, her hands were gentle as she examined Isabella for bruises. She was silent, not asking a single question, as she attended the puncture wounds on Isabella's shoulders.

"Did you see to Nicolai's wounds?" Isabella asked, catching the housekeeper's hand. "He fought off a pack of wolves." The hot water had taken the chill away, but she shivered all the same, remembering the terror of fleeing the hunting pack. Remembering the lion stalking her.

"He refused to allow me to aid him." Sarina hung her head. "It is uncomfortable for both of us. He prefers to be alone." She dried Isabella and slipped her nightgown over her head. She then held out a fresh robe.

"No one prefers to be alone, Sarina. I'll go with you, and we'll see to his wounds. He may need stitching." Isabella had to see him tonight. If she didn't, she feared for him, feared for herself. He broke her heart with his sad words.

Sarina began to comb the tangles from Isabella's long hair. "He's in a foul mood. I didn't dare take him to task for taking you out in the weather alone, with only your robe, and for entering the room while you bathed." She hesitated, floundering for the right words. "Did he touch you, Isabella?"

"He's in a foul mood because he thinks to send me away again for my own good. He's afraid he'll harm me."

Tears glittered in Sarina's eyes. "We all hoped you would be the one to help us. But it was wrong of us to sacrifice you. It's possible the *don* is right and you should go." Her hand brushed over Isabella's shoulder. "He is very dangerous. It's why he keeps to himself—to protect us all from the beast."

Isabella pulled away from Sarina in a fit of temper, her dark eyes stormy. "He is a man, and like any other man he needs companionship and love. Did it occur to any of you that had you treated him more like a man and less like a beast, you might have *seen* him as a man?" She paced the room in restless fury, then swung around to make her challenge. "He's sacrificed much for his people. Are you coming with me to look at his wounds?"

Sarina studied Isabella's furious face for a long moment. She sighed softly. "He'll not be happy to see us," she warned.

"Well, that's too bad. He'll have to live with it."

"And it's entirely improper for you to visit him in your nightclothes," Sarina pointed out, but she led Isabella out of the steamy room to the wide staircase leading to the upper stories.

Isabella's shoulders were stiff as she marched up the stairs, prepared for war. She was angry with the lot of them. And close to tears. That made her even angrier. She had fainted like a dolt. It was no wonder the *don* was ready to send her away. Her father had been right about her all along. She had never measured up, never had the courage to be sold into marriage to further the Vernaducci interests. Perhaps when *Don* Rivellio had first offered for her, had she accepted, her father would still be alive. Her brother would not have been imprisoned and their lands confiscated. She had been such a coward, not wanting to be touched by a grasping, greedy man with a sick, lustful smile and flat, cold eyes.

She had been twelve summers when *Don* Rivellio had visited their *palazzo* the first time, his gaze following her every move. He licked his lips often, and twice, beneath the table, she had seen him obscenely rubbing his crotch while he grinned at her. He had sickened her with his cold good looks and evil smile. After his visit, two of the maids had been found sobbing—raped, bruised, battered, and almost too frightened by his perverted tortures to tell their *don* what had taken place. Both claimed he had nearly killed them, deliberately strangling them to terrify them into silence. The bruising around their throats had convinced Isabella they were telling the truth.

A sob escaped, and she jammed a fist against her lips to choke it back. She knew she lived in a world where a woman was little more than a way to acquire property or heirs. But Lucca had valued her, had conversed with her as if she were a man. He had patiently taught her to read and write and speak more than one language. He taught her to ride a horse and, most of all, to believe in her own strength. What would Lucca think of her when she confessed to him she had fainted?

And *Don* DeMarco. He was so alone. So wonderful to her. A man like no other. Yet she had failed him as she had Lucca and her father. Nicolai needed her desperately, yet when it counted the most, she had let him down, taken the coward's way out. Fainted. She should have continued to call to him, to bring him back to her. She had had the strength to hold the other lion, yet she had fainted like a child when the *don* needed her.

"Isabella?" Sarina's voice was filled with compassion.

Isabella shook her head adamantly. "Don't. I don't want to cry, so don't be nice to me. I hope Nicolai is angry so I can be angry, too."

They were at the bottom of the staircase leading to the *don's* private wing. Sarina hesitated, glancing up fearfully, her hand on the head of a sculpted lion. "Are you certain you want to do this?"

Isabella went up the stairs quickly, staring down the guards in the hallway and defiantly knocking on the door.

She jumped when Nicolai flung the door open with a crash. A snarl was on his face, a mask of brooding anger. "I told you I did not wish to be disturbed for any reason!" he bit out before he focused fully on Isabella.

Sarina crossed herself and looked steadfastly at the floor. The guards turned away from the beastly sight.

Isabella stared directly, belligerently, into Nicolai's blazing eyes. "*Scusi, Don* DeMarco, but I must insist on your wounds being looked after properly. Growl all you want, it will do you no good." She lifted her chin defiantly at him.

Nicolai bit back the angry, bitter words welling up inside him. If he were any kind of a man, he would have the courage to send her away. He had sworn to himself he would get around the lions guarding the valley, even if it meant destroying them. Now, looking at her, he knew he wouldn't, *couldn't* send her away.

Without her he was lost. She took away the stark loneliness of his existence and replaced it with warmth and laughter, replaced his recurring nightmare with hot, erotic thoughts and the promise of a haven, a refuge in the pleasures of her body. Her mind intrigued him—the way she thought, how outspoken she was, not in the least coquettish but straightforward and genuine with her opinions. Where everyone feared and catered to him, she stood up to him with humor and bravado.

He needed her if he was to continue his own existence, if he was to continue protecting and guiding his people. He wanted to weep for her. For himself. He had prayed for the strength to send her away, but it wasn't there, and he found he loathed what and who he was.

She looked beautiful in her defiance, but beyond that, he saw her fear of rejection. A plea mixed with the storm in her gaze. A need to help him. A need for him to want her. Something hard and stony around his heart melted away. He reached out, right there in front of Sarina, in front of the guards, and caught Isabella by the nape of her neck, hauling her into the shelter of his body. Fastening his mouth to hers, he kissed her hard, deeply, with the intensity of his volcanic emotions. He poured his feelings into the kiss, fire and ice, love and regret, joy and bitterness. Everything he had to give her.

Isabella instantly went soft and pliant against him, completely accepting of his wild nature, returning kiss for kiss, demand for demand. Fire leapt between them, instant and hot, sizzling in the air and arcing from one to the other, not seen but certainly felt by the observers. They clung together, two drowning souls, lost in each other's arms, their own sanctuary, their only safe refuge.

A guard coughed delicately, and Sarina made a sound somewhere between outrage and approval. "Enough of that, young *signorina*. There is plenty of time after you are wed." The housekeeper feasted her gaze on her *don* while he was in Isabella's arms. Although she was beaming, she did her best to scowl at the couple.

Slowly, reluctantly, Nicolai lifted his head. "You may as well come in, as you are already here." He smiled at Sarina over the top of Isabella's head. "She tends to get into trouble quite a bit, doesn't she?"

"I had her safely locked in," Sarina reminded him.

Nicolai stepped back to allow them entry. "And we know that once we lock her door, she remains perfectly safe inside at all times." He flashed Isabella a shadow of his heartstoppingly boyish grin, but it was enough to earn him a small smile in return.

But Sarina took her role as Isabella's protector very seriously, and her amusement faded. Her scowl deepened, and she closed the door to Nicolai's room, shutting out the guard's interested expression. "She would have been perfectly safe if no one had crept into her chamber and taken her unaccompanied into the night," she said in reprimand. "You must wed immediately, before this night's misadventures come to light."

Nicolai nodded. "We will ask the priest to perform the ceremony as soon as it can be arranged. I, too, think it best."

"*Mio fratello*," Isabella reminded him. "He'll be upset if he isn't here to see me wed."

Sarina clucked her disapproval. "Take the *don's* hand," she directed. "I must see his wounds to know how to treat them."

"I have news of your brother," Nicolai said, his fingers tightening around Isabella's. "I sent one of my birds to *Don* Rivellio. The bird just came back with a message. The *don* has released your brother into my care. He is ill but is traveling. I'm to be held responsible for his future behavior." A grim smile touched his mouth, then faded away, as if the thought of *Don* Rivellio's holding him responsible for anything set his teeth on edge and brought out every predatory instinct.

He flinched as Sarina put a mixture of herbs on one of his deepest wounds. Isabella tightened her fingers around his.

"Your brother will understand it is best we wed promptly. His journey will be slow, as his escorts must travel at a speed safe for him." Nicolai brought her hand to his heart and pressed it to his chest.

"Once we wed, Nicolai, you don't intend to send me away, do you?" Isabella dared to inquire, her expression shadowed.

He risked Sarina's displeasure by holding Isabella close to him. His lips brushed her ear. "I should. You know I should. But if you are willing to risk your life, I am willing to risk my soul." Eternal damnation would be what he deserved if he ever turned on her.

Sarina pretended not to notice the unwed couple cuddling as she examined the lacerations, spreading the salve she had made from a mixture of herbs.

While the housekeeper worked, Nicolai held Isabella tightly, resting his head on top of hers. She could feel his heart beating. She could feel each wince. It felt right to be in his arms. It felt as if she belonged there. She closed her eyes, tired from her adventures and warm with his body heat.

She jerked awake when Sarina made a clucking noise. "It is done. Say your good night, *signorina*. You are falling asleep where you stand."

The *don* dropped a kiss in her hair. "Sleep well, Isabella. We will soon sort out everything to our satisfaction." His fingertips brushed down her cheek before he dropped his hand and moved back into the shadows.

Sarina took Isabella's arm and dragged her out of the *don's* room the moment she had completed her work. "It may be best if you see Isabella only in my presence," the housekeeper recommended to her master in her most severe voice before firmly closing the door.

Isabella laughed as Sarina hurried her down the stairs and

through the halls to her own bedchamber. She should have been terrified at the prospect of staying at the *palazzo,* but she felt nearly giddy with joy. Sarina opened the door for her and waved her inside. "Go straight to bed, young lady, and this time, stay there! I believe you are becoming unhinged from all these intrigues with the *don.*"

"*Grazie,* Sarina, for helping Nicolai." Isabella leaned out of the room to kiss the housekeeper's lined cheek. "You are an amazing woman."

Smiling, Sarina shook her head before turning the key in the lock.

Isabella patted the door when she heard the key turn. Nicolai hadn't given her away. Sarina had no idea she could come and go at will.

"Where have you been?" Francesca demanded petulantly. She bounced on the bed, kicked her feet idly, and fingered the coverlet in nervous agitation. "I waited hours to talk with you."

Isabella whirled around. "I was hoping I'd see you. I finally know where the secret passage is!"

Francesca grinned at her, a quick, forgiving smile that emphasized her beautiful features. "Have you been out exploring? They said you wouldn't, but I knew you would. I love being right."

"Where are the interesting wails and rattling chains tonight? It seems rather quiet without them. I'm not even certain anyone will be able to go to sleep without their unique lullaby."

Francesca laughed happily. "Lullaby! Isabella, that's wonderful. They love that. A lullaby!" She clapped her hands. "You don't mind, then? They thought you might be angry with them. They like to rattle and wail but not if it bothers you. I think it's good for them. It gives them something to do for fun and makes them feel important."

"Well, then." Isabella turned in a circle in the middle of her bedchamber, her arms outstretched to embrace everything. "I rather like the music. Not all night, mind you, but for a little while. People—even spirits, I suppose—need something to keep them busy. I'm so happy, Francesca! Remember I told you about *mio fratello*, Lucca? He's on his way to the *palazzo*. He's traveling right now. You'll like him so much."

"Will I?" Francesca looked up eagerly. "Is he young?"

"A little older than I am, and very handsome. He's wonderful, Francesca." Isabella flashed a conspirator's grin. "He's not yet wed or promised."

"Does he know how to dance?"

Isabella nodded. "He knows how to do everything. And he tells the most marvelous stories."

"I might like him, although most men annoy me. They think they can tell women what to do all the time."

Isabella laughed as she dropped her robe on the chair. "I didn't say he wouldn't tell you what to do. He certainly told me all the time. But he's so much fun." She slipped into bed and pulled the quilts up to her chin, thankful to lie down. Her body instantly relaxed. "I met Sergio Drannacia's wife, Violante, today. She was interesting."

Francesca nodded wisely. " 'Interesting' is one way to describe her. She likes being a Drannacia, that's for certain. When she was a girl, she used to tell her *famiglia* she would marry a Drannacia, and she did." Francesca flashed a mischievous grin. "She *seduced* him. She's way older than he is."

"She seems as if she could be quite nice, given the chance. I'm withholding judgment for the time being. I think she is more intimidated by the *palazzo* than she cares to admit. I felt a little sorry for her. She's afraid her husband doesn't look at her with the eyes of love."

"He probably doesn't!" Francesca sniffed, making her opinion known. "She's always ordering him around. She wants a grander home, to rebuild the Drannacia *palazzo*. She nags Sergio to ask permission from Nicolai, then mocks him that he needs the permission." She imitated Violante's strident voice. " 'That it has come to this, the Drannacia name every bit as good as DeMarco, groveling for his permission to rebuild what is already yours.' " She flipped her hair around, primping continually. "She thinks she's so beautiful, but really, if she's not careful, she'll end up with lines all over her face from frowning at everybody."

"It must be difficult to be older than your husband. Sergio Drannacia is handsome and charming. She probably worries that many women are attracted to him and willing to bed him."

Francesca twisted her hair around one finger thoughtfully. "I didn't think of that. I have seen some of the women flirting with him." She sighed softly. "That *would* be difficult. But she isn't very nice, Isabella, so it's hard to feel sorry for her. She didn't love him, you know. She just wanted a title."

"How do you know she didn't love him?" Isabella asked, curious. She tried unsuccessfully to stifle a yawn.

"I heard her. She told her *madre* she would have her own *palazzo*, and she didn't care what she had to do to get it. She seduced Sergio and then pretended she feared she carried a babe. Of course he did the honorable thing and married her, but there was no child then, and there hasn't been since. I think she's afraid that if her belly grows round, he won't want her."

"If she wanted power, why didn't she go after Nicolai?" Isabella couldn't imagine looking at another man while Nicolai was free.

Francesca looked startled. "Everyone is terrified of Nicolai. And Nicolai isn't one to fall for a woman because she bares her breasts for him. Nor would he let a woman treat his people unfairly or berate them for accidents. He wouldn't stand for Violante's vanity. She keeps the dressmaker busy all the time, and she's never satisfied."

"How sad. I think it's possible she's fallen in love with her husband." Isabella sighed and curled up beneath the coverlet. "There's a sadness in her eyes. I wish I knew how to help her."

YES! ☐

Sign me up for the **Historical Romance Book Club** and send my TWO FREE BOOKS! If I choose to stay in the club, I will pay only $8.50* each month, a savings of $5.48!

YES! ☐

Sign me up for the **Love Spell Book Club** and send my TWO FREE BOOKS! If I choose to stay in the club, I will pay only $8.50* each month, a savings of $5.48!

NAME: _____

ADDRESS: _____

_____

TELEPHONE: _____

E-MAIL: _____

☐ I WANT TO PAY BY CREDIT CARD.

☐ VISA   ☐ MasterCard   ☐ DISCOVER

ACCOUNT #: _____

EXPIRATION DATE: _____

SIGNATURE: _____

Send this card along with $2.00 shipping & handling for each club you wish to join, to:

**Romance Book Clubs
20 Academy Street
Norwalk, CT 06850-4032**

Or fax (must include credit card information!) to: 610.995.9274. You can also sign up online at www.dorchesterpub.com.

*Plus $2.00 for shipping. Offer open to residents of the U.S. and Canada only. Canadian residents please call 1.800.481.9191 for pricing information.

If under 18, a parent or guardian must sign. Terms, prices and conditions subject to change. Subscription subject to acceptance. Dorchester Publishing reserves the right to reject any order or cancel any subscription.

JOIN NOW!

GET UP TO 4 FREE BOOKS!

You can have the best romance delivered to your door for less than what you'd pay in a bookstore or online. Sign up for one of our book clubs today, and we'll send you **FREE* BOOKS** just for trying it out...**with no obligation to buy, ever!**

HISTORICAL ROMANCE BOOK CLUB

Travel from the Scottish Highlands to the American West, the decadent ballrooms of Regency England to Viking ships. Your shipments will include authors such as CONNIE MASON, SANDRA HILL, CASSIE EDWARDS, JENNIFER ASHLEY, LEIGH GREENWOOD, and many, many more.

LOVE SPELL BOOK CLUB

Bring a little magic into your life with the romances of Love Spell—fun contemporaries, paranormals, time-travels, futuristics, and more. Your shipments will include authors such as LYNSAY SANDS, CJ BARRY, COLLEEN THOMPSON, NINA BANGS, MARJORIE LIU and more.

As a book club member you also receive the following special benefits:

- **30% OFF all orders through our website & telecenter!**
- **Exclusive access to special discounts!**
- **Convenient home delivery and 10 day examination period to return any books you don't want to keep.**

There is no minimum number of books to buy, and you may cancel membership at any time. See back to sign up!

*Please include $2.00 for shipping and handling.

"She might try smiling once in a while," Francesca pointed out. "You're too nice, Isabella. She's not losing sleep over you."

"I also met Theresa Bartolmei, and our encounter was so embarrassing. Her husband had tried to save me from Alberita's wayward broom, and he gripped me by the wrist, so it looked as if we were holding hands." Isabella laughed softly. "You should have seen their faces, Francesca! Do you know Theresa?"

"I wish I had been there. That surely gave Violante food for gossip. No doubt she's still repeating the story to Sergio."

"He was there. And so was Nicolai."

Francesca looked shocked. "Nicolai?" she breathed in awe. "What did he do?"

"Laughed with me, of course, only not in front of the others. I felt sorry for Theresa, because the incident obviously shocked her."

Francesca tossed her head. "She's always crying and whining for her *madre*. And she isn't very good with the servants. She annoys them whenever she visits. And she's terrified of the *don*." Francesca said the last with satisfaction.

"Why would she be afraid of him?"

Francesca's gaze flicked away. "You know. Once, when he maintained his own visage, she was horrified by his scars. I heard her tell Rolando they made her feel ill." She rolled her eyes. "Nicolai shouldn't bother with the energy it takes to let her see him."

"You don't like her." Isabella wasn't feeling much disposed to like Theresa at that moment either.

Francesca shrugged. "She isn't that bad. She's terribly timid and not much fun. I don't know why Rolando chose her. Once they spent the night here in the *castello*, and when the wailing started, she shrieked so loudly that even the *don* in his wing heard her. She insisted on leaving the *palazzo*, but Rolando said no and made her stay." Francesca laughed.

"Why would somebody be so afraid of a little noise?"

"That's unkind, Francesca," Isabella said gently. "You're used to the noise, but in truth, the first night I was here, I was afraid. Perhaps you should be a friend and help her get over her fears. She is young and obviously misses her *famiglia*. We should do what we can to aid her in feeling more comfortable."

"She's no younger than you are. What do you think she would have done if a lion had crawled toward her the way it did toward you when you saved Brigita and Dantel? Everyone is talking about your courage. Theresa would have fainted dead away." There was a sneer in Francesca's voice.

"What would you have done?" Isabella asked quietly. She couldn't very well admit she *had* fainted when Nicolai needed her the most.

Francesca had the grace to look ashamed. "I would have fainted dead away, too," she admitted. She flashed her impish smile, assuring she was instantly forgiven. "Why didn't you faint?"

"I knew *Don* DeMarco would come. The lion didn't want to kill us, but something was wrong. Something . . ." Isabella trailed off, unable to put into words exactly what she had sensed in the lion.

Francesca took a deep breath as she looked around uneasily. "It's evil," she whispered it, as if the walls had ears.

Isabella's head went up, and she stared at Francesca in shock and relief. "You feel it, too?" She instinctively lowered her own voice.

Francesca nodded. "The others don't really know about it, but they feel it sometimes. It's why they put you in this room. It can't get in here. This room is protected. It's very dangerous, Isabella, and it hates you. I wanted to tell you, but I didn't think you'd believe me. You awakened it when you came into the valley."

A chill went down Isabella's spine. She had felt the disturbance even in the midst of her fear of the unknown *don* and the wild storm. Francesca was telling the truth.

"How is this room protected, Francesca?" Something inside Isabella went very still. She was almost afraid of the answer, afraid she already knew what it would be.

"This wing is part of the original *palazzo*. This was Sophia's room. See the carvings? The *don* had them done for her. *It* can't come in here. This room is the only place you're truly safe. I think the entity had something to do with your accident, when you nearly fell off the balcony."

Isabella nearly gasped but kept her voice calm. "How did you hear about that? I thought no one knew of it."

"I hear things others do not. If it is whispered, I know. I think this thing has arranged more than one accident to get rid of you."

Beneath the coverlet, Isabella felt herself shiver, her blood suddenly like ice. "What is it?"

Tears filled Francesca's luminous eyes. "I don't know, but you're its enemy. Please be careful. I can't bear to think it will harm you as it did . . ." She trailed off with a small sob and leapt to her feet, pacing halfway across the room toward the secret entrance, pressing a hand to her mouth.

"Francesca, don't go! I didn't mean to upset you. Please, *piccola*, don't be unhappy. Think of the fun we'll have when Lucca comes to stay. You can help me cheer him up. He's very ill and will need plenty of rest and entertainment."

Isabella threw back the coverlet, intending to comfort Francesca, but the girl was already gone, so fast, so silently, Isabella didn't even see her slip through the wall. Isabella sighed. Sophia's room. Of course her bedchamber would have to be Sophia's room. What could be more fitting? Or more frightening? What was the curse said to be? That history would repeat itself over and over. Sophia's husband had started out loving her, but in the end he had failed her, had condemned her to death. Nicolai believed that, as a DeMarco, he was part of that terrible curse, that in the end he would destroy her.

What of Francesca? How had she known of the accident no one had spoken of? She had access to Isabella's room.

And it had been a female voice luring her up the servants' staircase. Surely Francesca wasn't an enemy. Isabella closed her eyes. She didn't want to think that way, didn't want to be suspicious of Francesca.

Isabella finally slept, but she dreamed of wolves and massive lions. Of chains rattling and the wailing of ghosts. Chanting. Words in a language she didn't understand. She dreamed of Nicolai kissing her, holding her, his fierce features softened by love. It was so vivid she tasted him, smelled his wild scent. Abruptly he was pulling away, his eyes red-gold flames. He wore a demonic expression as he dragged her out to a field. He tied her to a large stake and built a fire as shadowy figures danced in a circle around her. Wolves looked on hungrily, and the lions roared approval. She heard the cackle of high-pitched laughter, women dancing merrily in flowing skirts as she begged for mercy. Francesca was there, smiling serenely, dancing around with her arms up as if she had a partner. Then the fire was out, and Isabella was kneeling with her head bowed, thankful to be alive. A shadow fell across her. Captain Bartolmei smiled at her while Theresa and Violante sang softly and Francesca clapped her hands in delight. Still smiling, the captain lifted his sword and swung it at her neck.

Isabella screamed in terror, the sound jarring her out of her nightmare. A hand caught her wildly flailing arms. "Shh, *piccola*, nothing's going to hurt you. It's just a bad dream." The voice was warm and soothing.

She wasn't alone in the bed. She could feel a warm body entwined around hers. Only the thick coverlet separated them. The fire had long since died, and not even an ember remained in the ashes, yet it mattered not at all. Nicolai DeMarco. She would recognize his scent, the feel of him, anywhere, no matter how dark the night. His voice was distinctive, low, a blend of menace and heat.

She turned her head slowly, cautiously. Nicolai's head was next to hers. She struggled to get her heartbeat under control. "What are you doing here, *Signor* DeMarco?" She sounded breathless, even to her own ears.

"I like to watch you sleep," he replied softly, unrepentant. His hands framed her face there in the darkness. "I come into your room each night and just sit and stare at you sleeping so peacefully. I love to watch the way you sleep. You've never had a bad dream until tonight." He sounded regretful. "I did that, Isabella, and I'm sorry I never should have exposed you to such danger."

"I often dream." She closed her eyes again, oddly secure now that she knew he was beside her. She inhaled deeply, dragging the wild, masculine scent of him deep into her lungs. The nightmare had shaken her, but the night was Nicolai's world, and she knew he could protect her as no other. He might fear that he would harm her, but Isabella felt safe in his arms. "Aren't you afraid Sarina might come in and find you here?" There was a teasing note in her voice.

He moved his head closer to press his lips against her temple. His breath was warm against her ear. "I have every intention of treating you honorably, however difficult that proves to be." There was self-derisive laughter in his tender tone. He wrapped an arm around her. "Go back to sleep. It makes me happy to see you so at peace."

"Why aren't you sleeping?" Her voice was drowsy.

His body hardened, making urgent demands, when all he had come for was contentment. "I don't sleep at night," he said softly, his fingers tangling in her hair. He closed his eyes against the memory of his own nightmare, welling unexpectedly, as if his heart needed to tell her his every boyhood terror. "Ever."

As if she could read his thoughts, she fit her body more closely to his, protectively. Her hand crept out from under the coverlet to cup his cheek, her palm warm against the scars of his childhood. "You can go to sleep here, Nicolai. I'll watch over you." The words were so low he barely caught them.

His insides melted. It had been years since anyone had

ever thought to protect him or worry about him or comfort him. She was turning him inside out without even trying. He buried his face in her hair, closed his eyes, and breathed her in. She had said he was the breath in her body, the joy and warmth in her heart. Well, she was the air he breathed into his lungs. She was his soul.

Don Nicolai DeMarco wrapped his arms possessively around her and closed his eyes, drifting as he listened to her soft breathing. There in the darkness, in the arms of a sleeping woman, he found peace.

Chapter Eleven

"*Signor* DeMarco! Just what are you doing in this bed?" Sarina's voice was shrill with shock and horror. Sarina slammed the door, keeping out any prying eyes and successfully disturbing Isabella's slumber.

Isabella opened her eyes reluctantly, her body totally relaxed and warm. "Do you have to wake me so early?" She groaned and attempted to snuggle deeper into her pillow. She found it was warm and muscular, a heart beating out a steady rhythm beneath her ear. Her shocked gaze flew to *Don* DeMarco.

He was lying beside her, one arm wrapped firmly around her. He bent his head to place a kiss in the hollow of her throat. "*Grazie, cara mia.* I have not ever had such a peaceful sleep." He rose with his fluid grace while Isabella gaped at him. His hair was wild, pulling loose of the leather tie he had used to tame it the night before. He made no attempt to straighten the long mane, and she thought it only enhanced his good looks. There was no remorse on his face or in his eyes for his improper behavior.

Isabella caught his hand. "Have tea with me."

Sarina's scandalized gasp should have made them both wince. "He will not have tea with you in your bedchamber!" She crossed herself and kissed her thumb.

"Not here." Isabella kept her gaze locked with Nicolai's. "In the dining hall. Out in the open, where everyone can see us together."

"He must leave immediately, this instant, and not through the door. No one can see him come from your room." Sarina wrung her hands in agitation. "I'll get the priest. You must ask him to perform the ceremony at once."

"I'll speak with the priest, Sarina," Nicolai said calmly, his gaze drifting over Isabella's face. "And do not reprimand Isabella. The fault lies with me alone. I came in when she was unaware." There was a soft command in his voice but a command nevertheless. His gaze flicked to Sarina, then back to Isabella. "I'd be pleased to share tea with you, *bellezza*." Calling her beautiful didn't seem to capture the way she took his breath away. He clasped her hand, his fingers sliding over hers slowly in an unhurried inspection of her skin before he brought her palm to his lips. He pressed a lingering kiss in the exact center.

Mesmerized, Isabella could only stare up at him, this man who had claimed her allegiance by saving her brother but who had stolen her heart away with his fierce pride and incredible tenderness. He stole the breath right out of her body. His eyes held a thousand secrets, dark shadows, and turbulent emotions. When he looked at her that way, she ached for him.

Don DeMarco moved across the room, his body fluid and powerful. Both women watched as he disappeared into the hidden passageway.

"I saw him." Sarina said the words aloud in wonder. "You weren't touching him, and I still saw him. As a man, Isabella."

"He is a man," Isabella said calmly as she pulled on her robe. Her body was sore and battered, but she ignored her protesting muscles as she went to the small alcove to wash and dress. The less she drew Sarina's attention to the previous night's adventures, the better off she'd be.

"You can't know what that means after all these years," the housekeeper whispered. Abruptly, as if her legs could no longer support her, Sarina sat on the bed and covered her face with her hands. Her thin shoulders shook as she wept without reservation.

Isabella saw the housekeeper sobbing and gathered her into her arms. "Sarina, what is it? Tell me. Is it Betto again? We can find him a healer. I've heard there are many who know much about herbs."

Sarina shook her head. "It's *Don* DeMarco. I watched over him as a little boy, so beautiful with his wild hair and laughing eyes. I loved him like my own." She wiped at the tears streaming down her face. "When he came in from the courtyard that day, that terrible day, covered in blood, his poor face torn . . ." She buried her face in her hands again in a storm of weeping. It was a few minutes before she recovered herself enough to lift her head and look at Isabella. "His *padre* loved him, you know. Loved him more than anything. I know he wanted to spare Nicolai the pain, the shame, of what he believed would happen to his son. He tried to kill Nicolai, not out of hatred but out of love. Love can be a terrible thing." She gazed at Isabella. "From that day to this one, I've never seen Nicolai as a man, not when he was standing alone."

"Sarina." Isabella took a deep breath, let it out, and forced herself to ask what was better left unsaid. "His *padre* believed Nicolai would kill his own wife someday. He believed it so strongly he was willing to destroy his own son to prevent it from happening. I know Nicolai fears it is possible. You know Nicolai, you know his true heart, and you love him. What do you believe?" Every muscle in her body clenched, waiting.

Sarina sighed softly, her shoulders slumping in defeat. She looked her age, thin and worn. "Forgive me, Isabella. I've grown so fond of you. I shouldn't have been so willing to risk your life for our sakes. None of us should have." She hung her head. "That first night, the night you arrived, do you remember the scream you heard, when the lions roared?"

Isabella turned away from the housekeeper, a shiver running down her spine. She had wanted to know. From the very first night she had wanted to know what had happened. Now she wasn't so certain. She backed away from Sarina.

"Nicolai had a meeting with his most trusted men, Sergio Drannacia, Rolando Bartolmei, Betto, and another man named Guido."

Isabella took another step back, shaking her head.

"You have to know," Sarina insisted tiredly. "You need to know. Nicolai loved Guido and trusted him as he does his captains. They were all boyhood friends. There was a terrible argument that night. Guido wanted Nicolai to send you away. Nicolai refused. No one really knows what happened—no one knows whether it was Nicolai or another lion that killed him—but Guido was torn to shreds. It was strange, the argument. They had never raised their voices at one another, they had never said cruel things, but that night Guido did." Sarina sighed softly. "Betto was very upset at what was said. He told me he hardly recognized Guido. Guido fancied himself a ladies' man, and he often was indiscreet with the maids, but he wasn't a man who raised his voice. Everyone ended up shouting at one another. Nicolai told Guido to go take a walk. The last anyone saw that night of Nicolai, he was walking away from the *palazzo*. The next time Betto saw him, he was standing over Guido's dead body, blood all over him. He looked a lion, with his great, shaggy mane, but it was Nicolai. To us, he is unmistakable."

Isabella twisted her fingers together behind her back to keep from trembling in front of the housekeeper. She could feel her heart pounding in alarm. She couldn't move, couldn't breathe.

Sarina rushed to comfort her, but Isabella shook her head and turned away, desperately trying to compose herself. She thought of Nicolai, his gentle touch, his smile. His eyes. How utterly alone he was in his *castello* of twisted legends. She knew what isolation did to the soul.

Isabella lifted her chin as she turned back to the housekeeper. "I am mistress of my own fate, Sarina. I entered into the bargain willingly. If I should change my mind, I'm certain *Don* DeMarco would allow me to leave. I'm no prisoner, no sacrifice."

"You're trapped here now. There's no way for you to leave," Sarina said sadly.

Isabella waited in stillness while her heart pounded out a rhythm of fear. Nicolai had grown from that beautiful child who brought joy to his people, to a powerful, dangerous man of mystery, one with a sinful smile and a promise of erotic ecstasy in his gleaming eyes. Her heart trapped her in the valley, her fidelity to a man who had been willing to bargain for the life of a stranger. She kept her promises. Her word of honor was her life. She wouldn't believe that anything else kept her there; that way lay disaster. She was mistress of her own fate.

"Nicolai won't harm me, Sarina," she said firmly. Her heart believed it was true, but her mind was stubborn, remembering the needlelike claws puncturing her skin. For one terrible moment the wounds burned and throbbed as a reminder. Had Nicolai killed his friend? A man who had trusted and served him? Was that possible?

Sarina went to the wardrobe. "If you're to meet him for your morning tea, you must hurry and dress. Something beautiful, Isabella, to give you courage." She flung open the doors to the wardrobe and cried out, the sound escaping before she could stop it.

"What is it?" Isabella pulled her robe tightly around her

and crossed the room to stare in horror at the floor of her wardrobe.

Captain Bartolmei's coat was lying there, shredded almost beyond recognition. Great, rending tears in the material made the coat nearly unrecognizable as anything other than scraps. There were claw marks on the floor of the wardrobe, great gouges, deep and angry, scoring the wood for all time. Beside the tattered remains of the coat lay the gown Isabella had been wearing the previous evening. It, too, was in ribbons, the remnants of the material mixed with the shreds of Captain Bartolmei's coat.

"Isabella." Sarina whispered her name in terror. "We must get you out of the valley. There must be a way."

Isabella wrapped a comforting arm around the older woman. "We must get me ready for tea. I don't want to keep *Don* DeMarco waiting. Betto must burn the coat and gown." She longed for Lucca, yet she was curiously reluctant to explain Nicolai's legacy even to her beloved brother.

"Isabella," Sarina protested again.

"Say nothing. Tell no one. Let me think on this." She used her most authoritative voice, hoping to ward off the housekeeper's objections.

As Sarina worked on her hair with trembling hands, Isabella attempted to puzzle out why she was so pulled in opposite directions. Could she have fallen in love with Nicolai? So completely in love with him that she was willing to risk her life? She had told him she would trade her life for her brother's life, and she had meant it. But why the unswerving loyalty to Nicolai, the need to stay and remove that look of utter loneliness from his eyes?

She shivered, her heart pounding at the thought of being ripped apart by a lion with blazing amber eyes. Nicolai feared that such a thing would happen. He had said as much to her. It was in the shadows in his eyes. In his nightmares. He had feared it from the very beginning, when he had asked her if she would trade her life for Lucca's.

Isabella closed her eyes tightly for a moment, trying to

still her nerves and quiet her rapidly beating heart. Lucca always told her to think things through, yet there was a strange buzzing in her ears, and her mind was in chaos. "I want to look my best, Sarina." She needed the extra confidence. "We'll take tea in the formal dining hall, not his rooms." Isabella was uncertain whether she feared being alone with him, or whether she wanted his people to see Nicolai behaving in a normal manner. All at once it seemed more important than ever that he eat with her out in the open as a gentleman would.

Sarina nodded her agreement. "It's time, I think."

Isabella took a last peek in the looking glass to see her appearance. Satisfied that her terror wasn't reflected on her face, she took a deep breath and swept out of her bedchamber and down the curving staircase. The gown clung to her figure, the soft material falling in folds and swishing lusciously while she walked. Her hair was in intricate braids, swept up on her head, giving her an elegance her lack of height often prevented. Her appearance hid her pounding heart and a mouth tasting terror. She walked with her head held high, regally, a member of the *aristocratizla*, born to wealth and position.

All along the hallway fresh tapers flickered in their sconces, throwing the carved lions with their teeth and claws into stark relief. The flat, cold eyes of the carvings stared at her, seeming to follow her every movement as she made her way down the hall. Isabella was all too aware of the wings on the crouching creatures, the plethora of claws stretching toward her. She found herself straining to hear a whisper of movement as she walked carefully to meet her betrothed.

Don DeMarco was already in the dining hall, pacing restlessly. She paused in the doorway to drink in the sight of him. He was tall and strong, his shoulders wide, his bearing straight. His long hair was tamed into a semblance of order, pulled back and secured at the nape of his neck. He didn't look like a killer. He looked handsome and dashing, a man born to rule. She saw his head go up as if he scented her in the air. He turned slowly, his gaze drifting over her face, her body. Desire leapt into the depths of his eyes. Stark. Intense. Hungry. For her alone.

It shook her, the way he looked at her. As if she were the only woman in the world. As if, without her, his life was empty and meaningless.

He crossed the gleaming tiles and clasped her hand. "Isabella, you take my breath with your beauty."

A smile curved her full lips. "You certainly make me feel beautiful, Nicolai."

He led her to a small table, ignoring the long dining table set with exquisite china and flatware. "I want to be able to talk with you, not shout from one end of the table to the other. The servants will frown at this, but if they give us too much trouble, I'll growl at them," he offered.

Humor was the last thing she expected. A small laugh escaped her, yet his teasing hadn't dispelled the wariness in her eyes. "What a useful asset you have. I didn't think of that." She leaned close and lowered her voice, determined to treat him as her betrothed. "Have you ever done it just to see what would happen?"

He grinned at her, a quick, boyish smile that took the shadows from his eyes. "When I was a boy, I couldn't always resist. Poor Betto—when he would try to get me to come in at night and go to bed, I'd hide in the shadows and growl very low." He shook his head at the follies of his youth as he held the back of a chair for her to be seated.

Her laughter spilled out, soft and infectious, finding its way into his heart. Her eyes were once again shining at him, accepting of him, daring to tease him, daring to share his youthful escapades and even the abilities that set him apart from all others. He couldn't remember his father ever speaking of the gift with him. He certainly couldn't remember even entertaining the idea of bantering about it.

Brigita entered, her eyes downcast and her shoulders slumped, as if she were walking to her doom. She shuffled across the room and served the food on the platters, careful not to touch the *don*.

"Good morn, Brigita," Isabella said brightly, determined to see the meal through. "All is well with you?"

Brigita curtseyed, nearly dropping a plate. "Yes, *grazie, Signorina* Vernaducci." Her wayward gaze shifted toward the *don* before she could stop it, and her eyes widened in surprise. Staring at him, she backed out of the room.

Isabella burst out laughing again. "I think you're much too handsome, Nicolai. Your people can only stare open-mouthed at you in silence."

"Why can't I have that effect on you?"

She studied him from beneath her lashes. "You do have that effect on me, *signore*." Her lashes fluttered down as color swept into her face. The good Madonna help her, he did have that effect on her. Captain Bartolmei's coat shredded from collar to hem lying atop her ripped gown meant nothing when he smiled at her. Isabella rubbed at her suddenly pounding temples. Was she so weak-willed that a man's smile could rob her of intelligence, of sanity?

"What is it, *piccola*?" he asked softly, and he took her hand. His thumb stroked a caress across her sensitive inner wrist, right over her leaping pulse. "There are shadows in your eyes that were not there when you woke."

"My life has changed so quickly, Nicolai," she answered. "I feel unsettled and confused. I wish Lucca were here."

"You have me, Isabella. You aren't alone."

"I know." She flashed a small smile at him and withdrew her hand to bring the teacup to her mouth. "It's simply nerves."

"Don't get nervous yet, because I've spoken to the priest. I didn't want to give Sarina another opportunity to berate us. He is willing to perform the ceremony in a fortnight. I'm sorry we won't have emissaries attending—you deserve that—but it's best we wed quickly."

"That doesn't bother me. I don't want all those people staring at me anyway," Isabella said. "I think a small cere-

197

mony would be perfect. But Lucca will be disappointed if he's not here." Her heart was pounding so loudly, she feared he might hear it. "He should be here very soon, Nicolai." Isabella was uncertain whether she wanted to wait until her brother could attend the ceremony because Lucca would want to be there, or because she was looking for a way to delay the inevitable. When she was with Nicolai, she felt strangely mesmerized, nearly overwhelmed by her attraction to him, by his need of her.

Nicolai carefully brought the teacup to his lips, his amber eyes holding her gaze steadily. It had been years since he had shared a meal with another human being. He had to learn manners all over again.

He could read her every expression, her every thought. Fear had crept into their relationship, and he had no way to alleviate it.

Isabella could see the slight tremble of his hand, the sudden shadows in his eyes, and despite her fear, her heart went out to him. "Nicolai," she said softly, "I know you're afraid for me. Tell me why you are so afraid. If you can control beasts as strong as lions, why should you fear for me?"

His gaze shifted away from her. Isabella's heart sank. She studied her food carefully, not trusting herself to look calm and serene as he revealed his most secret fears to her. She could feel her insides beginning to shake, tremors that threatened to spread to her limbs, and she hastily folded her hands in her lap beneath the table.

"I would spare you the truth." He offered it gently.

She lifted her chin, calling on every ounce of pride and courage. "I don't think it did much good to spare your *madre* the truth. I prefer to know as much as I can."

He set the cup carefully on the table, afraid he might crush it. One of the servants peeked into the room in awe but hastily backed out when the *don* flicked a brief, fierce glare at the interruption. "My ancestors have lived with this gift—or curse, whichever you prefer—just as I have. But there is one small difference." He sighed softly, raking his fingers through his hair so that it came out of its tie and fell around his face and shoulders like a wild, shaggy mane. "I could 'hear and understand' the lions when I was a babe. I would crawl to them, even go to sleep snuggled up beside them. As far as I know, that was unheard of. My ancestors' ability to control the lions and understand them always came much later in life."

Isabella touched the tip of her tongue to her suddenly dry lips. "How much later?" She dug her fingernails into her palms.

"Well after they became full-grown men." He looked at her then, his amber eyes alive with pain. "I loved the lions and my ability to communicate with them. It was a part of me, natural to me. I didn't think it was a bad thing. Not until the people began to see *mio padre* as the beast. They refused to look at him directly." He reached across the table as if he needed her hand to hold on to while the memories crowded in.

Unable to resist his silent plea, Isabella slipped her hand into his, noting the difference in size, how much larger and stronger he was. His fingers closed over hers, his thumb absently stroking caresses over her knuckles. "I was a mere boy when it happened to me. Don't you see what that means? It is strong in me. It is much stronger than it was in my ancestors. If I concentrate, I can hold the illusion of a man for a short time, but the wildness rises, and when I work at controlling my appearance, I can't talk with the lions."

Isabella let her breath out slowly. "Nicolai, the illusion isn't the man, it is the beast. You are a man, not a lion. You can't talk to the lions because you're so focused on your appearance, not because you become something you're not."

"You believe that, when *mio padre* hunted *mia madre* as if she were a deer in the forest?" He pulled his hand away, his expression darkening with emotion. Flames leapt into

199

his glittering eyes. As he jerked his hand from hers, she felt a stinging scratch along her skin.

Isabella tried to tuck her hand beneath the table out of sight, but his mouth tightened ominously, and he shackled her wrist, dragging her hand up for his inspection. For one moment the flames leapt and burned, an orange-red conflagration. He brought the back of her hand to his mouth. She felt the warmth of his breath, the touch of his perfectly sculpted lips, then the soothing velvet rasp of his tongue.

Abruptly he let her go, rising out of the chair so quickly it nearly fell over. He stepped away from her, his features a stone mask, but his eyes were alive with pain. He looked utterly and completely alone.

"Nicolai," she protested, sorrow welling up from deep within her. She ached for him, ached for his private nightmare, the pain of knowing he might be responsible for the death of someone he loved. That he very well might be responsible for her death someday.

"If you didn't move me, Isabella," he hissed in accusation, "if you hadn't stolen your way into my heart and soul, if you hadn't wrapped yourself so tightly inside me, there would be no danger. There's safety in not caring. If I don't feel, I stay in control. You've taken that from me."

"Do you want to live your life without caring, without loving, Nicolai?" She lifted her chin at him, storm clouds gathering in her eyes. "If that is the life you want, choose another to be your bride. You forced the decision on me, and I agreed. I accepted the risk, all of it. How dare you stand there and tell me you want a lifetime of emptiness?" She stood up, too, facing him squarely, uncaring that her hands were shaking. Let him see her fear. At least it was an honest emotion. "I'm not willing to live in emptiness, weighed down by sorrow and fear."

She turned away from him, terrified her temper would get the better of her. Terrified her runaway tongue would destroy what had been building between them. She had to think of Lucca, somewhere out in the wilderness, sick and in need of a healer and a warm place to pass the winter.

"I did not dismiss you, *Signorina* Vernaducci," *Don* DeMarco informed her, his voice a low whiplash of menace, of command. "You have all but accused me of cowardice." A soft, threatening growl rumbled in his throat, setting her heart pounding and her pulse racing frantically.

She stiffened in outrage but refused to turn and face him. Nor would she deny his charge. How dare he use his position as the *don* to control her behavior? She was seething with anger, wanting to throw the dishes at him. "I don't think I can take the credit for *your* feelings *signore*. They're all yours and have nothing to do with me."

He had hurt her with his twisted anger. He could hear it in her voice. Her face was averted, but he knew it would be plain to see in her transparent expression. Nicolai raked a hand through his hair again. He wanted to gather her into his arms and hold her to him. Offer protection, offer safety. "Isabella, did you not hear me? Or perhaps you didn't understand me. Not one of my ancestors ever had the strength of the beast—the calling—so early as I. There was no danger as long as I kept to myself, as long as I stayed in control. But I feel for you. Everything a man feels—more, even. The emotions are strong, and they rip my control to shreds."

The image of his words conjured up the memory of the tattered remains of Captain Bartolmei's coat. "Jealousy, Nicolai? Have you become jealous?" She asked it very quietly, careful to keep her back to him.

"*Dio!* Yes, I'm jealous. I hear your laughter, see the way men's eyes follow your every movement. I'm even jealous of shadows when they touch your body. I have lived alone since my twelfth summer, Isabella. At least apart. I accepted my life and my duties to my people. I tried to keep you from coming." He closed his eyes for a moment and rubbed a hand over his face tiredly. "I knew. The moment I heard your name. I knew what you would do to me, and you have. You found your way inside me, and there's no getting you out."

She did turn then, her eyes bright with tears. "Then you have to come to terms with what we are together. You have to believe in us. Not in yourself. In us."

He took a step toward her, then stopped abruptly, his hands closing into tight fists as he heard the soft footsteps of an approaching servant. "I don't want to hurt you." His voice was low, a caress so powerful her stomach clenched in reaction.

"Then believe in us, or let me go." She made it simple for him.

"*Don* DeMarco, the runners have arrived. They seek an audience with you immediately," Betto informed him.

Isabella knew by the older man's downcast eyes that he was unable to see Nicolai in his true form. She dropped a low curtsey toward the *don*. "*Grazie* for having tea with me, *signore*. It was . . ." Her lashes swept down demurely. "Interesting."

Nicolai shook his head and turned away from her, unable or unwilling to deal with her ire. "I will see you later, Isabella." It was a warning, nothing less. He stalked past her, hesitated, then reached out to shackle her wrist, drawing her close against his body. He bent his dark head toward hers, his mouth against her ear. "And I'll never let you go, Isabella. Never." Abruptly he released her and was gone.

Childishly she wanted to stomp her foot in sheer frustration. Instead she took a deep breath and let it out, rubbing at the fingerprints on her wrist as she did so. "How are you feeling, Betto?"

"Much better, *signorina*." He looked puzzled. "I still don't know what came over me. It was like being caught in a dream. I heard myself saying those terrible things to the poor boy, and I felt rage in my heart, but it wasn't real to me. I couldn't stop myself or control it until everyone began to say such nice things about me. In truth, it terrified me that I had no control."

"Has such a thing happened before or since?" Isabella laid a hand comfortingly upon Betto's arm.

"When I was a young man, I saw it happen to one of the woodsmen. He nearly killed *mio padre*. They were laughing one minute and at each other the next. I'd never heard either of them say such foul things." He scratched his head. "Funny, I haven't thought of that for a long time. It was right after Nicolai's *madre* came to the *palazzo*."

"But nothing more has happened to you?"

He shook his head and crossed himself, looking very reminiscent of his spouse.

Sarina hurried in, appearing a bit harried. "I'm sorry I left the serving to Brigita. Did she break anything or annoy Nicolai?" She gasped with dismay when she saw the food untouched on the table.

Betto patted her shoulder gently and went out, leaving the two women alone.

"I'm grateful you didn't send Alberita," Isabella said. "Sarina, I'd like to go to the kitchen and speak with Cook. Would you show me the way?"

Sarina looked puzzled. "Everything wasn't to your satisfaction?"

"On the contrary, it was perfect. I wish to thank the cook personally."

"But . . ." Sarina floundered, uncertain what to do. "You didn't really eat anything, either of you." When Isabella looked stubborn, Sarina sighed, not understanding. "I'll convey your appreciation to Cook."

"I don't want the cook's feelings hurt. It was a wonderful meal," Isabella insisted. "No matter what you tell her, if she sees we didn't eat, she will feel slighted. I want to thank her in person for going to such trouble."

"Isabella, it's her job to cook," Sarina said, following Isabella out of the room. *Aristocratici* were not supposed to go rushing down to the kitchens to soothe a cook's hurt feelings. It wasn't done.

"I thought Betto looked quite well," Isabella said cheerfully, changing the subject.

Sarina nodded, still frowning. "He said he didn't know

what happened to him. It's odd, but a couple of others have acted strangely, too. Cook is one of them. She threw a knife at the kitchen boy because he didn't build the fire fast enough. She's never acted that way before, no matter how difficult her life has been."

"And that was recently?"

"Just after you came. I didn't tell anyone, not even Betto, because I knew she was so upset over . . . things." She trailed off reluctantly.

"What things?" Isabella prodded.

Sarina looked around her as they stepped off the stairs and began to walk down the long hall toward the kitchen. "Her husband was caught with one of the maids. They were in the storehouse together. Janetta is wed to one of the grooms, and they've always been so happy together. I've never seen her look at other men. She's never been coquettish, not even as a young girl, and Eduardo, Cook's husband, is older and staid, not someone I would expect to dally about."

"How awful." Isabella sighed. "Did Eduardo deny what happened?" She kept her voice low to match Sarina's, not wanting anyone to hear.

The kitchen was a huge, open room with large pots and pans, long tables and cupboards everywhere, and a walk-in fireplace. The area was busy yet not chaotic, as if everyone had a job to do and was bustling about getting it done. Isabella lifted her skirts a little as they crossed in front of the wide hearth, not wanting to get ashes on the hem of her gown. She leaned toward Sarina to hear her whisper the rest of the story.

There was no real warning as a wall of flames flashed out of the fireplace to reach greedily toward them. The sound was like a clap of thunder, a roar of hatred and loathing. The heat was intense, engulfing Isabella, scorching her skin. The flash was so intense, fiery white light exploded in front of her eyes, obscuring her vision. Flames licked at the hem of her gown and raced up the material.

Buckets of water hit her from two sides, dousing the flames quickly enough that the fire had no chance to burn her skin. She stood drenched, shocked, her gown black and ruined, gaping holes in it. The smell of the burned frock was overpowering. She couldn't move, couldn't speak, so astonished that for a moment she scarcely heard the shouts all around her.

"Were you burned, Isabella?" Sarina caught her shoulders and shook her gently. "Sit down, *bambina*, before you fall." The housekeeper began examining her right there in the kitchen with the servants gawking.

Cook cuffed the ears of a gnarled old man, shouting hoarsely at him, fear twisting her face until she appeared demonic. The man was trembling visibly, his knees knocking. Isabella forced the terrible buzzing out of her mind to concentrate on what was being said.

"I did see them, Cook, as they were approaching," the man admitted. "I don't know what happened. I swear, I don't remember using the bellows to feed the air in. My hands were on them, but I didn't do it. I wouldn't endanger Sarina nor the *signorina*." He sounded close to tears. "I wouldn't do that."

"You nearly killed them," the cook accused. "I saw you do it, saw you deliberately work the bellows so that the flames roared."

He shook his head in denial and reached behind him unsteadily for a chair. "For a moment they were hideous to me." He rubbed his face, then buried it in his hands. "What am I saying? I felt such anger and hatred. I couldn't stop my hands. I was horrified. It was me. I did do it. *Dio!* The great Madonna save me from his wrath. He'll have me killed, sent away, but it's no more than I deserve."

Isabella made every effort to shake off the shock. The servants were murmuring angrily, glaring at the old man with twisted malevolence. She had seen that expression before. She took a deep breath and raised a hand, command-

Christine Feehan

ing silence. It was difficult to control the trembling of her body, but she managed.

"I am Isabella Vernaducci. I ask your name, *signore*." She kept her voice gentle.

A flood of tears greeted her simple question, a barrage of pleas for understanding and forgiveness. To Isabella's horror, the old man flung himself to his knees and attempted to wrap his arms around her legs.

"I don't believe it was intentional," she assured him hastily. Panic was welling up, and she wanted the comfort of her own room. Her gown was ruined, her face and body covered in soot, but she couldn't leave this poor man to face the wrath of the crowd. She gripped Sarina's hand tightly and looked at the sea of faces. "I'm certain you all know this man. Is he really the kind of person to deliberately harm two women for no reason?" Her gaze settled on Cook's face. "Surely you more than the others know that something else happened here." She stared without flinching.

Cook dropped her gaze and nodded sorrowfully. "Nothing makes sense anymore." She patted the old man's shoulder. "I don't know what happened today, but I felt the same thing."

Isabella nodded. "There is something at work here I don't understand, but this poor man has nothing to do with it, no more than Cook did when she felt it. We have to look out for one another. If something seems wrong, try to help one another and come to me, Sarina, or Betto. Let's work together on this." She forced a smile. "I think we need Alberita and the holy water."

A few of the servants managed answering smiles. Tired and drained, Isabella didn't have anything more to give. She leaned on the housekeeper as they made their way back through the halls to the sweeping staircase.

"You're going to tell Nicolai, aren't you?" Isabella said wearily.

Sarina tightened her arm around Isabella's waist. "Yes, he must know. That was good of you, Isabella. They were

206

all so angry at what he'd done, they might have attacked him."

"Were you hurt?" Isabella was struggling not to cry. The day had not started well, and she was terrified it would not end well.

"I'm fine. You were between me and the flames."

Betto appeared, anxious and a little out of breath, giving evidence that gossip was already spreading throughout the *castello*. Sarina gave a quick warning shake of her head, and he stopped where he was, staring at Isabella's ruined gown.

Chapter Twelve

The room deep beneath the *palazzo* was filled with steam. Isabella was grateful for the humidity and the vapor rising from the surface of the heated bath. At the last moment, just before entering her bedchamber, she had looked down at her hands and was appalled at the soot and grime. Tremors had nearly driven her to her knees. All at once it was the most important thing in the world to remove every trace of the incident. Sarina hadn't argued when she pleaded to be brought to the beautifully tiled bath.

Isabella left her ruined gown in a heap on the polished marble and slowly went down the steps, letting the water lap at her body. Her skin stung in places, but the water was deliciously soothing. Giving in to the terrible trembling, Isabella sank into the bath. At once Sarina began to pull the intricate braids from her hair.

The door flew open, and *Don* DeMarco stalked in. He looked powerful, angry, filled with turbulent emotions. He said nothing at first. Instead, he paced up and down the length of the room, his long strides betraying his agitation, a low, threatening growl emerging from his throat.

Intimidated by the *don's* barely leashed temper, Isabella glanced at Sarina for courage, but the housekeeper seemed more frightened than she. Isabella could tell by Sarina's downcast eyes that she was unable to see Nicolai in his true form.

Nicolai stopped pacing and turned the full force of his amber eyes on Isabella. "Leave us, Sarina." It was an order, and his tone brooked no argument.

The housekeeper squeezed Isabella's shoulder in silent camaraderie and allowed her young charge's hair to fall loose, hoping, no doubt, that the long tresses would act as some sort of covering. She retreated without a word. Nicolai stalked behind her, locking the heavy door, sealing Isabella in the room alone with him.

Isabella counted her own heartbeats, then, unable to stand the suspense, slipped beneath the surface to scrub the grime from her face and rinse the smell of smoke from her hair. She wanted to escape, simply to disappear. When she came up for air, Nicolai was standing at the top of the steps, looking wild, untamed, and very powerful. He took her breath away.

He padded across the tiles, his face shadowed, dark with his dangerous thoughts and inner turmoil. He was as silent as any lion as he stalked to the water's edge, to her ruined gown. He glanced at her once, then hunkered down beside the dress and lifted it with two fingers, staring at the black smudges and gaping holes. Nicolai straightened, a quick, fluid motion, naturally graceful. *Animalistic*. Swallowing visibly, he dropped the blackened gown upon the tiles and turned his glittering amber gaze to her face.

"Come here to me."

She blinked. It was the last thing she expected him to say. A shiver went down her spine despite the heat of the water. Her heart accelerated, and in spite of everything that had happened since she came to the *palazzo*, she tasted desire in her mouth. It blossomed low and pooled, a heated ache so intense she trembled. Isabella wrapped her arms around her breasts and looked up at him. "I have no clothes on, Nicolai." She meant to sound defiant. Or appeasing. Or anything but what she did, which was weary, with a huskiness that made her voice a soft, seductive temptation.

A muscle jerked in his jaw. His eyes grew hotter, more alive. "It was not a request, Isabella. I want to see every inch of you. I *need* to see every inch of you. Come here to me now."

She studied his face. She was infinitely tired of being afraid. Of coping with unfamiliar situations. "And if I do not obey?" she asked softly, uncaring what he might think, uncaring that he was one of the most powerful *dons* in the country, uncaring that he was soon to be her husband. "Go away, *Don* DeMarco. I can't do this right now." Her eyes were burning, and she would not, *would not*, cry again.

"Isabella." He breathed her name. That was all. Just her name. It came out an ache. Terrible. Hungry. Edgy with need, with fear for her.

Her heart contracted, and her body tightened. Everything feminine in her reached for him. "Don't do this to me, Nicolai," she whispered, a plea for sanity, for mercy. "I just want to go home." She had no home. She had no lands. Her life as she had known it was gone. She had nothing left but an all-consuming love that would eventually destroy her.

His gaze burned over her. Hot. Possessive. The merciless eyes of a predator. The hard line of his mouth softened, and his expression changed to one of concern, of comfort. "You *are* home, *bellezza*."

The brush of her gaze was nearly as potent as the touch of her fingers. If it was possible, his body hardened even more. "Are you afraid to come to me?" he asked softly, gently, a hint of vulnerability in his tone. What did propriety matter when there was such deep sorrow in her eyes? When she drooped with weariness? When she looked so sexy his body was going up in flames?

It was that slight break, that mere touch of an unguarded note in his voice, that changed everything for Isabella. He stood tall and enormously strong with nearly limitless power, yet he feared she might not want him with his terrible legacy. What sane woman would? He was seducing her with his voice. With his burning eyes. With the dark intensity of his emotions, with his loneliness and his incredible courage in the face of his heavy responsibilities. Who would love him if not she? Who would ease the pain in the depths of his eyes if not she? Isabella's gaze deliberately drifted over his body, settling for a moment on the thick evidence of his arousal beneath his breeches. Who would relieve the suffering of his body when no other woman could find the courage to look upon him and see beyond the ravages of an age-old curse?

Isabella lifted her chin, her eyes steady on his. She could spend a lifetime staring into his eyes. She allowed herself to be mesmerized, captivated. "Not at all, *signore*. Why would I be afraid of you? A Vernaducci is stronger than any curse."

She straightened, then tipped her head to one side to capture her long hair in her hands. It took a few moments to squeeze the moisture from the thick mass. She kept her gaze locked with his, needing his strength, needing his reaction. Isabella walked slowly toward the steps, the water caressing her every inch of the way. It slid over her skin, silky and wet, touching her breasts and her belly until she ached with need. Deliberately, provocatively, she dragged her feet and emerged slowly, coming to him through the steam and swirling water.

Nicolai knew he had made a terrible mistake the moment she took her first step toward him. The sight of her made his knees weak and his heart pound. His erection was a thick, pulsing ache. He was heavy with need, but it didn't matter. Nothing mattered until he examined every inch of her skin to make certain no harm had come to her.

His heart had stopped when they informed him of the

accident. His throat had closed, and for one terrible moment he couldn't breathe. Couldn't think. The beast had risen unexpectedly so that he wanted to kill. To maim and tear and destroy everything. Everybody. The sheer intensity of his emotions had terrified him.

He pulled her to him, crushed her against his body, buried his face in the wet mass of her hair. She soaked his clothing, but he didn't care. He held her tightly, trying to calm his wild heart, trying to breathe again. When the trembling stopped and he felt steadier, Nicolai held her at arm's length and began a slow inspection of her body. Very gently her turned her around and pushed the long rope of hair over her shoulder to expose her back to him. The talon marks were beginning to heal. His hands moved over her reverently, needing to feel her soft skin. He held her shoulders still as he bent to taste her. His tongue found the angry, raw marks of courage and lapped at the beads of water.

Isabella bit her lower lip and closed her eyes against the sensations his mouth was creating as he leisurely followed the contours of her back to her buttocks. His hands cupped her bottom, kneaded her flesh, then curved over her hips to slide up to her narrow rib cage. He pulled her back against him. She could feel his thick erection pressed hard against her bare skin, only his breeches separating them.

"Isabella." He breathed her name softly into the hollow of her shoulder. His teeth teased her neck gently as his hands took the weight of her breasts, his thumbs caressing her nipples. "I'm going to make you mine. I can't stop this time." He kissed the scratch on her temple. His tongue swirled over the puncture wounds on her shoulders, leaving behind a sweet ache. "I have to have you."

"I'm already yours," she whispered, knowing it was true. She belonged with Nicolai DeMarco.

He turned her face to him, wanting to see her expression. His hands framed her face, and he bent his head to hers. Her mouth was soft and pliant, opening to him so that his tongue could stroke hers. Fire swept through him, hot and fast, and he found he was ravaging her mouth when he wanted to go slowly. He forced himself to gentle his kiss, to keep from devouring her. When he lifted his head, she was looking up at him, bemused, so trustingly he fell to his knees with a groan, his arms wrapping around her waist, resting his scarred face against her belly. There where their child would grow.

The thought brought another wave of love, overwhelming, intense. His mind was roaring with hunger for her, with the need to bury his body deeply in hers and merge them together. He wanted her so badly he trembled with his need. His hands slid up the curves of her calves, her knees, found her thighs.

A sound escaped her. She was shaking. "I don't think I can do this."

"I have to have more," he whispered to her, and he slipped one hand between her thighs, caressing and stroking. Her soft moan tightened his entire body. He pushed his palm tightly against the hot core of her, felt it dampening, and smiled, pleased at the evidence of her arousal. He leaned into her and tasted her, his tongue stroking where his hands had been, determined that she would want him, would accept him, would feel nothing but pleasure.

"What are you doing?" she gasped, her hands fisting in his hair. She was afraid her legs would give out, but she didn't want him to stop. Ever.

His tongue stroked again. "You taste like hot honey," he murmured as he indulged himself, holding her to him while he fed, loving the way she clutched at him and her body tightened and trembled. "I could spend a lifetime tasting you," he whispered, rubbing his mouth on her stomach before standing up. "I'm taking you to my rooms." He lifted her high into his arms so her breasts nuzzled his chest.

Isabella wrapped her arms around his neck. "My room, please, Nicolai. We'll be safe there. I won't be afraid." She could hardly breathe with wanting him, and when he bent his head to flick her nipple with his tongue, she felt another wave of warm moisture seeping in invitation from between her legs.

He wasn't altogether certain he could walk, but he was not going to take Isabella's innocence on the tiles like a heated, uncaring youth. As he made his way through the hidden passage, he stopped to kiss her several times. Once, just outside her bedchamber, he allowed her feet to touch the floor while he pressed her against a wall and took her mouth with his, his hands wandering over her body.

Isabella found his mouth a wonderful mystery, a place of erotic beauty. He swept her into another time and place, where her body burned deliciously and she craved him, craved the feel and taste of him. She would never get enough of his kisses, never get enough of his body. Boldly she slipped her hands beneath his tunic to find the muscles of his chest. His skin was hot. She couldn't resist rubbing her hand over the large bulge in his breeches.

Nicolai nearly exploded. He came to his senses with his mouth at her breast and his fingers deep within her body. He was attempting to tear his breeches away, and the frustration brought him back to reality. He took a breath, breathed her in, and once more cradled her to him. She was offering herself to him without reservation, a gift he was determined to treasure.

Nicolai carried her into her chamber and laid her on the bed. Unable to take his eyes from hers, he pulled off his tunic and dropped it on the floor. She was beautiful, lying there completely naked, her gaze following his every move. He sat on the edge of the bed to pull off his boots and couldn't resist the temptation of the breast closest to him. He bent to suckle, his tongue teasing her nipple, his teeth scraping gently until she shuddered with pleasure and her legs moved restlessly.

Her belly was soft yet firm, and she jerked as his hand slipped lower. "Trust me, Isabella," he pleaded. "Just let me take care of you."

"Undress then," she said, trying to catch her breath. "I

want to look at you the way you look at me." It was broad daylight, and she should have been ashamed, but he filled every one of her senses until there was only Nicolai. Everything he did, everywhere he touched or tasted, brought her pleasure and need. Her body no longer felt like her own but was heavy and aching and desperate for release. She was hot, feverishly so, and she needed something. Needed his body.

He tossed his boots carelessly aside and stood to rid himself of his breeches. She found herself staring in apprehension at the hard, thick erection springing from between his legs. Nicolai smiled as she frowned at him.

"I think you may be too big for me," she said softly.

"That's not possible. You were made for me." He wouldn't let her be afraid of making love with him. There were many legitimate reasons for her to fear him, but his size wasn't one of them. "I'll make certain your body is ready for mine. Trust me, Isabella."

She reached out to wrap her fingers around his thickness. When she felt his shudder of pleasure, she slid the pad of her thumb over the soft tip to watch his reaction. Her stomach clenched hotly deep inside, every muscle contracting with anticipation.

"Later, *cara*, I swear, I'll show you many ways we can pleasure each other, but right now, I want you very much. I need to make certain you're ready for me."

"I feel ready for you," she said as he knelt between her legs, nudging her thighs wider. She felt ready to explode.

"We both thought you were ready for me before, *cara mia*, but I rushed you." He pushed his finger slowly into her tight sheath. Isabella gasped and nearly came off the bed. "This is what it's like, *cara*, only more, remember? There's nothing to be afraid of." He bent to kiss her belly as he withdrew his finger. "Now I'm going to stretch you a little, but it should bring pleasure, not pain." He pushed two fingers in very slowly, watching her face for signs of discomfort.

Her muscles clenched and tightened around his fingers, and he began to push deeper, a longer stroke that had her crying out. When he withdrew his hand, Isabella protested. "Nicolai." A soft reprimand that made him smile and shake his head.

"Not yet, *cara*. One more. I want to be sure you feel nothing but pleasure with me this time." Deliberately he inserted three fingers, more slowly, more carefully. Again he deepened the stroke and was pleased when she lifted her hips to meet his hand. "Ah, that's it, that's what I want." He leaned down to kiss her again as he settled between her thighs. "When I begin to move inside you, that's how you move to deepen the pleasure."

Isabella felt him pressed at her entrance and waited breathlessly as he began to push into her. He went slowly, his amber gaze holding hers. The feel of him stretching her, binding them together, her muscles tight and clenching around him, was almost more pleasure than she could bear.

His body shuddered in reaction to the exquisite torment. She was hot and tight and more than ready for him. He stopped when he encountered her barrier. Nicolai took her hands, stretched them above her head, and bent to suck on her nipple. He kissed her throat. "*Ti amo*, Isabella," he whispered. "I love you." And he surged forward.

She winced, and her fingers tightened around his. They looked at one another a long time, and then both smiled.

"It is done, *bellezza*." He kissed her again. "Take all of me now. Every bit of me." He pushed deeper into her. "That's it, take more." Nicolai pushed deeper still, another inch, and Isabella cried out, the sound muffled against his neck. He felt like shouting himself. She was a fiery sheath that gripped and teased and drove him mad. "We're almost there, just a little bit more, all of me, where I belong," he coaxed. He let go of her hands and caught her hips.

Isabella shuddered with pleasure as he withdrew and surged forward, gliding into her, out of her, slowly at first, then fast, faster still, deep, hard strokes that took her breath away and set her nerves screaming for more, always more. She could feel his rhythm now and began to meet his body with her own so that he clenched his teeth against the building pressure.

Nicolai wanted it to last forever, an ecstasy for both of them. It was building in him, wild and primitive. His woman. His mate. The roaring in his head increased. He gripped her hips harder, pulling her to him as he thrust forward with long hard strokes, so deep he wanted to find her soul. No other would know her, no other would have her, no other would give her a child. It ripped through him, a firestorm burning hotter than anything he had ever known. His body shuddered, tightened, hardened to a single purpose.

Isabella was watching him closely as his body began to pound hers in a near frenzy. At once the ripples began, spreading, encompassing her, taking her over so that she cried out with pleasure. It didn't stop. He kept going, taking her over and over so that her release seemed endless. She hadn't known what to expect, and she could only grip his arms for sanity as her body took on a life of its own.

He threw back his head, the wild mane of hair a halo around his head. As his seed poured into her, hot and fast, his hips pumping to send it deep, the roar deepened in his head and ripped from his throat.

Isabella's eyes stared directly into his. The amber was fiery orange-red, as if his body had truly started a fire and the flames were burning brightly in his gaze. His hands tightened around her hips, his fingers digging into her.

"Isabella." It was a soft, husky groan of defeat, of fear. "Run. Get out of here while you can." There was despair in his voice, but he didn't let her go, his body trapping hers beneath it. His hips were still surging forward as her muscles rippled and clenched around him. She felt a stab of pain in her hip, a needle puncture.

She stared directly into his eyes, holding him to her. "Nicolai," she said softly, "I love you. For yourself. Not as the *don*. Not as the powerful being who saved *mio fratello*. I love you for you. Kiss me. I need you to kiss me." She dared not look away from his eyes, dared not take the chance of the illusion taking hold, not now. Not in the midst of their lovemaking.

There was a silence as he stared down at her. Isabella remained calm, waiting. Watching. Her hands rubbed up and down his arms. She could feel his strong, hard muscles beneath his skin. Skin, not fur. The flames receded, and the needle slowly retracted from her hip. Her body still gripped his, her muscles clenching and unclenching as little after-shocks rocked her.

He bent his head and found her mouth, his kiss tender. "Did I hurt you?" He was afraid to look at her, afraid she would see tears swimming in his eyes. How could he ever trust himself with her again? He knew he would want her again and again, and each time he took her would become an experience in painful self-control. Sooner or later he would lose the battle, and it would be Isabella who paid the price.

"You know you didn't." She nibbled her way up his chin to the corner of his mouth. "Is it always like that?" His hair was brushing her sensitive skin, and deep inside, her muscles reacted by contracting again, sending another burst of pleasure rushing through her. Relief washed over her. She was certain they could find a way to be stronger than the curse. Of course, it was ingrained in Nicolai to believe in the curse, to believe he would one day kill the woman he loved, and she was afraid he was defeated before they even tried.

"You saw it, didn't you?" His hand moved over her hip and came back with a small smear of blood on it. "You saw me as the lion."

"No, Nicolai, I didn't see it. I saw you, only you." She held him close to her, their hearts beating frantically together. Needing comfort, he laid his head on her breasts while her fingers twisted in his hair.

"But you felt the lion, Isabella," he said sadly. "I know

you did. I know you heard him." Her nipple was too much of a temptation, and he took it into his mouth, his tongue teasing and stroking. Again he was rewarded when her body shuddered with pleasure, squeezing and tightening around him. He kissed her breast and lay quietly, letting her peace, her tranquility, seep into his mind so he could think clearly.

"None of that matters, only what we are together," she answered softly.

Nicolai lifted his head and stared down into her face. "I'm not going to marry you." His eyes gleamed at her, and his hair fell across her sensitized breasts, teasing her nipples to hard peaks.

She stiffened beneath him. He lay over her naked body, his naked body blanketing hers, entwined with hers, his arms holding her. They had just lain together in the way of husband and wife, yet he chose that moment to announce he had once again changed his mind. Isabella tried not to think it was due to her inexperience, due to the fact that she had given up her innocence without marriage.

"Please get off me," she said politely when she wanted to slap his handsome face. That she could still find him handsome frayed her temper even more.

"I'm sorry. Am I too heavy?" He shifted his weight immediately, one arm still around her waist, one leg thrown casually over her thighs. His breath was warm against her breast. "I don't know why I didn't think of it before."

"You did think of it before," Isabella pointed out dryly, and she shoved at him. "I must get up. Sarina will be wondering where I am. I trust your inspection of my body met with your approval."

"Isabella." He sat up. "What's wrong?" He rubbed the bridge of his nose, confused by her reaction. "You'll be my mistress," he reassured her. "I would never give you up. I'll send for another bride if I must, but you'll stay here and live with me."

Her chin rose a fraction. She rolled away from him, sat on the other side of the bed, and inspected the stained sheets, evidence of her lost innocence, her temper rising so that she struggled for control. "I suppose I deserve that, *Signor* DeMarco, and, of course, your will is my command. Will you have the decency to leave me now please?" *He would send for another bride*. He dared to say that to her while her body was still throbbing from the invasion of his.

"Isabella, it's the only way to get around the curse. Don't you see?" He reached for her, but she slipped off the bed and dragged on her robe, her dark eyes stormy.

"*Don* DeMarco, I'm asking you to leave my room. I have agreed to serve you in whatever capacity you require in exchange for Lucca's life. If you wish me to be your mistress, than I will do so. But I'm asking you to leave my room before I forget myself and throw something quite large at your head." She was proud that she managed to keep her voice pleasant.

"You're angry with me."

"How perfectly clever of you to guess. Get out!" She enunciated the words carefully on the chance he was impaired in some way. Perhaps that was what happened to a man after he lay with a woman. Perhaps they lost their senses and became perfect dolts.

"I'm protecting you, Isabella," he pointed out reasonably as he pulled his clothes toward him. "You must see that. We have no other choice."

"I have politely asked you to leave my bedchamber." Isabella assumed her haughtiest tone. "Unless I have no rights in our ever-changing relationship, I believe privacy is a small thing to ask."

"You have to see that I'm right in this," Nicolai said, exasperated with her. "*Dio*, Isabella, I might have killed you. And if you became my wife, one day I would."

"Ah, yes, that excuse again. A mere pinprick is much like the stab of a dagger. I think the stabbing has been done to my heart."

He took a deep breath and shook his head. "We were lucky this time. I felt it taking me. I nearly couldn't control the beast, with my emotions so intense. I won't risk marrying you and letting the beast take you, not even to appease your injured feelings. Propriety means nothing against the chance of losing you."

"Propriety may mean much to *mio fratello, signore,* and to my good name. I am a Vernaducci, and we, at least, do *not* go back on our word." She looked down her nose at him, every bit her father's daughter. She walked to the door and yanked it open, ignoring the fact that he was undressed. "Leave my room at once."

"Isabella!" Shocked, he snagged his clothes with one hand, his boots with the other, and hurried to the entrance of the secret passage.

Ignoring him, Isabella calmly yanked on the bell pull to summon a servant. She steadfastly refused to look back at Nicolai as he escaped into the passage. She stared resolutely out the door of her bedchamber, waiting for her call to be answered.

Alberita arrived, breathless. She curtseyed three times. *"Signorina?"*

"Please tell Sarina I need her immediately. And, Alberita, there is no more need for bowing."

"Yes, *signorina,*" the maid said, curtseying repeatedly. She whirled around and raced down the hallway at breakneck speed.

Isabella didn't move, standing beside the door waiting, her bare foot tapping out a rhythm of impatience, of temper, of mortification. Sarina hurried toward her, and Isabella caught her by the hand and dragged her into the bedchamber. She shut the door firmly and leaned against it. Tremors were starting from deep inside, spreading throughout her body.

Sarina looked from her pale face to the disheveled bed, the stained sheets. She looked back at Isabella. "I must get rid of the evidence immediately."

"There's no need." Isabella waved a hand and worked to keep her voice even, but it wobbled alarmingly. "I'm no longer his betrothed. He's informed me I am to be his mistress, and he will send for another bride." To her horror, her voice broke completely, and a sob escaped.

Sarina was astounded. "That can't be. You're the one. The lions know. They always know. Isabella . . ." she began, her gaze straying back to the stained sheets.

Isabella covered her face, ashamed to be weeping in the presence of a servant, but nothing would stop the flood of tears. She comforted herself with the knowledge that the DeMarco holding was different, the senior servants treated as family.

Sarina went to her immediately, swallowing every lecture and putting her arms around the younger woman, her expression compassionate. Isabella put her head on Sarina's shoulder, clinging to her. Sarina made little clucking noises, patting Isabella's back in an attempt to calm the storm of tears. "He couldn't have meant it. He wasn't thinking properly."

"I should have listened to you."

"If Nicolai thinks he's protecting you, it wouldn't have made any difference. Would you have told him no if he had wanted you as his mistress before he offered marriage?"

Isabella shook her head. "No." She had to be honest with herself and Sarina. She would have become his mistress if those had been the terms of their agreement, but she never would have allowed herself to be so drawn to him. At least she hoped she wouldn't have. A wife could eventually find a way to dispose of a mistress. "I would have done anything he asked to save Lucca. I still will, but it's different now, Sarina." She shook her head again and left the comfort of the housekeeper's arms to sit on the edge of the bed and survey the reminders of her sins. "Everything has changed."

"Because you love him." Sarina made it a statement.

Isabella nodded sadly. "And he would lessen what we have together. I have no choice but to accept what he decrees, but it will take some time to begin to forgive him. And I don't know what I'll do when he sends for a bride."

She rubbed absently at her throbbing temples. "Why didn't he just choose one from this valley?"

"No DeMarco chooses a bride from within the valley." Sarina sounded faintly shocked. "It isn't done. And what *famiglia* would risk such a thing?"

"Of course not, not when they believe the bridegroom might eat the bride." She made a small attempt at humor, but it came out bitter. "Better to bring in a girl from a holding who knows no such tale, who can't escape and is sold by her *famiglia* for profit." She squared her shoulders. "At least I choose my own fate, Sarina. I came here willingly, and he's told me what to expect."

She looked sadly around the room with its plethora of winged guardians and crosses. "I was supposed to be safe here. I thought that somehow she would protect me if I was in this room."

"I am certain the Madonna is watching over you, Isabella," Sarina assured her.

"She must be," Isabella agreed, "as I'm still alive in spite of the curse. But I was thinking of Sophia. This was her room. I feel her presence sometimes. It must be terrible for her to see what her words have wrought. I wish I could help her in some way. I think she must have suffered greatly."

"You are an unusual woman," Sarina said sincerely. "If *Don* DeMarco is so foolish as to allow you to slip through his fingers, then he doesn't deserve you."

A small, humorless smile touched Isabella's mouth. "I don't think it's in his mind to allow me to go anywhere, just not to marry me. I will live as his mistress while he chooses another bride."

"The curse is on Nicolai as the DeMarco heir, not on his bride. You are the one the lions have accepted. It won't matter how many other brides he chooses, nor how often he professes not to love you, he can't cheat his destiny," Sarina said sagely.

Isabella suddenly leaned into her and circled Sarina's neck with her arms, burying her face on the housekeeper's shoulder. Sarina couldn't resist the silent plea and held her tightly. "I think you're right," Isabella said. "I feel you're right. Nicolai can't defeat the curse by tricking it." She sighed softly. "But there was no talking to him. He thinks to protect me. In truth, he will make it more difficult for me." Isabella allowed herself a few minutes of comfort before determinedly getting up. "I would appreciate your aid, Sarina. My hair is a mess. Would you mind helping me again?"

Sarina was all business, choosing another gown for Isabella, carefully brushing out her hair in front of the fire to dry it before once more dressing it. Isabella lifted her chin and turned around to allow Sarina to look at her. "What do you think?"

"I think you'll do," Sarina said softly.

Chapter Thirteen

Isabella spent the remainder of the morning reading in the library. She knew she should be finding her way around the *palazzo*, familiarizing herself with the holding, but she needed to spend time alone, away from prying eyes.

Betto stuck his head into the room and beckoned her. "*Don* DeMarco has said you must go to him immediately."

She set her book carefully aside and rose with grace to follow Betto through the long halls and up the wide staircases. She moved without haste, making him wait for her several times. It was Betto who was forced to knock on the door of the *don's* inner sanctuary, as Isabella refused to do so.

Nicolai beckoned her.

She stood just inside the entryway, her chin up. "I believe you summoned me?" she said in her haughtiest voice. She kept her eyes fixed on the falcon standing on its perch in one of the recesses of the room. She didn't dare look at Nicolai, didn't want to feel that curious melting in the region of her heart, the butterfly wings brushing at her insides.

"Sit down, Isabella. We have much to discuss."

She tilted her chin at him. "I would rather stand, *Don* DeMarco, as I'm certain we have little to say to one another."

He sighed heavily, his amber eyes glinting at her. "You are being particularly difficult, when all I'm asking is that you sit in a chair while I give you news of *tuo fratello*."

He made her feel childish and silly and a little bit ashamed of herself. It wasn't his fault that she burned each time she looked at him. That after his possession, her body no longer seemed her own, but his. The craving for him was a terrible thing, and yet he looked upon her with his strange eyes and his mask of indifference. He wanted a mistress, not a wife. Her father had warned her never to give herself to a man without marriage, but once again she had chosen to go her own way, and disaster had followed. Isabella bowed her head to keep him from reading her humiliating thoughts and with great dignity seated herself in the high-backed chair farthest from the fireplace. "*Scusi, Signor* DeMarco. Please give me news of *mio fratello*, as I'm quite anxious for his arrival."

Isabella sounded so subdued, it nearly broke Nicolai's heart. She looked alone and vulnerable seated in his large chair. He desperately wanted to offer her comfort but didn't dare trust himself to get too close to her.

"I'm afraid the news isn't good, *cara mia*. Lucca is quite ill, and they have been forced to stop in hopes of aiding him. The *don's* escort sent word promptly that they were allowing him to rest before continuing the journey."

Isabella's dark eyes widened in shock, in fear. The compassion in Nicolai's voice was nearly her undoing. "The *don's* men escort him?"

"Rivellio insisted. He wishes to aid me in any way possible," Nicolai said dryly. "I suspect he really wants a look at this valley in the hope of one day acquiring it through some treachery or battle."

"It is likely they are killing Lucca. *Don* Rivellio detests *mio fratello*. He won't want him to live. I must go to him at once, *Signor* DeMarco. Please have my horse made available, and I'll pack a few things."

Nicolai was already shaking his head. "You know that is not possible, Isabella I have sent out several of my most trusted men, and they will see to it that Lucca is well enough to travel and escort him to the *castello* as soon as his health permits. Rivellio's men wouldn't dare bring me a dead man."

She jumped up from the chair and paced restlessly across the gleaming floor. The falcon flapped its wings in warning, but she sent it a single, ferocious glare, and the bird of prey settled down docilely.

Nicolai watched her, admiring the passion in her—so much passion her shapely body could barely contain it. His own body hardened with the relentless ache of need. Of hunger. Possessing her might not be enough. Devouring her would not be enough. She was fire and courage, the epitome of the characteristics he wanted in himself. She was a living flame, and making love to her was an endless journey into erotic ecstasy. He wanted to yank her to him, to crush her mouth beneath his.

She stopped directly in front of him, tilting her head back so she could look up at him. The action exposed the vulnerable line of her throat. Her large eyes blazed with temper, and her fingers curled into fists. "Perhaps you mistake me, *signore*. I did not ask for an escort. I am aware you have need of your people here. I am perfectly capable of finding my way to *mio fratello*." She was making every effort to speak politely, but her breath was coming fast, and even her sensual mouth gave evidence of her agitation. "I will not take a chance with Lucca's life. I prefer to make certain the *don's* men do not harm *mio fratello* in any way."

She was so beautiful, Nicolai wanted to drag her to him, crush her perfect, trembling mouth beneath his. Crush her body beneath the weight of his and bury himself deep inside her, where there would be white-hot heat. She made him wild, something a DeMarco could ill afford. He could feel his primitive nature rising, calling to him, demanding he embrace it, demanding he take what was his and hold her against all enemies. As a precaution, he slipped farther into the shadows. Was he so much an animal that he couldn't control his passions when she was near? His body was painfully hard, his erection thick and heavy with need of her. Even now, when he was delivering news that upset her, he hungered for the lush pleasures of her body. It was a frightening thought that the beast was gaining control faster than he expected.

"I did not misunderstand you, Isabella." His voice was gruff, a soft, warning growl escaping from deep within his throat. "I have many enemies who would love to get their hands on you, Rivellio being one of them. You are protected in this valley, and you will not leave."

Her eyebrows shot up. "That is ludicrous! I am no longer your betrothed. You have only to announce it to the world, and the threat is gone. In any case, I'm evidently in more danger here than I would be anywhere else—you told me so yourself. Nicolai, I am not running away from you. I'll return immediately. You know I must go to Lucca."

"And you know I cannot allow it." His voice was quiet, purring with menace.

With anyone other than Isabella, that dangerous note in his voice would have been warning enough. But eyes held the beginnings of a turbulent storm. "*Can't* allow it, Nicolai, or *won't* allow it?"

"If you like, I will send Captain Bartolmei along with those escorting our healer. He will personally see to it that your brother is fit for travel and escort him back as quickly as possible." He found himself trying to appease her.

"Then I will be perfectly safe traveling with the captain," she challenged.

He snarled. Actually snarled. But even that wasn't enough to express the intensity of his emotions. Another sound rumbled from deep within his throat, swelling in volume. A roar filled the room, an explosion of rage that shook the entire wing of the *palazzo*, set the falcon's wings flapping wildly in alarm and the lions in proximity answering roar for roar, as if the *don* were one of them. From deep within the shadows his amber eyes glowed with eerie flames. His hair was wild from the constant raking of his fingers. It spilled around his face, long and shaggy, reaching down his back. Fearing he would appear more the beast than ever, Nicolai slipped deeper into the alcove.

His gut clenched at the very idea of her traveling for days and nights in the company of Rolando Bartolmei. Boyhood friend or not, Nicolai didn't want Isabella seeking solace in the arms of another man. Even innocently. If her brother didn't survive, and she was grief-stricken, it would be perfectly natural for Bartolmei to console her.

Isabella swung around, all restless energy, her stormy eyes flashing fire at him. She stalked him into the shadows as he retreated farther. "Don't you snarl at me, Nicolai DeMarco, and don't you dare roar. I have every right to be upset with you and your dictatorship. You have no reason to be angry with me at all. I intend to go to *mio fratello* and ensure that his health improves. I have my own horse and don't need your captain or your permission."

"Don't threaten me, Isabella." His voice was low, controlled. He was careful to keep his hands to himself, though her scent filled his lungs and did wicked things to his body. "The healer will bring your brother to you alive and as quickly as possible. Let that be enough." Jealousy, an unwelcome and unattractive emotion, was gripping him. If Rolando brought her beloved brother back well and happy, would she be grateful to Bartolmei, look upon him with affection? Nicolai was ashamed of his thoughts, ashamed of his inability to control his emotions. He had always been so disciplined.

Her breath caught in her throat in pure outrage. She closed the distance between them in three angry strides, heedless of how reckless she was being. Anger was energy crackling in the room, fierce and passionate. "I can't believe you're *ordering* me to stay." The idea was so appalling, she clenched her fist and struck him hard right in the stomach. It made her even angrier that he didn't even pretend to wince, while her knuckles stung. She jerked her hand back, glaring at him.

A small smile softened the hard line of his mouth as he gently shackled her wrist and brought her throbbing hand to his heart. Because he couldn't help himself, he raised her hand to his mouth, his tongue swirling over her sore knuckles with soothing heat.

She was indeed all courage and fire; any other woman would have fainted away at the terrors of her position. Not Isabella, with her stormy eyes and passionate mouth. "You don't have the good sense to fear me, do you?" he observed. He feared enough for both of them. He had seen the evidence of the curse with his own eyes. He had felt the welling of savage excitement, known the hot taste blossoming in his mouth.

"I'm afraid, Nicolai," she admitted. "Just not *of* you. *For* you. For me. I'm not a dolt. I'm aware this could end badly. But we're in it already. I'm here in this valley, I've already met you, the pattern of our lives is already unfolding around us. Would it stop if I hid beneath a bed as a child might? What would that help, Nicolai? I want to live my life, what little I may have, not hide shivering beneath a coverlet." Her palm caressed the scars on his face, her heart softening, melting, at his expression.

"Isabella," he whispered softly, achingly, his throat clogged with such emotion he couldn't breathe properly. "There is no other like you." Sacrificing her for his people, for his valley, was a horrifying exchange. He knew how his father must have felt. The emptiness. The self-loathing. The despair. Nicolai had prayed, and he had lit many candles to the good Madonna. Still, danger surrounded every move Isabella made.

"I want you, Isabella," he said, his voice aching with need. "God help me, I want you again and again, when I should be locking you up somewhere far from me."

She looked up at him, and the simple act was her undoing. Desire blazed in his eyes. Possessiveness. Hunger. Love. It was stark, undiluted. Burning brightly.

Groaning, he bent his head and took possession of her mouth. Dominating. Male. Demanding her response. Devouring her. He couldn't get enough of her, couldn't get close enough to her.

Despite everything, she was kissing him back, feeding on him. A fire raged in her, burned out of control, a storm of such intensity she was swept up in it, no longer able to think, only feel. Her arms, of their own volition, crept around his neck, her fingers tangling in his hair. She felt weak with wanting him, craving his mouth, his body possessing hers.

His lips left hers to trail over her chin, down her neck, the column of her throat, leaving flames where his tongue swirled and caressed. There was no drawstring at the neck of her gown to give him access to her body. In sheer frustration he found her breasts right through the material of her dress. His mouth was hot and wet, pulling strongly so that the cloth rubbed her nipples, teasing them into hard peaks of desire. Her body went liquid with need. He bent her over his arm, tilting her breasts upward so that he could draw first one, then the other, from the neckline of her gown. The material cradled her breasts like hands, holding them up for his inspection.

"You are so beautiful." His breath was warm against her aching flesh.

Her body clenched, a heated pool settling low within her, demanding relief. His hands moved over her, thumbs teasing and driving her wild, his mouth strong and hot and persistent until she tugged at his hair, wanting more. She tried her own exploration, tugging at his shirt, at his breeches, but her legs threatened to give out when he lifted the hem of her skirt.

"You have too many clothes on," he muttered thickly.

"So do you," she answered breathlessly.

He was already yanking his out of the way, tearing away her undergarment to expose her bare skin. Then he was kissing her again, removing her ability to think, building the storm to the next level, his hand sliding beneath her skirt to her thigh, rubbing between her legs to feel her damp invitation.

"I love how you feel." Nicolai took her down to the floor, to the thick rug in front of the massive fireplace. "You're ready for me. I look at you across a room and wonder if your body will be ready for mine. If just a look would be enough to do this." His finger penetrated deeply, stroked and danced and caressed. "I just have to look at you, think of you, and my body is like this." He settled between her thighs, caught her hips, and pulled her toward him so that his thick erection was pressed against her entrance. "I'm so hard its painful, *cara*. I need to bury myself in you."

She gasped as he thrust forward, spearing her, stretching her tight sheath around him. He made a sound, somewhere between a growl and a groan of utter pleasure. He stopped, clenching his teeth, waiting for her body to accommodate his size, allowing her to become used to his invasion so he could inch more of himself into her. She was so hot and tight he was afraid he might not have the control needed to pleasure her, too.

"More, Nicolai," she pleaded. "All of you. I want all of you."

He caught her hips more firmly and began to move, surging forward, long, hard strokes, fast and deep. He wanted to crawl inside the haven she offered, the paradise he had never known so completely. He plunged his body into hers, watching them come together in perfect rhythm, wanting to stay there for all time. There was no give in the floor, and he was able to fill her, his every stroke shaking her body so that her breasts quivered invitingly and her eyes grew sultry.

He experienced no dark thoughts, only the ecstasy of her body, the pleasure he brought to her. He glided in and out of her, pushing deeply, feeling her response as her muscles clenched around him, the ripples spiraling outward until he was caught up in them, too. Until her body was gripping and milking his seed. It poured out of him, a hot stream of desire, of commitment, of love.

He bent forward and took one breast into the hot cavern of his mouth. Shuddering with pleasure, he held her to him, buried deep inside her, his mouth at her breast, as the ripples overtook her and she cried out his name and her fingers curled into fists in his hair.

At once, through his pounding heart and the fire sweeping his body, he felt the wildness rising in him, felt the beast wanting to mount her again and again, to ensure no other touched her, no other gave her a child. His thoughts were confused and primal, a fierce possessive streak shaking the very foundations of his soul. He nearly leapt away from her in fear, wanting to retreat into the shadows like the animal he was.

One moment his body covered hers in a wild, passionate exchange, the next he was wrenching himself away from her as if he couldn't bear the sight of her. Isabella didn't look at him, didn't want to see if the lion was blazing in his eyes. She didn't want to know if he was near the end of his control. She wanted more. Much, much more. She wanted him to hold her close, to cuddle her in his arms and whisper how much he loved her.

She closed her eyes against the pointless tears burning there. She couldn't blame Nicolai; she had been his willing partner each time. And she would be again. She could hardly deny it when her body still throbbed and clenched and craved his. She pulled her gown up over her breasts, her body responding to the feel of the fabric against her sensitized skin. Very carefully she sat up, looking away from the corner where she could hear his heavy breathing as he struggled for control.

At once she felt an edge of danger in the room. It had nothing to do with the strange entity and everything to do with the curse. The hair on her skin rose, a chill going down her spine. He was watching her from the shadows, and she didn't know if he was watching as a man or a beast, and for the very first time she was afraid to find out. Isabella rolled over and came to her knees, wanting to get up.

At once she sensed movement, a whisper of sound, hot breath on her neck. Nicolai stood over her; she felt the brush of his hair along her arm and back.

"Don't move," he warned. His voice was thick, strange.

"Nicolai." She knew her fear was between them, that he could smell it. Hear it.

"Shh, don't move." His hands shaped her bare bottom. "We haven't finished."

Isabella nearly jumped out of her skin. Her heart leapt in terror, then settled into a strong, fast, pounding rhythm. Hands, not claws, touched her body. It was fully Nicolai. He might be struggling, but he was with her.

His hands kneaded the firm flesh of her buttocks, then slipped lower to find her pulsing, wet core. He pushed into her with his fingers, immediately bringing her to a fever pitch again so that she moaned and cried out for him.

"*Dio, cara*, this is dangerous," he whispered. "So dangerous." But he didn't stop, pushing deeper until she moved against him with a small sob.

At once he caught her hips and thrust into her again, deeper and harder, filling her with his thickness, stretching her tight sheath, the friction almost more than either could tolerate. Having emptied himself into her once, he had more staying power, but he could feel the wildness rising with every stroke. His blood raced with fire; his belly burned with it. He reached for emptiness in his mind, sheer pleasure, no thoughts, no fear, just erotic pleasure.

Isabella could feel him surrounding her, his arms strong,

every muscle taut, his body surging in and out of hers. He was deep inside her, the pleasure building and building until she was swamped with it, until every cell in her body was stretched beyond endurance and she was shuddering with pleasure. Until her body was no longer her own but his, to teach and play like an instrument until she fragmented, exploded, dissolved. Until there wasn't a part of her that wasn't burning and spinning out of control.

She felt his body swelling, hardening even more, the friction so intense it was more than she could bear. It sent them both tumbling over a cliff and falling through space. Colors burst in her mind, whips of lightning danced in her bloodstream. This time he collapsed over her, driving her to the floor, where they lay in a tangled heap, too exhausted to move. They lay still for some time, hearts pounding, the heat so intense that beads of sweat formed between their bodies, but neither could find the energy to move away from the fire.

Nicolai's wild hair was everywhere, their clothes were disheveled, and their arms and legs were tangled together. Isabella turned her head. "What did you do to me? I can't move."

"I can't move either," he said, satisfaction purring in his voice. "Even if the beast wanted to leap out, it couldn't." He stirred enough to press a kiss against the nape of her neck. "I guess you'll have to spend your nights and days making love with me."

"We'll die."

"It's a better way to go," he pointed out. His hand stroked her bare buttocks, sending a fresh lightning whip sizzling through her body.

Isabella's answering laughter was muffled against the rug. She closed her eyes and rested, listening to the steady rhythm of his heart. She hadn't felt so at peace, such a sense of belonging, since she'd been in her own home. It was so *right* with Nicolai.

"What are you thinking?" he asked gruffly.

"That I belong here with you. That this is right, meant to be. I'm happy with you." She sighed softly. "I do miss Lucca and my holding, but I want to be here with you. My home was a happy place most of the time—if I could stay out of *mio padre's* way." She spoke unguardedly. "I loved him, but he was distant and disapproving of me. I never seemed an asset to him."

The sadness in her voice twisted in Nicolai's gut like a knife. He rolled over, taking her with him so he could sit against the wall, cradling her in his lap, his arms protective. "I believe you were more of an asset than he could possibly have ever known. You had the courage to come to me when most men refuse to brave this valley." He kissed the top of her head. "You saved your brother's life, Isabella."

"I hope I have. I hope that he comes here and recovers completely." Her eyes held shadows. "But then he will have to face what we don't want to face. That there is a lion who at every turn seeks to defeat us."

"Not a lion," he protested. "The curse. A lion is simply an intelligent beast, not necessarily vicious but acting instinctively."

His words told Isabella that he saw himself as part beast. The hope that had been blossoming in her died a quiet death. A shiver went through her. "Just as your instincts will tell you to kill me."

He held her in his arms, cradled her close to him protectively, brushing stray tendrils of hair from her face. "We'll find a way, Isabella. Don't give up on me. We'll find a way. I promise you. The beast was close this time, but it didn't win."

She thought he was wrong, but she said nothing. The beast had already won. Nicolai accepted it in his life, as part of who and what he was. He had always accepted his legacy, had always known he would take a wife who would provide him with an heir. Provide him with another guardian for the lions and the valley. And something would trigger the lion to kill her. He did not believe their combined strength and love could overcome the beast, the curse.

She closed her eyes for a moment and leaned against his warmth. Against his strength. It was the first time she felt so close to defeat. It was the first time she believed her husband might actually murder her.

All at once she wanted to get away from him, away from the *palazzo* where all things led back to him. She needed her brother. She needed normalcy. She couldn't allow despair to entrap her. "You have duties, Nicolai, and I need fresh air. I haven't seen my mare, and I think I'll take her for a short ride."

He stirred, a powerful man with too much knowledge in his amber eyes. "Riding her before she is trained to the scent of the lions would be dangerous, *cara*, and you will need an escort when you wish to travel these mountains and valleys. I'm certain your horse would welcome a visit in the stables, however. They are within the outer walls of the *castello*, and you should be perfectly safe."

Perfectly safe. She would never be safe again. But she was too tired to argue, too tired to do anything but get wearily to her feet and try to straighten her clothing. She couldn't look at him as she stood by the fire repairing the damage to her hair. She heard him dressing, taming his own hair into a semblance of order. When she felt she could be seen by others without inviting speculation or comment, she turned to leave.

Nicolai caught her at the door, all at once afraid of allowing her to leave his side, afraid he had lost her. He framed her face in his hands and kissed her soundly, kissed her until she kissed him back and sagged in defeat against him. When she was gone, he leaned against the door for a long time, his heart pounding in fear and his breath strangling in his throat.

Isabella hurried to her bedchamber to change her clothes. Her appearance still revealed too much evidence of Nicolai's possession, although she feared it showed more in her eyes than in her clothes. When she was satisfied she had chosen garb that wouldn't arouse suspicion—her riding outfit—she made her way to the lower story to locate Betto. He immediately provided her with instructions on how to find the stables. He offered her an escort, which she politely declined, wanting some time to herself to be able to clear her head and think. The gloom of her sentence was beginning to weigh heavily on her shoulders, and she needed breathing room.

Isabella inhaled the fresh, crisp air, grateful she was outdoors. The stables were inside the outer wall but some distance from the *palazzo*. She drew her cloak around her and stepped into the path, trodden by many servants and soldiers, leading toward the city. She followed the trail until it veered away from the direction she wanted to take. The thought of the city pulled at her, but she turned toward the stables. It had been too long since she had seen to her mare. The path to the stables had been tamped down by many feet, but it wasn't as wide or well traveled as the one leading toward the city, and the snow seemed to fall into her shoes no matter how carefully she walked.

Before she could enter the long building housing the horses, she caught sight of men walking their steeds back and forth through the fields. Each of the animals had cloth tied around its eyes and hooves. Some were sidestepping nervously, and others were tossing their heads in a fractious manner. The men reassured them, talking quietly, patting them as they paced back and forth and circled the field continuously.

Intrigued, Isabella wandered closer, careful to stay well back from the action. Someone shouted, waved a hand, and pointed toward a young horse that was rearing and snorting, its handler clearly having trouble coping with its fears. At the shouted instructions, the soldier took a firmer grip on the bridle, settling the animal, talking soothingly. Isabella recognized Sergio Drannacia directing the activities.

She waited on the edge of the field until he noticed her.

At once his face lit up. He said something to the man beside him and began to stride toward her.

As he drew near, she smiled and waved. "Sergio! What is it you're doing with the horses? Why do you have wraps on their feet, and why do you cover their eyes so?"

He hurried up to her. His handsome uniform accented his boyish good looks. "Isabella, what a wonderful surprise." Beaming at her, he took her hand and brought it gallantly to his lips. "What are you doing wandering around out here?"

She withdrew her hand and moved around him to watch the horses being walked or ridden up and down the field. "I wanted to visit my mare in the stable. Betto assured me she was well cared for, but I missed her. *Mio fratello*, Lucca, gave her to me, and right now she's all I have left of *mia famiglia*." Her voice was sad as she gazed out over the fields.

"Come watch," Sergio invited, taking her elbow to escort her. "We're training the horses for battle. We cannot have a beautiful woman feeling low on such a day as this."

"Aren't the horses already trained? They were prepared when we attempted to leave the valley, were they not?"

He shrugged. "It was a bad experience for them. We try to raise them with the scent and sounds of the lions to give us more of an advantage should we be attacked. It takes great patience on our part and great courage on the part of the horses; the lions are natural enemies to them, normally seeing them as prey. The incident near the pass was a setback to the horses, as one of the lions went rogue. If you noticed our mounts were nervous while we rode toward the pass, but they held steady. The lions were pacing alongside us just out of our sight."

"But the horses panicked."

"Only when the lions began taking up pack hunting positions. The horses were experienced enough to know the lions were warning us away from the pass. Now, however, it's imperative to retrain them and get them used to traveling with the lions close by."

"And the wraps on their hooves?"

"For silence. We cured and stretched skins. Times are uncertain, and our valley is rich with food and treasure. Although the cliffs and the narrow pass protect us, too many have looked upon our valley with greed. So we train hard and often. We've successfully fought off every enemy, but they will continue to try to take our lands."

"Are you worried about something in particular?" She felt a sudden tightness in her chest, a sudden knowledge. She saw too many horses for this to be simply a training exercise. "Is this because *Don* Rivellio has sent his men along with *mio fratello* to the valley? Is the holding in danger because of us?"

He smiled at her gently, a superior male smile meant to reassure her. "No enemy will get through the pass into the valley and live to talk of it. They will be buried here, and no one will go back and tell the tale. Thus we add to the legend of the valley."

Isabella could see the wisdom of his words. She had grown up listening to the mysterious stories of the DeMarco valley. No one knew whether to believe the tales, but the power of the unknown gave the *don* and his soldiers a tremendous advantage. Most armies already feared attempting to take over the holding. "Does it slow the horses down to wrap their hooves?"

He shook his head. "We take care to train them in the use of the wraps, and they become comfortable with them." He turned her around, leaning across her to point to the far side of the field. "Those are the younger, inexperienced horses. You can see they're having a harder time. Some are stumbling. The blinders are to keep them from balking at the sight of the lions."

"I don't see any lions," she said, looking around. Her heart beat faster at his words. She didn't think she'd ever get used to seeing the beasts up close.

"They're near enough that the horses pick up their scent, but we won't bring them closer until the younger horses settle down a bit," he explained.

"How do you control the lions? How do you keep them from attacking men and horses? Surely they have the inclination to eat your trainers." She shivered, rubbing her hands up and down her arms, remembering the utter terror of seeing one such beast up close, its eyes fixed on her.

"*Don* DeMarco controls the lions. Their behavior is his responsibility."

What a tremendous burden Nicolai had. And how terrible to live with a single failure. One misstep and a friend might die a death of pure horror.

A wild yell distracted her thoughts. "Captain Drannacia!" Alberita waved wildly to get his attention. She lifted her skirts and sprinted toward them, a flash of color, hair streaming wildly.

Isabella heard Sergio Drannacia's involuntary sigh of exasperation, and a long-suffering expression of impatience crossed his face fleetingly. As the servant girl came close, however, he smiled, his white teeth gleaming, his gaze running quickly over Alberita's curves as she halted, her breasts heaving beneath her thin blouse.

"What is it, young Alberita?" he asked kindly.

Apparently the mere fact that he had remembered her name and looked at her with recognition and approval had her breathless and staring up at him with utter devotion.

Isabella again saw clearly it was in Sergio's nature to respond gallantly to women no matter what their station or his interest. He flashed the exact same smile on anything female, though his gaze didn't trail after them as it did after his wife.

"Betto said to give you this missive from *Don* DeMarco." Alberita dropped a curtsey toward Isabella and squared her shoulders, looking important. "Sorry, *signorina*, but it's secret, to the captain only." She drew a small piece of parchment from the folds of her skirt, started to hand it to the

241

captain, drew it back to her as if she couldn't let it go, and then nearly threw it at him. It left her fingers before he could snatch it, and a gust of wind sent it spiraling away from them.

Alberita shrieked in horror, a high-pitched sound that hurt Isabella's ears, and raced forward, plowing into Sergio as he turned in an attempt to catch the willful missive. He caught Alberita's arms to steady her while Isabella pounced on the fluttering parchment as it landed in a nearby bush.

"*Signorina!*" Alberita wrung her hands, clearly distraught. "It's secret! It bears the DeMarco seal."

"I've got it behind my back, so I can't possibly look," Isabella assured her. "Captain," she continued soberly, her eyes meeting Sergio's with shared laughter, "you'll have to walk around me to retrieve your wayward message, as it must be of great importance. *Grazie*, Alberita. I shall tell *Don* DeMarco of your loyalty to him and the service you performed. You must go to Betto at once and tell him it is done. The missive is safe in the hands of Captain Drannacia, and all is well with the holding."

Sergio, seized by a sudden fit of coughing, courteously turned his back to them, his shoulders shaking. Alberita bowed and curtseyed, backing away until she tripped over the uneven ground. Then she caught up her skirts and ran toward the enormous *palazzo*.

Isabella waited until the young maid was safely out of hearing distance, then tapped Sergio on the back, laughing softly. "It's safe, Captain. She's gone and can't knock you to the ground or douse you with holy water or clobber you with a broom."

Sergio caught her shoulders, laughing so loudly she feared Alberita might hear all the way to *castello*. "Holy water? A broom? I don't know what you're talking about, but I'm certain that very frightening girl has something to do with it."

"She never walks anywhere—she's always running. But she's very enthusiastic about her work," Isabella was compelled to point out. She glanced toward the battlements and caught sight of Nicolai staring out across the fields at them. "*Don* DeMarco must be pleased with the training today. Does he always have to be present, whether the lions are near or not?" She waved toward Nicolai, but he either didn't notice or didn't acknowledge her.

Captain Drannacia dropped his hands from her shoulders the moment she called his attention to his *don*. He stiffened, nearly coming to attention. "He isn't watching the training, Isabella," he said thoughtfully, moving to put space between them. He opened the sealed parchment and scanned the contents, his jaw hardening. He stepped farther away from Isabella.

"That missive has nothing to do with secrets of state, does it, Captain Drannacia?" Isabella asked quietly.

"No, *signorina*, it doesn't," he answered.

She glanced up at the battlements again. Nicolai seemed a lonely figure, his long hair blowing in the wind, a tall, powerful *don* apart from his people. "Do you see him as the man he is, Captain Drannacia?" she asked.

"I see him as a dangerous predator at this moment," he replied gently. "In truth, *signorina*, more often lately I have seen the man, not the beast. I think he wants me to see the beast this time. As a warning, perhaps."

Her mouth tightened. "I grow tired of the way men think. Of their unfortunate and unbecoming jealousies." She glared up toward the battlements fiercely, whereas before her heart had gone out to Nicolai's solitude.

"Do you also grow tired of the unbecoming jealousies of women?"

A certain note in his voice warned her, and Isabella turned to see Violante in the distance. She stood watching them, a faint frown on her face, suspicion in her eyes. The moment she saw them turn toward her, she began approaching them. Isabella felt sorry for her. There was a lack of confidence in her step as she neared her husband, a basket on her arm.

243

Isabella waved a greeting. "I'm so glad you've come! I've been wanting to see you again."

"Violante." Sergio said his wife's name tenderly, and his dark eyes lit up at her approach. "What have you done for me now?" He reached for the basket with one hand and wrapped his other arm around her waist, bringing her close to him. "It is far for you to be walking without an escort," he said, as if they had discussed the subject many times.

"You must have your dinner, Sergio," she said uncertainly. "Isabella, I hadn't thought to find you here."

Isabella shrugged. "In truth, I needed the fresh air. I wanted to walk into the city, but Nicolai insisted I wait for an escort."

"I'd be most pleased to go with you tomorrow if it is convenient," Violante offered.

"I'd love that." Isabella could tell, as polite as both parties were being, that they wished her gone so they could be alone. "I'll take my leave and look forward to visiting with you on the morrow." She glanced up at Nicolai once more before walking toward the stables.

Chapter Fourteen

Isabella was feeling out of sorts when Sarina announced that Violante had arrived and was waiting for her in the library. She had spent the morning, as usual, attempting to familiarize herself with the *palazzo*. It seemed a huge task, more rooms at every turn, some of which had not been used in years, and an abundance of sculptures and artwork, treasures she could only gape at in awe. *Don* DeMarco was wealthy beyond her imagining. She knew if *Don* Rivellio had an inkling of the worth of the lands and property, he would be pushing to find a way to get his greedy hands on it.

She couldn't stop thinking of the despicable man who had condemned her brother to death. She knew he would always be a mortal enemy, one who would relentlessly seek her brother's demise. Lucca would have to spend the rest of his life looking over his shoulder, wondering when Rivellio would send out an assassin. Mostly she feared that the men traveling with her brother would be instructed to kill him the moment he was on DeMarco land, perhaps with a poisonous herb.

Isabella had hoped Francesca would visit, but she had waited in vain, finally drifting off to sleep. She had awakened several times, thinking Nicolai had entered the room, but if he had been there, he had only watched her from the shadows.

"If you are not up to visitors," Sarina said gently, compassion in her eyes, "I will send *Signora* Drannacia away."

Isabella hastily shook her head. "No, a visit is just the thing to cheer me up. She sent word earlier that she would escort me through the city and, if we had time, one of the many *villaggi*. I think the fresh air will do me good. It's stopped snowing, and the sun is out. It will be wonderful to be outdoors."

Violante stood and spoke as Isabella entered the room. "It's a wonderful day out. I hope I haven't kept you waiting. Sergio needed his lunch, and I prefer to bring it to him myself." She blushed a bit and patted her hair, as though it must be disheveled from a recent romp.

"Not at all, Violante," Isabella said. "I appreciate that you would want to take care of your husband. He's a very nice man, and he's lucky to have such an attentive wife." She blinked back tears that seemed to rise unexpectedly out of nowhere. Why hadn't Nicolai come to her in the night? Held her? She was badly in need of his reassurance.

"You look sad, Isabella." Violante laid a gloved hand on Isabella's arm. "I know we haven't become friends yet, but you may talk to me of what concerns you."

Isabella forced a smile. "*Grazie.* I can use a friend, Violante." She traced a finger along a smooth, polished table. "It's *mio fratello*, Lucca. He was traveling here, and I thought he'd arrive soon, but it seems he's much more ill than I knew. I can't go to him, and I don't even have a way of sending him a missive." Sorrow clawed at her, loneliness, and it was sharp and deep. Isabella turned away from the other woman to stare sightlessly at a painting on the wall.

"You know how to read?" Violante's voice held awe, admiration, even envy. "You can write? *Mia madre* believed a woman had no need to know such things." She sighed. "Sergio often reads, and sometimes he reads aloud to me, but once, when he was very annoyed with me, he said he wished I could read so our children would learn." Her expression mirrored a deep sorrow. "So far, I am a great disappointment. No *bambini*, and I can't read." She forced a laugh, but it held no humor.

"You'll have a *bambino*, Violante," Isabella said in an effort to console the woman. "Have you spoken with the healer? I know our healer offered much advice to the women in out *villaggio* when they wished to have a *bambino*."

"*Grazie*, Isabella. I hope you're right. But I'm afraid I'm too old." She turned her head away, but not before Isabella saw tears glittering in her eyes.

"Violante!" Isabella was shocked. "You're not that old. You can't be more than a couple of years older than I. You certainly are not too old to have a *bambino*. Speak to your healer, and if that doesn't help, I'll send word to my healer to see if she has any advice."

"You would do that for me?" Violante's voice trembled.

"Well, of course. I would like us to be friends and would hope our *bambini* would play together. Come, I'll show you how easy it is to make marks upon the page. I'll write your name for you." Isabella opened the great desk and searched until she found the small box containing dye and a quill.

Violante crowded close to her, and Isabella carefully made swirling marks along a piece of parchment.

Violante inhaled sharply. "That's me? That's my name?"

Isabella nodded. "Doesn't it look beautiful? I remember the first time Lucca showed me my name." She wrote her own name on the bottom of the parchment with a flourish. She studied it for a moment with a critical eye.

"What would you say in a letter to your brother if you

were to write to him?" Violante asked, curious. "How would you write it?"

Isabella smoothed the parchment with one fingertip. "I'd write his name here, just below where yours is." She did so and added a couple of sample lines. "This says that I miss him and wish he would hurry and join me. I'm not really good at all the letters. I don't practice enough. You see where some of the lines waver." She blew on the wet dye to dry it, pleased she had found a way to begin a friendship with Sergio Drannacia's wife.

"That seems many marks for those words," Violante observed.

Isabella swallowed hard. "I added that I love him—silly, when he'll never see it."

"You said your brother was being held in the dungeons of *Don* Rivellio," Violante remembered. "I'm so glad he was released. Theresa dislikes him intensely. The *don* has a reputation of being difficult."

"A nice word to describe him, *Signora* Drannacia," Isabella said dryly. "How in the world did *Signora* Bartolmei have dealings with *Don* Rivellio?" Isabella was curious, despite her dislike of gossip.

"You must call me Violante," the older woman implored. "Theresa is, of course, a cousin to *Don* DeMarco. She was raised on a farm, nowhere near the *palazzo*, yet she is an *aristocratica*." There was a hint of envy, of frustration, in Violante's tone. "She wed Rolando Bartolmei, who, like Sergio, also carries a great name. Naturally, she and her kin are invited to all the celebrations in the other holdings."

Isabella sat down at the table and studied Violante's face. The mixture of jealousy and relief she saw there was nearly humorous. But Violante's expression was serious. "Theresa and Rolando took Chanise, her younger sister, with them to a festival. *Don* Rivellio was there. He paid particular attention to Chanise, although she was but eleven summers."

Isabella's heart jumped. Very deliberately she folded her hands in her lap to keep from betraying her agitation. A child's fear was blossoming in her stomach and spreading rapidly.

"Theresa said the *don* was gallant and charming. They were all impressed with his attentions. Chanise seemed very enamored of him. But she disappeared. They were frantic and looked everywhere for her, but to no avail." Violante sighed. "Chanise was a beautiful child, very much loved. I used to wish I had a little *bambina* just like her."

Isabella rubbed at her suddenly throbbing temples. "Did they ever find her?"

Violante nodded. "After much time passed, *Don* Rivellio sent word that Chanise had hidden in his carriage and insisted on staying with him. She had a *bambino* but was very ill. There is a sickness the people of this valley get if we are away too long. If we don't return, we wither and die. Theresa and Rolando brought her home. She doesn't speak. Not to anyone at all." Violante sighed softly. "I go to see her often, but she won't speak to me. She stares at the floor. She has scars on her wrists and ankles. Theresa told me there are stripe marks on her back. The *bambino* is the only one she responds to. I think she would take her own life if she didn't have him. Rolando and Theresa loathe *Don* Rivellio, and I can't blame them."

"Does *Don* DeMarco know about this?" Of course he knew. He knew everything that went on inside and outside his valley. Isabella couldn't imagine Nicolai's allowing such an atrocity to go unpunished. She didn't believe for one moment that the child had chosen to go with Rivellio.

"He arranged for safe passage for Chanise and bargained with *Don* Rivellio for her release when the *don* pretended to be reluctant to let her and the *bambino* go. He claimed he wasn't certain, but the *bambino* might be one of his." Violante gave an inelegant sniff. "If Chanise was ever with any other man, it was because the *don* gave her to them. *Don* DeMarco paid a great deal of money to get her back— at least that was the rumor. Theresa doesn't talk about it at all. I think she feels guilty because she gave in to her sister's pleas to attend the celebration."

Violante shook her head. "In truth, no one could resist Chanise. She was like sunshine dancing on water. Theresa never speaks of it anymore, but the sadness and guilt will always be with her, and she deserves better."

"You feel sorrow, too," Isabella observed. "You must be very close to Theresa and her *famiglia*."

"Enough talk of sadness. I came to cheer you up." Determinedly Violante stood and looked around for her gloves. "We really should be going if I'm to show you around. Darkness falls quickly here in the mountains."

Isabella stood, too, pulling on her gloves distractedly. Along with Violante's story of *Don* Rivellio's debauchery and depravity came that sense of evil. It crept into the room, dark and malignant, as if the very name of Rivellio summoned what was already twisted. Isabella shivered and looked around her, wanting to be out in the open where she could see any enemy approaching. At times, she had discovered, she felt surrounded by enemies.

Violante shivered visibly, as if she, too, were affected by the very name of Rivellio. In her haste to leave the room, she moved too quickly and knocked a massive tome from the edge of a shelf. It slammed to the floor with a thud. Violante turned crimson and gave a mortified squeak.

"I've done it more than once," Isabella said hastily, knowing how chagrined Violante became over the slightest social error. She stooped to retrieve the large book. It was heavier than she had anticipated, and it slipped from her fingers to land with a second loud thud. She laughed softly, wanting to dispel the tension in the room, but it swirled in her stomach persistently.

She was more than happy to follow Violante out of the *palazzo* into the fresh, crisp air. Isabella inhaled deeply. The wind rustled through the trees, and the leaves glittered a beautiful silver. Branches swayed gently. The world seemed a dazzling place of silver and white. They followed the well-worn path that led from the large *castello*, a nearly impregnable fortress, past the outer walls to the city of houses and shops. The marketplace felt familiar—the smells and sights, the stalls, the narrow steps and small courtyards where people gathered to talk and to trade items of interest. Rows of buildings sprawled in every direction, creating a tight-knit community of people who lived and worked in or near the *castello*.

Isabella wistfully watched some children playing, throwing snow at one another. She had never done such a thing, and it looked like great fun. She stood a moment watching. "Where I grew up, we didn't have snow. Did you play like that, Violante, when you were a child?"

"Sometimes. Mostly *mia madre* refused to let me go outside with the others. It was important to her to choose my friends." She, too, was watching the children, a look of longing on her face.

Isabella looked around carefully to ensure no adults stood nearby. Then she stooped and gathered some icy crystals into her hand, shaping and packing them as she had seen the children do.

Violante backed away from Isabella, shaking her head in warning. "Don't you dare! We're hardly little ragamuffins to play at such things."

"Why should they have all the fun?" Isabella asked with a wicked grin.

A snowball landed on the back of Isabella's neck, splattering down the back of her dress. She squealed, whirling around, expecting to face the children. Theresa, a few feet away from her, was gathering more snow quickly, laughing as she did so. She looked quite at ease with the game, packing the ice crystals with swift, efficient movements.

Isabella hastily flung her snowball at Theresa, laughing so hard she nearly slipped and fell. Theresa was just straightening up, and the snowball hit her shoulder, the ice clinging to her sleeve. She hurled her compacted sphere back at Isabella, who leapt sideways, ducking as she did so, already reaching to scoop up more snow.

Violante screamed as snow splattered over her shoulder and neck. She stumbled backward and fell, landing in the wet flakes. "Ooh!" She spluttered for a moment, as if she couldn't make her mind up whether to laugh, be angry, or cry.

Theresa and Isabella were in an all-out war, hurling snowballs back and forth fast and furiously. Violante determinedly formed several spheres and threw them with unexpected accuracy at the other two women.

Both tried to retaliate, their gloved hands bringing up fistfuls of snow and flinging it back at Violante, their carefree laughter rising without inhibition to be carried on the wind.

"What is going on here, ladies?" The voice was low, amused. Male.

"Theresa!" The name was hissed in a stunned, embarrassed voice, stiff with disapproval and reprimand.

"Violante?" The third voice was more shocked than embarrassed.

All three women ceased instantly, turning to face the speakers. Violante's and Theresa's laughter died, replaced by horror and shame. Isabella's gaze danced with merriment and a hint of mischief as she looked at the *don*.

Sergio Drannacia and Rolando Bartolmei stood gaping at their wives in a kind of astounded silence.

Nicolai spoke first. "Ladies?" He managed a courtly bow, but he couldn't keep the trace of amusement from his voice.

"A battle, *signore*," Isabella answered, deliberately packing the snow in her hand tighter. "I fear it is unfortunate for you and your captains that you walked into the middle of it." Without hesitation she threw her missile straight at *Don* DeMarco. "You may get hit in the heavy action."

Nicolai deflected the projectile in midair, preventing it from hitting his head. Ignoring his shocked companions, he bent to scoop up handfuls of snow. "You just made a mistake, *signorina*. No one is better than I at this type of warfare," he declared.

Isabella took Violante's hand and began backing up, laughing. Violante caught at Theresa, who remained stiffly staring at the ground.

"With your permission to disagree, *Don* DeMarco," Sergio said, reaching for some snow. "I believe *I* used to be the champion." He fired off two snowballs at Nicolai, both hitting their target, then lobbed a third projectile playfully at his wife.

Violante lifted her skirts to run, but the ice crystals hit her shoulder before she could move. Without hesitation she caught up handfuls of the flakes and tossed them at her husband, running backward as she did so.

Isabella hit Rolando square in the middle of his forehead and doubled over laughing at his expression. Nicolai took advantage of her merriment, pelting her with snow until she was nearly covered in white flakes.

Rolando began to laugh, suddenly stooping to shape the snow into weapons of his own. He threw two at Isabella, who was laughing so hard she couldn't retaliate.

"Theresa! Help!" Isabella pleaded as Nicolai dove at her. Violante clearly had her hands full warding off her husband.

Isabella's pleas roused Theresa to action, and she proved to be the best of the women at the warfare, accurate and swift. Isabella loved the sound of Nicolai's laughter. More than anything else, she loved that the others saw him as she did. A man. He seemed young and carefree, the battle fast and heated, his worries set aside for the childhood game. She loved the feel of his arms around her waist as he rushed upon her, tipping them both into the snow. She felt the brush of his lips in her hair as he kissed her temple before firing off a flurry of snowballs at Sergio and Rolando.

It was all over much too soon, the men helping the women out of the snow and dusting off their clothes. Children had crowded around to cheer them on, most staring in awe at *Don* DeMarco, shocked and happy that they saw him out and about.

Nicolai brushed the snow from Isabella's hair and shoulders, his hand lingering against the nape of her neck. She looked happy, her eyes sparkling with joy. Everything in him melted as it always did when she was near. Isabella. His world. "Where were you going, Isabella?" he asked, his gaze scanning the crowds restlessly as if something or someone might harm her. "I wasn't informed you were going out."

"How dreadful." She reached up and brushed snow from his wild hair with her gloved fingertips. "You really must talk to those spies of yours. They aren't doing their job." Her gown was wet, and she was beginning to shiver despite her warm cloak.

He caught her chin firmly and forced her to meet his gaze. "You need to get warm. Go back to the *palazzo*," he ordered.

"You have incredibly beautiful eyes." She flashed a sassy grin. "Very unusual." She loved the color, gold with nearly translucent irises, loved his long, almost feminine lashes.

"You told me the truth when you said you did not understand the meaning of the word *obey*. You do not *obey* even the dictates of your *don*." He leaned close, so that his lips were against her ear, so that his body brushed hers, sending little whips of lightning dancing through her bloodstream. "Do not think to distract me with your pretty words."

"Never, *signore*. I would never consider such a thing." Her mouth curved in a tempting smile. "I believe you men have much to do, so we will, of course, excuse you to your more *serious* duties."

Nicolai couldn't resist the temptation of her smiling lips. He simply bent his head and fastened his mouth to hers. Just like that he created magic, fanning a fire from smoldering embers so that flames raced through her bloodstream and her body throbbed and pulsed in reaction.

Energy crackled around them, and the very air seemed alive. He lifted his head slowly, regretfully, oblivious of the children giggling and the four grown-ups staring in shock at him. His hands framed her face, and he kissed the tip of her nose. "It grows dark quickly in the mountains. Return home soon."

A bit bemused, Isabella nodded, touching her mouth, where she could still feel him, still taste him.

Nicolai clapped his hands, and the children scattered in alarm as he waved them off. Sergio and Rolando followed him as he strode away from the city and toward the dense forest. Isabella stood staring after the three men.

Violante and Theresa were grinning at her. Isabella's body was aching with need, with a hunger that was fast becoming familiar to her. Finally she blinked at the two women, as if she were astonished to see them standing there. "What?" she asked. But she knew what. Nicolai had rocked the world for her, set it on fire, and she would never feel the same, never be the same again.

"How is it I could see him?" Theresa asked, wonder in her voice.

Isabella pressed a hand to her stomach. "He's a man, Theresa. Why wouldn't you see him?" She felt strange, shaky. The feeling crept over her, and she shivered, drawing her cloak closer around her. "You should *always* see him as a man."

"I didn't mean to offend you," Theresa said stiffly. "I was amazed, that's all. He rarely makes appearances."

"I'm hoping to change that," Isabella answered with a small smile, trying to recapture the camaraderie of their game. She knew she had snapped at Theresa, knew the people in the holding rarely looked at Nicolai, afraid they would see the illusion of the lion. Isabella hadn't meant to snap, but she felt unsettled. It bothered her that no one seemed to consider the loneliness of Nicolai's existence, and that the way they all treated him might contribute to the illusion itself.

"The game was fun," Violante said, "but cold." She rubbed her hands up and down her arms to warm herself. "I couldn't believe it when Sergio began to throw snow at us." She attempted to pat her hair back into place, aware of her disheveled appearance. "I don't suppose I look very beautiful all mussed." Her gaze moved over Isabella and Theresa critically, enviously, the laughter fading from her eyes. "Theresa, your hair has fallen on one side, and your face is red. I guess it's impossible for us to look as good as Isabella does."

"But I'm a mess," Isabella said, surveying her wet cloak and gown. Her stomach was knotting, and she clenched her teeth.

"I noticed Rolando enjoyed the game while he was playing with *you*, Isabella," Violante chattered on. "If you hadn't thrown snow at him, he might have given poor Theresa another one of his lessons on how to behave."

"Well, there's no doubt Theresa's the best at our little war." Isabella beamed determinedly at her. "You hit your target every time."

"I have two younger brothers," Theresa admitted. "I've had lots of practice. I must go. I was visiting a friend but must get back." She lifted a hand and moved off, following the pathway that led to the rows of buildings.

Isabella watched her until she was out of sight. "I didn't know she had two brothers. She didn't mention them before."

"They're under Rolando's command," Violante said. "Theresa is lucky that her *famiglia* is so close. I would have thought being raised on a farm would keep one from being able to fit in at court, but her *famiglia* does it easily."

Violante's voice was so wistful, Isabella wrapped an arm around her waist and hugged her gently as they began walking. "I don't think any of us have your grace and presence, Violante, I grew up running *mia famiglia's palazzo*, and I still can't manage to look as confident and fashionable as you. I'm always saying and doing the wrong thing."

Violante looked down at her wet gloves. "I saw the way *Don* DeMarco held you and kissed you. I saw the love on his face. You have something I'll never have."

Isabella stopped walking to face the other woman. "I've seen your husband when he looks at you," she said softly. "You have no reason to fear he cares for any woman other than you."

Violante pressed a trembling hand to her lips, blinking rapidly to prevent tears from spilling over. "*Grazie,* Isabella. You are a true friend to say such a thing."

"I only tell you what I see."

"I just want you to be prepared, Isabella. Nicolai is a powerful man, a man other women will want. Once they see him, they will gaze upon him with lustful, greedy eyes. You will be unable to know what woman is friend or foe. A man can be weak when females throw themselves at him."

"Has this happened to you?" Isabella could not reconcile the man who had played with such glee in the snow with a man capable of betraying his wife.

Violante shrugged. "I see the way women flirt with him. And they think me old and barren."

"It matters little what other women think," Isabella said softly, "only what your husband thinks. And he sees you with the eyes of love. You must know you are beautiful." Isabella sensed that Violante was becoming uncomfortable with the private disclosures, so she searched for a distraction. "Oh, look! The marketplace."

Gratefully Violante turned her attention to the wares. They hurried to the long rows of stalls, exclaiming over the various treasures they found.

Isabella found the people of the holding pleasant and informative. They crowded around her eagerly, wanting to meet her. Violante stayed close, agreeable and friendly but making certain Isabella had room to move through the many stalls and stands. Violante became distracted when she spotted a carved box the perfect size for trinkets she had acquired, but as she reached for it, another woman lifted it up for inspection.

Isabella shook her head as an argument broke out between the two women. She knew the other woman would not get the carved box if Violante wanted it. Violante could be tenacious.

A fluttering of color caught Isabella's attention as a woman with a mane of flowing black hair disappeared around the corner of a building. She moved much as Francesca did and was of her height and build. Few women wore their hair unbound. The color of her gown was unusual, too—a starburst of royal blue she had seen before. Certain it was Francesca, Isabella hurried down the row and turned up a narrow walkway. No one was in sight. She quickened her steps, peering down several side paths that led to small courtyards and also to a network of other walkways that meandered through the city. After several minutes of searching, Isabella sighed and turned back toward the marketplace. No one managed to disappear quite as quickly as Francesca.

A long row of large buildings caught her attention. They were beautiful and carved with the inevitable lions. She walked slow toward them, studying the various renditions of the huge beast. Isabella found them fascinating. Something about their eyes, no matter how they were depicted, drew her attention. The eyes seemed alive, as if they were watching her from every direction. She turned first one way and then another, but always the eyes were watching.

Although the buildings blocked the wind, she shivered, drawing her cloak closer. It was growing late, and she found she was inexplicably weary. Shadows were lengthening, and the multitude of stairs and pathways grew gray. She became aware of the silence, and a chill slid down her spine. Isabella turned to head back in the direction of the marketplace. She slipped on a patch of ice and went down hard, striking her back against the corner of a building. The talon marks were healing, but they throbbed now, reminding her of her frightening encounter. She sat up carefully, looking around, wishing she were in out of the snow.

It took several tries to get to her feet on the icy walkway. As the shadows grew, the temperature dropped, and the cold was piercing. The walkway glistened with ice. It might be wiser to choose a less slippery path. Isabella took a narrow, less steep walkway without stairs and began to walk down it. She was hoping it would lead straight to the marketplace at the center of the city, but the path opened into a courtyard. Sculptures were scattered around, but she saw no people.

She stood still in a moment of indecision. If she took the time to find her way back to the marketplace through the unfamiliar maze of buildings and paths, it might be dark by the time she made her way out. It seemed a better idea to return to the *palazzo*. It was high above the city, and all she had to do was make her way uphill. There would be no missing the enormous *castello*. She was certain Violante would go there as soon as she realized Isabella had lost her way.

Lucca would laugh at her for getting lost. It wasn't often she managed to lose her way, yet twice now she had gotten turned around. *Almost as if everything had deliberately shifted on her.* The thought was chilling and brought back the strange sense of being watched. Isabella clamped down on her wild imagination. Buildings couldn't move. *But then, men couldn't become lions.*

The feeling of being watched persisted. Isabella glanced around. There was a large statue of a lion in the courtyard. It seemed to be watching her, but that didn't account for the heavy weight of malevolence she felt. Abruptly she began to walk along a narrow path that led upward. She was uncertain why she saw no people. Did they go into their homes as the sun went down to prevent a disaster with a stray lion? A chill went down her spine again at the thought.

She heard it then. Soft. Barely discernable. A huffing noise. A whisper of fur sliding against something solid. She began to walk faster up the path, huddling in her cloak, her heart pounding with each step. She felt its presence. Knew it was stalking her, following her scent. Moving deliberately slow to terrorize her.

Nicolai? Would he do such a thing to teach her a lesson? Was the curse unfolding because he had lain with her? He had watched her from the battlements as she spoke with Sergio. He had even sent Sergio some missive warning him away from her. She had been certain that he had come into her room the night before. That *something* had visited her room. She shivered again and rubbed her arms for warmth. She had felt eyes on her in the night. She should have felt Nicolai's arms, but he had left her alone. Was he jealous enough to stalk her, hunt her down, and devour her?

Isabella went very still, ashamed of herself. She recognized the subtle flow of power directed at her. It fed her doubts, fed her fears. If she didn't believe in Nicolai, in his strength, no other ever would. She would not think it was Nicolai. She would not give in to the curse. Nor would she allow the entity any influence over her. But she knew she was in grave danger.

Isabella clutched at the fastening of her cloak as if she could feel the lion sinking its teeth into her throat. She heard the peculiar grunting noise the lions often made. A beast was definitely trailing her. Isabella rounded a corner, and her heart nearly stopped. For a moment she was certain she had come to a dead end. A line of buildings blocked her way.

"Nicolai." She whispered his name. A talisman. "Nicolai," she said aloud as she raced toward two buildings that looked as if they might be homes. "Nicolai!" She called his name as loudly as she could, a sob in her voice as she rushed to the door of the nearest house and pounded on it. The lion huffed again. It was much closer. And no one was home, the door secure. Isabella felt the swell of triumph in the air. Of evil. She wasn't alone with the lion. The entity was there. Real. Seething with malevolence. It filled the small area between the houses with a thick cloud of venom.

"Isabella!" She heard Nicolai's voice and went weak with relief, sinking to the steps in front of the building. "Answer me!" There was panic in Nicolai's voice.

"Here, Nicolai, I'm here." She knew he would hear the fear and relief in her voice. "Hurry! There's a lion."

She saw it then, the dark shape hidden in the shadows. Its eyes glowed a fierce red loathing of her. Isabella stared back, mesmerized by such intense hatred. The creature sank into a crouch, watching her, hating her.

"Isabella! If anything dares to harm you, nothing, no one will be safe in this valley," he vowed. She could hear the pounding of his horse's hooves as he followed her scent through the maze of streets. There was an edge to his voice, as if he had reached out to control the beast and found it resistant.

She strained to see the lion, but it was well in the shadows. Only the eyes were clear, glowing at her with a wicked promise. The lion was aware of Nicolai's approach, and it snarled once, revealing huge teeth that gleamed at her from the shadows. Suddenly the beast whipped around and simply disappeared between the buildings.

Nicolai rode around the corner at a dead gallop and had to pull up his horse before it trampled her. He was out of the saddle before the animal even stopped. His face was pale, his hair wild. He dragged her into his arms and crushed her to him. "I'm going to tie you to my side." It was a vow, nothing less. His hands framed her face, forcing her head up so he could find her mouth with his. Fear welded them together.

His hands ran over her, searching every square inch of her, needing to make certain that she was all in one piece. It had driven his breath right out of his body, that sudden knowledge among the lions that his woman was being hunted. "Isabella, this can't go on. It has to stop. You're driving me out of my mind with your heedless ways." His hands tightened on her arms, and he shook her. "You're in danger. Why can't you understand that? From me, from this valley, from everyone. You're so fearless, so headstrong, you don't seem to be able to stay out of trouble for one moment." He shook her again and then once more blotted out the world, his mouth finding hers somewhere between anger and sheer terror.

And then they were both out of control, kissing wildly, tearing at each other's clothes, trying to find skin, oblivious to the darkness, the cold, the enmity of the lion that had been stalking her. She wanted the solace and heat of his body, the joining of their bodies. She wanted him to fill her completely so that she could think only of him, of pleasure.

He pushed her deeper into the shadows, forcing her against the wall of the building deep within the courtyard. His mouth was hot and dominant, a wild response to his fear. He tugged at the string of her neckline, loosening her top so that he could shove the material down, exposing her breasts to his exploration.

Isabella slid one leg up his, nearly as wild as he was, pressing tightly against his thick arousal, rubbing her body against his. It was wicked to be standing outside with her breasts exposed to him, but she loved it, loved watching him look at her. Her nipples hardened in the cold air, and she cried out when he cupped the weight in his hands and bent to suckle. At once his mouth was driving her crazy with need, making her weak so that she clung tighter to him, her leg wrapped around his waist to align her body more perfectly with his.

"It's too cold out here for you," he whispered as his teeth skimmed her nipples and his tongue stroked caresses over her breasts. His mouth, hot and moist, was branding her, claiming her for his own.

"Then warm me up, Nicolai, right here, right now."

"It's going to have to be fast, *piccola*. Are you certain you're ready for me? I don't want to hurt you." He was already checking for himself, sliding his hand up her thigh to find her heated, damp entrance. He pushed into her even as he pressed her tighter against the wall. "I want to make certain, *cara*," he said, lifting her to an outcropping on the wall, bunching her skirt around her waist. He wrapped her legs around his neck.

"Nicolai!" She sobbed his name, her fists clenched tightly in his hair for anchor as he stroked his thumb over her core.

He bent his head and replaced his hand with his mouth, his tongue stabbing deeply. Her body went wild, bucking against him, fragmenting, so that she was pleading with him to stop even as she held his head to her. He felt the orgasm take her, again and again, before he lifted his head, satisfied she was ready for him.

"You'll have to help me. It's cold tonight, and that can take away a man's ability," he said as he allowed her feet to touch the ground. He was unfastening his breeches, his body already hot and thick.

"Tell me, Nicolai," she pleaded. "I want you so much right now."

"Keep me hot. Take me in your mouth, Isabella." He guided her head. "Wrap your fingers around me and squeeze gently, firmly. *Dio!*" He gasped as her mouth took possession of him, hot and tight and untutored but willing. He guided her as best he could when he could barely stand with the waves of pleasure washing over him. His hands found the back of her head even as his hips thrust helplessly.

He watched her through half-closed eyes, marveling at her ability to please him in every way. He loved her body, her mind, and now even her mouth was priceless. Before he could embarrass himself, he dragged her up and simply lifted her in his arms, resting her weight against the building. "Wrap your legs around my waist."

Isabella pulled her skirt aside and locked her ankles behind his back. She could feel him pressed tightly against her. Slowly he lowered her body so that she settled over the thick length of him, inch by delicious inch, an agony of pleasure. At first Nicolai allowed her the lead, watching her face, her dreamy, sultry expression as she began to move, began to ride him. She was strong, her muscles firm and tight. She started slowly, loving the way she could lift her hips and clench her muscles to bring him even greater pleasure.

"You like that, don't you?" she whispered.

Nicolai nodded, unable to speak, as he tightened his grip on her hips. He began to thrust upward hard as he brought her body down to meet his. She gasped, clutching at his shoulders, fingers biting into his skin. He did what she needed most—drove out every worrisome thought until there was only the reality of Nicolai, his body taking hers with hard, long strokes, burying himself deeply inside her while her body gripped his and wound tighter and tighter until she let go, flying high, soaring free, exploding with sheer elation. They came together there in the darkness with danger surrounding them, with snow on the ground and in the midst of a city. They came together in fire and passion.

Chapter Fifteen

Isabella lay beneath the coverlet, grateful for the warmth of the fire. It lent the room a feeling of safety. She watched Nicolai light the candelabra on the mantel; watched the way his muscles moved and flexed beneath his shirt. She hadn't realized how cold she was until she dressed for bed. All too conscious of Nicolai intending to share her bedchamber, she had donned fine intimate apparel and found it less than satisfactory at keeping her warm. The lace hugged her breasts and slithered over her waist and hips, sinfully clinging to her every curve. Shivering, she almost exchanged it for a warmer gown, but its sensuous beauty was too much to resist.

For the first time she was confused, even embarrassed, over her wanton behavior with Nicolai. She had been so frightened, knowing she was stalked by a lion. Then she had been so relieved to see him, to know he wasn't the predator. Then . . . She bit her lower lip and turned her face into the feather pillow. She had been out of control, wanting him with every fiber of her being, wanting his possession of her to drive away all thought, leaving only feelings. The things they had done together . . . She wondered if it meant she was wicked beyond redemption. She wished her mother were alive to advise her. She had no one to turn to. No one other than Nicolai.

Nicolai had lit the fire himself, arranged for hot tea and biscuits, and had called his most trusted servants, Betto and Sarina, instructing them that someone was to be watching over Isabella at all times when she moved about the *palazzo*. It should have annoyed her, but it made her feel cherished. He had, of course, gone to his own apartments but had used the hidden passageway to return to her bedchamber the moment the *castello* settled down for the night.

Nicolai looked down at her pale face, the shadows that his valley, his people, even he, had put in the depths of her eyes. Unable to keep from touching her, he smoothed back her hair with gentle fingers. "I know this has been a trying day for you. I just want to hold you, *piccola*, hold you close to me and comfort you."

She turned over to lie on her back and look up at his beloved face, drinking in every detail, every line. She loved looking at him. His wild hair and unusual eyes. His broad shoulders and tall, muscular body. Even the scars on his face seemed to belong, giving him a mysterious, dangerous aura.

He was enormously strong, yet his touch on her skin could be incredibly gentle. His eyes could blaze with fierce possessiveness, burn hot with desire, or be as cold as ice, yet stark need would suddenly creep into his gaze. He exuded confidence, a man born to power, yet at those times vulnerability would be etched into every line of his face. He could make her weak with desire with one look; another look could have her struggling to control her temper. Nicolai DeMarco was a man who needed a woman to love him. And God help her, she did.

She couldn't resist him. She couldn't resist his need of

her, his elemental hunger for her. A part of her wanted to hide, to run away from all that had happened between them. Another part wanted comfort, wanted to be held in his arms, close to his body. She said nothing at all, just watched as he purposefully undressed, completely at ease with his nakedness. Propriety dictated she look away, not stare at him with such matching hunger, but it was impossible, and deep inside her the butterfly wings fluttered and warmth spread.

Nicolai lifted the coverlet and slid in beside her. "I know you're tired, *cara mia*. I see it in your eyes, and I want you to sleep. I just want to hold you close. You are so soft and warm, and you feel so right in my arms." His voice was a sorcerer's whisper in her ear. His breath was a warm enticement. He pulled her close to him and fit her tightly into the curve of his body. It all felt far too intimate there in the flickering candlelight with the memory of their recent, wanton passion still burning in her mind.

Isabella closed her eyes to block out the sight of him, but it was impossible to block out the masculine scent of him, the feel of his hard muscles imprinted on her body. His arms crept around her waist, his hands locked beneath her breasts. She was acutely aware of the way his fingers moved, seeking her skin beneath the lace of her gown. Her skin felt hot, and her breasts were full and aching for his touch.

They lay for some time in silence, with only the fire crackling and popping and the flickering flames from the candles throwing dancing figures on the wall. Feeling protected and treasured, Isabella snuggled closer against his solid frame.

Nicolai pressed his mouth into the nape of her neck, then felt his erection swelling and thickening against her body. He let it happen, savoring his need of her, determined he would let her rest. He could have her again and again. Share her bed. Her body. Her thoughts. Her heart and soul. Touching her would be enough for now. Tasting her. Knowing she was in bed beside him, that her body craved his with the same hunger he felt. He moved one hand up to her

267

breast to cup the warmth. Soft flesh filled his palm. Lazily his thumb caressed her nipple through the delicate lace.

Isabella shifted restlessly. "How am I supposed to go to sleep?" Her voice held a soft, sensuous note, a hint of laughter, and no reprimand.

He lifted his head to nuzzle the valley between her breasts, his tongue sliding over her skin, his hands carefully pushing the lace aside. "You go to sleep and dream of me. Take me with you wherever you go, *bellezza*. Take the feel of my hands and mouth with you so no one dares to creep in to disturb your dreams." His tongue flicked at a nipple, once, twice, his hand kneading with exquisite gentleness. He lowered his head and drew her into his hot mouth.

A rush of heat consumed her, and her legs moved restlessly. Her arms circled his head to hold him to her. Nicolai suckled there, one hand sliding down her back to press her against his painful erection, holding her there. Then, as he pulled strongly at her breast, his hand slipped lower, dragging the hem of her gown up over her triangle of tight curls.

Her body clenched tightly, the sweet ache becoming urgent and demanding. She moved her hips, but his hand pressed against her damp mound and held her still. "Just let it happen slowly, *piccola*. There's no need to rush. Let it happen." He circled her nipple with his tongue, and went back to suckling.

Isabella was acutely conscious of his hand moving, sliding over her, into her, picking up the rhythm of his mouth. His fingers were clever, caressing her, disappearing deeply, stretching her, exploring, finding her thighs again. Her body shuddered with pleasure. It was almost more than she could bear.

Nicolai abruptly lifted his head from the temptation of her breasts. Isabella heard the coughing grunt of a lion nearby. She watched him turn his head one way, then the other, as if listening. The silken fall of his long hair brushed her skin, sending flames licking along her nerve endings. She shivered beneath the onslaught. His fingers were deep inside her, stroking little caresses so that waves of fire seemed to wash over her, through her.

Nicolai pressed his forehead against hers. "I'm sorry. I meant only to hold you, not make you ache. I swear to you, I'll be back." Reluctantly he withdrew his fingers from her. "Intruders are approaching the pass. I must go."

Her body was begging for release, but she nodded at him, aware of the anguish in his eyes, aware he wanted to hold her and comfort her, aware he had meant to love her slowly and thoroughly. She hugged the knowledge to her and nodded again. "Go where you're needed, Nicolai." She needed him. Isabella curled her fists at her sides and kept her expression carefully blank.

Nicolai kissed her again, then regretfully pulled on his clothes with swift, fluid ease. "I'll be back, Isabella." He hesitated for a moment, searching for something to say to ease his leaving her, but nothing came to mind. Thank the good Madonna she didn't weep or beg; he would have hated that. Yet she looked so alone and vulnerable, it ate at his insides. *"Ti amo."* The words slipped out before he could stop them, straight from his soul. He turned and left the room by way of the hidden passage, careful of her reputation even with the lions summoning him.

With a groan, Isabella buried her face in the pillow and just breathed. Her body was on fire, her heart felt bruised, and confusion reigned in her mind. But he had said he loved her. She wrapped herself up in those words, in the sound of his voice, armor to shield her from her own fears.

A small sound alerted her, and she glanced toward the passageway, frowning, certain he couldn't have returned so quickly.

Francesca peeked around the doorway of the passage, one eyebrow raised, her impish grin engaging. "I thought he'd never leave. I've been shivering in the passage. It's freezing in there. I had to hide around the corner when he came out. I was waiting to speak with you." In the flickering of the fireplace, she looked a young, fey woman-child. She tiptoed

269

into the center of the room. "So where did he go?"

"I think he heard someone prowling around and went to inspect the premises," Isabella improvised, certain Nicolai wouldn't want her repeating the truth. She sat up, drawing the coverlet up over her, a smile on her face. "You disappear so fast, Francesca, and I can never find you."

"You've had company," Francesca pointed out. "And I'll have to listen carefully from now on, or he'll catch me in here."

"I've missed you. I went out today and had my very first snow fight. In the city. And yesterday I saw the horses being trained." She plucked at the quilts for a moment. "And a lion chased me."

"What?" Francesca swung around, her dark eyes sparkling with unexpected fury. Isabella had never seen even a flash of temper in the young woman. "That isn't possible. All the lions know you are the one."

"At least one of the lions doesn't want me to be the one," Isabella said wryly.

An expression of anger crossed Francesca's face, but then it was gone, the fury melting away as if it had been merely an illusion. Francesca smiled at her. "You've lain with Nicolai, haven't you? What's it like? I've thought about seducing one of the visitors—a young, handsome one who would tell no one and would go away quickly—just to see what's its like, but the thought of someone touching me so intimately has always been too disconcerting. Does it hurt? Do you like having him touch you? Is it worth having a dictator take over your entire life?"

Isabella supposed she should have been shocked. Francesca asked the most improper questions. "Nicolai isn't my dictator, Francesca. What a thing to say."

"He will be. All husbands rule their wives. And once their wives lie with them, the woman becomes silly and jealous and simpers around her husband to keep all the other women away. Her husband can lie with many women, but if she does such a thing, he will beat her or behead her. So the woman becomes a ninny. Is lying with a man worth such a fate?"

"You have a terrible view of marriage, and I doubt most women are that jealous."

Francesca shrugged and grinned. "Violante is jealous of any woman who looks at Sergio, but in truth, she is not alone. I watch people, Isabella. You choose to see the good in people, and you ignore the bad. Most women don't like others looking at their man. Rolando never looks at other women, yet Theresa is very jealous. She is certain he has found another woman."

Isabella looked up. "How do you know that?"

"Her brothers were talking about it. They didn't see me. They stopped by the falls to eat, and I stayed hidden from them. I guess they found her crying a few days ago, and she admitted it to them. They told her it couldn't be so—they're often with him—but she seemed certain." Francesca shook her head, sending her long hair flying. "If I had a man, I would never worry about such a foolish thing. If he wanted another, then he could go to her, but I would never take him back to my bed." She studied her nails. "What is the point of being with a man and then never enjoying it because you're angry or hurt all the time? I think it's silly. Theresa Bartolmei is perfectly silly."

"You don't believe Rolando has another woman."

Francesca's expression was faintly haughty, aristocratic, superior. Isabella found herself smiling, recognizing the DeMarco features. Was she one of Nicolai's cousins, like Theresa? She was so fey and imaginative. There was something magical about her. Isabella felt warm in her presence. "I see and hear all kinds of things. I would know. She worries for nothing."

"Sergio?" Isabella asked, curious, knowing she shouldn't persist in gossiping.

Francesca shook her head. "He looks, but that's all. I think he'd kill for Violante. She's just too silly to see it. I'm telling you, women lose their minds once they're married. I

271

wouldn't want to ever trade who I am for a man."

"Not everyone has your confidence," Isabella pointed out. "You're frightening sometimes with your confidence. Why don't I ever see you during the day?"

Francesca laughed merrily. "I don't want to be given duties or dress properly. I prefer to go where I want. People think I'm 'off,' you know." Her dark eyes danced. "Such a reputation allows me freedom."

"Why do they consider you 'off'?" Isabella asked.

The laughter died from Francesca's face, and she jumped to her feet to pace restlessly across the floor. "We're friends, aren't we?"

"I like to think we're very good friends," Isabella agreed.

Francesca stood a short distance from her, watching her closely. "I can talk with the others. I do it all the time."

Isabella could see how nervous Francesca was, so she took her time, choosing her words carefully. "The 'others'? I'm not certain I understand."

"You know." She twisted her fingers together. "The ones who make the noises at night. They're all trapped here in the valley and can't leave until you let them out."

Isabella blinked. "Me? Come here, *piccola*. Come sit by me and explain." She patted the bed. "I don't want you disappearing. You do it so quickly, and I'm not going to try chasing you through the secret passageway."

Francesca laughed. "You'd never catch me."

"I know that, and I've had enough misadventures for a lifetime, so please stay and talk with me. Who are the others?"

"Spirits. They're trapped here until you free them. Those born here in the valley can't leave for too long a time without wasting away. Even then their spirits return to the valley and must remain until the loved one of a DeMarco releases all of us from the curse."

Isabella could see that Francesca believed what she was saying. "So you believe the story Sarina told me, the story of Sophia and the curse she put upon the DeMarco *famiglia*, upon the valley?"

Francesca looked at her steadily. "Don't you, Isabella? You see Nicolai as a man, but you know that most in this valley see him as a beast. And why is he able to communicate with the lions if the legend isn't true? You know it is. And you know you are to be the bride of DeMarco. Every single man, woman, and child in this valley knows of the curse and knows you are our only salvation. If you fail . . ." Francesca shivered.

Isabella raked her hands through her hair and rubbed at her temples in agitation. "You told me that you could speak to the 'others.' Do you 'see' them, too, Francesca?"

"Not the way I see you. Mainly, I talk with them." Francesca sounded faintly defiant, as though she expected Isabella to try to talk her out of her fanciful notions.

"Have you ever spoken with Sophia?"

Francesca looked startled. "You can't be thinking of trying to get her to speak with you, are you? No one has ever dared. She knows things others don't. Isabella, she's a powerful woman."

"*Spirit*, Francesca," Isabella pointed out. "She no longer belongs here, and she must want to rest. Don't you ever think about how terrible it must be for her to watch history repeat itself over and over and know she's helpless to stop it? From what Sarina told me, Sophia was a good woman who loved her husband and her people. This can't be easy for her."

Francesca backed away from the bed, shaking her head and wringing her hands. "You can't be thinking of talking to her. *I've* never even tried."

"Has she frightened you in some way?" Isabella asked gently.

Francesca lowered her voice to a whisper. "The others are frightened of her. They don't go near her, and they don't speak of her. They hate her for what she did."

"Well, I don't think there's any harm in asking. Will you

try? Will you at least ask her to speak with me through you?" Isabella threw off the coverlet and quickly reached for her robe to cover her scandalous attire. "For me, Francesca. It might be the one thing that saves my life."

Francesca hesitated for a long, strained moment, then nodded. "I'll try, Isabella, for you. But she may not answer. They aren't like we are, and time seems different for them. But I'll try tonight."

"Since I'm asking favors, I need one more. *Mio fratello* means everything to me I know you know things others don't, things maybe even the healer doesn't know. Lucca will be arriving soon, and I'll need someone to help me care for him. I won't be able to be with him all the time, and Sarina has so many duties. I don't really know very many others. Please say you'll do it. And if anything should happen to me, promise me that you'll look after him for me."

Francesca nibbled thoughtfully at her lower lip, revising Isabella's opinion that she was wildly impetuous. Francesca was not about to give her word lightly. "I suppose being in charge of a man might actually be fun. I do know a few things that would help him . . . if I like him."

Isabella leveled her gaze at the other girl. Francesca rolled her eyes and shrugged. "All right, I'll help you take care of him, Isabella. But I hope you realize Sarina and Nicolai won't agree with your decision."

"It's my decision to make, not theirs." Isabella tilted her chin with a distinctly haughty air.

Francesca laughed aloud. "They think I've been touched by madness, and yet you're willing to put *tuo fratello*'s life in my hands. How perfectly extraordinary."

Isabella put her hands out toward the dying fire to ward off the sudden chill that crept down her back. "Why would they think you're mad? You and I can't be the only ones who hear the wails at night."

"Everyone hears them wailing. The 'others' want them to hear. It was a joke at first, something to do when they were bored, but I think they want everyone to remember they're still here in the valley, locked in it like the rest of us."

Something indefinable in Francesca's face, in her far too intelligent eyes, something about her mouth and chin, mesmerized Isabella. In the gathering darkness she tried to grasp what was eluding her.

"What are you doing here?" The demand was harsh, accusatory, the voice purring with menace.

Both women whirled around to face Nicolai as he emerged in his usual silent manner from the hidden passageway. He stalked across the room, inserting himself protectively between Francesca and Isabella. There was something frightening in his posture, in the line of his mouth.

Francesca backed away from him, clearly appeasing. "We were just talking, Nicolai, that's all."

Isabella started to walk around Nicolai, a sudden urge to comfort Francesca welling up in her, but Nicolai's long fingers wrapped around her wrist, locking her to him. "Just talking, Francesca?" His tone held disbelief.

Immediately Francesca drew herself up. "It's obvious you don't believe me, Nicolai, so I will take my leave. Good night, Isabella." She started toward the passageway. "As for tyrants and dictators, I give you my brother and thus prove my point."

"I did not dismiss you, Francesca," Nicolai bit out between clenched teeth. "Come back here immediately."

Isabella stared from one face to the other, shocked that, although she'd noticed a resemblance, she hadn't guessed the relationship immediately.

Francesca turned back slowly, her face sulky. "I don't much care for interrogations, Nicolai."

"Francesca," Isabella said softly, hurt in her eyes, "why didn't you tell me you were Nicolai's sister?"

Nicolai swept Isabella under the shelter of his broad shoulder, his hand finding her so. "What game are you playing now, Francesca? Why did you follow Isabella and frighten her this evening in the city?"

Isabella gasped and would have protested, but his fingers tightened in warning around hers.

Francesca looked bored, tapping her foot and heaving an exaggerated sigh. "Pray tell, why would I bother with such nonsense? You manage to frighten her enough for both of us." She steadfastly refused to look at Isabella.

"You dare to deny it, then?" A growl rumbled deep in his throat, a distinct threat. "You think I can't smell DeMarco blood? You stalked her through the streets and scared her for your own amusement. Did you think you could get away with such a thing?"

The blood drained from Isabella's face as she stared at the young woman she had come to feel affection for, the woman she called friend. It was a painful betrayal, unexpected and frighteningly sinister.

Francesca finally shifted her gaze from her brother to Isabella. "I adamantly deny your idiotic charge, Nicolai. Look elsewhere for your enemies. I've sought only to protect Isabella. You seem far too busy planning your battles to watch over her properly." There was accusation in her voice. "Sophia might protect her here in this room from the entity that mars our valley. Isabella awakened it—don't tell me you haven't felt it—and she should be protected at all times. Yet you leave her alone."

"No one but you would dare defy me, Francesca."

Francesca narrowed her eyes and lifted her chin. "That's sheer arrogance talking. You won't look at our history, won't acknowledge the old ones, because you want to think you control everything here in the valley, but you and I both know it isn't so."

"I scented our blood in the city, Francesca."

Isabella found Nicolai's softly spoken accusation, the coldness of his tone, far more intimidating than his hot temper.

"You can become the beast, Francesca?" Isabella was struggling to take it in, also remembering the feminine voice leading her up the *palazzo* stairs to the balcony, remembering she had nearly died.

"Of course. I'm a DeMarco. Why shouldn't I be able to become the lion? It is my birthright as well as my curse. Don't let him fool you, Isabella. He embraces his legacy just as I have. What do you think keeps our valley and our people safe from outsiders?" She tipped her head to one side and leveled a cool gaze on Isabella's pale face. "Tell me, what is one life, the life of a woman, an outsider, in comparison to ruling all of this?" She swept her arms wide to encompass the entire valley.

"That's enough, Francesca. Leave us now. I will expect to see you this afternoon in my rooms." Nicolai's voice was a whip of command.

"What?" Defiant to the last, Francesca lifted an eyebrow. "No tower for your mad sister, Nicolai? How very kind of you." She glanced back at Isabella. "Know your enemies, Isabella. That's my advice to you. You're surrounded by them." Francesca spun around and was gone, using the passageway to make her escape.

Isabella moaned softly and covered her face with her hands. "Go, Nicolai. You go, too. I don't want to see you either."

"Not this time, *cara mia*," he said tenderly. "You're not sending me away." He pulled her resisting body into his arms and held her close, stroking her hair, pressing her face into his chest as she wept.

She didn't even know why she was weeping or for whom. She simply wept. How could she find solace in Nicolai's arms when he was the biggest threat of all to her? Francesca had hit home with her poisoned arrow. *What is one life, the life of a woman, an outsider, in comparison to ruling all of this?* The words echoed over and over in her mind. Isabella had offered her life in exchange for her brother's life . . . and Nicolai needed an heir.

Nicolai lifted Isabella into his arms and cradled her against his chest. His ridiculous plan of keeping her out of harm's way by making her his mistress was flawed. The lions knew she was his true bride. He knew she was his true bride. The curse was already at work. The entity had awoken at her arrival, just as it had upon his mother's arrival.

He sighed softly, sat in a chair, and rubbed his blue-shadowed chin over the top of her head. "It isn't true, you know. What Francesca said to you. I didn't make a bargain with you expecting to trade your life for Lucca's. I tried to keep you out of the valley. I'd heard of you many times, of your courage and your passion for life. I knew what you would be." His fingers stroked her skin, traced her mouth. "Francesca is not quite sane, Isabella. She runs wild, has always done so, and none of us have had the heart to force her to heel."

"Why didn't you tell me about Francesca?" She sounded forlorn, vulnerable. She buried her face against his neck, her tears dampening his skin, tugging at his heartstrings.

"Francesca is different. No one speaks of her. They don't talk of their *don* and the way he is seen as a lion any more than we speak of my sister and her strange behavior. I should have told you, though it's ingrained in me not to. In all honesty, I felt you had enough to contend with when your betrothed was a beast a great deal of the time. You didn't need to worry about my half-mad sister."

She lifted her face to examine his golden eyes, her long lashes spiky from her tears. "You, *signore*," she said haughtily, "are no longer my betrothed. And I've spoken with Francesca nearly every night since my arrival, yet I saw no signs of madness. She's different, young, and obviously in need of guidance, but what makes you believe she is mad? Her ability to speak with the 'others'? Because, frankly, Nicolai, I don't think that's any more difficult to believe than your appearing as a beast."

The shift of her hips in his lap caused a pulsing ache, his body hardening despite his every resolve. "Stop moving, *bellezza.* You're not entirely safe from me with nothing between us but that gown."

She felt his body's reaction, the way he grew thick and hard, pressing tightly against her buttocks. Her heart jumped, her breath hitching in her lungs. Desire began to pool low, a sweet ache that caused her breasts, pressed tightly into his heavy muscles, to tingle with anticipation. Determinedly she looked away from the hunger flaring in his eyes.

"You should have told me about Francesca, Nicolai."

His hand began to make slow, lazy circles over the small of her back. "Yes, I should have, *cara*, but it never occurred to me that she might be dangerous to you." Heat flared between them, burning through the lace of her gown. "Francesca was only a babe, five summers, when *mia madre* was killed." His hand sank lower, rubbing her buttocks, his fingers kneading her flesh.

"She was there, too, wasn't she?" Isabella guessed, her heart immediately going out to Francesca. "She saw it. She saw her *padre* kill her *madre*." She held him close, wanting to comfort him, needing to ease the memory of that terrible afternoon. Her arms wound around his neck, her fingers tangling in the thick silk of his hair.

Nicolai nodded. "It was Francesca who called the lions to save my life. And she was changed just as I was." He touched the jagged scars on his face. "She was scarred on the inside, where no one could see. She didn't talk, didn't cry or make a sound for years. She wouldn't go near any of us, not even me. She would sit in a room with me, but she wouldn't let me touch her." Pain laced his voice. His hand slid up her back to her nape.

"And you think it's because she's afraid you'll kill her, just as your *padre* killed your *madre*?" Isabella found herself seeking to comfort him. "You don't understand Francesca at all, Nicolai. She loves you more than anyone, anything in the world. It's in her voice when she talks of you. If she did what you said and followed me, it isn't because she wanted to hurt you—or me. We had talked of jealousy. Perhaps she was trying to tell me something."

He pressed his lips to her eyelids; then his mouth drifted over her temple and down her cheek to the corner of her mouth. "What would she have to be jealous of? She's never wanted her place in the holding. She would no more run the *palazzo* or help Sarina with the details of everyday duties than she would become a soldier. She's refused to even consider marriage. She runs wild, and I should have put a stop to it some time ago."

His mouth was scattering her thoughts, nibbling gently on her chin, tightening her nipples into hard pebbles and causing her breasts to ache. His tongue stroked a caress over her chin, stroking a flame that raced along her nerve endings. Isabella squirmed, inciting him to harden more, to push tightly against her. His mouth wandered unhurriedly along the slender column of her neck, her throat.

"You can't know what it's like to touch you, Isabella, to be able to lose myself in your body. To know I can bring you such pleasure in return." He pushed the robe from her shoulders, then slid his fingers over the lace of her nightgown, making the bodice slither down to bunch at her waist.

She felt his gaze on her breasts, and immediately her body responded with a wave of heat. He didn't touch her, simply looked at her, watching her breathe in and out.

"You're so beautiful." He lowered his head and suckled her aching flesh.

Isabella nearly exploded, liquid dampening her thighs, her body clenching tighter and tighter. His hands bit into her waist as he bent her backward so that her breast thrust more fully into his mouth. She closed her eyes, threw her head back, and allowed the sensations to wash over her. She could feel him, so hard and hot now against her buttocks that she thought they both might go up in flames.

When he released her breast to run kisses up her neck, she carefully stood, bravely removing the shirt from his wide shoulders. He sucked in his breath and leaned back to allow her to unhook his breeches. Her fingers brushed over his hardened body, sending lightning streaking through him, shaking him to the very core of his being. He lifted his hips as she hooked her thumbs into the waist and tugged his clothes down to the tops of his boots. Nicolai bent, finding it somewhat painful, and pulled off his boots so he could rid himself of his clothing.

When Isabella would have turned to the bed, Nicolai caught her hand and brought her back around to stand in front of him. He seated himself in the chair and urged her closer. "Part your legs, *cara*." His hand went between her thighs, gently encouraging her to do as he bid.

Color swept her face, but Isabella obediently widened her stance. Nicolai watched the way the firelight cast loving shadows over her body. His erection was a hard, thick spear, the head glistening, pulsing with anticipation. He rubbed his fingers across her mound, finding her damp and ready for him. "I left you wanting me, didn't I," he murmured, his gaze on her face as his long fingers slid deeply into her body.

Pleasure heightened her beauty, put a sheen in her dark eyes. Nicolai pushed deeper, wanting her on fire, wanting this night to make a memory for both of them. His other hand caressed the curve of her buttocks, urging her to move, to find a rhythm with him. Then she was crying out, her body gripping his fingers tightly, squeezing so that his erection throbbed and pulsed.

Deliberately he brought his fingers to his mouth to taste her. The hand on her buttocks brought her forward, forcing her to straddle him. "I want you to ride me, *cara*, just as you ride that horse of yours, only I'll be deep inside you, and each time you slide your body over mine . . ." His voice trailed off wickedly, his hands biting into her waist, positioning her body directly over his. Very slowly he began to lower her body until the thick knob of his erection was pushing into her hot, wet core.

Her eyes widened in shocked surprise. He was stretching her, spearing her, his body so thick and hard he took her breath away. Isabella hesitated, gasping as he entered her, waiting breathlessly for her body to adjust to his size. Slowly, inch by inch, she lowered her hips, taking him deeper and deeper inside her.

Isabella was tight and hot, surrounding him like a silken sheath. She settled onto his lap, wiggling into a comfortable position, the action sending fire racing through his bloodstream. He bent to find her mouth with his, to taste her pleasure, to feed it. When she began to move, the breath left his lungs until he was burning for air, struggling for control. He wanted this time to be leisurely, tender, a joining she would cherish, but he was uncertain if his body could take the ecstasy of hers without going up in flames.

Isabella found she could experiment. She took her time to learn what felt best, starting with a slow, languorous ride, tightening her muscles and watching his face as she slid over him, back up, nearly breaking contact, then back down so that he filled her completely. She could feel his body's reaction, the trembling of his muscles, the shudders of pleasure, his eyes hot with desire.

He made a single sound as she began to pick up the pace, moving her hips faster, creating a fiery friction that left little beads of sweat on his forehead and a glow on her jutting breasts. His hands caught her hips, and he began to work with her, thrusting upward to bury himself deeply as her body came down to meet his, driving the breath from both of them. He was growing thicker and harder, filling every space, stretching her even as her body clenched and gripped, spinning them both into a mindless vortex of exploding colors and flames. They soared in perfect rhythm, bodies shuddering with pleasure so intense she didn't know where he started and she left off.

They clung together, unable to catch their breath, unable to move. Her head on his shoulder, they remained locked together while the earth rocked and the room spun around them. Their hearts were pounding, skin hot and damp, so sensitive that if either moved, it sent ripples of pleasure spiraling through both of them.

Isabella closed her eyes and savored being in his arms, his body deep inside hers. She felt boneless, floating, waves of delight washing over her. When he stirred, she tightened her arms around him. "Don't move," she murmured. "I don't want it to be over yet." There was no fear in her mind, no sorrow. No sense of betrayal. No danger. When they were alone together, when he was touching her body, everything they did seemed right and perfect. She wanted to simply stay where she was, locked with him, burning cleanly in the fire together. Without thought. In total peace.

"I think I can make it to the bed with you," he said, his hands stroking caresses along the line of her back and down the curve of her hip. "Keep your arms around my neck."

"I don't want to get up," she protested, her voice husky and sated.

"You don't need to. Lock your legs around my waist." With enormous strength he got out of the chair and made it to the bed, Isabella locked around him. The action sent her body over the edge again, so that she tightened around him, rocking with heat and sensation.

He lay over her, his arms tightly around her, kissing her face, her throat. His voice was tender, loving, whispering to her as she drifted to a place, half awake, half asleep. She dreamed of him, moving in her, his mouth and hands exploring every inch of her, over and over, his mouth drifting over her body so that her sleep was a sea filled with erotic images and waves of lust and love.

Chapter Sixteen

Far in advance of the soldiers escorting Lucca Vernaducci toward the pass, word reached the *castello* that they were on their way. A party of guards was instantly dispatched to ride to meet them and see *Don* Rivellio's men safely into the valley. No hint, no whisper, not the slightest murmur of lions was to be heard. The *palazzo* was teaming with activity. Servants prepared food in the kitchens, and the visitors' barracks were cleaned and made ready for the outsiders.

Understanding the way the household gossips worked, Nicolai knew Isabella would have been informed of these developments the moment she opened her eyes. He entered her bedchamber and found her already dressed to ride out to meet her brother. She flashed him a radiant smile, nearly knocking him over as she rushed into his arms. "I heard! I'm going to meet Lucca! I asked Betto to have my mare saddled."

Nicolai's hands framed her face with exquisite gentleness.

"Wait another hour or so. I know you're eager to see him, but it isn't safe. Those are *Don* Rivellio's men with him. If the soldiers were purely an escort, they would have turned back the moment they sighted the pass. I've word that a larger party of soldiers have been gathering a few miles outside the pass, and another is coming up along the entrance to the cliffs."

Her eyes widened. "You knew Rivellio was using Lucca as a shield to gain entrance to the valley? And you let him?"

"Of course. It was the only way to make certain *tuo fratello* was truly safe. If Rivellio had no further use for Lucca he would not likely trouble himself to keep him alive."

"I thought you were letting in spies, not an entire army," she said in alarm.

"An army could not enter the pass without my knowledge. And once it's in, it's trapped."

"Are the cliffs safe? They can't invade us from that direction, can they?" She was wringing her hands with such agitation that he covered them with his own long fingers, stroking soothing caresses over her knuckles.

"I'm assuming they have a spy in the valley already, or they wouldn't have tried that direction. There's an entrance, a tunnel that winds its way through the mountain. It's a maze deep beneath the earth, but if they have an ally, they may have a map of sorts."

"If they have a spy, they know about the lions and have probably prepared for them, too," Isabella pointed out anxiously.

She was frowning, her face so apprehensive Nicolai rubbed at the line between her dark brows with the pad of his thumb. "One cannot prepare for the sight of a lion, and certainly not in the heat of battle." His voice was gentle. "*Don* Rivellio only *imagines* he can sneak into my domain." There was a predator's gleam in his eyes. "I'll worry about *Don* Rivellio and what he may be up to, and you concentrate on *tuo fratello's* homecoming. He is safe now, though very ill. I have been told to prepare you for a vast difference in his appearance, but he is alive and therein lies hope. I will take care of *Don* Rivellio and his intended invasion."

Nicolai actually sounded as if he was looking forward to it, and Isabella gave him a quelling glance.

He reached out casually and caught the nape of her neck. "I must require you to remain within the walls of the *castello* at all times. I insist on your word."

She nodded immediately. "Of course, Nicolai. But I'd like to go up on the battlements and watch for Lucca's approach."

"I can't be with you—I'm needed to control the lions in the presence of strangers—but don't venture too close to the edge." He bent his head and kissed her. Slowly. Gently. Leisurely. His kiss held heat and promise, his tongue sliding along her bottom lip, tasting, prompting, until she opened her mouth to him.

She shivered with pleasure. It blossomed in her abdomen and spread, molten heat that began a slow burn. Nicolai lifted his head reluctantly and stared down with evident satisfaction at her half-closed eyes.

"I mean what I say, *cara*. No more accidents. I must turn my attention now to the *don* and his plans."

"I'll be careful," she promised him solemnly, finding it difficult to catch her breath when he seemed to have robbed her of the very air around her.

He bent to take one last, lingering kiss before he turned and strode away. Isabella watched him go, thinking him a man born to rule, born to battle. Power and responsibility sat well on his broad shoulders. The moment she heard *Don* Rivellio's name, a shiver of apprehension had gone down her spine, but Nicolai inspired confidence. He looked utterly, almost arrogantly, sure of himself, and she found herself smiling again, able to feel the joy of her impending reunion with her brother.

Isabella rushed up to the battlements, vaguely aware of the two men shadowing her. She paced back and forth, impatiently waiting. Sometimes she would stop long enough to stare down the valley, praying to the good Madonna for a glimpse of the riders. Other times she couldn't stand still.

A single rider came into view in the distance, nearly stilling her heart. She strained to identify him as he came nearer. He was riding fast, his horse covering the ground in long strides, the rider low over its neck. Her breath caught in her throat in anticipation. This was the forward runner, coming to alert them. He swept through the open archway of the outer wall, calling out to the guards and people waiting. At once commotion reigned, everyone scurrying to finish preparations for the visitors.

Isabella hurried down the steps and through the *palazzo*, uncaring of propriety, her heart singing at the thought of seeing her brother once again. She could barely contain her excitement, tears of joy sparkling in her eyes. She made her way into the courtyard, remaining within the walls, conscious of her promise to Nicolai. She saw them then: a long row of soldiers, a travois and a guard of four men on either side of it.

She jammed a fist to her lips and locked her muscles to keep from running forward. Sarina slipped up beside her to give her comfort.

The last few yards before the men entered the outer walls seemed a lifetime to Isabella, but she held her ground, having seen Rivellio's soldiers straining to catch glimpses inside the DeMarco holding. They were being led away from the massive structure to the barracks, used for visiting soldiers.

As the party made it through the archway, Isabella rushed to her brother's side, nearly knocking over his guards. Lucca attempted to rise from the travois to reach her, and then she had him in her arms, hugging him close, appalled at how thin he was. His dark hair, was streaked with gray, his face lined and pale, sweat dampening his skin, although he was shaking with fever chills.

"*Ti amo*, Lucca. *Ti amo*. I thought I'd never see you

again," she whispered against his ear, tears clogging her throat.

His body was thin and trembling, but his arms held her tightly, and he buried his face in her hair. "Isabella," he said. Only that. But she heard his choking sob, the love in his voice, and it was enough—worth every peril she had faced.

As a cough wracked his body, she pulled back to look at him. She saw the tears swimming in his eyes and hugged him close again before gently helping him to lie back on the stretcher. "Please be careful with him," she instructed the guards. Then she turned toward the housekeeper. "I want him put in a room near mine, Sarina." Isabella clutched her brother's hand, and he gripped hers just as tightly.

"*Don* DeMarco has said he is to have the room right next to yours," Sarina agreed, patting Isabella gently. "It is already prepared for him."

Tears in her eyes, Isabella walked beside the stretcher, her fingers entwined with Lucca's.

The room they carried him to was more masculine than hers. A fire crackled on the hearth, and soothing, aromatic candles also lit the chambers.

Two of the men carefully helped Lucca onto the bed. At the movement, he began coughing and held his chest as if he were in great pain. Isabella glanced anxiously up at Sarina, terrified that she might lose her brother when he had finally come back to her.

It had been nearly two years since she had last seen Lucca. Two years since he had helped her onto the back of her horse and sent her fleeing with their mother's jewels and what treasures they could gather quickly. He had been warned Rivellio's men were coming for him, that the powerful *don* meant to steal their lands and have Lucca assassinated or arrested and Isabella brought to him. Lucca had sent Isabella to a neighboring city, where friends watched over her while he was hunted. The moment she heard of his capture, she had begun the search to find the entrance to

Don DeMarco's land knowing he was the only one powerful enough to help her and Lucca.

She waited until the guards were gone and the door closed before falling to her knees beside the bed. Lucca wrapped his arms around her and buried his face in her shoulder, unashamedly weeping. She held him tightly to her, tears streaming down her face. Never in all her years had she seen him cry.

It was Lucca who pulled himself together first. "How did you manage to do this, Isabella?" His voice was low and husky, his fingers tight around her arm, as if he couldn't bear to lose contact with her. "When they came for me, I thought they were bringing me to the executioner. They said nothing. I saw Rivellio. He stood on the battlements and watched them take me away. He was sneering. I was certain he was up to some trick." He pulled her closer. "Are you certain DeMarco is not in alliance with Rivellio?"

"No! No, never!" Isabella was horrified that her brother would come to such a conclusion. "Nicolai would never do such a thing. He despises Rivellio. You're safe here. You really are." She smoothed back the tangle of his hair. He was so thin, every bone protruding, his skin gray, stretched over his lanky frame as if it no longer fit. Isabella thought her heart was shattering. "All you have to do is eat and sleep and grow strong again. You owe your life to *Don* De-Marco—your life and your fidelity. He is wonderful, Lucca, truly a good man."

Lucca lay back on the bed, his strength leaving him. "The rumors of him are untrue, then?" His lashes drifted down, though he strained to stare at his sister forever, afraid that if he closed his eyes he would wake up and find it all a dream. "Do you remember the stories of the DeMarco *famiglia* I used to tell to frighten you? Were they but gossip?" He closed his eyes, his body prevailing over his mind. "I owe you my life, little sister. My fidelity is to you."

She smoothed his hair as if he were a child. "Sarina will bring you a hot drink, Lucca, if you can stay awake." She didn't want him to sleep, she wanted to hold him. She leaned close. "Don't slip away, Lucca. Fight for your life. I need you. I need you here with me, in this world. I know you're tired, but you're safe here. All you have to do is rest."

For a moment his fingers tightened around hers, but he was too weak to open his eyes or rouse himself enough to reassure her. She remained kneeling beside him, watching him force raspy breaths in and out, watching a choking cough convulse him before he could once more lie quietly.

Isabella was grateful when Sarina bustled in and took over, propping numerous pillows under Lucca's shoulders and back, allowing him to breathe more easily. She directed Isabella to aid him as she pressed a hot drink of healing herbs to his mouth. He sipped, not attempting to hold the cup, his arms limp at his sides. He was asleep the moment they removed the cup from his lips.

Isabella clasped Sarina's hand. "What does the healer say? He's bad, isn't he?"

"The good Madonna will watch over him." Sarina's voice held a wealth of compassion. "With a little help from us." She patted Isabella's shoulder.

The housekeeper left the room, closing the door, leaving Isabella alone with her brother. She knelt close to the bed to keep vigil. To look at him. To drink him in. She stared at him, afraid that if she took her eyes from him he would disappear.

"Isabella?" The soft voice made her stiffen. "Please, Isabella, just listen to me before you hate me."

Isabella turned to look at Francesca, who was standing just inside the room. She appeared uncertain, even nervous, not her usual confident self. "I'm not angry with you, Francesca." With a small sigh, Isabella tucked her brother's hand beneath the coverlet and got to her feet to face the sister of the *don*. "I'm hurt and disappointed. I thought we were true friends. I let myself feel great affection for you, and I felt betrayed by your deceptions."

Francesca nodded. "I know. I know that what I did was

wrong. I should have told you immediately who I was. I didn't want to admit I was the *don's* crazy sister." She looked down at her hands. "You didn't know me. You didn't know anything about me. When I suddenly appeared in your room, you just accepted me." She rubbed the bridge of her nose, a gesture curiously reminiscent of her brother. "With you I could be anyone I wanted to be, not the *don's* half-mad sister. I'd grown tired of that role but had no way of changing it until you came into the valley."

Isabella saw the raw pain in Francesca's eyes, and it was impossible not to feel for her.

"You are the only friend I've ever had, the only person who ever talked to me as if what I said mattered." Francesca walked across the room to gaze down at the man lying in the bed, his breathing harsh and ragged. "You even trusted me enough to ask me to care for your brother. I don't want to lose our friendship. I've thought about it a lot, and my pride isn't worth what you gave me." She knelt beside the bed. "I didn't do what Nicolai said I did. I don't know why he would accuse of me of it, but I didn't do it. I would never hurt you. But I don't expect you to take my word over Nicolai's."

Isabella considered for a few moments. "Is it possible you don't remember? Are you really aware of what you do when you're the beast? Maybe without knowing, you don't want to share your brother with anyone. He's all you've ever had. Just as Lucca is all I've had." Her voice was gentle, compassionate. She knelt beside Francesca and touched her brother's hair.

Francesca shook her head stubbornly, a flicker of denial crossing her face. But when she opened her mouth to protest, she hesitated, and horror crept into her expression. "I don't know, Isabella," she whispered. "I honestly don't know. But I don't think so. I love having you here. I *want* you here." Her defiant expression crumbled, and she buried her face in her hands. "If I did that, if I stalked you as Nicolai said I did, then you have to leave here. I believed Nicolai would be the one, with you, to free the valley. But the beast isn't as strong in me; the voices are whispers, and the change rarely takes me. Nicolai is different; the beast is much stronger in him."

Isabella couldn't stand the sight of Francesca's slender shoulders shaking as the girl wept. She wrapped comforting arms around her. "Francesca, you don't know for certain. Maybe it wasn't you. A rogue lion went after me in the valley and again here in the *castello*. Both times I felt the presence of the entity."

Francesca stiffened, then slumped into Isabella's arms. She cried as if her heart were breaking. Over Francesca's head, Isabella saw her brother stir, his lashes fluttering open, his expression concerned. She shook her head in warning, and he closed his eyes again without protest. Holding Francesca, stroking her hair, she watched Lucca drift back to restless sleep.

"Shh, now, it's all right, *piccola*," she said when Francesca's weeping showed no signs of slowing down.

"Everything will be all right."

"Why would Nicolai speak to me like that? He sounded so cold." She lifted her tear-ravaged face to look up at Isabella. "I know he thinks I'm mad, but to have him think I would want you dead . . ." She trailed off miserably.

"I'm sorry, Francesca," Isabella murmured. "I know he wouldn't want to hurt you. I think Nicolai is afraid of what he might do to me. It's eating away at him, so he defends me all the more."

"I see it every night," Francesca whispered, casting a quick look toward the bed, making certain Lucca remained asleep. "Over and over I see *mio padre* ripping *mia madre* to shreds. There was so much blood. It was like a red river there in the courtyard." Sobs shook her again.

Isabella tightened her hold, knowing Francesca was that five-year-old child reliving a horror that had forever changed her life.

"I was frozen. I couldn't look away. *Mio padre* turned his

head and looked at Nicolai. I knew he was going to kill him, too. He didn't look at me; he didn't see me there. *Mio padre* used to carry me around the *palazzo*, whirling me in circles." Francesca covered her mouth as another sob emerged, heartrending, painful, torn from deep within her. "I loved him so much, but I couldn't let him take Nicolai. So I called the lions, and they killed *mio padre*. I couldn't let him have Nicolai." The large dark eyes looked at Isabella for forgiveness. "You see that, don't you? I couldn't allow it."

"I'm grateful to you, Francesca, as I'm certain your *padre* is grateful. You did the only thing you could do, a decision no child should have to make. Nicolai doesn't sleep at night either. He doesn't forget, and he blames himself for not saving your *madre*."

"But how could he have saved her?" Francesca protested.

"And how could you *not* save your brother?" Isabella kissed the top of her head. "We'll straighten this out, *piccola*. No more tears now."

Francesca flashed a wan grin. "I can't remember ever crying before."

Isabella laughed softly. "You do things wholeheartedly," she observed. "This, by the way, is *mio fratello*, Lucca."

Francesca gratefully turned her attention to the sleeping man. He looked young and vulnerable in sleep, the lines etched into his face visible but soft in repose. Without conscious thought she touched the gray streak in his dark hair. "He's suffered, hasn't he? That despicable Rivellio had him tortured."

Isabella sucked in her breath. Of course Lucca had been tortured. Rivellio would never have passed up the opportunity to inflict as much pain as possible on a Vernaducci. She hadn't allowed herself to think too closely about the atrocities her brother would suffer at the hands of the *don*. She nodded, reaching to touch his arm, his face, just to reassure herself he was really there.

"Will you still trust me to watch over him?" Francesca's

fingertips caressed the ribbon of gray in his hair. "I swear to you, I'll look after him." She held herself very still, waiting anxiously for the reply.

Isabella didn't make the mistake of hesitating. Every ounce of her was aware that Francesca was extremely fragile, and one wrong word would shatter her. "With all my heart, I'd be grateful to you if you would help me to bring his health back or make his last days more comfortable."

The DeMarco mouth tightened stubbornly. "They won't be his last days," Francesca vowed. "I won't allow anything to happen to him."

"It's in the hands of the Madonna," Isabella reminded herself and Francesca.

Francesca hugged her again. "I have to go. I look awful, and I don't want *tuo fratello's* first glimpse of me to send him screaming from beneath the coverlet."

"I doubt if that would happen—*tu sei bella.*" Isabella leaned to kiss her cheek as she assured Francesca she was beautiful. "But I understand the need to look just right when meeting a handsome man for the first time." She touched her brother's arm because she couldn't stop reassuring herself he was with her.

"He will live," Francesca promised. Jumping up, she retreated to the passageway, leaving silence behind.

Soft laughter escaped from beneath the coverlet. "You are the same, little sister, your compassionate heart unmistakable." Lucca's voice was dreamy, far away, as if the herbs in the tea had set him drifting. "Her tears were genuine. They tore at me until I wanted to hold her close. Who is she?"

"Francesca is *Don* DeMarco's younger sister. I thought you were asleep." Isabella tried to remember what had been said. She didn't want Lucca anxious over her relationship with Nicolai.

"I was asleep, in and out, and most of what I heard made no sense to me. I think I mixed up my dreams with reality, but someone should watch over her. No woman should have such a sorrow to bear."

"Sleep, *mio fratello*, you're safe here, and no one is happier than *tua sorella*." Isabella kissed his temple and stroked the hair from his face, grateful she could sit beside him and see for herself that he was alive. After a time, she laid her head down on the coverlet and, holding his hand, allowed herself to sleep.

She nearly jumped out of her skin when a hand clasped her shoulder. Nicolai. She knew his touch. His scent. The warmth of his body. He bent to kiss the top of her head in greeting. His hand stroked a caress over her hair. "The healer says Lucca will need much care. More than you can provide alone. Sarina will help, but you will need another to stay with him during the night." His voice evinced a quiet command. He pulled her to her feet and into the shelter of his tall, muscular body. "I know you would wish to stay by his side day and night to ensure his recovery, but you would make yourself ill, and your brother would not want that. You know I'm right, Isabella."

Isabella was too grateful for her brother's life to be upset that Nicolai was dictating the terms of Lucca's care to her. "I have asked a friend for help. She will spend the nights watching over him for me." Isabella slipped her arms around Nicolai's waist. "*Grazie*, Nicolai. I don't know how to thank you properly for what you've done. I don't know how to repay you." She laid her head on his chest, her ear over the steady beat of his heart. Love rose up, overwhelming her so that she felt weak with it. She knew in that moment that she loved Nicolai without reservation, unconditionally and completely.

"Lucca is all the family I have in the world, and you gave him back to me." She tilted her head to look up at the *don*, this man whom she loved more than she had ever thought possible. This man who believed he might someday destroy her.

His arms tightened around her. "You have more than *tuo*

fratello, cara mio. Never forget that." His voice was gentle, a soft, rumbling sound that seemed to seep into her heart and soul.

The sheer force of her feelings for him shook her. She stared up into his strangely colored eyes, mesmerized by him, caught by the intensity she saw there. His words brought the memory of his hands on her body, his mouth taking possession of hers. More than that, the words brought the feeling of him curled around her, his arms holding her close as they drifted to sleep together. With Nicolai, she knew a sense of peace, of rightness. They belonged together, tangled and soaring or simply lying quietly together.

A knock on the door had Nicolai fading back into the shadows of the room. He smiled at her, indicating the door. Isabella, cautiously opened it, requesting that the men standing there keep their voices low. "What is it?" she asked the two servants Betto had ordered to guard her within the *palazzo.* "Surely I can be alone with *mio fratello.*"

"*Signorina*, Sarina is calling for all to help in the kitchen. With so many soldiers to feed and watch, she needs us there. But Betto has said we must stay to watch over you."

Isabella glanced back for permission to *Don* DeMarco, who raised an aristocratic eyebrow at her, then grinned his quick, sardonic, little-boy smile that always tugged at her heart. She turned back to the guards. "I'll be safe in this room with *mio fratello.* You help Sarina and then come back. I'll be all right, I promise."

"But, *signorina*," one protested, clearly torn.

She smiled in reassurance. "I doubt if a lion will find its way in here with the door firmly closed. Let me know when you've returned." She closed the door to prevent further conversation.

Nicolai reached for her, drawing her into the shadows with him. "But the lion's already in the room with you," he whispered against her ear. His tongue stroked a caress down her neck, sending a shiver of heat curling through her stomach. "You would not be safe if I had the time. But the lions are restless, and keeping them quiet is a full-time job. I will be most grateful when the trap is sprung, and our rabbit, *Don* Rivellio, is caught in our snare."

"Go to work, then. I will sit here with Lucca and see that he sleeps without disturbance." Isabella gave Nicolai a push toward the passageway.

He caught her face in his hands and kissed her soundly, leaving her breathless.

Isabella searched for the sewing Sarina had thoughtfully left for her, but she was unable to think straight. She dropped several stitches before she managed to get her breathing back under control. Then she heard someone at the door again. The knock was so soft she nearly missed it.

"*Signorina* Vernaducci?" Brigita was wringing her hands even as she curtseyed. "I can't find Sarina or Betto, and there's a problem. Would you come?"

"Of course. But I will need a maid to sit with *mio fratello*. Please find one at once. *Signorina* DeMarco will be along soon, but someone must sit with him until then."

Brigita's eyes widened in shock. Her face paled "*Signorina* DeMarco?"

"There is no need for a maid," Francesca announced, moving out of the shadows, obviously having used the hidden passageway. "And you've no need to hurry, Isabella. I'll watch over him." She looked the young maid up and down, her expression haughty.

"Thank you, Francesca," Isabella said with obvious relief.

"What is it?" she inquired as she followed the maid through the halls as the girl walked faster and faster, her shoulders stiff in silent disapproval.

"A woman has come from one of the farmhouses. Her husband died several days ago of fever, and she has four *bambini*, the oldest but nine summers. Their storehouse burned to the ground—a dreadful accident. She is asking for supplies to see her through until they can plant and bring in crops. Without a man I don't know how she'll manage to do that," she added gloomily.

"Has this been brought to the attention of *Don* De-Marco? The woman will need workers to see her through." Isabella was already calculating what help the widow would require for her family.

"He's busy meeting with *Don* Rivellio's men. Betto is at the barracks, and Sarina is in the kitchen helping Cook prepare meals for everyone. I didn't know what else to do," Brigita wailed. "You'll help her, won't you, *signorina*? I couldn't send her away."

"Of course you couldn't," Isabella said briskly.

Brigita led her to a small room off the servants' entrance. The widow's face still held stunned shock. She looked thin and tired and without hope. She curtseyed immediately and burst into tears at the sight of Isabella. "You must help me to see the *don, signorina*. I have no food for my *bambini*. I'm *Signora* Bertroni. You must help me. You must!" She clutched at Isabella, her cries growing louder.

"Brigita, tea at once, and please ask Cook to include honeyed biscuits. Have Sarina give you the key to the storehouse, and send two manservants to meet us there in a few minutes." Isabella helped the woman into a chair.

Brigita bobbed a quick curtsey and hurried away from the wailing widow. Isabella murmured soothing condolences until Brigita returned with the tea. "Enough now, *Signora* Bertroni. We must get to work if we are to save your farm for your sons. Dry your eyes, and let us get to the planning of your future."

Isabella's calm words and tone brought an end to the woman's wild, abandoned weeping. "Where is your eldest boy? Is he old enough to aid you?"

"He is waiting outside with the little ones."

"Brigita will mind the little ones while I take you and your son to the storehouse for supplies. I have two men waiting to help us load your wagon. I'll send workers to your farm to plant your crops when it is time, and your son can labor with them and learn."

"*Grazie, grazie, signorina*."

In her haste to complete her task, Isabella didn't take time to throw on her cloak before braving the outdoors. Gray clouds were spreading across the sky and casting dark shadows across the land. The wind tugged at her thin gown, whipped at her hair, and numbed her fingers.

The storeroom was some distance from the *palazzo* but still within the outer wall. She glanced around for her two guards, then remembered she had sent them to help Sarina. Brigita had not come with her, so she had no one to send back to the kitchen for her guards or her cloak. Sighing, Isabella resigned herself to a cold journey and a lecture from *Don* DeMarco when her guards reported she had not stayed where she promised.

The storage house was enormous, a great, hulking building that loomed up very close to the outer wall. The two servants were waiting as Isabella and *Signora* Bertroni hurried up to them.

It took some time to find torches and lamps to adequately light the cavernous storehouse in order to find the supplies needed. Then Isabella directed the two men and *Signora* Bertroni's young son to carry out grain and dried fruits in sufficient quantities to see the family through the cold season. She carefully noted each item on a parchment to give to *Don* DeMarco. The task took longer than she expected, and night had fallen by the time the wagon was loaded.

Isabella realized just how cold she really was as she turned back to extinguish the torches. It crept in then. Slow. Insidious. That terrible, stomach-churning knowledge that she was not alone. She looked around carefully, but she knew the entity had found her.

It seemed wrong to send the widow and her children alone to the farm without an escort when the wind was once again howling and the wagon heavily loaded. She feared for them in the darkness with the spiteful, malevolent being waiting to strike. "It is best if you go with *Signora* Bertroni," she said to the two servants. "Escort the wagon to the farm, unload it, and remain for the night if necessary and report back in the morning."

Annoyance crossed the face of the younger man. "I have a home to go to. A woman waiting for me. It's cold and late. Let Carlie go." He indicated the older man with a jerk of his thumb.

"*Both* of you must go," Isabella said sternly, her expression every bit that of an *aristocratica*. "You cannot allow this woman and her children to travel unescorted in the darkness. I will hear no more about it."

The man glared at her, his black eyes snapping with repressed fury. For a moment his mouth worked as though he might burst into a protest, but he set his lips in a hard line and brushed past her, knocking into her hard enough to send her staggering. He kept going without apology, not looking back.

Isabella stared after him, wondering if she had somehow put the widow in danger by supplying her with a bitter, reluctant escort. Shivering uncontrollably, she hastily snuffed out the remainder of the lights, with the exception of a lantern she needed to see her way back to the *castello*.

Through the open door she could see mist covering the ground. The fog was thick and swirled like a gray-white shroud in the darkness. "Just what I need," she muttered aloud, feeling in her pocket for the key to the storehouse door. It wasn't there.

She held the lantern high, looking around the floor, trying to locate the exact spot where the younger servant had bumped into her. The key must have slipped from her skirt when he sent her stumbling backward.

A torrent of expletives exploded from the doorway, hate-filled and frightening. Isabella's heart jumped, and she swung around to see the young servant, his face twisted with malice, swinging the heavy door closed.

"No!" Isabella rushed toward him, her heart pounding with fear. The door clanged shut solidly, cutting her off from the outside world, imprisoning her within the huge storage room with no heat and no cloak.

Chapter Seventeen

Carefully setting the lantern on the floor, Isabella tried to push the heavy door open. It was locked, the mystery of the missing key solved. The servant must have been adept at picking pockets and had cleverly extracted it when he slammed into her. She stood very still, shivering in the cold air, aware of how wet her shoes were. Her toes were freezing. She rested her head against the door, closing her eyes briefly in dismay. The light from the lantern cast a dim circle around her but didn't extend more than a scant few inches beyond the hemline of her gown.

She was afraid to move deeper into the storage house. She wanted to be able to shout for help should she hear anyone nearby. The cold had crept into her bones, and she was unable to stop her helpless shivering. Rubbing her hands up and down her arms generated the illusion of warmth but little else. She stomped her feet, paced back and forth, and pumped her arms, but her toes were so cold she thought they might shatter.

Isabella refused to entertain the idea that she might freeze to death. Nicolai would come looking for her. The moment he found her brother with Francesca, the moment he saw her bed empty, he would turn the hold upside down looking for her, and he would find her. She held that knowledge close to her.

Deliberately she avoided looking into the black, empty maw of the darkened building. It had taken on a disturbing feel, as if hundreds of eyes stared at her from the shadowed interior. Each time her gaze was inadvertently pulled in that direction, shadows moved alarmingly, and she looked away. Only silence stretched endlessly before her. She detested the lack of sound, far too aware of her teeth chattering and how alone she was.

A whisper of movement caught her attention, and her heart stilled. She turned to peer into the darkness. The noise came again. A scurry of tiny feet. Her heart began to pound out a rhythm of terror. She inched her hand toward the lantern. When her fingers closed around it, she lifted the light higher, hoping to cast the circle of illumination wider.

She saw them then, a flash of furry bodies running along the shelves. Her entire body shuddered in horror. She detested rats. She could see their beady eyes staring at her. The rats should have turned away from the lantern, but they continued running toward her.

She realized they were agitated, dashing away from a predator. As terrified as she was of rats, whatever was scaring them frightened her even more. The rats rushed around her feet, scuttling toward a hole she couldn't see. She cried out as she felt them brush against her shoes, her ankles, in their hasty exodus. Isabella clutched the lantern and stared into the cavernous interior, trying to pierce the veil of darkness to see what had sent the rats dashing for safety.

Only then did it occur to her. As much as she detested rats, with grain and food items in the storage house, she had seen only a handful of them. There should have been many, many more. Where were they? She raised the light higher, her mouth dry with fear. *Why weren't there more rats and mice? Where could they all be? And what had frightened them more than her lantern, more than a human?*

A cat yowled. A high-pitched scream like that of a woman in terror. Another cat answered it. Then another. So many that Isabella feared the building was overrun with felines. She clapped her free hand over one ear to drown out the increasing volume of the cats' cries. The lantern swung precariously, flickering and sputtering, and she held her breath, afraid the flame would go out. As she carefully righted the lamps, fights broke out, cats clawing at one another, a continuous yowling of starving animals desperate for food.

The cats prowled, eyes glowing in the darkness. One leapt onto the shelves above her head, hissing and clawing at the air.

Terrified, Isabella pressed herself against the door, trying to stay out of the animal's way. Ears flat against its head, the cat snarled at her, exposing long, sharp claws and needle-sharp teeth. Though pitifully small in comparison with a lion, the animal was still dangerous. The cat hissed and spit, its eyes feral. Without warning, it launched itself into the air, claws extended toward her face. Isabella screamed. She swung the lantern at the cat, connecting solidly and flinging the animal away from her. For one heart-stopping moment the light dimmed, flickered, the liquid wax-splattering across the floor. She held her breath, praying, until the flame steadied.

The cat screeched, landed on its feet, and turned to snarl, crouching low as it watched her. The other cats hissed and yowled, the din frightful. Isabella didn't dare take her eyes from the cat stalking her. It was small, but it was wild and hungry. It could do much damage. She knew that if she stayed as she was, cowering against the door, others would join the bold one in attacking her. Summoning up every bit of courage she possessed, Isabella began to inch her way toward the nearest torch.

At her movement, the cats became agitated, raking the air with their claws, spitting, hissing, the hair on their backs and tails rising. Some of them attacked one another. Two somersaulted from a shelf and landed with a thud at her feet. One struck out at her, raking across her shoes before leaping away. As she reached for the torch anchored to the shelving, one of the cats swiped at her arm, ripping the sleeve and laying open a long scratch.

She lit the torch from the lantern's flame and held it high. At once the cats screamed in protest, most slipping back into the shadows. But a few of the bolder cats advanced on her, hissing their defiance. She swung the torch in a semicircle, retreating toward the door. After she made a few whirling passes, even the most aggressive animals stayed back. Only when she placed the lantern on the floor did she realize she was still screaming.

Isabella slid down the door to sit on the floor, clapping a hand over her mouth, ashamed of her inability to stay calm. Loss of control was never allowed. She repeated the words in her mind, using her father's voice. Silent, she huddled on the floor, shaking from the cold, her hands and feet numb. She held the torch like a weapon, terrified it would burn out before Nicolai came for her.

She had no idea how long she was actually in the storehouse; it seemed as if most of the night had passed. The lantern's candle had burned down to the size of her thumbnail, the flame sputtering. The torch was reduced to a glowing ember. Occasionally the cats ventured close to her, but for the most part they kept a respectful distance from the circle of light. She was too cold, too frightened to move when the door finally began to creak open.

"*Signorina* Vernaducci?" Captain Bartolmei's tall frame filled the doorway, his eyes narrowing when he spotted Isabella.

Isabella lifted her head, fearing she was hearing things. Her muscles were locked in place, and she couldn't find enough strength to get to her feet.

Captain Bartolmei uttered a startled imprecation when his light spilled over her. At once he stepped inside, crouching beside her. "Everyone is looking for you. *Don* DeMarco sent a party out to the farm to find the woman Brigita said you aided. He is searching for you in the nearby forest while others scour the city."

Isabella just looked up at him, afraid he was going to ask her to stand. It was physically impossible.

"You're freezing, *signorina*." Captain Bartolmei removed his coat and put it around her shoulders, drawing her close to him to share his body heat.

"I seem to be collecting your coats, *signore*." Isabella made a weak attempt at humor, but her shaking didn't stop.

Bartolmei had to lift her, a most unseemly and humiliating moment in her young life. She couldn't manage more than circling his neck with her arms to hold on. "Found!" Captain Bartolmei shouted. "Light the signal fire atop the battlements. *Signorina* Vernaducci has been found."

Isabella could hear the cry, carried from man to man, telling the seekers of her rescue, alerting the servants to prepare for her arrival. Word spread fast, a wildfire of gossip. Rolando Bartolmei hurried across the uneven, snow-covered ground. The lantern swung crazily as he carried her.

They neared the entrance to the huge *palazzo*. White clouds of vapor streamed from their mouths. Fog swirled around their feet. Without warning a huge lion leapt onto the top stair, the shaggy mane wild, eyes fiery red in the night, mouth snarling. Rolando froze in place, then slowly lowered Isabella to her feet and thrust her behind him, a small protection for her should the beast attack.

"I thought all lions were to be kept out of sight in case *Don* Rivellio's men should be sneaking about," Isabella whispered close to Rolando's ear. She was clutching at him, her legs too unsteady to hold her up on their own.

"Evidently it's a faster means of travel," Captain Bartolmei responded, clearly recognizing the animal.

Isabella peeked around his shoulder, but the lion took a second gargantuan leap, disappearing into the swirling mists. "It's safe now," she said, her teeth chattering so hard she could scarcely get the words out.

Rolando swung her back into his arms and almost ran straight into *Don* DeMarco. He loomed over them, tall and powerful, his expression grim. Nicolai reached out and wordlessly plucked Isabella out of the captain's arms, securing her against the protection of his chest. Captain Bartolmei's coat fell unnoticed to the ground.

Isabella caught a brief glimpse of Theresa and Violante standing together, clutching hands as they watched Nicolai carry her into the house. Theresa caught her husband's arm. Violante reached down to retrieve the coat from the snow, handing it to Sergio to return to Rolando.

Isabella burrowed closer to Nicolai in a futile attempt to get warm. She buried her face against his neck. He carried her swiftly through the *castello*, straight to her bedchamber. Sarina was already there, wringing her hands, distress plain on her face.

"She's freezing, Sarina. We must warm her immediately." Nicolai's voice was tight with control, but a fine tremor ran through his body, the only indication of the volcanic emotions roiling deep in his belly.

"She's injured!" Sarina gasped.

"We have to warm her before we attend to anything else," Nicolai insisted. "The underground baths will be too hot."

"I've asked for the small tub. They are heating the water."

Sarina and Nicolai talked as if Isabella weren't present, but she couldn't seem to summon the energy to take offense. She was so tired, wanting only to sleep.

Nicolai looked down at her tear-stained face. The thought of what could have happened to her had they not found her when they did tore at his soul, turned his blood to ice. Questions clamored in his mind, but he kept quiet. He had never seen Isabella look so vulnerable, so fragile. His arms tightened around her, and he held her to him.

There was a knock on the door, and Francesca swept in. "Sarina, I've summoned the healer." She turned to her brother. "I will care for Isabella while you find the one responsible for this, Nicolai. I'll send for you the instant she's in her bed."

Nicolai hesitated, for the first time indecisive. His gaze locked with his sister's.

Her eyes remained steady on his. "I'll see to her myself, *mio fratello*. I won't leave her side until you are once more with her. I give you my word of honor, the word of a DeMarco. Leave her to us, Nicolai."

He didn't want to leave Isabella, not for even a few minutes. But he intended to know what had transpired. His men would bring the widow and the two kitchen servants to him. Nicolai bent his head to brush a kiss along Isabella's temple. "I'm putting my heart in your hands, Francesca," he said softly, his voice rumbling with menace.

"I'm well aware of that," she answered.

Nicolai reluctantly placed Isabella on the bed. The healer had entered the room. Nicolai stood there, looking at the three women. "See to it that she recovers quickly." Something unfamiliar clogged his throat, and he spun away from them, his fingers curling into fists. This would stop. It had to stop. It was bad enough that Isabella faced a very real threat from him, but to have these *accidents* occurring so regularly whispered of a conspiracy.

Francesca closed the door behind her brother and turned to the healer. "Tell us what to do."

The three women stripped Isabella and put her in the bath. Even the lukewarm water was painful to her, and she cried out and tried to squirm away from them as they gently rubbed life back into her limbs. The healer attended the wicked scratch, even as Sarina called for steaming water to make the bath hotter. Tears streamed down Isabella's face as her body began to warm. The shaking persisted, the remnants of horror in the depths of her eyes. Francesca rocked her gently, while the healer poured strong, honeyed tea down her throat.

When Isabella was finally dressed in her warmest nightgown and tucked beneath the coverlets, Francesca sat beside her, stroking back her hair.

She waited until the healer and Sarina had bustled out of the room, taking their supplies with them. "You frightened me, *sorella mia*. You can't disappear like that." She leaned close, whispering words of encouragement. "I held watch over *tuo fratello* for you. He is sleeping peacefully. Nicolai loves you very much. You have become his life, you know. His heart." She took Isabella's hand in hers and leaned closer still. "You're the only friend I have, the only one who can lead me back from a dark, empty place. I don't want to live there anymore, Isabella. Stay with us. Stay with *mio fratello*. Stay with me. We live in a world you can't hope to understand, but we need your courage."

Isabella's fingers tightened around Francesca's just for a moment, then went slack. Francesca sighed and tucked Isabella's hand beneath the coverlets. Nicolai was waiting impatiently, nearly growling at his sister as he prowled into the room like the restless lion he was.

"Let her sleep, Nicolai," Francesca advised. "What have you found out?"

"My men are bringing the woman and the servants. We'll have our answers when they arrive." He touched Isabella's hair, a tender caress, then resumed his pacing.

"She was attacked by the cats. There are deep scratches on her arm." Francesca inhaled at his murderous expression and tried to explain hastily. "The cats take refuge in the storehouse to keep from being eaten by the lions. They keep the rodents down. We need them, Nicolai. You can't destroy them. The poor creatures are hungry and were only protecting their territory. They have nowhere else to shelter. Everyone knows that." Her words trailed off as the import sank in. She raised her eyes to her brother's "Nicolai." She breathed his name in horror.

308

Flames burned in his eyes, orange-red, a reflection of his inner turmoil. He continued to stare down at her.

"Nicolai, you can't still persist in thinking I would want harm to come to her." There was pain in her face, in her eyes.

"I don't know what to think, only that her life is in danger from something other than what lives within me."

"What would I have to gain by her death? What would be my reason? I'm the one person you can trust with her life. The *only* person. You're *mio fratello*. My loyalty has always been to you." She lifted her chin. "Isabella has given me a task. I've given her my word of honor, and I intend to keep it. If you'll excuse me . . ." She squared her shoulders and walked toward the door.

Nicolai raked a restless hand through his thick mane of hair. "Francesca." His voice stopped her, but she didn't turn around. "I don't even trust myself," he admitted in a low voice.

She nodded, looking over her shoulder sadly. "Nor should you. She's in more danger from you than from any traitor living in our holding. We both know that. And she knows it, too. The difference is, Isabella is willing to take a chance on us, live with us, make a life for herself and those around her. We chose to lock ourselves away, watching life and love pass us by. Without Isabella, neither of us has much of a chance at a life."

"And with us," he answered, "what chance does she have at living?"

Francesca shrugged. "As with every bride before her, the beast will wait until an heir is secured. She has those years, Nicolai. Make her happy. Make her sacrifice count for something. Or decide to break the curse."

"You sound as if I have a choice." His hands knotted into fists, and, with the intensity of his emotion, needles punctured his palms. "How?" There was rage in his voice, hopelessness. "Does anyone know how it is done?"

Christine Feehan

Francesca shook her head. "I know only that it can be done."

Nicolai watched his sister leave the room. He paced restlessly, padding in silence, his mind working furiously. From the moment Isabella had come to the valley, a killer had stalked her. He had to find the traitor and dispose of him . . . or her.

Isabella stirred, shadows creeping into the peace of her expression. At once he went to her, sliding his large frame onto the bed to stretch out beside her. He gathered her close to him, his arms circling her, drawing her against his heart. Nicolai rested his chin on top of her head, rubbing his jaw gently along her hair in a gesture meant to soothe. He wasn't entirely certain whether he was soothing Isabella or himself.

"Nicolai?" She whispered his name uncertainly, caught between a dream and a nightmare.

"I'm here, *cara mia*," he assured her. The intensity of his emotions gripped him, tears welling up, choking him. "Think only of happiness, Isabella. *Tuo fratello* is safe within the walls of the *palazzo*. You are safe in your bedchamber, and I'm with you." He pressed a series of kisses along her throat. Gently. Tenderly. "*Ti amo*, and I swear to you, I'll find a way to keep you safe."

"When you're with me, Nicolai, I feel safe," she murmured. "I wish you would feel safe when you were with me," she added wistfully. "I want peace for you. Just accept what you are, Nicolai. Accept who you are. My heart. That's what you've become. My heart." Her lashes fluttered, her soft mouth curving. "Be with me, and let the rest take care of itself."

"I can't protect you from the traitor in our home," he said in despair. "How can I protect you from what I am?"

She rubbed her face against his chest. "I don't need protection from a man who loves me. I'll never need protection." She sounded drowsy, sexy, her voice so soft it crept under his skin and wound around his heart. "I'm so tired, Nicolai. Maybe we can talk later. I saw Theresa and Violante. Keep them safe, and Francesca, too. I should have warned them."

He looked down at her face, her long lashes two thick crescents. Duty was ingrained deeply in her. "The captains and their wives will be spending the night here in the *palazzo*. I intend to find out exactly what happened." He kissed her temple. "Sleep now, *piccola*. Just rest, and be assured the others are safe."

As he watched her sleep, he realized there were no chains rattling, no wailing in the halls. Even the ghosts and spirits were reluctant to disturb her. When he was certain she was in a deep sleep, he left her to conduct his investigation.

Isabella didn't sleep for long. Nightmares assailed her, jerking her awake despite her terrible fatigue. She needed company. She needed to see her brother.

Isabella pushed open the door to her brother's room and was surprised to see Francesca jerk away from Lucca's bedside, two bright spots of color in her cheeks. Her eyes were over-bright. Isabella looked from her brother to the *don's* sister. "Is everything all right? Is Lucca better?"

"He's doing very well," Francesca assured her, pacing a short distance from the bed.

"*Grazie*, Francesca. I appreciate your seeing Lucca through the night for me. He looks better." Isabella brushed at the waves of hair framing her brother's face. "Has he been resting?"

"I'm right here, Isabella," Lucca reminded her. "Don't talk as if I'm a *bambino* with no sense."

"You act like a *bambino*," Francesca accused. "He refuses to take his medicine without first knowing every single herb in the mixture." She rolled her eyes. "He doesn't have a clue what herb treats what ailment, but he insists just to test my knowledge." She glared at him.

Lucca took Isabella's hand, looking as pathetic as possible. "Who is this *bambina* you have watching over me? She's power-hungry."

"*Bambina?*" Francesca spluttered, her eyes hot. "You are

the *bambino*, afraid of every little drink or ointment. You think because you're a man you can question my authority, but, in truth, you're weak as a babe, and without me you can't manage to hold a cup in your hands."

Lucca shook his head and looked up at Isabella. "She likes to put her arms around me. She uses my illness as an excuse to stay near me." He shrugged carelessly. "But I'm used to attention from females. I can put up with it."

Francesca sucked in her breath. "You . . . you arrogant *beast*! If you think your ridiculous delusions will get rid of me, you are sadly mistaken. And I won't be driven off by your bad temper, either. I've given *tua sorella* my word that I'll attend to you, and the word of a DeMarco is *gold*."

Lucca lifted an arrogant eyebrow at her furious face. "Instead of chattering uselessly so much, you might help me to sit up."

Francesca hissed between her teeth. "I'll help you to sit up all right, but you may find yourself on the floor."

His laughing eyes assessed her small frame. "A little thing like you? I doubt you can assist me to sit. Isabella is much sturdier. I think I'll need her."

"Stop teasing her, Lucca," Isabella ordered, trying not to smile at the evidence of her brother returning to his old self. "It's his odd way of showing appreciation," she told Francesca, who looked as if she might fling herself on Lucca and assault him. She stepped closer to aid her brother.

"Don't you dare." Francesca bit out the words. "It's my job to see to him, and I'll sit His Majesty up." She smiled with feigned sweetness at Isabella. "You won't mind if I bind a scarf around his mouth so he ceases his endless prattle, will you?" She caught at Lucca's arms to help him up.

His body was instantly wracked with coughing. Lucca turned his head from them and waved Francesca away. She ignored him and held a handkerchief to his mouth. Her hand pounded a rhythm on his back, bringing more spasms of coughing until he spit into the handkerchief.

Francesca nodded approvingly. "The healer said all of

that must be gotten out of you, and you will once again be strong."

Lucca glared at her. "You don't know when to give a man his privacy, woman."

She raised an eyebrow. "At least I've become a woman. That's something. You need to eat more broth. You can't expect to recover unless you eat."

Isabella looked from one to the other. "You two sound like adversaries." She wanted them to like one another. Francesca already felt like a sister to her. And Lucca was her family. Francesca had to like Lucca.

Francesca smiled at her. "We spent most of our time talking of pleasant things," Francesca reassured her. "He's just feeling out of sorts at the moment. It makes him grumpy." She waved a careless hand. "It's of no importance."

Lucca raised an eyebrow at his keeper. "A Vernaducci is never grumpy. Or out of sorts. I can scarcely make it to the alcove on my own, and she refuses, *refuses*, to call a male servant. The next thing you know, she'll ask to assist me." He sounded outraged.

Francesca attempted to look blasé. "If you're embarrassed about what you look like, I suppose I can provide a cover."

"Have you no shame?" Lucca nearly roared. That brought on another spasm of coughing. Francesca dutifully held him. "Do you spend much time looking at the naked bodies of men?" His hot gaze should have seared her. "I intend to have a word with *tuo fratello*. He has much to answer for."

Francesca hid a grin behind her hand. "I'm not your concern, *signore*."

"Lucca, she's teasing you," Isabella explained, hiding her own smile. Lucca looked weak and thin, but he was always a forceful personality, and she was happy to see him chafing under the restraints of his illness. "You make a terrible patient."

"Isabella?" Sarina opened the door after a perfunctory knock. "*Don* DeMarco wishes an audience immediately in his wing." She beckoned her young charge into the hall, lowering her voice to keep Lucca from hearing. "The servants have arrived from the farm along with Widow Bertroni."

Francesca followed them into the hall. "He has the man who locked you in the storehouse. Nicolai will have him put to death."

Isabella's breath caught in her throat. She glanced toward her brother through the open door. Lucca attempted to prop himself up. "What is it, Isabella? Is something wrong?"

She shook her head. "I must go to *Don* DeMarco. Just rest, Lucca. Francesca will look after you."

"I'm not a *bambino*, Isabella," he snapped, looking mutinous. "I don't need a nursemaid."

Francesca assumed her haughtiest look. "Yes, you do. You're just too arrogant and stubborn to admit it." She waved at Isabella. "Don't worry. No matter what he says, I'll see to it that he takes his medicaments." Firmly she closed the door.

Isabella found herself smiling in spite of the grimness of the situation. She followed Sarina up the long, winding staircases to the huge wing of the *palazzo* reserved for *Don* DeMarco. She had no idea what to think or feel, facing the person who had locked her in with the feral cats and the freezing cold. He had gone off to the widow's farm and never thought to send word back to have someone let her out. It must have occurred to him that she might not survive the night, yet he hadn't turned back to free her.

With some apprehension she entered the *don's* apartments. His two captains, Sergio Drannacia and Rolando Bartolmei, were there along with the two kitchen servants and the widow. Isabella swept across the room to Nicolai's side, taking his hand as he seated her in a high-backed chair. She could smell fear in the room. She could smell death. It had an ugly, pungent odor, and it sickened her.

She felt Nicolai's hands on her shoulders, bringing her a

feeling of safety and comfort despite her trepidation. When she looked directly at the man who had locked her in the storehouse, she saw he was sweating profusely.

"Isabella, please tell us what happened," Nicolai prompted gently.

She reached up to entwine her fingers with his. "What are you going to do, Nicolai?" Her voice was steady, but she was shaking inside.

"Just tell us what happened, *cara*, and I will decide what needs to be done, as I've been doing for most of my life," he reassured her.

"I don't understand what this is all about," the widow began.

Don DeMarco made a soft, menacing sound, cutting off any further speculation. His eyes burned with fury. The servants squirmed visibly, and the widow blanched.

"Brigita asked me to help *Signora* Bertroni, because her storage shed had burned to the ground and her man died recently," Isabella said. "The family needed to be seen through the winter. You were busy, as were Betto and Sarina. I took her to the storehouse, within the walls of the *castello*." She glanced up at Nicolai. "I kept my promise to you."

"We are here to find the one guilty of attempted murder, *cara*, not to accuse you of anything." Nicolai brushed his lips against her ear. He wanted to make it abundantly clear to all present that Isabella was his lady, his heart, and his life. The good Madonna could have mercy on the soul of any who attempted to harm her; they would find none from him. "Continue with what happened, Isabella."

"I had two servants sent to aid us." She indicated the two men. "Those two there. The wagon was loaded, very heavy, and night had fallen. I was afraid for *Signora* Bertroni and her *bambini*. I ordered the two men to accompany the wagon to the farm." She nodded toward the older man. "He agreed without dissent, but that one"—she looked at the younger man—"became angry. He knocked into me as he left the storehouse. I remained to extinguish the torches. The door was closed and locked behind me. He must have taken the key from my skirt."

At her words Nicolai's features went carefully blank, only his eyes alive. The flames seemed to have disappeared, to be replaced with sheer ice. There was a sudden chill in the room. Isabella's voice was barely audible. "He deliberately shut me in." In spite of her resolve to remain calm, she shuddered at the memory.

"No! *Dio*, help me! It wasn't me! I don't know what happened! I don't!" the servant burst out. He jumped to his feet, but Sergio caught his shoulders and slammed him back into the chair.

"I didn't know what he'd done, *Don* DeMarco," the older servant, Carlie, cried, obviously horrified. "I didn't see the *signorina* once she sent us away."

"Nor I," the widow added, wringing her hands. "May the good Madonna strike me dead if I lie. I would never have left her there. She was an angel to me. An angel. You must believe me, *Don* DeMarco."

Rolando gestured to the widow and the other kitchen servant, beckoning them to follow him to the door. "*Grazie* for your time. *Signora* Bertroni, you'll be escorted back to your farm." He gestured toward the guards outside the door to take the widow and servant from the *don's* wing.

Nicolai moved around in front of Isabella's chair, blocking her view of the groveling servant. He lifted her fingers to his mouth. "Go back to your bedchamber, *piccola*. It is finished here." His voice was gentle, even tender, completely at odds with his ice-cold eyes.

Isabella shivered. "What are you going to do?"

"Don't concern yourself with this any longer, Isabella. There's no need." He brushed a kiss on top of her silken head.

The servant broke into a torrent of weeping, of pleading. Isabella flinched. She wrapped her fingers around Nicolai's wrist. "But I'm a part of this, Nicolai. You haven't heard everything. We weren't alone in the storehouse. I felt the presence of evil." She whispered the words, afraid to allow any other to hear. "It isn't over."

Nicolai swung around to stare at the servant, his eyes flat and cold. "It is over. I'm looking at a dead man."

His voice chilled her. The servant shrieked a protest, throwing himself on Isabella's mercy, apologizing profusely, denying he had known what he was doing.

"Nicolai, please, hear him out," she said, holding the *don's* gaze with her own. She felt the energy in the room, the subtle influence of evil feeding the anger and disgust. It fed the servant's fear right along with her own. She glanced at the two captains, noting they were watching the servant with the same loathing as their *don.*

"This is no longer your concern." Nicolai was staring over her head, his gaze locked on the hapless servant, a hunter eyeing its prey.

"I want to hear him speak," she answered, her tone gentle but insistent. She didn't dare allow the entity to influence her or give it more of an opening to the men.

"Grazie, grazie!" the man cried. "I don't know what happened, *signorina*. One moment I was thinking of the journey and how best to unload the supplies when we reached the farm, whether to wait until morn or just take care of it immediately. All of a sudden I was so angry I couldn't think. My head hurt and buzzed with a noise. I don't remember taking the key from you. I know I did because I had it, but I don't remember taking it. I sat in the wagon, and my head hurt so much I was sick. Carlie can tell you, I leapt down and was sick." His eyes pleaded with her for mercy. "In truth I don't remember locking you in, just that closing the door and turning the lock seemed the most important thing in the world."

"You knew she was in there," Nicolai said, his voice purring with menace. "You left her to freeze to death or to be torn to shreds by the feral cats."

"*Signorina*, I swear I don't know what happened to me. Save me. Don't let them kill me."

Isabella turned to Nicolai. "Allow me to speak with you alone. There is more at work here than what we can see. Please trust me."

"Take him out," Nicolai ordered.

His two captains looked as if they wanted to protest, but they did as Nicolai commanded. Neither was very gentle with the servant.

Nicolai began to pace. "You can't ask me to let this man go."

"Please, Nicolai. I think there's truth in the legend of your valley. I think that when its magic was tampered with, it did become twisted, and something evil was let loose here. I think it preys on human weakness. Our failings. It feeds anger and jealousy. It feeds our own fears. There have been so many incidents, and each person tells the same story. They don't know what happened; they acted differently than they normally would have."

A growl rumbled deep in his throat. "You want me to let him go," he repeated, his amber eyes gleaming with menace.

She nodded. "That's exactly what I want you to do. I believe there is an entity loose, and it is responsible, not the man."

"If this *thing* influences what a man is capable of, then this man has a sickness that he would dare risk your life."

"Nicolai." She breathed his name, a gentle persuader.

He muttered an imprecation, flames flowing in his eyes. "For you, *cara mia*, only for you. But I believe this man has forfeited his right to live. I should banish him from the valley."

She crossed to his side and stood on tiptoes to press a kiss along his set jaw. "You will give him his job back. Send him home. Your mercy will earn his loyalty tenfold."

"*Your* mercy," he corrected. "To me he is already dead."

When she continued to look at him, he sighed. "As you wish, Isabella. I'll give the order."

"Grazie, amore mio." Smiling, she kissed him again and left him to his pacing.

Chapter Eighteen

Sarina was in Lucca's room, fussing and clucking over him. Lucca, looking desperate, gestured to Francesca behind the housekeeper's back, clearly expecting her to save him. Francesca and Isabella grinned at each other, the smirk of conspirators.

"Sarina," Isabella said, using her sweetest voice. "Francesca and I have one small errand to run. Please see to *mio fratello* until we return."

"It's the middle of the night," Lucca hissed between clenched teeth. "Neither one of you should be going anywhere unescorted."

"We'll be perfectly safe," Francesca assured him with a bright smile. "We'll keep to the passageways. Sarina will take excellent care of you in our absence."

"Isabella, I forbid you running wild! Have you lost all sense of propriety?" Another spasm of coughing shook him.

All three women rushed to aid him, but it was Francesca he leaned against, accustomed to the firm feel of her arm around his back and the square of cloth she pressed into his hand. Weak, he bent nearly double and clutched her arm to prevent her from moving.

When the spasm had passed, Lucca looked up at Francesca. "You can see I need you here with me."

"Just try to sleep," she replied sweetly, patting his shoulder. "I'll be back before you know it."

"I should speak to *tuo fratello*," he snapped, disgusted. "And you, Isabella, have much to answer for. Francesca has told me of your betrothal."

Isabella laughed softly and kissed her brother on the top of his head. "It's too late to worry about my running wild. I came to this place all by myself. I think *Don* DeMarco intends to speak to you about my wayward manner."

Lucca's dark eyes flashed, momentarily revealing his proud, arrogant nature. "If he wants to talk to me about your behavior, he might want to explain why his own sister is allowed to be unescorted in a man's bedchamber."

"I'd love to hear that particular discussion," Francesca said as she took Isabella's hand. "Pay him no attention when he's rambling, Sarina. It's the illness."

Isabella and Francesca escaped into the passageway. The moment the hidden door had swung closed behind them, they burst into laughter. "He's very demanding but so sweet, Isabella. He said he likes my hair." Francesca patted her upswept hairdo. "I asked Sarina to dress it for me."

The taper Francesca held was sputtering. She raised the flickering flame to a torch. Light leapt and danced as they hurried along the narrow corridor.

"Lucca isn't normally so demanding, Francesca. I don't know why he's clinging to you the way he is or why he's teasing you so much." Isabella rubbed her temples. "I hope he won't really talk to Nicolai. We shouldn't let the two of them ever get together."

Francesca looked vulnerable for a moment. "No one has ever talked to me as Lucca does. He seems so interested in my life, in my opinions. Once, when I was quoting *mio fratello*, he became impatient and demanded to know what *I* thought. Only you and *tuo fratello* have ever asked me what *I* think."

Isabella smiled affectionately at her. She studied the young face, finding her vulnerability touching. She couldn't imagine the beast overtaking Francesca. Or Francesca leading her to her doom off a slippery balcony, or stalking her through the city streets. She sighed softly. If Francesca hadn't stalked her, that left Nicolai. "Lucca believes a woman should speak her mind, yet he is extremely protective. He might well speak to *Don* DeMarco."

"He couldn't sleep, and he told me the funniest stories. I love his voice. I loved his stories." She ducked her head. "I hope you don't mind that I told him of your betrothal. I assured him Nicolai loves you."

"What did he say?" Isabella gripped Francesca's arm as they began the descent to the bowels of the *palazzo*. Isabella hadn't been looking forward to telling her brother, knowing he would guess how the match had come about.

Francesca looked down at her hands. "He seemed pleased. Nicolai is a good catch, but I couldn't bring myself to tell Lucca about the lions. I wanted to. I didn't want to lie to him. When he looks at me, I want to tell him everything." She sighed and smoothed her dress. "He says the nicest things to me."

"I'm glad he hasn't been too difficult with you. I owe you so much, Francesca. It must be hard for you to be indoors so much after all your freedom." She looked at the young woman. "Your gown is beautiful. Did Lucca notice it?" It was like her brother to observe details.

"Do you like it?" Francesca asked shyly, pleased that Isabella had noticed. "Sarina is always after me to wear the gowns Nicolai has had made for me. I usually give them away to the young women who really want them. Lucca thought it becoming." She shook her head. "Lucca knows something is wrong. He keeps asking me. I told him he was to sleep, but he wanted to know why I was sad."

"We'll find a way to tell him the truth."

"What truth? That I'm Nicolai's half-mad sister who turns occasionally into a beast?" Francesca's voice shook. "I *really* like him. I don't even know why, but I don't want him thinking ill of me."

Isabella glanced at her. "Lucca has no reason to think ill of you."

Francesca was no longer paying attention. Her hand gripped Isabella's wrist. They were in a small room deep beneath the *castello*. It was bare, empty, a stark, almost ugly place, unlike any other room Isabella had seen.

Isabella shivered in the cold. "What is this place?"

"This is where Sophia was buried, here beneath the floor." Francesca spoke in reverent tones, indicating the cross carved into the marble in the middle of the floor.

"But there's nothing here," Isabella protested. "She should have candles, something to honor her. She wasn't guilty of the crimes they accused her of. Why isn't anyone taking care of her resting place?"

Francesca looked astonished. "Because of her curse, of course."

"And if the entity was already loose in the valley, preying on human weaknesses, don't you think, in that one moment, when her friends betrayed her, when her own husband betrayed her, it would feed her natural anger?" Isabella shrugged. "I find myself thinking of her often, wishing her well. What a terrible torment she has lived through. I hope at last she is with her husband and has found some happiness."

"They all despise her—the 'others,' I mean. They blame her for locking them in the valley. None of them go near her. I don't know about her husband."

Francesca made a soft sound of warning and turned her head to the side, her eyes closing. "She is here with us now." She was silent a moment, listening to whispers Isabella had no hope of hearing. "She thanks you for your generosity and kind thoughts. She warns you of great danger, of betrayal." Francesca entwined her fingers with Isabella's as if she could somehow hold tightly to her, prevent the dire predictions, the ominous warnings. "The evil was awakened when you arrived in the valley, and you are its greatest adversary. It is preying on Nicolai." Francesca looked stricken. "On me and all others it can use to harm you."

"Please tell her I'm so sorry for all her pain and anguish. I hope to set her free. If I cannot, I look forward to meeting her in the afterlife." Isabella felt her heart pound at the thought of how she would meet her death.

"She can hear you, Isabella, but she cannot aid you. Those trapped within the valley cannot give aid to the living. She says she can only remind you that she, who was strong and very much in love with her husband, fell prey to the entity. Your task is twofold. She is sorry for what she caused." Tears filled Francesca's eyes. "She's weeping. Alexander, her spouse, is in eternal torment, unable to reach her, unable to be with her, nor can she reach him."

"Nicolai is a good man, well worth saving. I'll do my best. It's all I can do," Isabella said softly.

Francesca heaved a sigh of relief. "She's gone now. I don't feel her." The cold had seeped into her blood. "Let's go quickly."

Isabella allowed Francesca to drag her back through the maze of corridors, not really paying attention to the directions they took. Sophia had warned her of the danger Isabella had known all along was there. She couldn't abandon Nicolai and his people. She had grown to care about them. Rubbing her hands up and down her arms for warmth, she forced her mind from thoughts of Nicolai and the beast. She was determined to think of him only as a man. Someone had to see him as a man instead of a beast.

For most of his life he had been shaped by his legacy, shaped by his isolation and his people's downcast eyes. If she gave him nothing else, she would give him the gift of his own humanity. And while he was hers, she would cherish him. She became aware of Francesca's silence. Glancing at her, she noted the stricken look on her face.

"What is it?"

"Didn't you hear what she said? She said the entity was preying on *me*. She warned you of betrayal and danger. *I* was the beast following you through the city. Nicolai smelled me. Isabella, what are we to do? I don't even remember I could harm you. Nicolai could harm you."

Isabella stopped in the passageway and hugged Francesca to her. "Sophia didn't say you were the beast. We already knew there was a possibility of danger and betrayal. We'll figure it out together, you and I and Nicolai. We just have to watch one another, try to be prepared for the entity when it feeds our weaknesses."

Francesca nodded mutely, looking as though she might burst into tears. She took a deep breath and found the panel that swung the hidden door to Lucca's bedchamber open. They extinguished the torch before entering.

But it wasn't Sarina waiting for them. *Don* DeMarco was pacing, his long strides taking him back and forth across the floor in his silent, fluid manner. He swung around as they entered, his amber eyes burning with fury. He moved so fast that Isabella's heart jumped as he shackled her wrist and, right in front of her brother, dragged her against him.

"Where have you been? Don't you think I was worried enough about you tonight without another disappearance?"

His voice was so soft with menace, Isabella shivered. She glanced at her brother. He was watching them, speculation and knowledge in his gaze. Lucca and Nicolai both turned to Francesca at the same moment.

She lifted her chin. "My movements are of no concern to *anyone*. I'm certainly not used to having my activities questioned." She tried to sound haughty, but her voice trembled a little.

"I can see I've been far too lenient with you, Francesca," Nicolai answered, retaining his hold on Isabella when she would have gone to her brother's side. "Your safety is of paramount importance. Enemies are within our valley, and we have a traitor among us. I must insist you conduct yourself properly and with circumspect behavior. I am *tuo fratello* and your *don*. You must answer to me."

Francesca glared at Lucca. "This is your doing. You've said things to him."

Lucca lay back, lacing his fingers behind his head, a satisfied expression on his face. "We've had a most informative talk," he admitted without remorse.

Nicolai looked down at Isabella's upturned face. "*We* need to have a most informative talk," he said grimly, "right now, just the two of us. Say good night, Isabella." It was an order.

Lucca bristled visibly at the proprietary tone used on his sister, but he remained silent when she brushed a kiss on the top of his head. "Good night, Lucca. I'll see you first thing in the morn. I'm so happy you're finally here."

Nicolai's fingers tightened on her wrist, tugging her away from the bed. He barely restrained himself as he escorted her to her bedchamber, using the hidden passageway so he would not have to leave her in front of the servants and return later. He was seething with anger, fear gnawing at him until he was afraid he might explode. The fire was burning brightly, and a cup of steaming tea waited on the nightstand, evidence Sarina had prepared the room. Nicolai stalked to the door, ensuring it was locked, before turning to face her.

Isabella tilted her chin. "Am I to report my every movement to you?"

He let his breath out in a single rush. "Absolutely you are. You have no idea what you mean to me, what I've discovered myself capable of. *Dio*, Isabella, all this time I've wasted worrying about what I might do years from now. I should have been getting as close to you as possible. Binding you to me in every conceivable way so that there's no doubt between us."

She raised an eyebrow. "Doubt, Nicolai? What is it you find yourself doubting? Surely not my fidelity?"

He raked a hand through his hair, leaving it wild and rakish. "I have heard several . . . unpleasant whispers."

She stared up at him, her entire body stiff with outrage. "And do you, even for one moment, believe those unpleasant whispers?" She held her breath, waiting for his answer, needing it to be the right one. Everything she was, her heart and soul, was her word of honor. If Nicolai doubted that, he knew nothing of her.

A slow smile softened the hard line of his mouth. "You look at me with such trust, such belief that I'll say and do the right thing. I *fear* for you, Isabella. I fear that everywhere you go eyes watch you with petty jealousy, and that already the curse is bringing about its finale. There is more at work here than my controlling or not controlling the beast. You said it yourself. I trust no one with you." He crossed to her side and reached to pull the pins from her hair. He watched it cascade like a silken waterfall, thick and luxurious, below her waist.

"Francesca loves you, Nicolai. She won't betray you."

"I never doubted that *mio padre* loved *mia madre*, Isabella, but in the end he betrayed her." He bent his head to her mouth, needing to taste her, needing to shelter her close to his heart. Her lips were warm, melting beneath his. Her body came into his, soft and pliant, molding to his harder, more muscular frame.

Isabella lifted her head to look into his strange, amber eyes. "Maybe she betrayed him, Nicolai. Not with her body, but with her mind. Maybe she didn't love what he was."

"A beast acts on instinct, Isabella, not reason," he cautioned. "How could a woman ever love that part of him?"

"Sometimes, Nicolai, a woman acts on instincts, too. If the beast resides in you, then it is a part of you. A woman doesn't pick and choose what she loves in a man. She loves all of him."

His hands framed her face. "Do you love all of me, *cara*, even my wild side?" His voice was a low caress, playing over her skin like the touch of his fingers. Butterfly wings brushed along her insides.

"I love every part of you," she whispered softly. "Your voice, the way you laugh, how gentle you can be. I love the way you love your people, the way you've dedicated your life to them."

"And my wild side, beautiful one—do you love that part of me?"

"Most particularly, *signore*," she agreed.

His thumbs trailed down her neck, her throat, slipping along the neckline of her gown. Isabella shivered as the pads of his thumbs rubbed her exposed skin.

His gaze was moody, brooding, a dark quagmire of love and despair. He wanted her; desire burned fiercely in him. He had lived with the results of his legacy; Isabella had not. Still, she believed she saw matters more clearly.

"Are you correct, *amore mia*? Do I place my entire faith in you and trust that you are capable of securing our future for us? There is no giving you up, no turning back, as much as I have tried to pretend that we could. Keeping you as my mistress would change nothing."

She shook her head. "No, it wouldn't." Her voice was a shivery whisper. His fingers were loosening her gown, allowing it to gape open, spilling her breasts into the shadows of flickering firelight. The light and dark seemed to caress her curves, and the brush of his fingertips over her flesh sent heat curling deep in her very core. "What other choice do we have but to live our lives, Nicolai?"

His hands framed her face again, his amber eyes alive with love, with tenderness. "I want to make a vow to you. I'll love you with everything in me. I'll bring you as much happiness as I can give you. But I cannot allow your death, not at my hands. You're more important than I am." His mouth found each of her eyelids, then drifted down her cheek to the corner of her lips. "Don't protest. Just listen to me. I've thought about this for a long time. Your life is in danger. You've accepted that, and you're willing to chance our love. But I couldn't live with your death at my hands. I can't, Isabella." He kissed her mouth, her soft, pliant lips, drawing strength from her, her endless courage becoming his.

When he lifted his head, his amber gaze drifted over her face. "After our child is born, an heir for our people, when I see the beast grow stronger I'll end my life."

She cried out, a shocked protest, but his arms tightened around her, crushing her against him, crushing her objections. "I'm placing my trust and faith in you, all of it, that your way is the right path for us, but you have to allow me this way out. You have to promise, give your word of honor, that you will raise our children to love this valley, the lions, their legacy. I won't have regrets, Isabella. Your life, our lives together, are worth it."

She slid her arms around his waist, afraid to speak, afraid of saying the wrong thing. What could she say? She heard the finality in his voice. She had to guide them through the dark passages and into the light. There had to be a way. She was certain the key lay within her. And she refused to lose him.

"I've been so alone, apart from life, not really knowing why I was so empty. You've filled all those empty places, *cara mia*. I sleep with you in my arms and have no nightmares. I open my eyes and look forward to each hour, to hear your laughter, to watch you move through my home. Your smile takes my breath away."

She looked up at him, love shining in her eyes, complete acceptance. Nicolai kissed her again, allowing the fever to rise, allowing his possessive, passionate nature to the forefront.

He wanted to look at her there with the firelight caressing her body. His hands made short work of her gown, leaving it lying in a frothy pool on the floor. He wanted nothing in his way, not the thinnest barrier. When she was naked, only the fall of her hair to tease him, he moved to stand some distance away from her.

Isabella stood in front of the fireplace, her hair shining with blue lights. The shadows caressed her breasts, her belly, her legs. She watched his expression, saw the blossoming lust mixed with his love. She saw his breeches grow snug, taut, the material stretching to accommodate him. It was exciting to be entirely naked before him while he was fully clothed. Her nipples were hard peaks of desire, and her body ached with a curling heat she recognized.

Nicolai walked around her, not touching her, simply looking, drinking her in, devouring her with his hot gaze. He gestured to the bed as he crossed to the bottle of wine sitting on her nightstand. "Go lie down." His voice was husky, a testament to his arousal. He poured himself a glass of wine and sat in the chair beside the fire.

Isabella walked across the room, aware his eyes tracked her, aware of the sway of her hips, her breasts. She lay back, feeling more sensuous than she ever had in her life. He hadn't touched her, yet every part of her body was alive and pulsing with need.

"Bend your knees and spread your thighs wide so I can see you, Isabella."

She watched his face, the hunger etched there so deeply. She was bringing him pleasure, and it was as arousing to her as it was to him. Slowly she obeyed him, allowing the flickering light to shine between her legs, revealing the glistening invitation.

Nicolai took a slow sip of wine, allowing it to trickle down his throat. She was so beautiful, so *everything* to him. "Feel your breasts, Isabella. I want you to know your body the way I know it. How perfect it is. Slide your hand down your belly and push your fingers deep inside yourself."

He expected a shy protest, but Isabella had courage, and she wanted his pleasure as much as her own. She cupped the weight of her breasts in her palms, her thumbs sliding over her nipples. Her breath caught in her throat.

Nicolai's breath caught in his. His body tightened to the point of pain. His gaze was riveted to her hands, to the beauty of her full, firm breasts spilling out of her palms. He watched as her fingers slid slowly over her curves, caressing her belly, the curve of her hip, then tangled in the tight curls of her mound. His lungs nearly exploded as her fingers disappeared inside her body, as his had often done.

Her face was turned toward his, flushed with passion, pleasure heightening her beauty. He watched her until her breath was coming in short gasps and her body was quivering, until he could no longer stand to be apart from her. He stood up, set his wineglass down, and began to remove his clothing.

Isabella lay back and watched him. He looked like a magnificent god, with the firelight stroking the hard angles and planes of his body, with his erection thrusting large and insistent toward her. Nicolai reached out, caught her wrist, and sucked her fingers into the hot, moist cavern of his mouth. Her entire body clenched.

"Nicolai," she said softly, almost reverently.

He knelt on the bed between her open legs. "There is no other like you, Isabella." He meant it, too. His head was roaring, his mind numb with need. His body was a fierce ache that felt as if it could never be assuaged. He was enormous, thick and hard and throbbing with urgency. He caught her hips and thrust hard, burying himself deeply with one desperate stroke. It was the most important thing in his world to take her, possess her, to love her to distraction.

As he pumped his hips hard, guiding her hips with his hands, he watched her face, watched the play of the flickering firelight on her breasts. He watched their bodies come together in perfect accord. Her sheath was hot and tight and fit him as though she'd been made for him. She tilted her hips to take all of him, greedy for every inch, unashamed to show she wanted him the way he wanted her.

He pounded into her, deep and hot, taking her higher and higher. He felt her body tighten, ripple, clench around his. She cried out, her fingers digging into his arms as she went over the edge. Nicolai kept his gaze glued to hers, woman to man, man to woman, even though his body was primitive with a lusting he'd never experienced. He thrust hard, stroke after stroke, keeping her pleasure so heightened that she was in tears, crying his name, pleading with him.

When his release came, he poured into her, emptying himself completely. He slumped over her, kissing her breasts, sucking her nipples into his mouth so that her body continued to clench and spiral out of control. They lay together, hearts pounding, breathing hard.

When he found he could move, he rolled to one side, easing his weight from hers, pulling her onto her stomach. Nicolai trailed his fingertips down the curve of her back. "Do you know what's so beautiful to me? I think of you all the time, the way you are, like this. So willing to let me love you any way I wish. Your trust in me when I have you all to myself."

"You always bring me such pleasure, Nicolai," she said softly. His hands were kneading her buttocks, her thighs, caressing the small of her back. She loved every new lesson he brought to their bedchamber. She felt lazy and content, as sated as she could possibly be, yet when he bent his head to kiss the side of her breast, his hair spilling across her body, she shivered in reaction.

He heard the drowsy note in her voice. It teased his senses, heightened his pleasure even more. She was nearly purring with contentment. Nicolai settled close to her, his hand cupping her breast, his thumb sliding over her nipple. "Sleep, *amore mia*, for now. You'll need to rest. I'm not finished this night." And he knew he wasn't. Her body was warm and soft. Her trust in him, her acceptance of him, her complete giving of herself into his hands, was becoming as necessary to him as breathing.

Isabella drifted to sleep with a smile curving her mouth. She awakened twice during the night to his lips moving erotically over her body, his hands exploring, memorizing her intimately, his body taking hers. No matter how he possessed her, fast and hard or slow and tender, he ensured she found that ultimate rush of pleasure and then he would kiss her back to sleep.

Her body was deliciously sore when she awoke in the early-morning hours. She felt well used, happy. Nicolai had crept out, not disturbing her, and the first rays of light were just beginning to slip through the colors of her window. Isabella took her time dressing, often touching the pillow where his head had rested. Their bodies had remained tangled together throughout the night. She knew it was right, meant to be. She belonged with Nicolai. They shared something deep and intimate and well worth fighting for.

She relieved Francesca, who looked very tired, having spent the night trying to entertain Lucca. He had been restless, coughing, sometimes out of his head with fever, other times teasing her and telling her stories. Isabella watched Francesca tuck the covers around her brother before slipping out to get much-needed rest. Isabella settled down to her sewing. Her tea and breakfast were served to her in her brother's room, and the morning passed quietly until Lucca woke.

He smiled at her, his dark eyes alive with love. "You did it, Isabella. You saved my life. A miracle. But have I tied you to a monster? What is he like, this *don* who has claimed my sister?"

She blushed, feeling the color climbing up her neck. "You've met him. He's wonderful." When he continued to stare at her steadily, she sighed. She had never been able to lie to him. "The stories are true, Lucca. Of the legend, the lions, the man. It's all true. But I love him and want to be with him. He tries to protect me, but in truth, we haven't discovered how to defeat the curse." She blurted it all out to him, every last detail, other than the fact that she had already lain with the *don*.

He rubbed his temples, his dark eyes reflecting his inner turmoil. Lucca never wasted time on regrets, on circumstances one couldn't change. "If I can arrange your escape, would you leave?"

She shook her head. "Never."

"I was afraid you would say that." Admiration crept into his gaze. "Then I guess I have no choice but to get well and guard your back. What of Francesca? I can't imagine her slinking around trying to murder you. She has shown me every kindness."

Isabella looked at him sharply. There was a note in his voice she had never heard before. "She is a remarkable woman, different, with extraordinary gifts. You be nice to her, Lucca. I see that teasing light in your eyes when she's around."

He grinned, unrepentant. "She rises so beautifully to the bait, how can I resist?" His smile faded. "Go carefully, Isabella, until I'm stronger and can aid you. If we think this through together, we should be able to find a way out of it."

"I won't leave him," she declared staunchly.

Francesca entered with the briefest of knocks. "How are you this morn, Lucca? I awoke and thought I'd come sit with you if you want the company. Isabella, do you have things you wish to be doing?"

Isabella saw the quick, welcoming smile on her brother's face for the *don's* sister. She stood up with a small sigh. Lucca had no land, nothing to offer should he decide he wanted Francesca, and she carried the DeMarco legacy in her blood. *"Grazie,* Francesca." She kissed the top of her brother's head. "I think he's feeling better, so watch out for his teasing." Brushing back his hair, she smiled at Lucca. "You behave."

Lucca flashed a smirk at her, warming her heart. He was becoming more like his old self every hour.

Isabella made her way through the *castello,* aware of the two shadows, the guards Nicolai had ordered to watch over her. She ignored their presence, heading toward the library, her one sanctuary. She was turning over the matter of Francesca and Lucca in her mind. Deep in thought, it took her a while to become aware that the servants she passed were whispering together in groups. Their voices were hushed and agitated.

She stopped in the middle of the great hall, suddenly afraid the battle with *Don* Rivellio might have started. Surely Nicolai would have told her, although he had left her bed in the early-morning hours. Worried, she turned toward the nearest group of servants, determined to find out what had made them nervous.

The whispers stopped the moment Isabella approached, the servants suddenly extraordinarily busy. Even Alberita was dutifully scrubbing at an imaginary speck on the gleaming table in the formal dining room. She kept casting surreptitious glances toward Isabella and then hastily looking away.

Annoyed, Isabella went in search of Betto. He was talking softly with two other men near one of the entrances to the servants' passage. They stopped speaking and looked at the floor the moment they spotted her.

"Betto," she said, "I must speak with you."

He didn't look happy but obediently took his leave from his companions, who hastily escaped. "What is it, *signorina*?"

"Exactly the question. What is it? The *palazzo* is a hotbed of gossip. I've been caring for *mio fratello* and have not heard it, but it obviously concerns me."

The man cleared his throat. "I can't possibly know what the servants are gossiping about now."

Her gaze pinned him. "It's better I hear it from you, Betto. If it is something upsetting, I prefer to hear the news from a trusted friend."

His shoulders sagged. "Better you hear it from *Don* DeMarco. He has said if you inquire, I'm to bring you to him."

She stared at the servant for a long time, so many thoughts racing through her mind she was afraid to move or speak. Surely Nicolai hadn't sent for another bride. Rivellio's men were in the valley. Nicolai would never betray her in a power play. She knew he was busy with his captains, preparing for battle. Why would he have her brought to him simply to repeat gossip?

She followed Betto slowly up the sweeping staircases to the wing of the *don*. At his gruff command, she entered his rooms with trepidation. At once his captains excused themselves. Isabella faced Nicolai across the room.

They looked at one another for a long time. She couldn't read his expression at all, which was faintly shocking when she had just spent the night in his arms. When his body had been buried deep inside of hers. When they had clung to one another, whispering together, sharing laughter, sharing plans. Nicolai looked almost a stranger, his amber eyes flat and hard. He didn't approach her, didn't smile in welcome.

"What is it, Nicolai?" Deliberately she addressed him informally, hoping to break through his icy demeanor.

"The servant, the one who locked you in the storehouse, is dead," he said starkly, without inflection.

A shiver went down her spine. Her blood turned to ice. She kept her gaze locked with his. "How did he die, Nicolai?" Her voice betrayed her, husky with emotion.

"He was found this morning, murdered. There were signs of a struggle. Someone stabbed him numerous times." His voice was still devoid of expression.

She waited, knowing there was more. Her heart seemed to be thundering in her ears. She couldn't equate the gentle, loving man she had lain with to someone capable of such a brutal act. Yet Nicolai had gone into many battles, defeated many enemies, was a feared and respected *don*. He was capable of ordering death and just as capable of killing.

"There were paw prints all around the body in the snow, though all the lions are hidden. There were no signs of a human approaching him, only the tracks of a lion." He didn't take his eyes from her face, watching her with the unblinking stare of a predator focused on its prey.

"Am I to believe that you murdered this man, Nicolai? You were with me last night." Her throat felt swollen, threatening to cut off her air.

"The blood on him was fresh. He was killed in the early-morning hours. I left you well before that time."

Her lashes swept down to break the contact with his hawklike gaze. He missed nothing; she had no way to hide her slightest thought from him. He read her so easily. Isabella didn't know what to think. She didn't know what he was trying to say. She lifted her chin. "I won't believe it, Nicolai. Why would you murder him? You could have ordered his death, and no one would have blamed you."

He did move then, turning away from her with a fluid, catlike gesture, power and coordination rippling through his body. His dark hair spilled down his back, a wild mane as untamable as the man. "I despised that man, Isabella. I wanted him dead. Not just dead, I wanted him to suffer first." He made the admission in a low, compelling voice "I let him go because you asked it of me, not because I agreed with you. I wanted to leap on him and tear him to pieces the moment he was brought before me for what he had done to you. For the hours of fear he caused you. For the danger he put you in. For his cowardice in not returning immediately when he realized he had the key, if his story was the truth. I wanted him dead."

"Wanting him dead doesn't mean you killed him, Nicolai."

He spun around to face her, looking dangerous and powerful. "I don't care if I did kill him," he said, the words cutting deeply into her heart. "I care that I don't remember. I went out this morn, and I ran. I unleashed the beast to run free."

She took a moment to compose herself. "Why would you use a knife, Nicolai? That makes no sense. If you used a knife, you would have remembered."

He shrugged. "I remember last eve when he stood in this room and admitted he locked you in that storehouse, I wanted to shove my stiletto through his throat." His gaze met hers without flinching. "I won't apologize for who I am, Isabella. And I'll never apologize for wanting to destroy any enemy who dares to try to take you from me. I'll never apologize for my feelings for you. Not only am I willing to die for you, but I'm more than willing to kill for you. And I'm not apologizing for that either."

"I've never asked you to," she replied quietly. She was grateful for her father's training, for the composure she managed when each of his revelations had shaken her to her core. "If you'll excuse me, Nicolai, I must attend *mio fratello*."

He padded across the floor then, his footfalls silent, his amber eyes burning. "Not yet, Isabella. Don't leave me yet. I want to look into your eyes and see what I've destroyed between us."

She titled her head, her eyes meeting his without flinching. "I don't think you *can* destroy anything between us. I love you with all my heart. All my soul. Confess all you want, Nicolai, show me your worst side, I will still love you." She reached up, caught his face in her hands, and kissed him hard. Her eyes blazed into his. "And know this, Nicolai DeMarco. Should the worst happen and the beast is let loose and destroys me, I will never regret what we share, what we are together. I love every inch of you. Even that part of you that is capable of destroying me."

When she would have turned away from him, he tightened his hold on her and brought his head down to hers to claim her mouth. Love welled up, nearly overwhelmed him, nearly unmanned him. It swept through him with the force of an avalanche and shook him to the very center of his being.

Chapter Nineteen

The knock on the door made Isabella's heart pound. It was loud, insistent, heralding grim news. Nicolai retained possession of her wrist but turned toward the sound, his face once more an expressionless mask.

Captains Bartolmei and Drannacia hurried in, sketching quick salutes. "He's on the move, *Don* DeMarco. One of the birds has returned and brings word." Drannacia glanced at Isabella and bowed low, apologetically. "We feared the news couldn't wait."

"*Grazie*," Nicolai said and bent unhurriedly to once more take possession of Isabella's mouth. "There's no need to worry," he whispered against her lips "I'll return shortly."

She suddenly found that she loved the savage side of him, reveled in it. That part of him would enable him to defend their valley, defeat Rivellio. That part of Nicolai would keep him safe for her and return him to her. "I shall be very, very angry should you receive so much as a scratch from that hateful man," she cautioned him, keeping a smile plastered to her face in spite of the tightening in her chest.

"And I shall be very, very angry with you if you are not waiting here when I return. No adventures, *cara mia*." The pad of his thumb slid in a long caress over her sensitive inner wrist.

"I have plenty with which to occupy myself," she replied. "I'm most grateful. Theresa and Violante are here already. When the people come in from the farms and *villaggi*, I will need their assistance."

She took her leave, her heart pounding out a rhythm of fear. Nicolai had led his soldiers to victory many times; she had to believe that nothing would happen to him now. As she closed the door, she heard Rolando Bartolmei's voice. A note of accusation caught her attention, and she lingered to hear him speak.

"Before we go into battle, *Don* DeMarco, let me ask if I've done something to offend you or make you question my loyalty."

There was a brief silence. Isabella could well imagine the look on Nicolai's face, his eyebrows raised, the censure he conveyed so silently. "Why would you ask me such a thing, Rolando?"

"I was out patrolling this morn, long before the sun was up, and I was followed. I never saw the lion, but the tracks in the snow followed my mount everywhere I went. There are no lions loose at this time, yet those same tracks were found near the body this morning, too."

Isabella pressed a hand against her mouth, her breath catching in her throat. The memory of Rolando Bartolmei's shredded coat rose up to haunt her. She waited for Nicolai's answer. It was a long time in coming.

"I have no reason to doubt your loyalty, Rolando. If you know of such a matter, feel free to confess it to me now, that we might lay the matter to rest."

"I have always served you loyally." Bartolmei sounded stiff with outrage. "I've never given you cause to doubt me."

"Nor I you," Nicolai returned softly.

Isabella closed her eyes briefly, hoping Rolando could hear the sincerity in Nicolai's voice. She was afraid he wouldn't, afraid that small surge of power she felt was subtly influencing the emotions of the men. There was little she could do but trust in Nicolai and the loyalty of his people. Isabella moved slowly down the long, curving staircase. She had duties to perform. She called Sarina and Betto to her, preparing them for the invasion by *Don* DeMarco's people who lived outside the safety of the walls of the *castello*.

Theresa and Violante were everywhere, Violante, well trained and in her element, directing the food preparations and locating supplies. Theresa worked closely and efficiently with both Isabella and Violante, following all instructions so things went smoothly.

Isabella took a short break the moment she had a chance, hastening to her brother's bedchamber to check on his progress and apologize to Francesca for leaving her so long without anyone to relieve her.

Francesca glanced up and gestured for hushed voices, a small smile curving her mouth. "I just got him back to sleep. His cough is still very bad, but the healer was here and said he looked stronger. I think sleep will help. He's been coughing so much he can't rest." She smoothed back the tangle of hair from Lucca's face with gentle fingertips.

"I told him everything, Francesca," Isabella confessed. "I should have warned you that he knows about the DeMarco legacy."

To Isabella's surprise, Francesca blushed. "We talked about it. He's just so . . ." She broke off, at a loss for words. "We talked all night long. I could listen to his voice forever. Most of the time he's funny and makes me laugh. He always says nice things about the way I look. He said he thought I would be an invaluable asset in destroying the curse. I think he meant it, too." Her eyes were shining as she looked at Isabella.

"Lucca rarely makes mistakes in his assessments, Francesca. I'm counting on you helping us to destroy the curse."

341

She patted Francesca's arm. "Just bear in mind, we no longer have lands, so Lucca has nothing to offer a wife. Certainly not enough to offer the sister of a *don*."

Francesca's elegant eyebrows arched. "I've never allowed others to dictate my actions. I doubt I would start now." She suddenly seemed to become aware of the unusually bustle of activity outside the room. She went very still, knowledge seeping in. "It's begun, hasn't it?" Francesca said. "Rivellio is invading our valley."

Isabella swallowed her fear and nodded. "Nicolai's gone out to meet him."

"I know you're afraid for Nicolai, Isabella, but he is a master at warfare. He plans every battle carefully. His men will watch his back, and should he call forth the lions, it will be over swiftly," Francesca reassured her.

A soft knock on the door heralded Theresa's arrival. She beckoned to Isabella, summoning her into the hall.

"Go ahead, Isabella. I'll watch over Lucca," Francesca assured her.

Isabella slipped out of her brother's room to face Theresa. "What is it?"

"Rolando has sent a request that we bring the men bandages and salves and also the mixtures for poultices. They want to treat the wounded quickly and then transport them back to the *castello*. The healer must stay here. I have some knowledge of wounds but very little. Sarina said you had some knowledge of treating injuries. Will you come with me?" She looked very anxious, visibly upset, wringing her hands.

Isabella nodded immediately. "I've treated wounds many times. I'm certain we can manage, Theresa." She had set up temporary camps for the wounded when needed at her father's holding. "Have you heard if many are injured?" She tried to keep the fear out of her voice.

Theresa shook her head. "A runner went out but has not returned. I had horses saddled for us, and the supplies are on a packhorse. I hope that was all right. I would have asked

Sarina to accompany me—she's good with wounds—but she's too old to weather the trip easily. I thought it would be better to go ourselves."

"We'll be fine," Isabella concurred. "We'll leave word to be relieved as soon as possible. I'll meet you in a few minutes."

Isabella hurried to her bedchamber to retrieve her cloak and gloves. Theresa met her at the side entrance closest to the stables. A packhorse was tethered alongside two mounts.

The day was shrouded in gray, the mist nearly impenetrable. The world seemed closed in, a dark veil draped over the *castello*. The animals seemed nervous, eyes rolling, heads tossing, hooves shifting and dancing in agitation. Isabella paused, her hand resting on her horse. Her stomach was rolling gently, a subtle warning. "I've forgotten something, Theresa." She kept her voice calm. The swelling triumph, the surge of power, thickened and grew around her. She knew it was too late. Far too late.

The blow had hard, passionate hatred behind it. Isabella crumpled to the ground, darkness claiming her.

She woke, upside down, her stomach heaving, her head throbbing. The horse raced through the mist at Theresa's urging. With her hands tied together and Theresa holding her face down as she rode, Isabella was sick, horribly so, twice, before Theresa halted the sweating animal and dismounted. Isabella slid from the back of the horse and fell, her legs too rubbery to support her. With her bound hands tied in front of her, she wiped at her mouth as best she could while she looked carefully around her. She was somewhere near the pass.

Theresa paced back and forth, her anger growing with every step. She whipped around to glare at Isabella. "You won't be so calm when he gets here."

"By *he*, I presume you mean *Don* Rivellio." Isabella kept her voice low. "You're the traitor who's been feeding him information."

Theresa lifted her chin, eyes glittering dangerously. "Call me whatever you like. You're the perfect bait to get him into the valley. He's such a coward, sending his men to certain death, but even with all the information I gave him, I couldn't lure him inside until I promised to deliver you. He knows that if he has you, *Don* DeMarco will trade his own life for yours." There was a sneer in her voice.

"How would he know such a thing?" Isabella asked softly.

Theresa shrugged. "I would do anything to get *Don* Rivellio into this valley. He thinks he has all the plans, but he knows nothing of the lions. His men will be defeated, and I'll kill him myself." Her voice held a wealth of satisfaction. "He deserves death after what he did to my sister." She turned her head to look at Isabella. "And you deserve it for stealing my husband."

Isabella stared up at Theresa in shock. Her head was throbbing so hard, for a moment she thought she hadn't heard correctly. She hastily bit back words of denial. Theresa was in no mood to listen to reason, nor would she believe protests of innocence. It would only serve to anger her further.

"Theresa, did you kill the servant who locked me in the storehouse?"

"I didn't kill him," she denied. "He overheard me giving information to one of Rivellio's men. They killed him. There was nothing I could do. I couldn't allow anyone to know, so I erased the footprints around the body."

"I can understand your wanting to kill *Don* Rivellio, but it's impossible. He'll have guards, Theresa, even if he comes. How could you possibly think you would be able . . ." She trailed off as it all began to fit together like pieces of a puzzle in her mind. The shredded coat and gown in her closet. The female voice calling to her, luring her up the stairs to the balcony. A voice like Francesca DeMarco's. The woman in the marketplace with long black hair, with DeMarco features. Like Francesca, only not Francesca. The lion following her through the narrow streets and staring at her with hate-filled eyes. The lion tracks in the snow surrounding the servant's body. The lion pacing after Rolando Bartolmei. Francesca DeMarco could become the beast. And Theresa was a first cousin to Nicolai and Francesca.

Isabella shook her head. "Theresa, think what you're doing."

"I'm doing what should have been done when he took my little sister against her will and used her the way he did. Nicolai should have sent out assassins to kill him." Theresa's voice hissed with hatred. "She was a *bambina!* Rivellio destroyed her. She's an empty shell now. It's hideous that he could get away with such a thing."

"He had *mio padre* murdered," Isabella said softly. "He tortured *mio fratello* and would have executed him." She lifted her tied hands and pushed at the hair tumbling around her face. When she looked up, her stomach did another somersault, her heart began to pound loudly, and she tasted fear in her mouth.

Through the gray mist she could see soldiers riding in tight formation around a single imposing figure. "Go, Theresa. You can still get away before he gets his hands on you," Isabella whispered, the blood draining from her face. She struggled to her feet. She would never meet an enemy cowed and shrinking. Without conscious thought, she placed her body protectively in front of the other woman. "They haven't seen you yet. Run. You can get away."

Isabella kept her eyes fixed on the man riding in the middle of the group. He looked a devil to her. He was evil incarnate, every bit as twisted as the entity feeding the hatred and jealousies in the valley. Isabella felt the rush of cold, felt a strange disorientation as the malevolent being eagerly reached out to embrace *Don* Rivellio, deserting all others now that it had an evil mind to control.

Behind her, Theresa moaned softly. "What have I done? What's happened to me? Rolando will never forgive what I've done." She reached around Isabella, a sharp blade slicing cleanly through the ropes. The stiletto was pressed into Isabella's palm. "When I allow the beast free reign, you run, escape into the woods. It's all I can give you." A sob welled up, but Theresa held it back, fighting for control.

The soldiers had spotted them. Several kicked their horses into action, rushing toward the two women. Isabella didn't bother to run. She lifted her chin and assumed her haughtiest expression.

"I'm sorry," Theresa whispered. "You had no right to lie with my husband, but this was wrong of me."

"If we both die here today, Theresa, I want you to know, Rolando has never given me any indication that he wanted more than courtesy between us," Isabella said sincerely.

The soldiers scouted the area surrounding the two women, leery of finding the two alone so far from the protection of the *castello*. *Don* Rivellio sat astride his horse, his eyes crafty and greedy as he looked at Isabella. The mist turned to a fine drizzle of sleet, the clouds darkening the skies overhead.

"I can't do it," Theresa murmured in fear. "I can't bring forth the beast. I've tried, but it's gone."

Isabella's heart was so loud, it was matching the throbbing in her head. She kept the stiletto hidden in the folds of her skirt.

"You look a bit the worse for wear, *Signorina* Vernaducci." *Don* Rivellio smirked at her, his lecherous gaze running deliberately over her. "Has *Don* DeMarco already sampled the goods? I do hate seconds." His eyes narrowed. "If I find it's so, I shall punish you severely. That can be quite delicious . . . for me."

The surrounding guards laughed aloud, leering at the two women. Isabella lifted her chin a little higher. She kept Theresa behind her by holding her in place with her free hand, not liking the look on *Don* Rivellio's face.

Somewhere in the distance came the screams of men in the throes of death, of terror. The sounds cut through the dismal sleet to send a chill through all of them. The men looked at one another in sudden anxiety. *Don* Rivellio smiled pleasantly. "That is the sound of my men killing any poor dolts who would stand in my way. My men have taken the valley. I have you, *Signorina* Vernaducci, as I was always meant to. If DeMarco should escape, he will no doubt attempt a rescue and place himself in my hands. I have such wonderful plans for you."

The *don* leaned forward on his horse, staring directly into her eyes, allowing her a glimpse of pure evil. "Pain is very close to pleasure, my dear. We shall see if you enjoy my little diversions as much as I do." His gaze moved from her face to Theresa's. "And you—how well you've served me. DeMarco has never learned a woman's place in his holding. You will learn it well in mine. I have a room right off the stables where you will be stripped naked, tied spread-eagled, and left for my soldiers to do with as they please. Your sister learned her lesson in that room—so tedious with her constant tears, her begging to go home." He laughed, sharing his amusement with his men. "They always enjoy my little gifts to them."

Isabella felt fear mixing with fury rushing through her bloodstream, felt the answering tremor run through Theresa. She gripped Theresa's arm. "Stay silent. Make no sound at all. Nicolai is here. Look at the horses," she whispered.

Her words were so low Theresa almost didn't catch them. She was reaching for the beast within, trying to recapture her hatred and rage now, when she needed it the most, when the disgusting creature who had dishonored and raped her sister was standing in front of her, threatening her with his vileness. The horses were indeed beginning to show signs of nervousness. Moving restlessly, tossing heads, some rearing until the soldiers were forced to dismount to calm them.

Isabella allowed herself a brief glimpse of the surrounding countryside. Through the gray sleet and gloom she caught the glow of feral eyes, the whisper of movement among the trees and boulders. More than one beast stalked the group of soldiers.

"I detest this place," *Don* Rivellio snapped. "Get the women, and let's get out of here." The agitation of the horses increased even as he spoke. The animals plunged and bucked, whirling to dislodge their riders. The soldiers fought with their mounts to stay astride. None of them were able to obey Rivellio's orders.

The lion came out of the gray veil, huge, nearly eleven feet of solid muscle, exploding through the sleet to hit the *don* solidly in the chest. Horses squealed in terror. Men screamed, faces blanching in horror as the world erupted into madness. The lead lion was not alone, a pack having surrounded the column of men. Sprays of crimson shot across the snow, trees, and bushes.

Theresa drove Isabella to the ground, wrapping her arms around Isabella's head to prevent her from seeing the horror. "Don't look! Don't look at this!"

Isabella had no way to see, but she couldn't drown out the sounds of terror. Of the crunch of bones and the sound of flesh being stripped from limbs. It went on and on, the terrible screams of men dying, the heavy breathing of the lions, the fierce growls that were spine-chilling, the horses shrieking in fear.

Theresa held her down, shaking as badly as Isabella. It seemed an eternity. *Don* Rivellio howled with pain, his pleading cries mingled with the sounds of flesh tearing and great teeth chomping through bone and muscle. Eventually his screams died away. And then it was eerily silent.

Isabella felt Theresa move off her, but she couldn't stand, didn't want to look. She buried her face in her hands and burst into tears. Nicolai had done this. Intelligence had been behind the attack. It had been well thought out, the lions moving into position, holding off their ambush until directed to strike hard and fast. They had virtually shredded the enemy. Even now she could hear the sounds of lions feasting. Warning growls rumbled in the night, reverberating through her own body.

Her fate. This would be her fate. Unbidden, unwanted, the thought took hold.

"Isabella." He said her name as if reading her thoughts, denying the truth.

She was sobbing when he lifted her from the ground, her face ravaged with tears, streaked with spattered blood. Her hair was disheveled, falling from its intricate arrangement to cascade down her back and frame her face. Nicolai dragged her against him and held her tightly while he glared over the top of her head at Theresa.

"Fortunately, I had two of my most trusted guards watching over my betrothed." His eyes burned with fury. "We heard every condemning word you spoke." His hands were gentle in Isabella's hair, completely at odds with the lash of his voice as he spoke to his cousin. "Take her to the *castello*. She is charged with treason and attempted murder. Gather my council at once. Captain Bartolmei, if you can't do your part of the job, you are excused and can await the outcome." Nicolai's voice was as cold as ice.

Bartolmei didn't so much as glance at Theresa. "I have never failed to do my duty, *Don* DeMarco, and my wife's treachery changes nothing."

Isabella clung to Nicolai, holding him tightly, smelling the wildness still rising from his skin and hair. "Take me home," she pleaded. She pressed her hands over her ears, trying desperately to muffle the sounds of the lions feasting on human flesh. She kept her eyes tightly shut, her breath coming in shuddering sobs.

Hatred and malevolence, blood and violence swirled in the air around them. She would never be able to forget the sounds of death, the cries and pleas of the soldiers for mercy. The sheer savagery of the night, of the beasts, of *Don* DeMarco, would haunt her for all time.

"Isabella." He said her name softly, whispered it over her

skin, calling her back to him, needing to comfort her almost as much as she needed to be comforted.

Nicolai caught her chin in one palm, tilting her head to the side to give him a view of her face. Above her eye was a bump, a trickle of blood, the skin already turning black and blue. Flames leapt into his eyes. His thumb removed the blood from her temple, and he pulled her once again into his chest to prevent her from seeing the killing fury burning in his eyes. She could feel him trembling, could feel him solid and real, could feel the volcano threatening to erupt. He held on to his rage with tenacious control.

Isabella was in far too fragile a state for Nicolai to indulge his anger. He wanted to get her into the safety of the *palazzo*, where the horror of this night would fade. Nicolai lifted his betrothed onto the back of his waiting horse, his arms and body sheltering her close to him. Nuzzling her hair, he turned his mount away from the sea of bodies and the beasts devouring them. She wept quietly against his chest, her tears soaking his shirt, breaking his heart. Building his hatred and need for retaliation against anyone, anything that had caused this great a sorrow.

Sarina was waiting at the *palazzo*, and she enfolded Isabella in her arms as if she were a child, taking her to the sanctuary of her room, where a bath and a fire awaited. She let her young charge cry out her storm of emotions. Tea and the hot bath helped to revive her for the coming ordeal. It wasn't over, and Isabella knew it wouldn't ever be over unless she could defeat the entity, her most powerful enemy.

"Have they said whether any of Rivellio's men escaped the valley?" she managed to ask as she sipped the steaming tea sweetened with honey.

"The patrols have been sweeping the valley," Sarina answered. "The pass and the tunnels in the caves are well guarded. It would be nearly impossible for any to slip through. Rivellio and his men will become, as so many others, part of the legend: would-be invaders who never returned to their holdings. Who's to say what happened to them? The evidence will be long gone should any seek information."

Isabella shuddered. Her hand was shaking as she set her teacup aside. She would need all her strength, all her determination, to face her craftiest, most evil enemy.

She wanted yet feared to see Nicolai before she entered the room where the court was assembling, but he hadn't come to her. Rivellio and his men had invaded the valley with the purpose of taking over the holding. *Don* DeMarco had a duty to protect his people from all invaders, and he had done so with the least amount of bloodshed to his own soldiers. She pressed a hand to her stomach. In all her experience, Isabella had not been prepared for such a killing field. It had been a nightmare, a horror. In truth, she didn't know if she would ever be able to overcome the sounds and sights, knowing the identity of the beast leading the killing spree.

She took another sip of tea as the knowledge of Rivellio's death finally began to sink in. The enemy of the Vernaducci family was truly dead. Her breath hitched in her throat. Nicolai DeMarco had the power to restore the Vernaducci's honored name. She had no doubt he could do it, even restore their lands. That would clear the way for Lucca and Francesca to be together. Carefully Isabella set the teacup on the tray, smiling as the thought of the look on her brother's face, the light in his eyes as his gaze followed Francesca. Between Isabella and Francesca, Isabella was certain that, with Nicolai's help, Lucca would find the happiness he deserved.

Isabella dressed for court with great care, making certain that every hair was in place, that her gown was regal and becoming. There was nothing she could do to overcome her pale features or the bruise darkening one side of her face and eye. Her stomach was tied in knots, but she would not plead the vapors and hide in her room weeping. She swept through the halls to the tower room where they were holding court. Theresa's trial. She looked neither right nor left, aware of the servants crossing themselves as she passed them, of young Alberita sprinkling holy water in her direction.

The room was filled with people, some officials she had never met, some she recognized. Captain Bartolmei stood stiffly to one side. Captain Drannacia was very close to his wife, Violante. Theresa stood in the center of the room, facing *Don* DeMarco. He was motionless, his features dark and implacable, only his eyes alive, burning with intensity, with rage.

"Now that my betrothed, Isabella Vernaducci, has arrived, we may continue. You have brought grave charges against her, claiming she had been unfaithful to me and had lain with my trusted captain." As he spoke in a flat, expressionless voice, Nicolai's gaze burned over Isabella.

She felt the impact like a blow, but she stood unwavering, silent, listening without protest.

"You have admitted to us that you betrayed your people and that you stalked and attempted to kill *Signorina* Vernaducci. You have admitted to us that you have the DeMarco ability to become the beast, and you used your ability in your pursuit of *Signorina* Vernaducci. How is it that you kept this talent from your *don*, and from your husband?"

Theresa took a deep breath. She was fighting for more than her marriage; she was fighting for her life. "The first time the beast overtook me was a few months after my sister returned. I was so filled with rage, I couldn't contain it. I went out into the forest and screamed. It just happened. I didn't know how. I thought it was a dream, a hazy dream. It didn't happen very often, and when it did it was always when I was enraged." Theresa glanced at *Don* DeMarco, looked quickly away, and allowed her gaze to stray toward her husband. She stiffened, her face crumbling when he refused to look at her. "The second time it happened was the first night *Signorina* Vernaducci arrived. I had gone to the *castello* to wait for my husband. . . ."

"Continue." It was a command.

Theresa shivered at the tone. "Guido was out walking and spotted me near the stables. He said things to me. He wouldn't stop. He insisted I wanted him." Tears glittered in her eyes. "He ripped my gown and threw me to the ground. I was so frightened, so angry, it—it just happened. I didn't try. I didn't know until later."

"You knew everyone thought I had killed him," Nicolai said softly, his voice a condemnation. "You said nothing. And the servant? Did you kill him, too?"

She shook her head. "No, Rivellio's men did that. *Signorina* Vernaducci will tell you. They killed him, not I."

"But you tried to kill Isabella." Nicolai was relentless.

"No!" Theresa shook her head in denial. "I don't know. I think I wanted to frighten her away, but the rage grew and grew until I just wanted her gone. Then I knew I could use her to destroy Rivellio. He forced me to spy for him. He wouldn't return my sister unless I agreed to supply him with information on the valley. I would have agreed to anything to get her back."

A single, strangled sound of horror escaped Rolando Bartolmei's throat.

"I couldn't really tell him anything," Theresa explained hastily. "I wasn't really spying. I didn't know anything. But I wanted him dead. I *had* to have him dead. He should have been punished for what he did." She twisted her hands together. "I knew I could lure him to the valley. He would come for *Signorina* Vernaducci. He thought to trade her life for *Don* DeMarco's. He was certain he could use her brother to invade the valley and defeat our men. I planned to kill him."

"Using Isabella." Nicolai's tone held accusation, threat, the promise of death.

"She betrayed you with my husband. With my Rolando!" The allegation burst from Theresa. For a moment her eyes flashed with anger; then, humiliated and ashamed, she resumed looking at the floor.

"You have proof of this." Again it was a statement.

Theresa shivered. She nodded, her gaze once more sliding to her husband, then quickly away.

The room was silent, the hush of expectancy. Isabella stood in the center of the room, looking as serene as she could manage, grateful for her father's training. All eyes were focused on her. She didn't flinch, but rather faced her accuser calmly.

"Let me see the proof of my betrothed's infidelity," Nicolai said softly. "The proof of my captain's betrayal." His voice was a low purr of menace. His tone brought the tension in the room up another notch. He held out a hand.

Isabella blinked rapidly, mesmerized by the sight of Nicolai's large hand. It was a giant paw, covered in fur, razor-sharp claws glinting like stilettos. She heard a collective gasp go around the room. She lifted her gaze to meet his, but he was focused fully on Theresa, watching her with the unblinking stare of a predator.

Theresa stepped toward the *don*, her outstretched hand holding the evidence of Isabella's treachery. She stopped short, her face pale, her hand shaking. No matter how hard she tried to force herself forward, she couldn't take the step to put the damning proof in that huge paw. Nicolai refused to move forward to take the scrap of parchment. He continued to stare at Rolando Bartolmei's wife, orange-red flames burning in his eyes, daring her to place the damning proof in the huge paw.

It was Isabella who broke the impasse, taking the missive from Theresa and putting it in Nicolai's open palm. She watched Nicolai's face as he read the words aloud " 'I miss you so much. Please hurry and join me. I wish I had told you the last time I saw you how very much I love you.' It is signed, 'Isabella.' " He lifted his gaze from the parchment and looked directly at her. "Did you write this, Isabella?"

"Yes, of course I did," she answered easily, quickly, into the expectant silence.

The silence stretched nerves to a screaming point. Theresa attempted to look triumphant. Rolando looked stunned. Isabella only had eyes for Nicolai. She watched his face for any fleeting expression, anything to give her a clue to his thoughts. He said nothing, simply waited in the vacuum of silence.

A sob escaped Theresa's throat. She jammed a fist to her mouth and averted her face from her husband. Rolando shook his head again.

"Where did you find my letter, *Signora* Bartolmei?" Isabella asked without rancor. Her voice was gentle, soft, non-threatening.

Behind her hand, Theresa's voice was muffled. "In the pocket of my husband's coat." Another sob escaped.

Isabella's eyebrows went up. "Really." She said the word thoughtfully and turned her head to search the room for a face. Her gaze settled on Violante. She remained silent, just watching the other woman.

Nicolai kept his attention centered on Isabella. There was no other in the room who could command his attention . . . and his control. He could feel his fury building, not white hot but ice cold, the beast raging to be released. Isabella was covered in bruises, in lacerations, subjected to this humiliation, this speculation, before the court. Anger and jealousy mixed with his icy rage until he shook with the need to explode.

Violante turned a bright crimson, glanced at her husband, then at the floor. Sergio Drannacia looked at his wife, inhaled sharply, and reached for her hand. As she looked up at him, understanding seemed to pass from one to the other.

Violante squared her shoulders. "I don't know what made me do it. I took the letter from the library when you picked up the book," she said to Isabella. "I just wanted to have it, to look at my name. I thought I might trace over the marks you made until I learned them."

She forced herself to look at *Don* DeMarco's motionless figure. He was so still he could have been carved from stone. "She wrote my name on the top, a short missive to her brother, and her name at the bottom. She was showing me how to write. I tore my name from it to keep it. I still have it in a box at my home."

Tears shimmered in her eyes as she looked at Theresa. "I'm so sorry. I don't know what came over me. I don't know why I said those things about your husband and Isabella. I kept trying to stop myself, but I couldn't. I remember putting the missive in the coat when I picked it up from the ground and gave it to Sergio to give to him. I just don't know why I did such a thing."

Theresa stared at her, clearly stricken. "Oh, Violante," she whispered, shaking her head. "I betrayed my people, my husband, my *don*, while you fed my jealousy and rage. How could you do such a thing?"

Sergio protectively drew Violante beneath the shelter of his wide shoulder.

"I don't know. I couldn't stop myself. Isabella, Theresa, I'm so sorry." Violante didn't dare look at the *don*. She had committed an unpardonable sin, treachery against his betrothed.

"You stalked Isabella Vernaducci and tried to kill her because you thought I had betrayed you?" The words burst out of Rolando Bartolmei. He was trembling with rage as he faced his wife. "You betrayed our people? *My* people? *Mio don*? You gave information to Rivellio that might have enabled him to invade our land? You did all of it? Even stalked me through my morning patrol to make me doubt *mio don*? I have known him since childhood, yet you sought to drive a knife between us?" He looked at his wife as if he'd never seen her before, as if she'd suddenly become a loathsome creature. "You believed I would dishonor *mio don*, my friend—dishonor *you*?"

Theresa sobbed loudly, the sound heart-rending. Humiliated and shamed by Theresa's deceitful deeds, Rolando turned on his heel, prepared to walk out and leave his wife to the *don's* doubtful mercy.

"Do you think yourself blameless in this, Captain Bartolmei?" Isabella said softly to his retreating back.

Bartolmei stiffened but didn't turn around. A soft sound escaped *Don* DeMarco. A low, rumbling growl that stopped Bartolmei instantly. The growl swelled in volume, shook the room, reverberated throughout the *castello*.

Nicolai paced across the room until he stood before the trembling figure of Theresa Bartolmei. He towered over her, a dark, angry cauldron of rage. "You *dared* to make repeated attempts on my betrothed? You conspired to make it look as if she were betraying me, while all the time you were betraying your *don* and your people? And for what, *Signora* Bartolmei?" His form shimmered between beast and man. "Chanise is part of my family. Assassins were in place to take care of the matter. You would have known that if you had had the sense to come to me. Not that I should have to explain my actions to you or anyone else. *Don* Rivellio was a dead man. He was dead the moment he put his hands on my cousin."

He stalked the length of the room and back again, his hair wild, his eyes blazing, power and fury in every step he took. He stopped once more in front of Theresa. "As *you* were dead from the moment you touched Isabella." He held out a hand, only it was a huge paw stretching toward her, one curved, stiletto-sharp claw, touching her chin. "Had I not had men watching her, you would have delivered her into the hands of a devil such as Rivellio. You disgust me."

He spun to glare at his guards. "Take her to the courtyard at once. *At once!*" He roared the order, orange-red flames burning in his eyes.

Chapter Twenty

Theresa screamed as the two guards caught her arms and dragged her from the *castello* and out into the dark night. Tendrils of fog lay along the ground, swirling into ribbons of mist. With the snow covering the rocks, the courtyard had the appearance of a graveyard, stark and eerie and hideously vile.

Isabella eluded *Don* DeMarco's outstretched hand and raced after the guards "What are you doing? You can't do this, Nicolai." There were tears in her voice.

Violante burst into a torrent of weeping. "*Don* DeMarco, I beg you to reconsider. Don't do this."

Sergio tried to silence her, terrified by the *don's* fury, terrified it would be turned on his wife for her part in the entire mess.

Nicolai leapt after Isabella. He caught her arm as she tugged at one of the guards in an attempt to set Theresa free. As he yanked her toward him, she felt the needles puncturing her skin, a certain sign of the beast's aggression.

"Go to your room, Isabella, until it is finished here." The flames in his eyes were burning out of control, his voice a dark rasp of authority.

Isabella quelled her first reaction to fight him. Stubbornly she shut off the fear and horror gathered in her soul. She stood still in his grip, forcing her mind to think. At once awareness crept into her heart, into her mind. Here, in the courtyard where Sophia was beheaded, where everyone believed it had all begun. Where Nicolai's father had killed his mother. Where the entity slept and awakened and orchestrated the hatred and fear that perpetuated atrocity on the entire valley.

She took a deep breath and forced it through her lungs. And she inhaled the entity's sour odor. Malevolence. Hatred. Pure evil. She was in its territory, and it was feeding Nicolai's rage, feeding his weakness, his utter belief in his destiny that he would kill the woman he loved above all others.

"We are not alone out here, Nicolai," she announced, looking to the others who had followed them. Even Francesca had arrived, alarmed, out of breath, frightened by her brother's roaring. "If you're very still, you'll feel it. The influence is subtle, but it can't hide the surge of power when it manipulates us." The needles in her skin flexed, and she felt hot breath blast her face, the warm trickle of blood down her arm that would only serve to call to the beast.

"It has influenced everyone to act differently than they normally would, building on their failings. Failings we all have. Jealousy, hurt, anger, distrust." She looked at Rolando. "Pride. What else would cause a man to leave his wife to a death sentence, a wife he loves. Even poor Sophia, a woman who by all accounts loved her people and her husband, who certainly loved her children. She never would have cursed them for all time without something evil compelling her to do so." She was alone, fighting an unseen enemy who was swelling in power and gloating at her inadequacy. She looked around her at the faces white with shock from *Don* DeMarco's orders. No one seemed to comprehend what she was saying. "Don't you see it? None of us would do these things." She was unashamedly pleading with them. Pleading with Nicolai.

Francesca rushed to her side and caught her hand in a show of solidarity.

Rolando took several steps toward Nicolai. "My *wife* is your *famiglia*. Your cousin," he reminded him. "You would see more DeMarco blood soak into the ground?" His hands were knotted into tight fists at his side. Fury had stolen into his eyes.

"If you have no mercy, Captain Bartolmei, for your own *wife*, why would I as the *don* have mercy for a woman who betrayed me?" *Don* DeMarco snapped his fingers, and the guard obediently forced Theresa to her knees.

She screamed in terror again, tears burning down her cheeks.

"This will not happen," Bartolmei objected, his hand on his sword. "If you're so eager for blood, take mine."

"No!" Violante protested from where she was huddled in Sergio's arms. "I'm the guilty one. I provoked her."

Fury swept through Nicolai, pure, undiluted rage. He threw back his head and roared at the defiance of his orders. The sound set the lions in the valley roaring until the night was filled with the brutal, primitive sound. His people scattered in all directions. Nicolai spun in a circle, scratching a deep line down Isabella's arm as he thrust her away from him. His long hair haloed his head and fell around his shoulders and back in a wild mane.

"Nicolai." Isabella whispered his name aloud in despair. She watched his powerful shape shimmer, the white mist swirling greedily around him, devouring the man, revealing the beast.

The lion stood in the center of the courtyard, a magnificent animal, enormous, heavily muscled, the shaggy mane adding to its bulk. Its eyes were burning with hunger, a dangerous, wild warning to those in the courtyard.

"*Dio*, it's happening again! I'll have to call the lions!" Francesca cried out, and she buried her face in her hands.

"No!" Isabella's voice was a whip of authority. She lifted her head and walked toward the crouching beast. Her arms were spread out away from her sides in a gesture of supplication. "I love you, Nicolai. It isn't going to take you from me. If you kill Theresa, we have nothing. It knows that."

The lion swung its massive head toward her, eyes flaming with the need to kill. The mouth opened, revealing huge, sharp teeth. Another roar split the air. Above their heads, the dark clouds split and poured down rain.

Isabella lifted her face to the drops, allowing the rain to bead over her face and wash away the terror of the moment. She looked back and met the lion's focused stare without flinching. Her heart was pounding, her mouth dry, but there was a sense of peace deep inside her. "I won't see you as the beast, Nicolai. I won't."

The lion shuddered and sank into a crouch, staring at her without recognition. Francesca stepped up beside Isabella. "I won't see you as the beast either, *mio fratello*."

Sergio and Violante took up positions on Isabella's left side. They refused to look away from the slavering lion. The beast shook its massive head, eyes glowing red in the night.

Isabella, always sensitive to the malevolence of the entity, felt it gather itself for the final attack. She knew its ultimate target was Nicolai. It fed the beast, fed natural instincts, hunger and rage, until the emotions swirled together, culminating in the lion's need to kill. In concentrating its entire power on the *don*, the entity had to leave the others alone.

Captain Bartolmei caught his wife's arm, pulling her away from the two cowering guards. The soldiers broke and ran some distance away, terrified of the crouching beast. Rolando and Theresa stepped up beside Sergio and Violante to face Nicolai.

Without further warning, the lion exploded toward them. Theresa and Violante both screamed and retreated behind their husbands. The captains backed up. Francesca covered her face. In that split second, time stopped for Isabella. Terror was a living, breathing beast in her heart. But this was the man who had rescued her brother from certain death. The man who carried the weight of his people on his back, carried a legacy others would have crumbled beneath. This was Nicolai. *Her* Nicolai. Her heart and soul, the laughter in her life, the love. This creature was her man.

Isabella flung herself forward to meet the attack. She would *not* allow the entity to take him from her without a fight. "Nicolai!" She called his name, wrapped her arms securely around the shaggy neck, and embraced death.

The great lion snarled and shook his head to throw her off. Her hands bunched tightly in the mane. Isabella buried her face in the wealth of hair. She felt the jaws close around her ribs and shut her eyes, breathing a final prayer.

"Nicolai!" Francesca launched herself forward, her arms circling the lion's massive head. "*Mio fratello. Ti amo!*"

The great beast shuddered with indecision.

Rolando Bartolmei and Sergio Drannacia followed the lead of Nicolai's betrothed, braving certain death to close their arms around the large creature. Their wives stumbled forward in their wake, touching the monstrous animal, praying to keep up their courage.

"Sophia's here," Francesca said, awed. "Sophia and Alexander. They're together, touching Nicolai. And the 'others.' All of them. They're here with us."

Isabella felt them, the spirits surrounding her, surrounding Nicolai, lending their strength to hers to battle for possession of *Don* DeMarco.

"My boy." Sarina and Betto were there, tears in their eyes. They led the servants to the courtyard. "We see only the man, Nicolai, nothing else."

The hot, panting breath heating her side was all at once against Isabella's neck. She could feel his face, not a muzzle, pressed tightly into her shoulder. She clung to him with every ounce of strength she possessed, whispering words of love, of hope.

The entity had pulled back, realizing it was fighting for its life, not just power. But, regrouped, it struck at Nicolai again with all its energy, pouring the malevolence, the hatred, the dark, twisted power into the being shimmering somewhere between beast and man.

Isabella felt the fur, the teeth, the claws, but she held her ground. Nicolai could have killed her in seconds, yet he hadn't. "Listen to me, my beloved," she whispered against the shaggy mane. "You never lied to me. I've always known of your legacy, and I've always chosen you. *You*, Nicolai. Beast or man, you and I are one. I haven't run, and I won't run. Choose for us. I love you enough to accept your decision. This *thing* that threatens us can't take that from either of us."

She heard a growl first, a rumbling. The words were raspy as they reached her ears. "*Ti amo, cara mia*, I love you. I can't harm you. I can't allow anything else to harm you." Nicolai's lips moved up her neck, her chin, and his mouth found hers, settling there to devour the sweet taste of her.

His kiss rocked the earth beneath her feet. His arms were hard bands around her, his body solid, muscular, the frame of a man. The ground shifted and rolled again.

"Nicolai! Isabella!" Francesca screamed the warning even as the captains dragged the couple from the courtyard.

They stumbled back out of the area, watching in horror as the ground buckled and split apart to form a deep chasm. Rain poured down. Jagged streaks of lightning danced across the roiling sky, veins of white-hot energy.

"Get back!" Francesca called as she rushed for the safety of the *palazzo*.

A bolt from the heavens slammed to earth, deep into the yawning chasm in the courtyard. The blinding impact knocked some of them off their feet. The sound was deafening. The air crackled around them. Noxious smoke arose from the deep hole, then dissipated in the cool, clean rain.

Nicolai pressed Isabella tightly against the wall of the *castello*, protectively shielding her. The ground buckled and rolled. Isabella attempted to peek under Nicolai's arm. Reluctantly, he moved slightly to allow her to watch the earth roll and heave, to cave in on itself to repair the deep crack. She breathed deeply, dazed by the events, her fists clenched tightly in Nicolai's shirt to anchor him to her.

There was a stunned silence while they looked at the courtyard and each other. For a long moment no one spoke. No one moved. The rain poured down on them, not dark and dismal but clean and refreshing.

Nicolai spoke first. "Is everyone all right? No injuries? Sarina, check inside. See to Isabella's brother, please."

They all looked at one another, inspecting for damage.

"It's over," Francesca announced. "You did it, Isabella. You freed us all. Sophia is with Alexander, and she says to convey the gratitude of all the 'others.' She thanks you for releasing her and Alexander from their torment."

"The entity's gone?" Isabella stared at the blackened courtyard. "It was locked in the earth, then?" It was nearly impossible for her to take it in. Now that it was over, her legs refused to support her. She leaned heavily against Nicolai. "Is it over? Can you tell? Are you certain?" She looked into his mesmerizing eyes and was caught and held by the mixture of sorrow and joy she saw there.

"I can hear the lions and communicate with them, but when I reach for the beast, it is no longer there." He looked lost.

Isabella tightened her arms around him. "It must be frightening to have a part of you missing."

"I don't feel it either," Francesca admitted.

"I could never become the beast unless I was violently angry," Theresa whispered from the safety of Rolando's arms. "I'm glad it's gone. It terrified me."

Nicolai gathered Isabella to him. His salvation. His love. A tremor ran through his body. "It terrifies me that it's gone." His whisper was against her ear, for her alone, his face buried in her hair. "It terrifies me that you are mine when I'll never deserve you."

"You'll get through this. We'll get through this together." Isabella framed his face with her hands. She went up on tiptoes to rub her lips gently against his. A soft caress. The merest contact.

And it shook him right to his soul. His fingers tangled in her hair and bunched there tightly. "You're my life, Isabella. You know you're my life." He kissed her with exquisite tenderness. "*Ti amo, cara mia.* For all time."

"*Don* DeMarco?" Rolando Bartolmei spoke gruffly. "I ask for an official pardon for my wife."

Nicolai lifted his head and swung to face his cousin, Isabella beneath his shoulder. "Theresa, we all made mistakes. I hope you forgive mine."

Theresa cuddled closer to her husband, tears glittering. "I'm truly sorry."

"None of us are blameless," Nicolai said, looking straight into Isabella's eyes. He smiled at her.

And took her breath away. Their fingers tangled together.

"We have much to celebrate," Sergio pointed out. "We defeated an invasion, brought justice to a rogue, overcame the curse, and banished the entity. Not bad for a single day's work." He bent to kiss his wife, right there in front of everyone.

"Betto, go get the priest and bring him to me," Nicolai ordered. Unable to keep his hands from Isabella, he buried his hands in her hair to drag her head back, giving him access to her soft, inviting mouth. He felt desperate, disoriented without that part of him that had always been. But her mouth was hot with promise, with temptation, as she met him kiss for kiss, oblivious of their interested audience.

At last, when Nicolai lifted his head, Isabella smiled at him, her heart shining in her eyes. "I think it's over," she said. "I don't think we need the priest, Nicolai."

Nicolai groaned and pulled her back against his aching body. "Believe me, Isabella, we need that priest immediately."

"I should say so." Sarina was scandalized. What did spirits and lions and the ground opening matter? Propriety was important in front of the servants. "Betto, get him at once! And, Isabella, come out of the rain this minute!"

Isabella glanced down at her wet gown, showing entirely too much beneath the now nearly transparent material. "I'm getting married now, like this?"

Nicolai bent his head to hers, his mouth inches from hers. "I'm giving you a *bambino* tonight, wed or not. If you prefer unwed and an audience . . ." he added wickedly.

Isabella tried to look scandalized, but she couldn't copy Sarina's expression. Happiness was blossoming, the realization that she had a future with the man she loved. She leaned close to him and tilted her head to look up at him. "Unwed is fine, Nicolai, and if we must wait much longer . . ." There was pure seduction in her voice.

His eyes glinted at her for a long moment. He raked a hand through his hair in agitation, making it wilder than ever. "Betto!" he roared it, ever the lion. "Where is that priest?"

CHRISTINE FEEHAN
DARK MELODY

Lead guitarist of the Dark Troubadours, Dayan is renowned for his mesmerizing performances. His melodies still crowds, beckon seduce, tempt. And always, he calls to *her*. His lover. His lifemate. He calls to her to complete him. To give him the emotions that have faded from his existence, leaving him an empty shell of growing darkness. *Save me. Come to me.*

Corinne Wentworth stands at the vortex of a gathering storm. Pursued by the same fanatics who'd murdered her husband, she risks her life by keeping more than one secret. Fragile, delicate, vulnerable, she has an indomitable faith that makes her fiery surrender to Dayan all the more powerful.

DEVIL IN THE DARK — EVELYN ROGERS

He rides out of the Yorkshire mist, a dark figure on a dark horse. Is he a living man or a nightmare vision, conjured up by her fearful imagination and her uncertain future? Voices swirl in her head:

> They say he's more than human.
>
> A man's life is in danger when he's around . . .
>
> And a woman's virtue.

Repelled yet fascinated, Lucinda finds herself swept into a whirlwind courtship. Yet even as his lips set fire to her heart, she cannot forget his words of warning on the night they met:

> Tread softly. Heed little that you see and hear.
>
> Then leave.
>
> For God's sake, leave.

Whether he is the lover of her dreams or the embodiment of all she fears, she senses he will always be her . . . devil in the dark.

___52407-4 $5.99 US/$6.99 CAN

The Trelayne Inheritance
COLLEEN SHANNON

Women are dying, the blood drained from their bodies and two mysterious pinprick marks imprinted on their necks. Angelina Corbett cannot help wondering whether the whispers of "vampire" haunting her uncle's isolated estate might have a basis in fact — especially after meeting their enigmatic neighbor, the earl of Trelayne.

Locked in his powerful embrace, Angel feels rational thought flee. His voice mesmerizes her, his eyes silently beseech her, his touch enflames her and leaves her longing for fulfillment. She knows he is her soul mate, but will his dance lead her to the heights of ecstasy or the downward spiral of the damned?

CALL
OF THE
MOON
RONDA THOMPSON

Jason Donavon walks in darkness, seeking release from his curse. It has the power to destroy everything — to take his humanity. In a world where he no longer belongs, he feels eyes watching him. Something even more sinister than himself stalks the night.

The woman who materializes to save him from the forces of darkness holds answers to the questions he's been afraid to ask. She takes him to her world, to the wilds of the North. Yet in a place where nature rules supreme, Jason knows danger awaits. He will be forced to fight his love for a woman forbidden, and discover whether salvation will come from resisting the seductive light of the moon — or in surrendering to it.

THE Ghost OF Carnal Cove
Evelyn Rogers

"I am a man without conscience," claims the dark stranger who accosts her amid the pounding surf and tearing winds of Carnal Cove. Taunting her with legends of the place, Captain Saintjohn accuses her of being a seductress herself. Little does he know that Makenna Lindsay has come to the isolated Isle of Wight to escape just such temptations. But her troubled mind seems to conjure equally disturbing hallucinations at every turn: the piteous crying of an abandoned child, the silvery figure of a ghostly woman in white. But is her enemy her own imagination or the all-too-tempting promise of passion with a lover as wild and remorseless as the sea itself?